ALSO BY JENELLE LEANNE SCHMIDT

Turrim Archive
The Orb and the Airship
Mantles of Oak and Iron
Hearts of Stone and Steel
The Prisoner and the Pirate
Towers of Might and Memory

A Classic Retold
Steal the Morrow

The Minstrel's Song
King's Warrior
Second Son
Yorien's Hand
Minstrel's Call

The Faelands
An Echo of the Fae

Children's Picture Books
'Twas an Evening in Bethlehem

THE PRISONER AND THE PIRATE

BOOK 4 OF THE TURRIM ARCHIVE

JENELLE LEANNE SCHMIDT

The Prisoner and the Pirate

Volume 4 of The Turrim Archive

By Jenelle Leanne Schmidt

Copyright 2025 by Jenelle Leanne Schmidt

Published by Stormcave

www.jenelleschmidt.com

The Prisoner and the Pirate

ISBN-13: 978-1-960357-02-1

Cover art by Dragonpen Designs

Book design and maps by Declan Rowe

For Evan: My brother. My hero. A true Bruce.

THE WORLD OF TURRIM

Turrim is a single-continent world with six separate cultures and a calendar that looks slightly different from our own.

Turrim's year is only 336 days long, separated into twelve lunats (what we would call months) and each lunat is exactly 28 days long, separated into 4 sennights (what we would call weeks). Their seasons are much as our own, following the same pattern of fall, winter, spring, and summer.

Their new year begins on what would for us be September 21st, or the Fall Equinox.

The months of the year (starting at the beginning of their calendar year) are named thus:

Chanjar	October
Deepthen	November
Darkthen	December
Edrian	January
Tella	February
Malla	March
Urin	April
Paute	May
Avar	June
Mirad	July
Avest	August
Felling	September

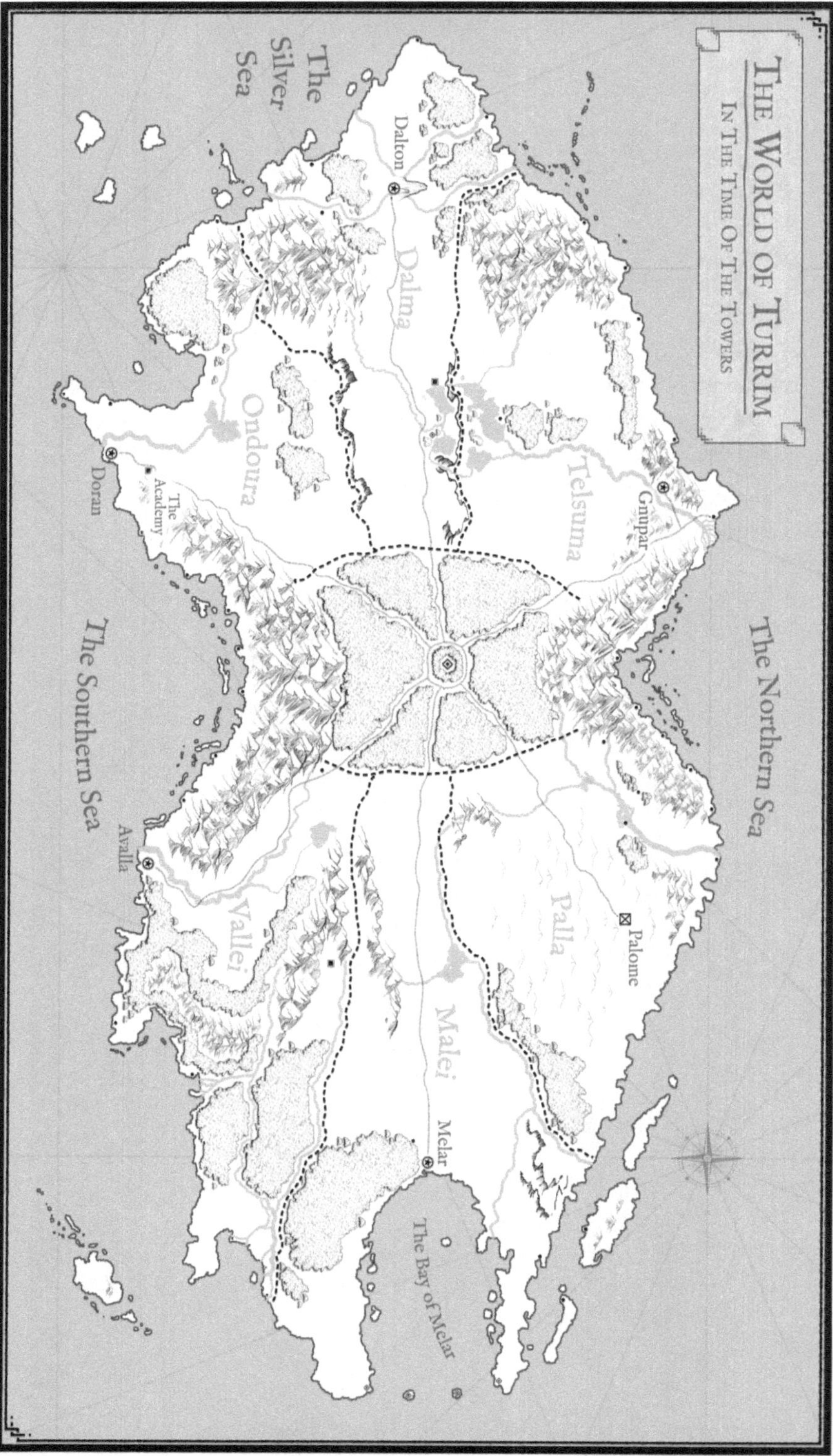

THE WORLD OF TURRIM
In The Time Of The Towers
The Silver Sea
Dalton
Dalma
Telsuma
Gnupar
Ondoura
Doran
The Academy
The Northern Sea
The Southern Sea
Avalla
Vallei
Palla
Palone
Malei
Melar
The Bay of Melar

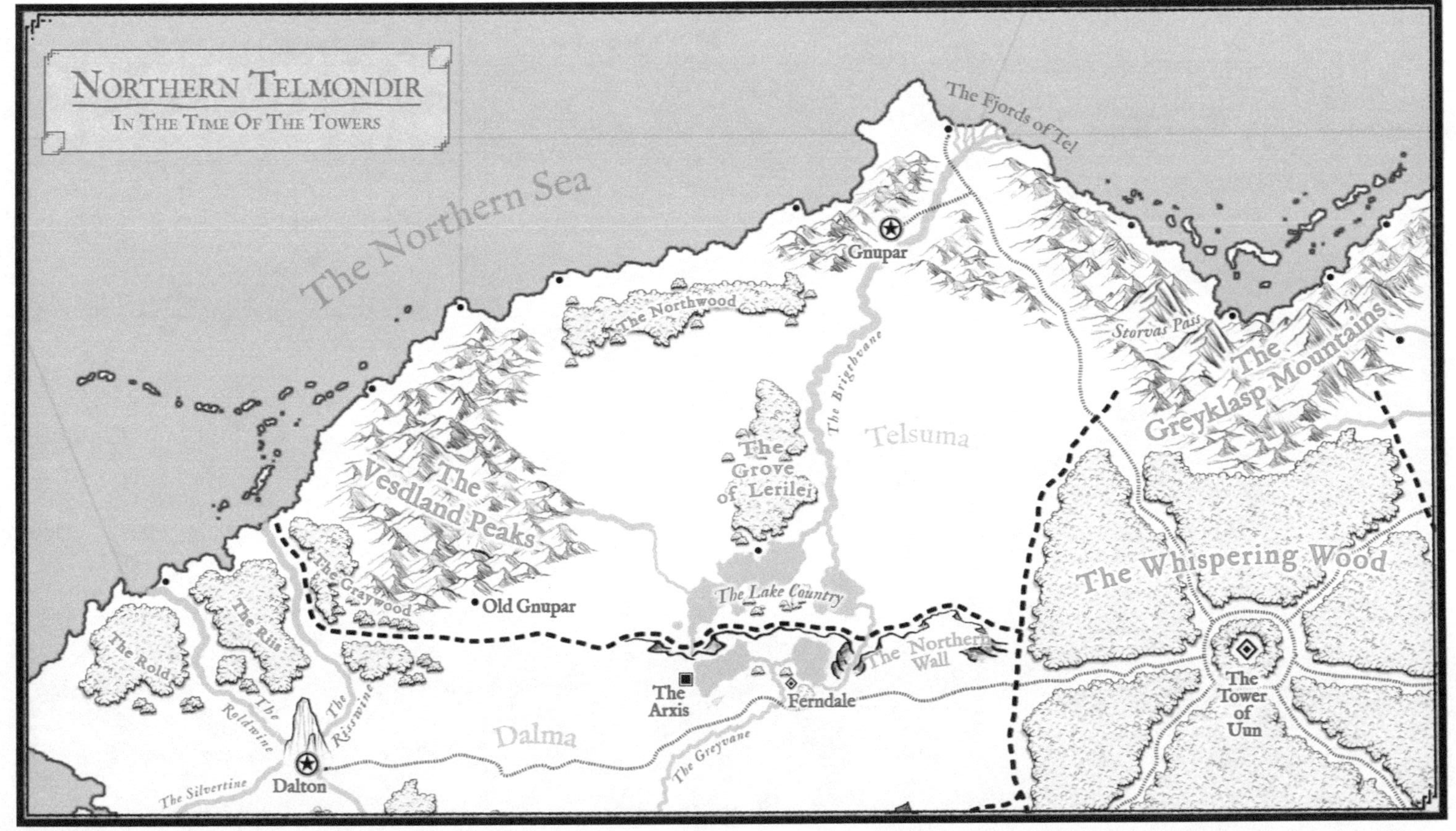

Northern Telmondir
In The Time Of The Towers
The Fjords of Tel
The Northern Sea
Gnupar
Storvas Pass
The Northwood
The Brigebvane
The Greyklasp Mountains
Telsuma
The Grove of Lerilei
The Vesdland Peaks
The Graywood
The Whispering Wood
Old Gnupar
The Lake Country
The Rold
The Riia
The Northern Wall
The Arxis
Ferndale
The Tower of Uun
The Roldwine
The Risswine
Dalma
The Greyvane
The Silvertine
Dalton

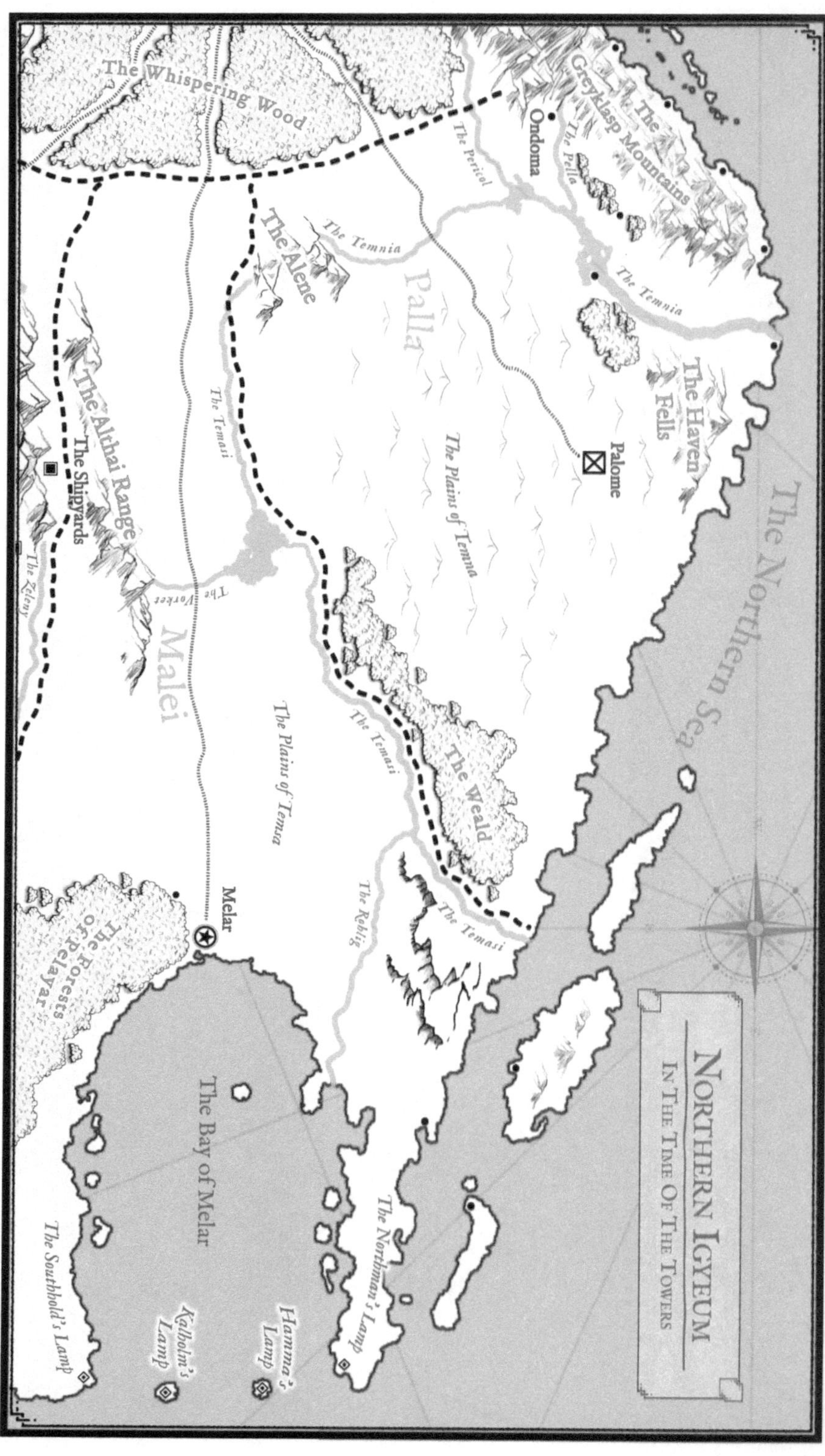

The Whispering Wood
The Greyklasp Mountains
Ondoma
The Periol
The Pella
The Temnia
The Temnia
Palla
The Haven Fells
The Alene
The Plains of Temnia
Palome
The Althai Range
The Shipyards
The Temasi
The Vortex
Malei
The Zeleny
The Plains of Temna
The Temasi
The Weald
The Northern Sea
The Forests of Pelayar
Melar
The Reblig
The Temasi
The Bay of Melar
The Northman's Lamp
Hamma's Lamp
Kalholm's Lamp
The Southhold's Lamp
NORTHERN IGYEUM
IN THE TIME OF THE TOWERS

THE SOUTHWEST OF TELMONDIR
The Roldwine
The Risswine
Dalton
The Silvertine
The Emewood
The Greyvane
The Southern Wall
Dalsea
Elricht Harbor
The Empela
Telseren Grade
The Tyveden
Attatoire
The Obuna
The Living Wood
The Academy
Khosha
Doran

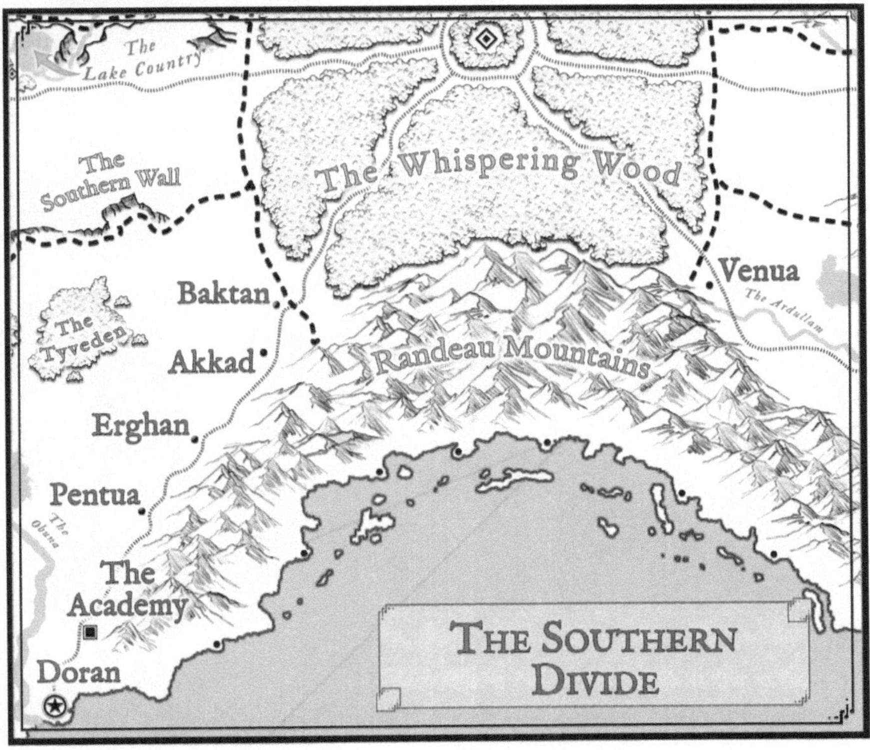

The Lake Country
The Southern Wall
The Whispering Wood
Venua
The Ardullam
Baktan
The Tyveden
Akkad
Randeau Mountains
Erghan
Pentua
The Obuna
The Academy
Doran
THE SOUTHERN DIVIDE

PROLOGUE

"Shiori!" Dalmir called in the darkness. "I'm lost, Shiori. I can't find my way home."

Dalmir groaned. His body ached as it hadn't ached since... well, he couldn't remember ever being in this much discomfort, but certainly it had been before the Builder granted him the gifts of immortality, knowledge, and power. Everything hurt. His body seemed to be on fire. Nightmares swirled around him in the darkness and he cried out again.

"Shh, it's all right, I'm here."

That voice! A treasured thing, that voice, from a long-lost memory or dream. Could it be her? Or was this just a fever dream brought on by his brush with death? Or perhaps he had died. What had happened?

Memory pierced like an arrow.

Or... wait... not memory. A real arrow. The arrow brought the memory, and with it, another surge of pain. But this time he embraced the pain, for it was no less than what he deserved.

"I'm sorry," he whispered. "So sorry."

"You are forgiven. Rest now, dear one. You have work still to do when you wake." The voice from his dreams spoke again, a gentle whisper that calmed the raging inferno inside.

Cool liquid brushed his lips and offered relief from the burning fire within. It trickled gently down his throat soothing his pain, and then darkness claimed him once more.

1

Ericole Niveya gazed out the window. Smug satisfaction filled him as he dipped his quill into the inkwell once more and continued his letter, the words appearing beneath his fingers in simple, elegant lines. He could have used a regular pen, but he preferred the elegance of writing with quill and ink. And such a letter as this demanded the extra level of care. The satisfaction of forming each perfect letter matched his feelings about the subject perfectly.

My dear Lord Adelfried, the note began. *I am pleased to inform you that Regeont Roshana's murderer has been dealt with and will no longer—*

The door to his study burst open. Ericole raised his quill smoothly, not marring the letter with even a drop of misplaced ink. He glanced up.

"Yes, son?"

Ettore, the image of his mother, yet with something softer around his eyes, strode to his father's desk. "The Igyeum has taken an Ondouran city."

"Village," Ericole corrected, lowering his quill to the paper once more.

"City, Father. They've taken Baktan."

Ericole's hand shuddered. A drop of ink dripped off the end of the quill. Niveya swiftly moved the paper so that the letter suffered no harm, then set the quill aside and turned his full attention on his son. "Baktan? Are you certain?"

Ettore nodded. "Just this morning."

"They have moved swiftly," Niveya muttered. "Just a sennight ago they were still encamped in the Whispering Wood."

"Our spies say the Igyeum has grown bold since learning of the Regeont's death. Without a leader, perhaps they see Ondoura as the easiest path for them into Telmondir."

A feathery mantle of guilt settled over Niveya's shoulders. He had sold that information to the Igyeum, just sennights ago. At the time, he had thought little of it, certain that Regeont Roshana's assassination had been a machination of the Igyeum anyway. It had seemed a pittance, even a bit clever, selling them key intelligence that was already theirs.

Of course, the investigation had eventually revealed that her murder had not been a plot of the Igyeum's after all, but rather an internal affair. Roshana had been murdered by her own nephew who had his eyes set on her position and power. Thus, knowledge of the Regeont's assassination had been far more valuable to the forces of the Ar'Mol than Ericole had intended. A serious misstep on his part, indeed.

"I should have demanded a higher price," he muttered.

"What was that?"

"Nothing." Niveya waved a hand. "Nothing important. Just the cost of doing business." He opened his mouth to say more when the door burst open again and a petite woman stormed into his office.

"Yes, Nira?" he asked, repressing a sigh. She wanted the same thing she always wanted.

"It has been lunats, Ericole," she hissed. "Nearly a year since my son was killed. What have you done about it? Where is his murderer?"

Niveya rose from behind his desk, stepping quickly to his

sister's side and clasping her hands in his own. "Nira, I told you these things take time..."

She looked up at him through red-rimmed eyes and all the fight seemed to go out of her. "Aubri told me about your work in Doran," she said, her voice dull. "You brought the Regeont's murderer to justice in a few sennights. But your own nephew— my son—goes unavenged."

Ericole cringed inwardly. Nira quiet and dull was so much worse than Nira storming and screaming. It always meant she was on the verge of doing something extremely ill-advised.

"Dianira..."

"You know who is responsible, don't you?" Her voice was little more than a whisper. "You told me you had suspicions, but you have more than that, don't you? Don't lie to me, brother."

"Yes."

"You know who is responsible for my son's death?"

Niveya regarded her calmly. "I know who carried out the deed and who ordered it done."

She closed her eyes and nodded. "And there is a good reason you have not moved against the murderers?"

"I *have* moved against them, Nira. But I must be cautious in how I do so. I have the whole family to think about, and the guilty party is powerful. We must bide our time and wait for exactly the right moment to strike."

"Do not wait too long, brother," she said. "Don't forget that I have my own sources I can go to. If you will not avenge my son, I will."

Tugging her hands from his grasp, she whirled in a hurricane of skirts and scarves and glided from the room. The door slammed behind her.

Lord Niveya took his seat once again and returned his attention to the missive he had been writing, pulling the paper toward him and glancing over what he had already penned. Without looking up, he asked, "What have you learned about the Igyeum's new weapon?"

"It is devastating, Father," Ettore replied. "They call it the cynderblast."

"Have you seen it in action?"

"Yes. The Telmondir troops will not be able to stand up to it."

Niveya tapped his chin thoughtfully. "We will need to get our hands on one of these cynderblasts. Perhaps if they had the device in hand the artificineers of Telmondir could construct something similar…"

"Rumor has it that the Telmondir artificineers are already working on their own version," Ettore interrupted his musing.

"Ah." Niveya allowed himself a slight smile. "Of course they are. Very good. Make sure that our people get samples of both versions, then."

Ettore frowned. "Father?"

"Yes?" Ericole glanced up, his musings interrupted.

"Which side are we actually on?"

Niveya gave a tight, grim smile. "Whichever side makes us richer."

Ettore gave him a small, troubled look, which Niveya ignored. The best way to play his hand must be to never let anyone glimpse all the cards he was holding. Not even those closest to him. Especially not those closest to him.

He set the pen's tip to the paper and began to write once more, quietly dismissing his son. After a few breaths, he heard Ettore's feet retreating from the room and the click of the door shutting behind him. Niveya did not bother to look up from his work. He had a letter to finish.

2

———————

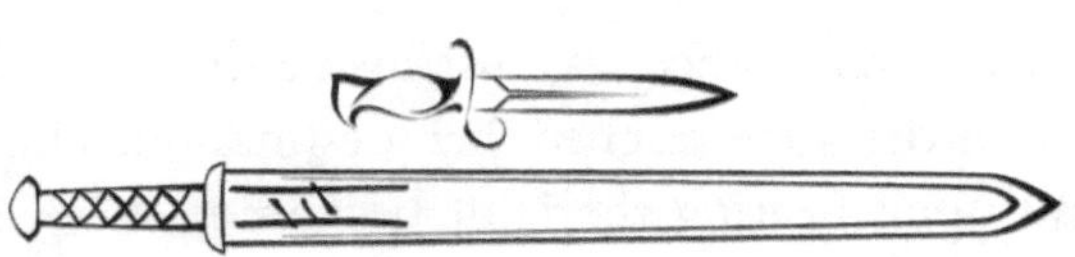

I t felt like coming home, Grayden thought, as the carriage rumbled through the enormous gates of the Academy and pulled up to the main building. With a quick word of thanks to the military driver, the two men disembarked. Standing beneath the impressive colonnades in the sweltering heat of mid-summer, Grayden pondered how far he had come since the first time he stood in this place. He had been so young when he started out from Dalsea, nearly an entire year ago now. Just a boy when he left home, now a battle-tested soldier, desperately missing his family and the life he loved, yet eager and proud to stand with his brothers-in-arms. He squinted his eyes at the massive columns, wondering fancifully if he might yet catch a glimpse of that youth he had been, so eager to leave Dalsea and dive into adventure, with so little understanding of all that he would experience, and none at all of the losses he would suffer.

Grayden's fingers rose involuntarily to the insignia pinned to his collar, his thumb brushing strangely over the new double chevron that marked him a first lieutenant: their reward for capturing those responsible for the assassination of the Regeont. Beren noticed his slight gesture and gave him a grin.

"Still adjusting?"

"It's like wearing a coat two sizes too big," Grayden admitted. "I still don't feel like I earned it."

"Our commanding officers disagree," Beren replied.

"It seems quiet."

"The new year hasn't started yet," Beren replied. "No new students getting lost yet."

"No, it's more than that," Grayden murmured as he followed Beren into the vast building.

The headmaster's office was just inside the front doors, and Beren and Grayden soon reached their destination. They knocked smartly and upon hearing the faint beckoning voice inside, the two men entered and saluted.

"Reporting as ordered," Beren barked.

Headmaster Freidzen barely spared them a glance from where he stood bent over a map laid out over a large table. "At ease," he muttered.

The two men stood waiting until Freidzen finally straightened and gave them his attention. "Ah, Beren and Grayden! It is so good to see you both. Forgive me if I seem somewhat distracted." He paused and focused on Beren. "I wish there could be time to catch up properly, nephew, I have heard of your exploits and read the reports, but it isn't the same as hearing the stories in person. However, events are moving too swiftly for such niceties."

Beren nodded. "I heard there had been some incursions. The war has truly begun, then?"

"Begun?" Freidzen shook his head. "More than begun, I'm afraid. Igyeum forces began amassing along our border inside the Whispering Wood shortly after the Regeont's murder. We originally believed this to be an indication of their guilt in the matter, since it seemed unlikely they could have learned of our lack of leadership so swiftly otherwise. However, as we now know they were not responsible..." Freidzen trailed off. "Clearly, they have good informants somewhere."

Grayden's eyes met Beren's and held for a brief instant. Grayden saw his friend's jaw harden, and he felt his own mouth twist into a grimace of displeasure. They both had the same suspicion as to who had fed the Igyeum such intelligence.

Freidzen was still speaking. "We received word this morning that the Igyeum forces have taken Baktan."

"Baktan?" Beren sounded horrified.

"But isn't Baktan a fairly sizable city?" Grayden asked, his thoughts wrenching away from their recent mission in Doran and turning to current events, trying to remember his geography lessons. "How have they managed to move beyond our borders so swiftly and take such a large prize?"

"It seems that they were already in position inside the forest for quite some time," Freidzen replied. "Our own superstitions that have kept us well away from those accursed trees blinded us to the danger building on our border. We were not able to meet them quickly enough, and they advanced unchallenged for too many miles. The Southern Command has been assembled and sent to stop them, but the Igyeum army is well supplied and dug in, with plenty of air support and a new weapon we have no answer for."

"Sir?" Grayden stared at the headmaster, his thoughts whirling with confusion.

"Uncle Freidzen, what are you talking about?" Beren finished the question.

Freidzen blinked. "I forgot, you've been fairly isolated for the past lunats. The Igyeum has developed something called a cynderblast, a weapon that scorches the earth with a beam of fire. They are retrofitting their airships with these weapons as fast as they can build them."

"What are our orders?" Grayden asked.

"I am sending you both to the front for now," Freidzen replied grimly. "Our forces are doing their best to hold back the Igyeum, but we need every defender we have." He pointed to the map and Beren and Grayden moved to join him. "I want you to report to the Eighth Battalion here at Akkad under Captain Bast. They are fortifying their position in Erghan. The Eighth Battalion there has taken heavy casualties. I'm sending three additional platoons to reinforce their position which is less than I had hoped for, but the two of you will certainly help to cover any shortage. We'll send a full regiment as quickly as we can. We've been hit and hit hard and are staggering a bit for a response. Time is what we are fighting for so we can develop that response. Is that understood?"

"Aye, sir," Beren and Grayden said together.

"Check with the supply officer over in the mess: he'll put you to work getting those supplies loaded." Freidzen paused and looked at them with solemn intensity. "Beren, Grayden... fight hard and look out for each other."

As they made their way to the dining hall, the Academy was a flurry of preparation, all in the framework of an eerie silence. The faculty and defenders were making ready for battle, not a new school year.

Grayden followed Beren, allowing his enormous friend to weave through the crowd and blaze the trail for him. They arrived at a long wagon being hitched to horses, with a solemn older man overseeing the loading, an open notebook in his hand.

"Are you the supply officer?" Beren asked.

The older man nodded, not looking up from his notebook. He checked off items as they were loaded.

"Yes, who wants to know?" the man asked.

"First Lieutenants Adelfried and Ormond, reporting as ordered, sir," Beren barked.

The man did glance up now. "Ah, the replacements I was told about. Yes." He pointed to a long table. "Check in with Trooper Feldan over there and make sure you have all the requisite equipment. Then help load the wagons. We move out in an hour."

The hour passed in a blinding haze of monotony underscored by rising adrenaline. Sooner than expected, Grayden stood in line with three platoons of men ready to march to the front lines and fight in the war they had spent the past year preparing for. He patted the front pocket of his jacket and felt the reassuring crinkle of paper, the yet-unopened note from his father. It wasn't something he was avoiding, but his father had told him to open it when he most needed to hear words from home, and although the past year had by no means been easy, it had never felt like the right time.

Someone barked the order to move out. The wagons rolled forward as the drivers twitched their reins. With clopping hooves and swishing tails, the horses pulled the wagons out of the Academy courtyard, through the gates, and onto the main road leading north. Grayden and Beren fell into step behind the wagons.

They marched.

The road rose before them, clear to the horizon. Approximately one hundred miles lay between them and Akkad, where the Eighth Battalion awaited reinforcements. It would take them five or six days to make the trip, and much could change in that time. Grayden looked around at the fresh faces surrounding him, faces he did not recognize, faces that seemed too young to be Academy students.

"What's your name, defender?" he asked one of the men closest to him.

"Luc, and I'm just a trooper," the other replied in a sort of nervously eager voice. "I didn't go to the Academy or nothin'."

"Where are you from, Luc?"

"A little town east of Doran."

"What made you want to join the defenders?"

The young man shrugged. "When we got word that the Igyeum army had marched into Ondoura and taken some villages, a bunch of us with some knowledge of how to swing a sword volunteered. Well, and a few who didn't know which end of the sword to hold," he admitted. "But that was two sennights ago. The trainers at the Academy gave us some lessons while we waited for supplies."

"Have the Academy students all been sent to the front, then?" Grayden asked.

Luc nodded. "Far as I know. Always hoped to go to the Academy, but I..." He stopped speaking abruptly.

Grayden frowned, a sudden suspicion dawning. "How old are you, trooper?"

Luc paused. "Eighteen last lunat."

Grayden considered the youth striding next to him. The boy stuck out his chin and marched with great purpose, keeping his eyes straight ahead, as though unwilling to meet Grayden's gaze. Surely the boy couldn't be a day older than sixteen, Grayden thought. His own nineteen years seemed suddenly far more numerous than they were. He opened his mouth to say something, and then shut it again, General Freidzen's words ringing in his ears. "They need every defender they can get." He couldn't prove the boy's age, and he might be wrong. What right did he have to deny the lad his desire to defend his homeland? And yet, the question continued to gnaw at him throughout the day.

They marched well past sunset. As they set up their camp for the night, Grayden asked Beren what he should do about the young man who had lied about his age.

"Did he admit to the lie?" Beren asked.

"No," Grayden replied. "I didn't challenge him on it."

"Then there's nothing to do," Beren said. "He convinced the officers at the Academy he was telling the truth. Maybe he just looks young. Or maybe you're just getting old," he joked.

Grayden let out a strained chuckle. "Maybe so."

"We've seen more fighting and death than many defenders twice our age," Beren said after a slight pause to unroll his blankets. "And we're not exactly ancient, ourselves."

"Words of truth."

"Once we join the battle, we'll all be the same age."

Grayden nodded and let the matter drop. He thought of Hunter and Burke back home. Would they lie about their ages and join the defenders as scripts, too? Although, he reflected, Hunter wouldn't have to lie. Burke would, though. Would he see his childhood friends on the front lines somewhere? He fervently hoped not.

Home.

It had been a place he had been both eager and reluctant to leave. Somehow over the past year it had become more dear to him, not less. He had worried about all he would miss, but now he just hoped he and the other defenders would be enough to protect it from the scourge of war descending upon Telmondir.

Laying himself out on top of his blankets, Grayden let the warm darkness of the summer night enfold him. He closed his eyes and let his mind drift back along the familiar paths of Dalsea, across the river—where it trickled as little more than a playful stream—through his family's orchards, and down a grassy knoll into the cozy log cabin his father had built with his own hands. There was the table around which the family had sat for so many meals. There stood Seren in the door, outlined in gold, her hair a wispy tangled mess like a halo above her grinning face. There was his mother, apron covered in flour, strong, gentle hands working a ball of dough on the counter. In strode his father, sun-browned and smiling, his eyes earnest and kind. He ached to see them again. Had it only been a year? Not even a year?

Ailwen.

Her pretty face and nose gentle-flecked with freckles floated into his memories and a pang of loneliness shot through him. Why had he never said the words that threatened to burst his heart open? Why had he left without telling her how much she meant to him? Would she have waited for him had he asked?

His thoughts tumbled together beneath the starry sky until they became indistinguishable one from the other, and then the peace of sleep welcomed him into its embrace and he thought no more.

3

Marik sat on one of the long benches that the Adelfrieds now used in their dining room since they had so many long-term guests to fit around the table. He stared thoughtfully out the window, holding a steaming mug of coffee in one hand, his other hand resting on his cane. Cathrine Adelfried sat outside on a stump, a large group of children gathered around in the grass and staring up at her with adoring eyes as she read to them from a brightly-illustrated storybook. She was not strikingly beautiful. Much about her could be called "plain." And yet, there was something about her that continually drew his attention. Her easy smile and gentle patience with even the most unruly of the small children was lovely to behold.

It had been her hands changing his bandages and cleaning his wounds, her footsteps coming down the hall carrying countless trays of food, her voice urging him back to health these past long sennights. He had come to rely on her, looking forward to their conversations that helped pass the slow, boring hours of his convalescence in the Adelfrieds' home and gracious care. She had spent so much time sitting at his bedside, entertaining him with stories about her younger siblings or the antics her students got up to. He had learned much of her life and found her to be a thoughtful person of deep reflection. But though her manner was reserved, he had also observed her in moments of excitement or delight, surrounded by her family, and he knew there was more spark in her than was readily apparent—but that insight was reserved for family and close friends, not strangers. She had kept him from going insane with boredom, and for that he was eternally grateful, but there was something more that kept her ever-present in his thoughts.

Much as he enjoyed Cathrine's company, it was good to finally be able to leave his room under his own power. Hobbling across the highly polished wooden floors while leaning heavily on a cane wasn't exactly freedom, but he would never take independence of movement for granted again. His injuries had been severe: a broken leg, broken collarbone, and three cracked ribs had kept him confined in a bed for an entire lunat. His leg was still encased in a cast, but the physician who came to check on him had assured him that the plaster could be removed in another two sennights. Even then, it would take time for him to get back to his old strength and mobility. The physician had cautioned him to be patient and warned that he might have a permanent limp even once the cast was off.

"At the very least, your leg will require time to gain its old strength back. You will have to do exercises every day," the physician had said.

But Marik could not dwell on these grim promises. Time was already slipping away far too fast. Outside, the late summer sun gleamed through trees that would soon begin to change their garments, trading out gowns of emerald for those of scarlet and gold. All too soon, autumn would grow cold and the deep snows of a Telsuman winter would bury his hopes of finding Raisa.

A rustling noise made him glance toward the next room. The other patient sat near the fireplace, huddled in a blanket, though the late summer air was quite warm even this early in the morning. Though Dalmir's external wound had healed, not even leaving a scar behind, Nadia and Cathrine still discussed his injuries in hushed tones. The man had lain unconscious in bed for many sennights with a raging fever that had worried everyone. The fever finally broken one night and Dalmir awoke, but his recovery continued slowly. The only thing that seemed to pull him out of the brooding darkness surrounding him was little Hubert, whose cheerful insistence on turning anything and everything into some sort of building materials always brought a glimmer of a smile to Dalmir's lips.

A tall man strode into the room, interrupting Marik's thoughts. He nodded good morning as he poured himself a glass of water and stood with his back to the window, leaning against the counter.

"Ioan, right?" Marik asked, attempting to rise and offer his hand at the same time. He made an unsteady hash of it.

Ioan grinned and gripped his proffered hand, helping ease him back onto the bench. "First time out of bed is always the hardest," he assured Marik. "I should know, I've broken my fair share of bones."

"This is my first," Marik replied with a grimace. He studied the man before him now. Although he had seen Ioan from a distance, they had not been formally introduced. There was a strangeness to Ioan's eyes that he could not quite place; they were a brilliant green, almost emerald in their brightness, and the pupils seemed to be the wrong shape. The skin of his hand was rough, and when Marik glanced down, he saw an intricate pattern in the brown skin that resembled the bark of a tree.

"Captain Marik," Ioan replied. "It is a pleasure to meet you. And it is good to see you up and out of bed. Uncle Thorben has told me a little about you." He blinked, and Marik found he could not tear his gaze away from the young man's strange eyes. They seemed familiar. Where had he seen eyes like that before?

Ioan's brow furrowed under Marik's gaze, and he turned his head away, seeming uncomfortable. As he did so, Marik also noticed that the man's ears were slightly pointed at the top, leaf-shaped, he thought to himself.

Marik shook his head. "Forgive me, I am still recovering. You are Lord Adelfried's nephew?"

Ioan gave an easy smile. "Ours is an adopted relationship. I heard about your crash. It's a wonder you survived at all."

"Someone was looking out for me," Marik shrugged. As he glanced out the window, a memory struck him like a blast of wind.

It was dark. The cage atop the cart stood in the middle of the road. All around him rose the sounds of fighting, but he ignored the clash of swords and the shouts of the men and women he had led here. Instead, he leaped up onto the cart, fumbling at the lock, desperate to open it.

Raisa's hand stopped him. He looked up into her eyes... eyes so brilliantly green they glowed in the darkness like a malkyn's... but Raisa's eyes had always been dark, a murky hazel... She leaned her head against the bars for a moment, her hair falling forward over her ears, long ears that pointed slightly at the top...

Marik bolted to his feet. Even in his rescue attempt he had been too late. What had they done to her? What more might they be doing? What horrors would she suffer, waiting for him to rescue her? His broken leg could not support him and he toppled sideways, reaching for the rough-hewn wood of the table. His hand missed and he felt himself falling. Marik squeezed his eyes shut, bracing himself for the pain of hitting the floor. But instead hands caught him, arresting his fall. He opened his eyes and stared into Ioan's somber face as the younger man helped him back to the bench and the security of his cane.

"Are you well?" Ioan leaned down and peered into his face, his brow furrowed in concern. "Maybe you shouldn't be up and around yet. Especially if you're going to go leaping about like a rabbit."

Marik nodded dumbly. "I'm fine. I—I'm sorry. Your eyes reminded me of someone else."

Ioan's gaze sharpened with sudden interest. "They did? Whose?"

"One of my crew," Marik replied. "She was taken prisoner by the Ar'Mol when we were in Malei. It was my fault, I shouldn't have let her go alone... she was in the dungeons for lunats..." He shook his head. "We attempted a rescue, but failed. But for the brief moment when I saw her... I don't know how to explain it, she just seemed... different. Her eyes had changed. I didn't think much of it at the time, but when I saw your eyes... I apologize, this must seem incredibly rude. It just struck me that her eyes looked exactly the same as yours, but that can't be right." He shook his head. "Raisa's eyes aren't green, they're hazel," he muttered to himself. "I must be remembering wrong."

Ioan sank into a chair on the other side of the table. "Is it possible?" he whispered, his voice sounding hoarse.

"Is what possible?" Marik asked the question, though he was not sure he wanted to know the answer.

Ioan shook his head. "It's hard to explain, but I'll try. You see, there was this madman in the mountains..."

———

MARIK SAT BY THE RIVER, tossing rocks idly into the water as it slid lazily by. His chest ached and his leg throbbed. Hobbling down the footpath had taken every last ounce of strength he had, and he wasn't sure he would be able to get back to the Adelfried home on his own, but it had been worth it to get outside. He had needed to get out into the open air after his conversation with Ioan.

The defender's story had shaken Marik more than he'd like to admit. But in the end, they both agreed that the most likely explanation must be that Lorcan, the madman, had somehow made his way back to Malei and used what he had learned from his experiment on Ioan to alter Raisa. This confirmed Ioan's suspicions that the man was in the employ of the Ar'Mol, or rather, the Ar'Molon, as they were beginning to realize the true power behind the throne of the Igyeum.

Marik had in turn told Ioan more of the durven's story, and the man had listened raptly. Ioan had met the durven, but he had not heard their full story. Eighty years ago, their people had suffered as experiments under the hands of Lorcan, the same man responsible for Ioan's transformation. The durven were a shy, reclusive people, though they seemed to be settling in down in the valley that Thorben had gifted them until they could be restored to their homeland.

Marik shuddered. He, of all people, knew what the Igyeum was capable of. But this atrocity of manipulating a person's very being and turning them into something else crossed a line he hadn't known existed. Worse, Ioan had hinted that Lorcan had seemed intent on creating new soldiers for the Igyeum. Marik hated to think about what that might mean for Raisa. That she might be forced to fight for the very ones who had killed her father, destroyed her home, and robbed her of the life she should have had was more than he could bear. He had to get to her, to rescue her, but how? He could barely walk short distances and he had no airship. He didn't even know if Raisa was alive. He banished the thought as swiftly as it occurred. She was alive. She must be alive! If Ioan's story and his own memory of the failed rescue so many sennights ago were true, then Raisa was alive. Lorcan would not let another "experiment" slip through his fingers.

"Hold on, Raisa," Marik mumbled grimly. "I'm coming."

A scuffling sound made him turn to see Wynn making his way down the path toward him. A moment later, Wynn had joined him. The younger man took a seat beside the pirate on the smooth pebbles of the riverbank.

"Ioan said you'd come down this way and might need help getting back," Wynn offered by way of explanation.

Marik heaved a sigh. "He's probably right."

"He told me what you talked about."

Marik nodded, staring at the water. It was too much to take in. Too heavy a burden to bear.

"I wanted to ask you something," Wynn said, his words tumbling out of his mouth in a rush. "You can say no. I know it's presumptuous of me. You might not like the idea of change... I've been meaning to ask for a while but you were still recovering..." He stopped and stared out across the river, unable to meet Marik's gaze. Marik waited, but Wynn did not continue.

"Just spit it out," Marik encouraged.

"I'd like to fix up the Hawk for you," Wynn said. "But I also want to make a few changes. Daegan and Molly and I... we've been learning a lot about cynders, and I'm sure I could make a few adjustments that would increase the efficiency of her engine. Might even be able to make her faster, too. I'm not certain what the possibilities are, but I think you'd like them."

A sudden lump filled his throat. Marik tossed another pebble across the water. It skipped a few times before sinking beneath the ripples. In his mind's eye, he pictured his airship the way she had always been before he rammed her into the Igyeum airship and took a sun-bolt meant for another: whole and perfect and poised for flight. He held the image gently in his thoughts, but like a broken vase the pieces collapsed. The Hawk was not whole, and he had been grieving her like the loss of a loved one.

Wynn shifted, the eagerness in his expression fading as the silence stretched between them. "I understand if you don't want me to."

"You think you can fix her?" Marik finally managed.

Wynn's eyes lit up and he nodded enthusiastically. "Definitely! We have all the parts we need right here, and Keene can fashion new spars. I think there are some things I can do to the sails, even. I've been thinking about this a lot, and wishing I had a small airship to try out some of these ideas on... I'm convinced they're sound... but without a ship, they are just theories. And building something from scratch seemed so impractical, but if you'd be willing to let me do some experimenting..."

"She'd still be the Hawk, right?" Marik interrupted again, staring hard into Wynn's earnest face.

Wynn gazed back steadily, and understanding lit his expression. He nodded firmly. "She'll be your Hawk," he assured Marik. "Just... maybe a little faster."

Hope flared in his chest with a burning warmth that was almost painful. Marik gave a terse nod. "Do your worst, then." He grinned. "Not that I think you can actually improve upon perfection... but I will admit, she's a little banged up right now. We make a good pair, me and the Hawk, be a shame to break up our team. I've got one favor to ask, though."

"Name it!"

"Can you help me get back to the house?"

Wynn laughed, and after a moment, Marik joined him. Their laughter filled the air, wafting across the river like a song of joy.

4

Raisa spat dirt out of her mouth and rose painfully to her feet, glaring at the man holding the whip. She wanted nothing so much as she wished to wrap her hands around his throat and squeeze until he stopped breathing. With her new strength and agility, she could kill him easily, she needed no sword or dagger. The training of the past sennights—or had it been lunats? The weather in this part of Palla was so stable and her training so rigid that it was impossible to keep track of time, the days all blended together in a haze of heat—had honed her into a weapon. But she could not risk it. There were too many soldiers in the Weald, and nowhere to run should she try to escape. She had already tried it once.

* * *

It had been raining that afternoon. She had only been in the Weald for a few days, still learning the limits of her new abilities, still learning the exacting discipline and merciless nature of her new masters. Torrents of water broke loose from the sky with an unexpected force, sending everyone running to their tents. In the confusion, Raisa had been left alone for a blissful moment. Without thinking, she acted, bursting into a sprint and racing into the forest. She pushed through large, leafy plants and dodged around tree trunks, her legs pumping as she forced herself to run faster and faster. The huge trees surrounded her, stretching up to the sky, a testament to the age of the forest, but she had no time to admire them in her panicked flight.

Her body, strengthened by whatever Lorcan had done to her, did not tire. She ran for ten minutes, fifteen, twenty, mentally counting the seconds. Her lungs began to burn and her muscles screamed at her to stop when she had burst suddenly through the last of the trees. Despair welled up within her as she realized why the guards had not bothered to chase her, or even keep a close watch on her. There was no need for bars or chains. There was nowhere to go. Stretching in every direction, sand filled her vision: vast expanses of sand, rolling dunes spread across the horizon beneath the dark storm front of turbulent clouds winging their way across the sky. With a sinking feeling like she had just swallowed a rock, she recognized her location: she was somewhere within the vast Plains of Temna, a barren desert that stretched across the entirety of Palla's southern half. Other than a few nomadic tribes, nobody lived in those desolate wastes, with good reason. Scorching hot by day, freezing cold by night, the Plains were inhospitable in the extreme. She stood there, considering; did she dare brave that barren expanse?

"No escape." The voice cackled in her ear and she whirled, hands raised to defend herself.

Lorcan hopped down from the crook of the tree he had been sitting in and Raisa recoiled, hating his nearness, hating everything about him.

"Isn't my Weald lovely?" he crooned, his hand caressing the trunk of the tree. "Oh yes, this forest oasis is all mine, all my doing. Grew it overnight. Nobody else could do that," he bragged. Then he grinned, his gaze suddenly sharp. "No way out for you, pretty pet. The perfect prison for such a dangerous soldier. Until she can be tamed and trained..." He nodded absently. "She will be good, a good soldier for Lorcan, won't she? She cannot run away, no. She would not survive out there." He gestured at the endless vista of rolling sand dunes, turning dark beneath the pelting rain. "She must survive here, where there is water enough. Must train and become an obedient soldier. Yes."

All hope of escape vanished in that moment, washed away by the storm. That had been the last time she attempted to flee or rebel. From that moment on, she had worked at her training, throwing herself into it with grim determination, doing her best to convince them they had broken her. She knew her only chance to leave the Weald rested on her ability to convince her captors that she was theirs, body and soul, their obedient soldier. In order to succeed in her deception, she had to be meticulous in her obedience, taking care to never give any indication that she had disobeyed.

* * *

The man towering over her cracked his whip, its stinging bite forcing her back to the present. "Again!" he barked.

Dutifully, her face schooled in impassivity, Raisa rose to her feet. Urging her aching body to its limits, she ran to the first obstacle, a twelve-foot wall affixed with sharp spikes jutting out on either side. She leaped into the air, catching hold of one of the longer spikes and using her momentum to fling herself over the wall in a wide arc. She dropped into the river on the other side, swimming across with quiet, powerful strokes. The course was part of her daily routine, but the obstacles themselves were altered often to prevent her muscles from simply memorizing the movements. Captain Virtanen insisted that she be trained adequately in learning to deal with surprises. Most of the time, the surprises were simple, various aspects of the course placed in a different order or combination, but some days they involved an ambush she had to fight her way through.

She focused on the next obstacle, a long field of deep, watery mud covered by a web of razor-sharp wire. The wire crisscrossed the ground only a couple of inches above the mucky bog, which meant she would have to immerse her entire body in the ooze in order to cross. Trying not to think too much about what she was doing, she lowered herself into the mud and began the tedious, swimming crawl.

Her body wove its way through the rest of the obstacles with a grace she had never before possessed. This time, she did not falter at the end, and the man with the whip gave her a reluctant nod.

"Better," was all he said.

Inside, she raged and howled. Outside, she stood stoic, awaiting her next orders.

"Clean yourself up and go back to your tent," the man ordered, tossing a damp rag at her. "We will continue in the morning."

Raisa caught the rag and wiped her arms and face, wondering why the captain couldn't have arranged it so that the mud-dive came before the swim across the river? He'd probably done it on purpose, she decided. But unless it was part of her training, she was not allowed to wander down to the pond, so she did the best she could with the rag and then made her way back to her tent.

She tried to ignore the accusing glares of the other prisoners as she passed the cages they sat huddled inside. They considered her a traitor. Well, they could think what they wanted. Her tactics had gotten her out of the cage and into a tent of her own. The freedom she had bought with her seeming cooperation had given her access to knowledge about where they were, and it gave her the opportunity to explore her new abilities and test the limits of her new form. If she seemed a traitor... well... that was a price she was willing to pay for the chance to be ready when an opportunity for escape presented itself. She could not help the others by remaining in the cage with them. But perhaps she could help them from out here. And she did. They were not aware that it was Raisa who deposited the gourds of fresh water within their ranks in the middle of the night, nor did they know to thank her for the odd blanket or handkerchief full of meat and bread she smuggled into their midst. They did not know that she often went hungry so that the little ones could eat. How could they know? She had to be extremely cautious about when she brought the offerings, only when they slept so that they could not give her away even involuntarily. Still—Raisa grimaced—they might have guessed that their benefactor was not one of the soldiers.

With a weary sigh she threw herself inside her tent and lay on the hard ground, considering her options and trying to ignore the grime still coating her body; experience had taught her the mud would flake off easily once it dried completely. There was little she could do until then, and she had been given explicit orders to return to her tent, which left no room for misinterpretation. With a stick, she scratched at the sandy ground, trying to come up with a plan.

A plate of food was tossed through her door; it landed with a thump and the dried meat slid off the misshapen tin into the dirt. Raisa pounced on it, brushing it off. The hard, cracker-like bread that lined the tin sat in several pieces. She waited, but nothing more appeared through the door of her tent. Her stomach flipped uncomfortably. Setting the tin carefully to one side, she poked her head through the opening and called out to the retreating soldier.

"Water!"

He stopped and turned to face her. "No water rations for you tonight," he barked.

She rose, drawing herself up and glaring at him. "I need water! I cannot train without it."

The soldier, not much more than a boy, gazed at her and gave an apologetic shrug. "Nothing I can do about it. Orders came from Lorcan himself."

Gritting her teeth, Raisa did not reply; she understood the madman more than she wished to. After all this time in the Weald, she recognized a summons when she saw it. If she wanted water, she would have to go speak with him. Her skin crawled with a discomfort that could not be accounted for just from the mud coating her body. His mad ravings were difficult to endure, and his moments of sinister clarity were even more unsettling; this was a man who knew exactly what he was doing, and he enjoyed it. She sighed. But enduring his conversation for an hour meant that she would walk away with a double portion of water, and perhaps even some extra food. Her gaze drifted to the pitiful group huddled inside the cage and her resolve hardened. They were worth it, even if they hated her. Reluctantly, she rose. Then her thoughts brightened. If the madman was in an especially good mood, she might even be allowed to go for a swim and clean the muck from her hair and clothes.

Knowing that he would not be pleased with her appearance, she dragged her fingers through her hair and did her best to force it into some semblance of a braid before leaving her tent. She crossed the camp and found Lorcan sitting on a log. A small fire inside a ring of stones flickered with new life, as though it had only just been started. He did not look up at her approach, but his face wrinkled into a hideous smile.

"Ah, my Raisa. My good Raisa," he purred.

Bile rose in her throat, but she choked it down with her true feelings, hiding them deep within herself. She sat down on the other side of the fire. "Master." She ducked her head.

"Yes, my Raisa. The only one of my children to respect me the way a father should be respected."

Unbidden, a memory of her own father rose in Raisa's mind. His face swam in her vision: the sun-darkened skin of his face creased in a smile, the scratchy feel of his beard on the top of her head as he held her in his arms, comforting her when she awoke out of a nightmare, the smell of woodsmoke and sawdust that clung to his rough woolen shirt. For a moment she could feel his strong arms wrapped around her, lending her his strength even now, so many years after his death. The insane creature before her was nothing like the man who had cared for her, loved her, and protected her even with his final breaths. She banished the memory with a shake of her head, clamping her teeth down on the angry, stinging retort she wanted to throw back at him.

"The soldiers would not give me water. I cannot train without water," she said instead, reciting her part dutifully.

"Ah." Lorcan frowned. "You must always come to me when

you are sad or if someone hurts you. Yes. Like a good daughter."
He handed her a cup filled with water.

Raisa just managed to keep from snatching at it, but could
not prevent her hand from trembling slightly as she raised the cup
to her lips. She drank deeply, the cold water soothing her throat
and her temper.

His sharp gaze caught hers above the rim of the cup. "Would
you like to meet your brother?"

She lowered the empty cup and frowned, suddenly thrown
off-balance. "My... brother?"

He grinned at her puzzlement. "It was unkind of me, perhaps,
that I kept him from you. But he does not seem to understand, as
you do, how to treat his father. I wondered if you might speak
with him? Explain to him? He is angry and frightened. I
wonder..." Lorcan trailed off for a moment. He shook himself. "I
believe it is because he did not know I was alive."

If that's the case, then he's probably angry to find out that
you are still alive, Raisa thought.

"You will speak with him?"

Raisa shrugged. "If you wish it."

"My good girl. I do." Lorcan rose and beckoned, so Raisa
followed. He led her across the camp and deep into the trees to an
area she had not yet explored. He wound his way through the
forest. As they left sight of the camp, Raisa wondered if this
might be her chance to kill the man. She pushed the thought
away. Just because it seemed like they were alone did not mean
that they truly were. She had seen his tree-men—he called them
his "generals" and the other soldiers referred to them as "baumen"—had seen what they were capable of. They mostly stayed
quiet and still on the outskirts of the Weald. Their presence
agitated the soldiers, which had prompted Captain Virtanen to
order Lorcan to keep the baumen out of sight. As he had orders
from the Ar'Molon himself to obey Virtanen, Lorcan had been
forced to comply, but he clearly resented it. Raisa understood
why the men were nervous about the baumen. Even with her new

strength and speed, she doubted she was a match for even one of them by herself, especially with no weapons, and it was certain Lorcan would call to them if she attempted any sort of attack. No, now was not her moment. Besides, she was intrigued to meet this "brother" he had spoken of. Not her real brother, of course —she was an only child—but in his insanity, she was certain he meant another like her, someone who had once been human, and then had undergone changes at his hands. Her curiosity was piqued. Lorcan had made it clear that she was the first of her kind, that his other attempts had been failures. Had he lied to her?

Now that they were quite a ways into the forest, Lorcan paused at a rocky hillock; across the side of the mound great roots twisted together like a giant, tangled spiderweb. At a tiny gesture from the madman, the roots unknotted themselves and pulled back, revealing the mouth of a dark cave.

Lorcan gestured. "He is inside. Won't you go in and speak with him? I will wait here."

Trepidation rose in Raisa's heart. What was this? Had he discovered her minor rebellions? Did he intend to close the cave behind her, sealing her in a tomb to die? But no. That did not match anything she had seen of the madman. When he delivered a punishment, he was swift and callous about it and he always made sure she knew her crime. To lure her into the woods and leave her to die took more premeditated vindictiveness than Lorcan seemed to possess.

Steeling herself, she ducked into the cave. Her eyes adjusted quickly in the darkness, another benefit to the changes Lorcan had made to her. She scanned the interior of the cavern.

Seeing no one inside, she hesitated, still half-afraid Lorcan meant to seal her inside. But she dismissed the thought, knowing that if she dwelled on terror she would soon find herself paralyzed, and then Lorcan's anger would be wakened. She had been careful; she was certain she had done nothing to arouse his suspicions. Still, she risked a swift glance over her shoulder at the entrance; it remained open and Lorcan still waited outside, craning his neck to peer after her.

"Hello?" she called out in a gentle voice. "I'm not here to hurt you."

Silence.

She took a few cautious steps farther into the cave. "Hello?" she called again.

Out of the corner of her eye, she saw the briefest glimmer of movement. Quietly, she crouched down in an attempt to appear less intimidating, and waited.

Minutes ticked by.

Her legs were starting to cramp, complaining that she had pushed too hard, asked too much of them today. She ignored the pain, holding herself as still as a tree.

Then, she caught a flicker of movement once more. She turned her head slowly toward the movement. He was so still and small, she almost missed him. But then he lifted his head and she saw his face. Their eyes met and she could tell that he knew he had been spotted.

"Who are you?" he whispered, his tone suspicious.

"I'm Raisa. Who are you?"

He looked about furtively. "Are you working for... him?"

Raisa very slowly and very deliberately shook her head. No.

Out loud, she said, "Yes."

He squinted at her, his expression a mixture of confusion and wariness. "Wait... you said your name was Raisa?"

"Yes."

He dropped his voice to a whisper. "Did you work for a pirate crew?"

It was Raisa's turn to be startled and wary. Who was doing the interrogating, here? Could this be a trap of Lorcan's? He might not be vindictive, but she wouldn't put this kind of mental torture past him, especially if he wanted to ascertain her true loyalties.

"Maybe," was all she said.

"What was the name of the airship?" the small figure demanded. "I won't speak to you any more or believe a word you say until you tell me the name."

Raisa hesitated, not wanting to give this stranger, or Lorcan, any information they did not need. But Lorcan already knew this. It was worth the risk. "The Valdeun Hawk."

His expression relaxed and he stepped away from the wall. He was short, no taller than Mouse. "My name is Olin," he said, his voice low. "Is the madman listening?"

"He is waiting for me at the entrance," Raisa whispered back. She raised her voice. "Our father is kind and only wants what is best for you, you do not need to be afraid."

"Your captain, Marik, convinced my people to help him in an attempt to rescue you in Malei," Olin confided. His voice rasped, as though he were recuperating from an illness. He crossed the cave to another wall and began clanking about with some items stacked there. "I got separated from the rest of the group in the confusion and the soldiers captured me and sent me here." Raisa caught the snap of a match lighting, and then a soft glow illuminated the cavern as Olin turned back to face her, lantern in hand.

For a long, frozen moment they stared at one another.

Olin's skin was a strange shade of grayish-green and covered in a pattern that looked like scales, and what he lacked in height he made up for in stocky width. He wore a thick leather vest and strips of leather banded his bare, muscular arms. His dark hair fell in coils and braids to his shoulders, and a dark beard covered the lower half of his face.

"What are you?" Olin whispered.

Raisa recoiled as though he had struck her. She was too shocked to reply. The question froze her to the heart of her being, a shard of ice jammed into her chest, a chill spreading across her with icy tendrils, repeating the question over and over, the question she had been avoiding since Lorcan had conducted his experiment: What are you? She had tried to ignore what Lorcan had done to her. In the Weald, it had been easy. Mirrors were a closely guarded luxury, and while she knew many of the soldiers had small ones they used when shaving, these little treasures were kept hidden away in their tents or pockets. Other than a single, horrified glimpse of herself that Lorcan had allowed her to see in the mirror he had held before her eyes just before they escorted her out of the palace dungeons, Raisa had not really seen herself since Lorcan's alterations took hold.

Olin stared at her, stricken. He seemed to understand the pain his question had caused and he took a tentative step forward.

"He did this to you." It was not a question, and Raisa knew instinctively which "he" to whom Olin referred.

Raisa nodded mutely. "And you?"

"Yes," Olin replied, his voice grating, as though the admission cost him.

"He called you my brother," Raisa told him, not bothering to keep her voice down; Lorcan would get suspicious at too much silence.

"In a twisted way, that is correct," Olin muttered. "Not that we are blood kin, but because he is responsible for what we now are." Olin's head listed to one side, as though studying her. "Though with you, he appears to have understood what he was doing. My people were his accident." His shoulders slumped. "We tried to remain hidden from him, but I was careless." He looked up at her, his dark eyes huge and pleading. "Do you know if there are any others like me here?"

"I didn't even know you were here," Raisa replied. "But... I don't think so. I haven't seen anyone else like you."

"That is good. I worry that I have put my people in danger. They... tortured me, and I fear I gave them the information they wanted."

"If you were helping Marik, then he will watch over your people," Raisa said, trying to infuse as much confidence into her tone as she could. "If they were in danger, you can be sure that he would not leave them." Her conscience winced as she spoke. Would he? Until recently, she had not even known the whole truth about Marik's past. She had trusted him implicitly since she and Oleck joined his crew, but could she still trust him, now that she knew the truth?

"I believe you," Olin said. "But why did Lorcan bring you here?"

"I don't know." Raisa raised her voice. "He just asked me to speak with you. To... explain things to you... though I'm not sure I know what that means." Raisa shrugged and lowered her voice again. "He is insane, that much is clear."

"The most dangerous kind of insane," Olin agreed. "He wishes to know more about my people, but I have done what I can to keep the details from him. He must never learn the things he wishes to know."

Raisa's curiosity rose, but she refrained from asking. She could not betray what she did not know, and she was still not certain how much control Lorcan had over her. So far, he had not demonstrated an ability to force her to do anything, but she had not given him reason to try.

"Daughter?" Lorcan's voice rang down the tunnel, making Raisa jump. "Time to go home."

"Coming, Father!" she called back, using the term to appease the madman. She turned to Olin and whispered in a rush, "You know he is insane. He thinks of us like his children." She shuddered. "If what you've said is correct, then you're not in immediate danger... yet. He's curious about how he created you. It seems he has been attempting experiments like this for a long time without any success. But at any moment he might decide there are quicker ways to get the answers he's looking for, answers that don't require you to be alive. If you show him a little deference, it goes a long way. You don't have to give him any secrets, just make him think you're coming around. At the very least, it might convince him to bring me back here. Perhaps together we can figure out a way to escape."

Olin's lips thinned, disappearing behind his thick beard. "You do not know what you are asking."

"I'm asking you to survive," Raisa whispered.

"Daughter!" Lorcan's voice sounded more demanding.

"I will think about it," Olin relented. "But I make no promises. That man... you don't know all he's done."

"Maybe not. But you won't be able to do anything about it if you're dead." Raisa turned and hurried back down the tunnel. When she reached the entrance, the vines and roots were already beginning to twine their way across the opening. Trying not to show her panic, she stepped through the swiftly closing gap.

Lorcan glanced at her, his eyes bright. "Did you explain things to him? Does he understand?"

"I think he is beginning to," Raisa replied, still at a loss about what it was Lorcan had wanted her to explain to Olin. "I might need to come talk with him again."

"We will see," Lorcan mused. He seemed about to say more, but instead he let out a pained, guttural cry and fell to the ground where he convulsed, huddling in on himself. Raisa frowned, torn. On the one hand, her tormentor lay vulnerable at her feet but on the other hand, the Weald was not large enough for her to hide in, and she knew she would never survive the desert on her own. So instead of using the dagger she had managed to steal and conceal at her ankle, she feigned concern.

"Father?" she said, spitting the vile lie from her mouth. "What is wrong?"

Lorcan clasped his hands to his head and moaned like a lost child. "He is coming."

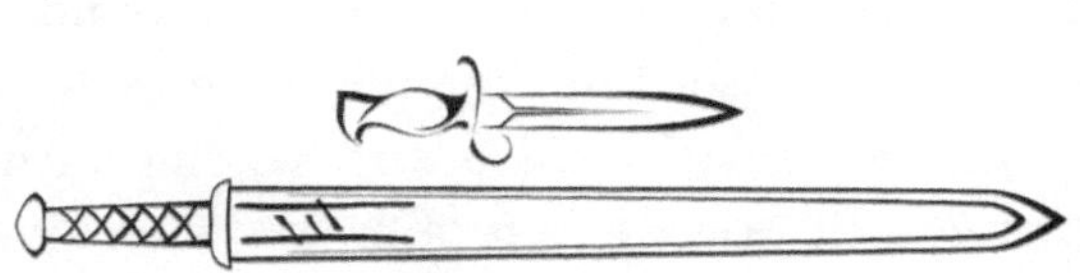

Beren lay flat on his stomach in the shallow ditch, his arms and face caked with mud. Great pines towered above him, lining the road leading into the nearby village and providing sparse cover for the soldiers. He glanced sideways to see the dim shapes of Grayden and the rest of their battalion stretched out along the winding line of the ditch, awaiting the signal. The stealthy swish of feet reached his ears and he saw the line of heads raise slightly, senses alert to the possibility of an enemy presence. Up and over the rise along the tree-lined road came a wave of Igyeum soldiers, slinking through the midnight blackness. Beren kept an eye on Captain Bast, awaiting his commanding officer's signal.

A flash of a hand, pale in the dark night, caught his gaze. Beren surged up from his hiding place, sword already raised and swinging down at the nearest enemy soldier. The man twisted and met Beren's swing with his own blade, but was unprepared for the sheer amount of force that the eight-foot-tall Telsuman could bring to bear. The soldier's arm buckled beneath the blow and the man fell to the ground without a sound. Behind Beren, the Eighth Battalion leaped from the ditch with a roar that shook the night.

Swords clashed, the resounding ring of steel on steel filled the darkness. Men cried out in startled pain as crossbow bolts found their marks. Torchlight flared suddenly, casting an orange glow on the battle.

The fighting raged swift and fierce, but the element of surprise did not last nearly long enough to matter. Soon, the greater numbers of the Igyeum army turned toward their position and the Eighth Battalion was forced to give ground, retreating into the village. Men rushed to close the crude gates, sealing the enemy out for now. Bast barked orders, sending men up onto rooftops to use their bows; a rain of arrows forced the Igyeum soldiers back down the road and out of range, but not before the deadly arrows had done their work.

The Eighth Battalion surged back through the gates, chasing their enemy, now thrown off-balance by this tactical ploy of retreat-and-advance. Beren led a platoon down the road after the fleeing soldiers, but when it became apparent that the enemy had no intention of stopping and regrouping, Beren ordered his men back to the village.

Once inside the village walls, Beren sought out Grayden and found him pumping water into buckets for the men. Beren waited until the line had dwindled and the men had departed.

"They've taken every settlement between Baktan and here in less than a lunat," Beren commented.

Grayden dunked his own head beneath the water pump and then straightened, giving his dark head a shake and throwing droplets of water everywhere. "They didn't take this village tonight, though."

Beren grimaced. "Bast's tactic won't work twice. They'll be ready for the ambush next time."

"Then Captain Bast will come up with something new. He's devilishly clever." Grayden grinned and held up a bucket. "Wash water?"

Beren nodded wearily and took the bucket. He scooped a handful up over his face. "How long can we last here? We keep falling back from one village to the next. The enemy has greater numbers and better supply lines, and they march toward Doran with purpose."

"But we only have to hold the line," Grayden reminded him. "They have to advance in enemy territory and travel hundreds of miles beyond their base of supply. Eventually, they'll spread their forces too thin. Besides, Southern Command will get the supply lines figured out. They'll send us more defenders, too. We were caught off guard, that's all. The road into Ondoura is the easiest route, and it makes sense they'd come this way with knowledge of the assassination..."

Beren's lip curled.

Grayden raised a hand. "We have no proof it was Niveya who told them."

"I don't need proof," Beren muttered.

"My point was simply that everything isn't as hopeless as you make it seem here."

"I hope you are right, my friend." Beren clenched his jaw. "But I cannot help but feel like we could be doing more."

"We are giving these villagers time to evacuate," Grayden reminded him, "and we're slowing the Igyeum down. Every hour we hold against them is another hour for our commanders to develop our response."

Beren nodded glumly. "You are right." With a sigh, he turned with his bucket and headed to a nearby barn to wash the mud from his face and arms.

———

EARLY THE NEXT MORNING, Beren woke to someone roughly shaking him by the shoulder. He peered up into the angry face of Captain Bast.

"Captain?" A glance at the sky showed him it was not quite dawn. Instantly alert, Beren scrambled to his feet. "What is it? An attack?"

"No," Bast growled. "New orders. Grab your gear and follow me."

Mystified by his commander's obvious anger and wondering what he had done to cause it, Beren rose and followed the captain along the hard-packed road. The man paused in various places, rousing other soldiers from their sleep, pulling men away from where they stood watch. Eventually, ten defenders in all, including Beren and Grayden, were trailing after their commanding officer. He led them out of the village through the southern gate. Beren halted in his tracks at the sight of a huge, flat-bottomed airship sitting in a large pasture.

"Here they are," Bast barked, gesturing at the soldiers behind him. "My ten best, as ordered."

A shock of dismay coursed through Beren at this. They were being reassigned? He turned to stare at the figure Captain Bast was addressing.

He was a tall, slender man with graying hair. The triangles of a major gleamed on his collar. The man returned Captain Bast's salute in the early gleam of predawn light. "Good work, Captain Bast, you have done well here at the front. I am pleased to be able to inform you that a whole regiment marches this way, fresh from Southern Command. They should arrive by nightfall to relieve you and your men, who will fall back to Command Hearth in Erghan."

Bast grimaced. "About time. We've been in slow retreat from Baktan for the past two sennights. My men are exhausted."

"They'll get a rest back in Erghan," the major replied. "It won't be as long as they deserve, but at least they'll get a few days."

The captain gave a short nod. "It's small comfort, knowing that my battalion will be back on the front lines in a sennight less my ten best soldiers."

"You'll get replacements."

"I'd need fifty replacements to make up for these ten."

"And that is exactly why we need them." The major's voice was impassive, his face expressionless.

"Yes, Major." Captain Bast's belligerent tone faded. He turned to the men behind him. "You all have orders to go with the major on a new assignment."

"Sir!" Beren protested. "Permission to argue this decision."

Bast's expression softened to one of pride. "Son, I hate to lose you. Every one of you has made a difference here, and it hasn't gone unnoticed. But orders are orders, even if some are harder to obey than others." The captain's face and tone hardened. "You leave now. Anything you didn't grab on your way out, you'll have to replace at your new quarters." He stood back and saluted. "It has been an honor serving with each of you, and I hope to do so again before this is all over. I turn you over to your new assignment and the major, here." He gave a curt nod and then turned and marched back into the village as the sky above turned a paler shade of blue.

Beren caught Grayden's mystified gaze and returned it, a rising sense of outrage building within him.

"Right," the major said. "I'm Major Semiv, commander of the Forty-Seventh, your new regiment. Everyone onto the troop carrier."

"Sir," Beren began as they moved to obey. "May I ask where we are going?"

"Attatoire."

The word meant nothing to him, and Beren's anger simmered further. He resisted the urge to look back over his shoulder at the men who had swiftly become like brothers to him.

"Why are we being called away?" he asked.

"Not my place to say. You'll find out soon enough." Semiv didn't pause, but marched toward the airship with long strides, forcing them to follow him.

Frustrated, Beren joined the other men as they jogged across the field to the massive waiting airship. As their feet pounded up the ramp, he found himself next to Grayden.

"You all right?" Grayden asked.

Beren unclenched his fists and heaved a sigh. "Yes."

Grayden peered at him in curiosity, but said nothing.

After a moment, Beren heaved a deep sigh. "It's just that I don't like being called away from the front lines. It feels like a giant step backward. We worked so hard to get there, and then to be pulled away just when we were finally doing some good..." He trailed off.

"I know you entered the Academy with a different goal in mind than most of us," Grayden said after a pause. "And I know that you felt like you lost time when we were working with Niveya this summer. But I think you might be forgetting that we have done good. We discovered Lorcan and chased him out of Telsuma. We discovered a viper in our own nest when we found the Regeont's murderer. Our road has not been conventional, but maybe it's all been preparing us for something."

"What?"

"I don't know. But something. Captain Bast said we were among ten of his best, as ordered. Wherever we're going, I think it's going to be important. If we have to fight, don't you want to fight alongside the best of the best?"

Slowly, Beren's anger cooled as he considered his friend's words. Maybe Grayden was right. It didn't erase the sting of frustration, but it did ease it somewhat. He gave a slow, thoughtful nod. "Perhaps you are right. That is, indeed, why I wanted to attend the Academy in the first place. However, the best of the best will have to be special indeed to surpass the men we have already fought alongside."

"Agreed."

The troop carrier was different from any airship Beren had ever ridden on, and he had flown in quite a few in the nineteen years of his life. As the oldest son of a Council member, he had been privileged to participate in far more travel than most men his age. He couldn't count the number of diplomatic trips he had taken with his father; he was well-acquainted with air travel. But now he found himself in wholly unfamiliar surroundings. For one thing, the troop carrier was vast, far more enormous than even the cargo cruiser that he had climbed aboard to journey to the Academy. For another, it boasted no masts; the entire upper deck was wide and flat and no sails stuck up from the middle of it. Large trim sails extended from either side as normal, but Beren wondered how the ship could be maneuvered without sails. He voiced this question to Grayden, who dragged him over to the back of the ship and had him look down.

As the airship lifted off the ground, a huge sail unfolded from the bottom of the ship, pointing down at the swiftly dwindling earth.

"It acts like a rudder on a sea ship," Grayden explained. "We studied them in my aeronautics class. Wynn could explain how it all works better than I, but from what I remember, it's basically the same principle as having the mast on top of the ship."

"How do the sailors get around in the rigging down there, though?"

"They don't," Grayden replied.

"But how do they furl and unfurl the sails and things like that?"

"The sails down there aren't canvas," Grayden explained. "They're made of a much more rigid material, so they don't need so many minor adjustments. It's something our own artificineers have come up with. Don't you remember Wynn telling us about them?"

A vague memory of a very long evening in their room at the Academy flickered through Beren's mind. "I think I stopped listening when he started talking about the benefits of various theories on aerodynamics and wind flow or something."

"He can get a little long-winded." Grayden gave him his patented grin and raised his eyebrows, inviting Beren to join him in a joke.

Beren frowned at him. "Yes…" he said slowly, trying to figure out why Grayden was suddenly fighting against laughter.

"Wynn-ded?" Grayden asked. "Wynn…ded?"

Beren blinked at him. "Ah," he said, finally understanding. "Yes. Amusing."

Grayden shook his head with a wry chuckle.

"Sorry, my friend. After all we have seen and survived this past year, I find little use for laughter," Beren whispered. He didn't mean for Grayden to hear, but the other caught the words, perhaps flung to him on the breeze of their takeoff.

"I have to laugh, Beren," he said, suddenly sober. "It keeps the fear at bay."

6

Raisa stared down at the quivering mass Lorcan had suddenly dissolved into. Warring emotions clashed within her: disgust and loathing filled her being, along with a powerful desire to flee, even if it did mean facing the desert on her own. But a strange, fragile thread of pity also wound its way around her heart. In her mind, she raised her foot, preparing to stomp on that thread and grind it beneath her heel. But then she paused. If she could use that thread of pity, perhaps she could begin to gain the madman's trust. With his trust, she might even find a way to escape.

Gritting her teeth, Raisa squeezed her eyes shut and clung to the flickering thread, coaxing forth the reluctant sensation of sympathy for the man who had destroyed her. She knelt on the sandy ground next to him, murmuring a soothing sound through clenched teeth. Lorcan remained huddled in a ball, rocking slightly and whimpering. Raisa's impatience rose; even the glimmer of pity was not enough to compel her to reach out and touch him; he did not deserve comfort. No one who could have so little care for life as he did deserved anything better than contempt. No one who saw people as nothing more than machines for his own twisted experiments should be allowed to roam free. And yet, his distress was obvious and real, so real, he had not noticed her shift in behavior.

"Who is coming?" she asked, at last.

He looked up at her, his eyes glassy. "The Ar'Molon," he gasped.

Raisa frowned in confusion. "Ar'Molon Uun? Why does that bother you? Don't you work for him?"

Lorcan pushed himself up to his knees and studied her warily. "What do you care? You care nothing for your father. You seethe with hatred. Run away. You dream of it, while pretending to play along. LIAR!" His voice rose into a snarling scream and he reached out, wrapping his fingers around her throat.

Raisa's breath quickened, turning into short, frantic gasps as the madman's hands began to cut off her breath. Even in her altered form, she knew he was stronger than her; it was one of the first things she had learned upon arriving at the Weald. The man had clearly turned his experiments on himself at some point, though there were no visible evidences of his tampering like the ones she bore. It was the main reason she had not attempted to escape. What he said about not surviving the desert was true, but more than that, she knew he would hunt her down and drag her back. She had seen what happened to the soldiers who displeased Lorcan, and she had no desire to be permanently bonded to a tree. The changes he had wrought already were bad enough, but that... she shuddered even now as the thought flitted through her mind. To be forever trapped in that dark silence was too awful to contemplate. She stared into his face, keeping the panic from her expression as he tightened his grip, slowly, slowly—her air was not cut off completely, but every breath became a long, agonizing struggle. The need to breathe consumed her, blocking out every other thought and desire.

"Defiant one." Lorcan's whispered words crooned in her ears as though from a great distance. "Dear one. If only you could see and understand how very precious you are. My greatest creation. If only you would serve me faithfully, if only I could trust you."

He released his grip and Raisa fell forward onto her hands as she gulped in great mouthfuls of air. Lorcan spun away from her, but she didn't care what he was doing or where he was going. All that mattered was breathing. Gratitude for every breath welled up within her and splashed down on her hands in the form of tears.

"What did he say?" Lorcan demanded.

Raisa looked up, confused, her vision blurry. Why was he still here? What did who say? "What?"

"Your brother! I could not hear his words, only yours." Ugly suspicion glinted in his eyes.

"Oh." Raisa took another breath, balancing her thoughts, sifting through them for a truth that revealed nothing. "He... he asked me what I was."

Lorcan's gaze sharpened. "What did you tell him?"

"I... I didn't tell him anything." She rubbed the back of her wrist across her eyes, dashing away all signs of weakness, furious with her traitorous emotions. "He confirmed that he is my brother, that we are both as we are now because of you."

"And did he tell you what happened to him? How or when?" Lorcan leaned toward her, his gaze hungry.

He doesn't know. The thought shot through her like a sudden surge of wind in the sails of an airship. He knows he is responsible in some way for what Olin has become, but he has no idea how he did it. And on the heels of that thought she realized something else. He must never find out. That is the terrible secret Olin and his people are protecting.

"No," Raisa admitted, thankful she had not pressed Olin for answers. "He did not. I don't know if he even knows. He's confused and frightened."

Lorcan bared his teeth in frustration. "We will return again in a few days. Perhaps he just needs more time to get to know you, to trust you. He will tell you. And then you will tell me, like the good daughter you are."

Raisa kept her face impassive. "Yes, Father."

"Come. Our master has landed in the Weald. He will desire an update."

Lorcan strode away without a backward glance, but Raisa did turn to look at the root-covered opening to the cave. Through a small opening, she imagined she saw the glint of dark eyes watching her. She wished there were some way to reassure Olin that she was not working with Lorcan, that she despised the madman and only wished to escape, but Lorcan would be sure to notice if she lingered behind, and leaving anything in writing was far too dangerous. With a sigh she followed Lorcan. She would continue to play the part she had set for herself; it was the only option left to her. Even if she could not convince the madman of her compliance, perhaps she could convince his master. A trickle of dread snaked its way through her soul. She had only met Uun once, and that encounter had ended with her being thrown in the Ar'Mol's dungeons and changed into... whatever she was now. What this meeting might mean for her future was too terrible to contemplate.

They arrived just as an airship settled down in the serene lake at the center of the Weald. Raisa stared. This was not the freighter in which she and the other hapless prisoners had been brought to the Weald, this was a massive beast unlike anything she had ever seen. Armored plating covered the hull, and enormous rivets lined each seam. The airship had five masts sticking up proudly from its deck, the numerous sails tightly furled for landing. The airship settled, consuming the entire lake with its bulk. Raisa's stomach did a fearful somersault as a long staircase slowly unfolded from the side of the ship and two figures stood in the doorway; they were merely silhouettes at this distance, but the knowledge that one of those men was the Ar'Molon remained ever-present in her thoughts.

Raisa glanced down at her arms, turning her hands this way and that as they waited for the new arrivals to disembark. Her bare arms were darker in color than they had been before. She had always been pale, envying Shaesta's dark beauty, wishing that the sun would bronze her skin instead of burning and blistering it. Now, her skin's color stood somewhere in between, but it also contained a subtle pattern of lines, like faint tattoos. Long V's and concurrent arches were etched across her entire body as if someone had lightly painted her skin to resemble the bark of a tree. Lorcan had held a mirror up for her just once before he escorted her out of the dungeon, and even now, the memory was emblazoned on her mind, a picture she could never forget. To look in that mirror, but not to recognize her own features, had been the strangest and most surreal experience of her life. Raisa shuddered. Those bright green eyes, not quite the right shape, staring back at her where her own had always been a muddy blend of brown, green, and gray before had been bad enough, but to see the very shape of her face elongated, and her ears... even now, she resisted the urge to reach up and check to see if they were still pointed at the top, like leaves. She considered the paucity of mirrors in the Weald a blessing, though she had managed to secure a fragment of broken glass a few sennights ago and smuggle it into the stash of useful items she continued to collect against the day of her eventual escape.

Next to her, Lorcan bent at the waist in a deep bow as the two figures stepped off the stair. He nudged her, but Raisa remained standing straight and tall. She would not bow, not even to save her own life. To do so would break the fabric of her soul, a consequence she could not bear. As she understood it, the madman had achieved her alterations by somehow blending her with the attributes of a tree. Well, she could use that. Trees did not bend without breaking; neither could she.

Ar'Molon Uun strode closer until he towered over them. He did not appear to notice or care about her lack of respect. In fact, he did not so much as glance Raisa's way. His full attention was on Lorcan, still bowing.

"Have you discovered the secret of that other one?" he asked, not bothering with even a mask of nicety.

Lorcan straightened. "No, my lord. He has not been forthcoming, not forthcoming at all. But I have introduced him to his sister, and she"—Lorcan cast his arm wide, indicating Raisa—"she has been a good girl and will bring to light all that he attempts to conceal. Nothing will remain hidden. Nothing."

Uun turned his gaze on Raisa, looking her straight in the eye, and she was startled to discover that where he had towered above her at their first meeting, she was now nearly as tall as he, but she contained the grimace she felt. Just one more difference. One more thing to set her apart. There was not time to ponder how her crew would feel about all the changes wrought on her. Even after lunats in the Weald, she'd barely had time to ponder how she felt about them.

Uun studied her with a scalding glance that she could feel all the way to her bones. His gaze seemed to take in every corner of her thoughts, every secret she had thought so well-concealed, every inch of her character until she knew she could bear it no longer, and then his eyes flicked away, dismissive and unconcerned. Raisa resisted the urge to wrap her arms around herself and cower into the bow she had refused to bend for a moment earlier.

"What other progress have you made?" Uun asked Lorcan, his attention back on the madman.

Lorcan began to detail the number of baumen he had crafted, how he impatiently awaited his lord's permission to begin transformations on the other prisoners, and Raisa's own "training," discussing her as though she were a piece of property, a weapon to be aimed and nothing more. But Raisa kept her rage on a quiet simmer deep within herself and walked a few paces behind them like an obedient servant.

"I would see a demonstration of this one before I make a decision about the others," Uun said.

"She is ready at any time, my master."

"Good. I will observe her first thing in the morning."

The other man who had exited the airship walked next to her. She had been unable to notice him while locked beneath Uun's gaze, and she dared not turn to study him now. Curiosity was not a trait anyone desired in a weapon, and she must continue to play her part if she wished to survive.

Lorcan took Uun past the camp and then glanced back at Raisa and gestured at her tent. Despite her desire to continue listening to the conversation, and perhaps gain valuable information, Raisa immediately made a sharp turn and left their company: she had been dismissed and, like a good weapon, she obeyed.

7

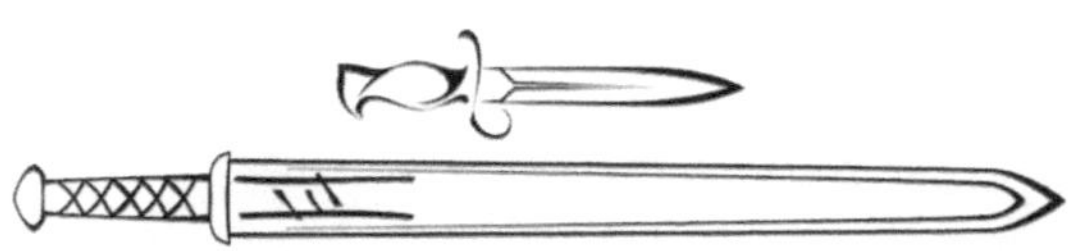

It seemed impossible for something so large as the troop carrier to move swiftly, even through the air, and yet by the next morning they were approaching a landing zone at the base of a small mountain range. The airship settled to the ground and the defenders filed out of her in orderly rows. Once outside, Grayden stared up at the mountains, feeling thoughtful. The mountains seemed familiar, and that familiarity infused him with a rare sense of peace.

"Major Semiv," he asked, catching the man as he walked past. "What mountains are these?"

"The Telseren Grade," Semiv said, barely glancing up.

He moved on, leaving Grayden staring up at the shadowy peaks, his insides shaking as though someone had replaced his bones with a ringing gong. He had already guessed the answer to his question, and yet, to hear it affirmed left him suddenly breathless.

Beren jostled up next to him. "Well, here we are, Attatoire, wherever that is. I guess we're supposed to make our way over to the barracks first. What's wrong?"

"That's the Telseren Grade," Grayden whispered, a terrible

ache filling his chest as if someone had carved everything out of his rib cage and left it hollow.

"Ah." Beren nodded. "So we're tucked up against the northern border of Ondoura. I didn't know there was a base here."

"My home is just on the other side of those mountains," Grayden whispered in a hoarse voice. "My sister and I were named for those mountains. Those peaks shelter and shadow my family at this very moment, as they have always done."

Beren did not reply. Grayden glanced at his friend and saw understanding etched in every line of Beren's face.

"Home," Grayden whispered. "So close I could almost touch it." He patted his vest pocket where the letter crinkled with familiar reassurance.

"Are you ever going to read that?" Beren asked, a slight twinkle in his eyes.

"Yes," Grayden replied.

"When?"

"When I need it most."

Beren's lips quirked up at the corners, but his voice came out low and serious. "Well, we've been attacked by pirates, abducted by mercenaries, watched our friends die in the Greyklasp Mountains, survived an avalanche, fought a madman who commanded walking trees, tracked down an assassin, worked hand-in-hand with one of the most dangerous men in the world, and we just spent two sennights fighting an invading force bent on conquering all of Telmondir. If you haven't needed to read your father's words, hear his voice in all of that... when will you?"

Grayden felt his face grow warm. "It's not that I haven't needed his words in all of that, Beren," he said quietly. "It's just that I can still hear his voice in my head. Sure, we've faced trials, fairly large ones, even, but through it all, I could close my eyes and know what my father would say to me. I could still feel home in my heart. I'll read the letter when I can't do that anymore."

Beren studied him. "Aye," he said at length, "wisdom, my

friend. More than most." He jerked his head. "Come on, we'd better get to the barracks to stow our gear."

Grayden followed his friend, his eyes continuing to stray toward the familiar peaks. They were backwards from how he usually saw them, and differently shaped on this side, and yet they plucked a chord in his heart that warmed him through. He closed his eyes and pictured it all, just as he had left it: the town decorated for the Harvest Festival; Seren, her hair up in bows; the sweet and savory scents of baking emanating from the kitchen; his mother in her apron, arms covered to the elbow in flour; his strong father grinning in the doorway, pruning shears leaning against one broad shoulder; Seren, dancing into his outstretched arms as he swung her up into the wagon for the ride into town. Later, they would be out in the village, the mayor would be making a speech, the musicians would be priming their instruments as someone lit the massive bonfire. There would be dancing...

Ailwen's pretty face flashed through his memory and he winced as a pang of regret pierced his heart.

The urge to read his father's letter nearly overwhelmed him, but then someone bumped into him, jostling him out of the daydream and pushing him toward the barracks.

"Grayden, come on." Beren had turned back, noticing his absence. "You don't want to get in trouble on our first day by being last to follow instructions, do you?"

It took some effort to push away the flood of images and emotion, but Grayden managed it, locking it all back in his heart. He gave his head a quick shake and then jogged to catch up with Beren.

In the barracks, they found bunks and stowed their gear. Grayden watched Beren greet the other defenders who were settling in nearby, asking where they had arrived from. Most had come from the Northern and Central Commands, and many had already been in Attatoire for several sennights.

"Have you seen much fighting?" Beren asked one man who said he had been recalled from the Northern Command.

"Nah," the stocky Telsuman replied. "Mountains up on the Telsuman border are too difficult to march an army over, and the passes are well-manned. Nothing's been moving anywhere close to our regiment." The man eyed Beren. "Young Adelfried, isn't it?"

Beren nodded and shook the man's offered hand.

"I thought it was you. Look just like your da, you know. I'm Venson," the other supplied. "Alhage Venson, but everyone just calls me Jerky."

Grayden chuckled at the joke and even Beren's normally serious face quirked into an amused grin.

"And I'm Shep"—a lanky man with dark hair and bright blue eyes joined the conversation—"because my family owns the largest flock of sheep in northern Dalma." He gave his head a wry shake and looked appraisingly at Grayden. "You're Dalman, too."

"Yes," Grayden replied. "Grayden Ormond. Or just Gray if it's easier. Where did they pull you two from?"

"I was up at Fellhammer Outpost," Jerky said. "Mostly a boring assignment. Been here nearly a sennight."

"I came from Central Command, patrolling the border," Shep added. "Been here two sennights, our group has been here the longest."

"There's a long stretch of fairly easy terrain along that border," Grayden said, looking at Shep. "Did you see the Igyeum forces out there?"

Shep shook his head. "All's quiet. Word is the only real incursions have happened in Ondoura. Heard they took a whole city there, don't know if it's true, though." He eyed Beren and Grayden.

"It is true," Beren supplied. "We just came from there. The Igyeum forces hold Baktan."

A low whistle greeted this news.

"You both arrived on the carrier coming from the Southern Command then?" Shep asked.

Grayden nodded.

"You make it to the front?" Jerky's question was eager.

"We did," Beren replied.

"Then you boys have seen some action already." Shep's voice rose in excited pitch.

Grayden nodded. He could feel the weight of questions about to spring forth, when an officer barked a command from the doorway and they all straightened to attention.

"Follow me, men," the man in the doorway shouted.

He led them to the field and then stood at attention himself as Major Semiv strode to the front of the group and turned to face the soldiers arrayed before him. Grayden glanced to his right and his left and did some quick estimating. There was easily an entire regiment assembled in the yard.

"Welcome to Attatoire," Major Semiv said. His voice carried over the grassy area. "You have been assigned here as part of the Gray Malkyns, a new division that the marshals of each army have been putting together for the past six lunats. You men represent the final regiment of this division to arrive."

Grayden caught Beren's eye. A whole division? What could the marshals be planning that would require forty-five thousand men to be pulled out of the three commands and reassigned?

"For this new initiative, we have been seeking out the best of the best. This division requires men who have already demonstrated their courage and fortitude in the face of danger. Many of you have already seen actual combat, as well, not something all defenders can say."

The men shifted uneasily under the implied praise.

"Your missions will place you behind enemy lines, preparing openings for the infantry divisions to come through," Major Semiv continued.

"And how will we do that, sir?" a man called out.

"With these." Semiv gave a subtle signal and three men standing near him moved suddenly, a huge piece of black fabric stretching open between them in a roughly rectangular shape.

Long ropes were attached to the fabric in various places, all coming together in a harness around the third man.

Grayden and his fellow defenders stared for a long, uncomprehending moment.

"With these skysails, gentlemen," Major Semiv continued, "you will learn to fly. And this is how we will defeat the Igyeum. Welcome to the Skyborne."

Skyborne. Fly. The words rang through Grayden's being like the little shocks Seren loved to treat him to after scuffing her stockinged feet across that thick throw rug their father had bought for their mother as a special gift one Midwinter's Night Feast. But those little tingling sparks faded swiftly, while this continued to course through him, buzzing in every inch of his being. It was just a word, but somehow it inspired him. For just a moment, his thoughts soared through the clouds, full of the possibilities the major's simple words had evoked.

Major Semiv continued speaking, his voice and demeanor perfectly calm. "You will see a demonstration tomorrow morning. You will train and learn all that is needed to carry out this great effort. That is all, gentlemen!"

The noise of thousands of voices rose up from the field as every man turned to his neighbor to verify what they had just heard. The mass of defenders made their way to the large main building in the complex.

Grayden turned to Beren, wondering what his friend thought of everything they had just heard. He raised his eyebrows and Beren replied with a nervous sort of smile.

"Crazy, right?" Beren asked.

"I must be," Grayden replied, eagerness brimming within him. "I can't wait to try it."

"Truly?" Beren asked.

A wild laugh burst from Grayden's mouth before he could stop it. "Yeah."

"You're right," Beren said, his eyes turning serious.

"About what?"

"You are crazy."

The line before them moved slowly, but eventually they made it to the table.

"Ormond." The trooper sitting at the table looked through several papers. "Ah, yes. You'll be in the Eighth Company under Captain Argond." He handed over a large packet. "Welcome to the Skyborne."

Grayden wandered back outside and waited for Beren, who joined him a few minutes later.

"Eighth Company," Beren said.

"Me too. Must be our lucky number," Grayden replied. "Should we go report to Captain Argond?"

Beren nodded and they hiked across the open field together. Grayden opened the large sack he had been handed and began examining the contents.

"What's inside?" Beren asked, digging into his own bag.

"I think it's a coat," Grayden said, pulling out the largest item and holding it up in front of his chest. It seemed to be made entirely of leather, but was shorter than most jackets and boasted no tails. It had large buttons up the front and a flash of color that caught Grayden's eye. He turned the coat to inspect it more closely. "Patches," he said.

"What?" Beren asked.

Grayden turned the jacket from side to side. "Patches on each shoulder."

"Ah." Beren nodded. "That makes sense. What's on them?"

"Malkyns on one side," Grayden said. He squinted at the other one, confused.

"Seems like they should have picked something with wings," Beren said.

"That's what I was thinking. But malkyns are fierce fighters and good hunters, so maybe it makes a sort of sense."

At that moment, Shep and Jerky jogged over to join them. "So, now we know what this is all about," Shep said, his wide, honest face breaking into a questioning grin. "What company did they put you in?"

"Eighth," Beren said.

Jerky slapped his hands together. "Black Dragons, same as us."

"That's what's on the other patch, then?" Grayden asked.

Shep grinned. "Yeah. Not a very good likeness, is it?"

Grayden shrugged. "Considering they went extinct a long time ago, I guess it's as good a likeness as it can be."

They continued to examine the items they had been given. In addition to the leather coats, they each had a fur-lined leather helmet, a long, black silk scarf, and a pair of sturdy goggles.

"What's the scarf for?" Grayden asked.

"Keeps your neck warm," Jerky replied.

"And keeps your coat collar from chafing your skin," Shep added.

"Where are you two headed, now?" Jerky asked.

"Supposed to report in to Captain Argond," Beren said.

Shep brightened. "Follow us, we'll take you to him."

Captain Argond had a tent-like hut to himself, but he was not in it when they arrived. Instead, he was over by the door to their barracks, greeting the men who had just arrived and been assigned to his command. His piercing dark-eyed gaze swept over both Beren and Grayden as they introduced themselves, and a slight furrow creased his brow as he shook their hands in turn.

"A bit young for first lieutenants, I would have thought," the man said.

"A bit young for everything," Grayden agreed. "We were part of the accelerated class at the Academy last year. Beren and I were promoted just recently for helping hunt down the Regeont's murderer."

"Ah." Captain Argond nodded. "I have heard rumblings about several young prodigies recently. That would be the two of you, then?"

"It wasn't just us," Beren said. "Quite a few students last year ended up on the accelerated track."

"But only two of them ended up here." Captain Argond studied them both through narrowed eyes. "Is it because you've truly earned it, I wonder? Or is there favoritism at play?"

Beren held his gaze. "I guess you'll find out soon enough, sir."

Argond eyed him sternly, but a light of approval seemed to glint in his eyes, then he shifted his gaze to Grayden. "And you, young Ormond?"

Grayden clasped his hands behind his back and stared straight ahead, not saying a word.

After a long, painful silence, Argond gave a brief nod. "I don't like to jump to conclusions, myself. If the two of you are here, you must have impressed someone. That says quite a bit. I'm pleased to have you both here in the Eighth. The men have started calling our company the Black Dragons."

Grayden felt a thrill rush through him. He wished he could have seen those majestic creatures before they died out. It seemed right, somehow, to revive their memory in this way.

"That is all for now," Argond continued. "Best get your belongings stowed and get some rest. Training begins tomorrow, and I guarantee you that the most difficult thing you've ever done will seem easy in comparison."

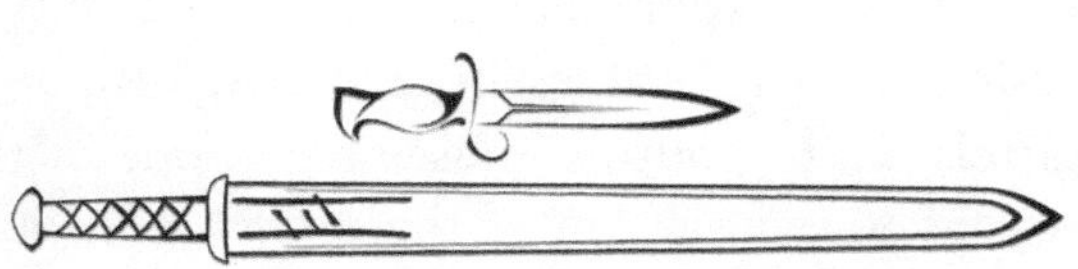

8

Beren watched as the defender drifted through the pale morning sky above him, the enormous, rectangular skysail slowing his descent considerably as he soared through the air like a leaf on the wind. Seconds later, the man landed in the grassy field nearby, hitting the ground at a run, the black sail fluttering to the ground behind him.

Those standing in attendance burst into cheers as the defender unclipped his harness and raised his arms, proving he had touched down safely.

Beren shook his head. "I saw it happen," he muttered. "But I'm still not sure I believe it."

Grayden turned to him, a wild light in his eyes. "I wonder how soon they'll let us jump for ourselves."

Beren stared at him. "Are you telling me that you are actually excited at the prospect of jumping off a perfectly functional airship?"

Grayden grinned. "Sounds fun."

Beren shook his head. He had never been afraid of heights, but the idea of willingly throwing himself off a flying airship and trusting his life to a piece of fabric was not instantly appealing. He would do it, of course, when the time came, but that did not mean he would enjoy it.

Captain Argond addressed his company. "Of course, most of our jumps will be scheduled at night, when our sails won't be as easy to spot. And the terrain we jump into won't always be as unobstructed as this field. There will be many factors to think about: wind speed and direction, how to maneuver your skysail, how and when to open your sail, and how to land with precision. You will master all of these things. But for now, form up into your assigned patrols. Each group will assemble at one of those platforms." Argond waved an arm at the eastern end of the field, where a dozen deck-like structures stood in a line. "The first thing you have to learn is how to land a jump without breaking your legs."

Beren grimaced, but he directed the men in his patrol to line up behind him. He led them over to a white platform and climbed up the short ladder. At the top, an older man pointed at the sand pit below.

"Landing technique!" the sergeant standing on the platform explained. "Once you have gained enough experience, you will be able to stay on your feet while landing as you just saw demonstrated, but we'll start with learning the correct way to fall so that we avoid injuries until then. You have all learned forms of falling in hand-to-hand combat training, but this is a new technique. First, you want to protect your face and throat, so cross your arms over your chest like so." He demonstrated. "Next, you should always hit the ground with your feet first, so you will jump backwards off the platform and strike the ground with the balls of your feet. As soon as your feet touch the sand, you will throw your body sideways, trying to distribute your fall evenly along the side of your leg, hip, and lower back, as I will now demonstrate."

Beren watched as the man carried out his own instructions, rolled back up to his feet, and climbed out of the sand pit. He gave Beren a nod, and Beren stepped to the edge of the platform.

It was not high, just below shoulder height, and yet it felt suddenly like an enormous drop because of all it represented.

Taking a deep breath, he hopped off the platform.

His feet struck the ground and he tried to throw himself sideways, but his well-trained instincts kicked in and he found himself rolling backward and propelling himself back to his feet, ready to fight.

"That's exactly how you should fall with a sword in your hand," the sergeant shouted, loudly enough for everyone behind the platform to hear. "But if you do that while harnessed to a skysail, you'll just end up tangling yourself in the rigging and more than likely getting hurt. Next!"

The next man managed to follow the correct movement, but he did so with exaggerated slowness.

"Better to practice the correct motion slowly than the wrong one fast," the sergeant barked when a few of the defenders waiting in line laughed. "You're going to be practicing this technique for an hour every morning before breakfast and an hour every evening before you turn in. The faster you get the motion down, the fewer casualties we'll have when you start jumping for real."

The next hour dragged by in a blur of waiting, watching, climbing, jumping, and falling. By the end of the hour, Beren's side ached and he was starving. It was a relief when Captain Argond called a halt and sent them to the mess hall to get breakfast. Beren found Grayden and they stood in line together waiting for their bowls of porridge.

"How'd it go?" Beren asked.

"My body kept trying to land wrong," Grayden replied. "I thought I had already learned all the different ways to fall, but this feels all wrong."

Beren nodded. "I struggled as well. I am not looking forward to repeating this exercise tonight."

Grayden held his bowl out and received a large serving of porridge, then made his way over to a table that also held Shep and Jerky. The two men grinned at them as they sat. "Sore yet?"

Grayden nodded. "What else do we have to look forward to?"

"Running," Shep said.

"So much running," Jerky agreed. "While carrying all the gear and weapons and armor they are making us take with us into the mission."

"And we have to take everything with us because we're going in behind enemy lines without the support we normally have in combat," Shep said.

"I hadn't thought about that," Beren said. "But it makes sense."

"Learning how to get in and out of the harness, and how to make sure your skysail has been prepared correctly in its pack so it deploys," Shep continued listing off things they could look forward to.

"Beyond that, we don't know. That's as far as we'd gotten before you lot showed up. But now that the entire division has been assembled, we'll probably get to start learning actual skysailing," Jerky said. "Best eat up, lads, it's a long time till lunch."

Captain Argond met them at the door on their way out of the mess hall.

"Gentlemen, grab your gear and be on the field in ten minutes."

Shep groaned. "There's that running we were talking about."

Ten minutes later, Captain Argond strode up and down the line of men, inspecting their weapons and uniforms. He made a few comments here and there, but for the most part he seemed pleased with what he saw.

"Now that we have a full company, we can begin training in earnest," he informed them. "Those of you who arrived first will have an advantage, but I expect to see you helping the new arrivals. We'll start slow. Fifteen minutes running around the training field." The captain held up a chronometer. "Go!"

Beren started forward alongside the rest of his company. Although he had considered himself to be in good condition, the other defenders set a swift pace and Beren's legs and lungs began to burn long before Captain Argond shouted that their time had ended. He stopped immediately and doubled over, panting for breath. Someone's hand landed on his back.

"You should walk a bit," Jerky said from somewhere above him. "Everything in you will want to stop and lie down, but it's better to walk it off. Get a sip of water from your canteen, too. Just a sip, mind. If you need more, swish it around and spit it out or you'll get side cramps."

Beren nodded and tipped his flask up to his lips, letting the cool liquid pour into his mouth. Then he straightened and began walking slowly back and forth until his breathing returned to normal. He glanced around and saw that others were doing the same.

"Not great," Argond barked when they had formed up once more. "But not terrible, either. I can work with what I just saw. You'll all be running three miles in twenty minutes before your first mission."

"Sir," one of the men who had arrived on the airship with Beren and Grayden spoke up.

"Yes, trooper?"

"What does running have to do with fighting or our assignment?"

Argond considered him for a minute and Beren expected the captain to explode at him like he had seen Captain Bast do on the front lines. But instead, he simply looked at the rest of the men.

"Does anyone have an answer for the trooper here?"

Shep stepped forward. "We will be sailing far behind enemy lines without easy access to the support other defenders are used to, sir. We need to train our bodies to endure difficult conditions, and there may be times when we have to move quickly in order to survive, sir!"

"Soldier Shep is exactly right," Argond said. "For now, we will finish our time with some additional strength training before you head to your next duty."

When Argond finally let them go, Beren dropped his gear off

back in the barracks and then followed his company to a large tent where a sergeant handed them each an empty pack attached to a harness. Then he gave them a large piece of folded-up material and showed them how to attach it securely into the pack.

"This is your skysail," he told them.

"It's so light," a defender said, fingering the fine material. "How is something so flimsy supposed to prevent us from crashing into the ground?"

"The sails and lines are made of the strongest Ondouran silk," the sergeant replied. "The lightest and strongest fibers we know of for creating fabric. It will be your responsibility to inspect your skysail and pack it before every jump. You will also check the packs of two other members of your platoon so that every single skysail is checked by three different sets of eyes. We will do this drill so often you will be able to pack and check your skysails in your sleep. If this skysail is folded incorrectly, attached incorrectly, or secured incorrectly, the man jumping with it will die."

The men nodded soberly and set to their work learning every knot, every clasp, and every fold in the fabric. Once they had each successfully packed a skysail, the sergeant then walked them through how to climb into their harnesses. He made them put the harnesses on and take them off at least a dozen times.

The leather harness was awkward and bulky, and Beren couldn't imagine trying to put it on along with the rest of his gear. He fumbled with the clasps and grew frustrated more than once as he tried to force his fingers to learn the correct motions. He heard a low muttering nearby and looked up to see Grayden having an argument with his straps; he seemed to be having trouble getting out of the harness. The other man looked up and saw Beren watching him. A look of mutual frustration passed between them. Beren raised his arms in a helpless gesture and Grayden's expression shifted to one of wry humor. As Beren watched in growing amusement, Grayden pushed the straps down off his shoulders and then slid the entire pack to the ground, stepping out of it like a pair of pants. Then he looked back up at his friend and grinned. Beren couldn't hold back his laughter, and a quiet chuckle burst past his lips.

"Eyes up here!" Captain Argond's booming voice behind Grayden made everyone jump and stop what they were doing. All eyes turned to Grayden, whose face darkened in embarrassment. Captain Argond bent down and picked up Grayden's pack, holding it up so that everyone could clearly see that all the clasps were still fastened tightly together.

A few men grinned, and a few soft sniggers rippled through the room. Grayden's face turned to stone.

"Do you find this training to be humorous, First Lieutenant?" Captain Argond bellowed.

"No, sir," Grayden replied.

"Do you find it to be boring or do you think it is somehow unimportant?"

"No, sir!" Grayden barked back.

"Do you find it to be frustrating?"

Beren saw a slight flicker of confusion ripple across Grayden's features. "Yes, sir," he admitted in a lower voice.

Captain Argond nodded and turned to the rest of the men in the tent. "You men have been pulled out of your other divisions, regiments, and companies because your leaders saw something in you that we desperately need. The Skyborne is something completely new and untried. You will all face moments here that frustrate you. And at times, you will need to be able to get creative in the way that you solve the problems set before you." He hefted the skysail pack. "As First Lieutenant Ormond just did." He handed the pack back to Grayden. "Before our first mission, it is my job to ensure that you are more familiar with these skysails than you are with your own name. You will take them with you everywhere. At any moment, any officer above you can ask you to unpack and repack your skysail or demonstrate your ability to get in and out of your harness. However, once you leave this facility and go on your mission, you need to understand that there will be obstacles we cannot prepare you for. When you leap into enemy territory, you may end up hanging by your skysail from a tree. Or your harness may become damaged in some way and you may find yourself unable to work the clasps. There are hundreds of things that can go wrong on a mission, and you will need to be able to do what the first lieutenant just did, and come up with a quick solution on the spot." Argond gave Grayden a nod. "Well done. Now, do it correctly."

Grayden saluted smartly and began working the clasps as Captain Argond strode away, his attention now held by another defender. Beren also returned to the harness, and somehow he found that the clasps were not quite as frustrating as they had been a moment before.

In between learning to fall and becoming well-acquainted with every element of their skysails, there were other lessons as well. They spent hours poring over maps of the Whispering Wood, as well as studying detailed maps of various areas inside the Igyeum. There were mock battles between companies, where one group would be assigned to play the role of skysailers jumping into a camp and the other group played the Igyeum forces ready to defend themselves.

Shep had not been exaggerating about the running, either. Every morning after breakfast, Major Semiv ordered them to pack up all their gear, including their skysails, fully arm themselves, and run up and down the trails in the foothills surrounding the camp. These started easy, with slow jogs for just a few minutes like on the first day, and gradually worked up to longer and longer runs. Some days the major would simply have them do a long march instead of running. But they always had to carry all their gear with them.

At first, Beren fell into bed each night covered in bruises and with every muscle in his body aching. But each day, he felt his body growing stronger and more accustomed to the tasks he was given. By the end of three sennights, he could run for miles, then leap from the platform and throw himself to the ground a hundred times over and barely notice.

9

"You cannot put this off any longer."

Dalmir did not look up at Frieda. "I am building a castle with Hubert," he said, carefully placing a pebble on the wall he and Beren's five-year-old brother were working on in the garden. The Chanjar breeze held a chill and there was a scent of snow in the air, but the rays of the sun were still warm on their heads, and the trees still held a myriad of crimson and gold in their boughs. With enough water, Dalmir had been able to turn the frostbitten dirt into mortar for Hubert's construction project. The little boy slathered a pebble with mud, his pudgy fingers patting the "mortar" into place. His small face and round cheeks were set in studious concentration, the castle at hand the most important project of his young life.

"You have a responsibility," Frieda insisted. "It is... my purpose."

"Your purpose is to watch over the villagers." Dalmir tied a tiny banner to a stick and poked it carefully into a patty of mud.

"That was my purpose," she said. "Until you came."

Hubert looked up at the aton. "We have to keep the bad guys out," he said earnestly.

The aton's head turned toward the boy. "That wall will not

even... prevent a single insect from crossing it. Master Dalmir, I do not... understand your reluctance. Lord Adelfried found a new... location for the Maleians lunats ago, my duty... to protect them has ended. Your own wounds are... healed. You know what you must do, why do you not... attend to your duties?"

Dalmir stood in a rush, scattering stones and sticks as he did. "Because it will destroy you!" He stared at the aton's expression-less visage for a long moment, then sank back down to his knees, carefully rearranging the piles of building materials. "Forgive me, Hubert," he said to the wide-eyed little boy. "I made a bit of a mess, didn't I? I don't think I did any damage to our tower, though. We can keep working."

Hubert's face relaxed once more into a happy smile, his building partner's outburst immediately forgiven and forgotten; he hummed as he dug a moat in the hardened dirt.

"Look," Dalmir muttered at Frieda. "Perhaps my body has healed, but my mind... my soul..." He shook his head. "I know I can't put this off forever. But I did promise Hubert I would build a castle with him. Another day. One more sennight. A lunat at most. I promise."

Frieda stared at him, her mechanical gaze impassive and unreadable as ever. After a long moment, she made a whirring sound. "Two lunats hence. By Longnight Feast," she intoned. "Promise me."

Dalmir bowed his head. "Longnight Feast," he promised, a sense of defeat flooding through him.

The aton turned and walked away. Her movements were strangely fluid and perfect, neither jerky nor mechanical, but not organic, either. Daegan and Wynn had been immediately intrigued by Frieda's construction, but Dalmir could not answer most of their questions about how his brother had built her. He had not known Tel was working on such a creation. It bothered him, that Tel had done so much in secret, had kept so much from him. It hurt even more that Shiori had clearly been involved—bringing that group of Maleians and Mulemo's orb to Chasm, the enormous area above Tel's sunken tower, and placing it within Frieda so that they would have light and warmth and the ability to grow their own food. Why had Tel and Shiori not confided in him? He had thought once—but no. He pushed that thought from his mind. Any hope he had ever had in that direction died long ago. Shiori would never... not after he... He turned his attention back to the project at hand.

They continued to work, the old man and the young boy, building the walls tall and thick. Together, they fashioned towers at each of the four corners of the castle and dug a deep moat around it. Then Dalmir showed Hubert how they could use seeds and sticks and roots to fashion tiny furniture. As they worked, Dalmir lost himself in the creative process. He had always enjoyed building things, and doing something so tiny and intricate satisfied him in a way his larger construction projects never had. He enjoyed using his hands and none of his power to bring this project to completion. The thought of his own tower in Dalton reminded him of his excursion through Tel's sunken one, which brought Frieda to the forefront of his mind once more. Dalmir frowned and sat back on his heels.

"What's wrong?" Hubert tilted his head to one side, his small face scrunched into a frown. "Don't you want to play buildings with me anymore?"

Dalmir tried to smile. "Of course I do, Hubert. This is one of the few true pleasures left to me. I just... I have to do something I don't want to do."

"Oh." Hubert's curiosity was appeased. "We need more rocks!" He bounded up and away to fetch more pebbles and Dalmir could not repress a grin and a shake of his head.

"Ah, to have the resilience of youth once more."

The feeling of another presence made him turn. Cathrine stood at the edge of the garden, hands on her hips, a grimace pinching her expression. Dalmir was suddenly aware of the mess he and Hubert had been making of her garden.

"I'm sorry," he apologized, standing and holding his dirty

hands up before him. "It never occurred to me that... we..." He glanced about and then back up at the young woman, a sheepish chuckle emanating from his lips. "We have made rather a bit of soup out here, haven't we? Don't blame Hubert; building our castle out here in the garden was my idea."

Cathrine's mouth twisted to one side and she heaved a deep breath. She waved a hand. "It's not like it matters, I harvested the last of the vegetables sennights ago." She let out a wry chuckle. "You merely took me by surprise, that's all. Mother wanted me to let you know that it is time to wash up for dinner."

"Ah. Well, we are almost finished here. There's just the one wall left, and I think Hubert mentioned wanting to dig a leythan pit over there..."

Hubert came up the path, struggling to drag a large bucket of pebbles with him. His grunts with each pull could be heard across the garden. Dalmir strode over to him and lifted the bucket.

"I'll help with that. I think you gathered enough rocks to build a second castle!"

Hubert trotted along beside Dalmir. "I thought we could build another one. Then they can be neighbors and borrow things from each other! Look at what we're building, Cassrin! I made that part, and this is the garden, just like yours! And over here we're going to dig a pit for leythans, so that bad guys will fall into it if they try to sneak up on the walls."

Dalmir chuckled at the boy's enthusiasm, banishing all thoughts of the unpleasant task Frieda wished of him. There would be time enough for that later. For now, he had a five-year-old to entertain. He carried the bucket over and set it down, giving Cathrine an apologetic grin. She shook her head and rolled her eyes. However, a moment later, she was crouched over the castle with them, holding her skirts up out of the mud with one hand and helping place rocks with the other.

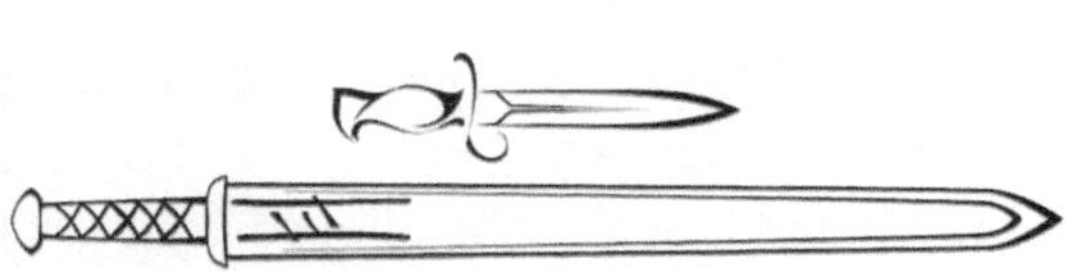

10

Grayden's heart raced as he darted through the trees, staying in the shadows as much as possible. He tried to run softly, but the thick layer of crunchy leaves covered in frost on the forest floor made it impossible to keep his steps completely silent. He peered out from behind a tree and threw himself to the frozen ground in a dense thicket of tangled vines, breathing hard. He had made it to the top of the hill.

Raising his head slightly, he caught sight of Beren standing casually at the base of a tall rock formation that rose high in the air. Grayden's eyes traveled up the rocks and caught a flicker of orange.

There!

He had found the other team's flag. But how to reach it with Beren standing guard? His sixth sense had not been working since getting to the Academy, and Grayden had begun to suspect that it had something to do with his distance from Dalmir's orb, though it was just a guess he couldn't prove.

He caught a flicker of movement on the other side of the hill and recognized Hans, one of the men on his own team. His heart pounded. If they could coordinate, they might have a chance to get the flag away, but it was clear Hans hadn't seen him, and

Grayden couldn't signal his teammate without giving away his own position to Beren. But then, maybe that was exactly what they needed.

Grayden inched his way through the thicket, creeping as close as he dared to Beren's location. Then, in a rush, he burst out of the shrubs, a few meters away from where his friend stood.

Beren didn't hesitate but leaped toward Grayden. But this was exactly what Grayden had been hoping for and he veered away, darting back into the trees. He glanced over his shoulder, but Beren had not followed him as he had hoped, so Grayden wound back to the clearing, as though attempting to go after the strip of orange cloth from a different angle. Knowing he had to convince his opponent of his commitment, Grayden darted toward the rocky spire. Beren came after him, and Grayden narrowly avoided being captured by leaping sideways. He dashed around a tree, swinging himself around its trunk and back toward the flag once more. Once again, Beren blocked him and Grayden had to dance away; this time, Beren gave chase. Grayden wound through the trees in a circle around the hilltop, as though looking for an opening to race Beren back to the flag, but widening the circle as he ran so as to take them slowly farther and farther away from the flag to give Hans a chance to get in and out without being noticed.

Grayden wove and darted through the trees, grateful for all the running they had been doing every morning for the past three lunats. His legs felt fresh and he breathed easily despite the frigid air of late autumn as he pushed himself to run faster, using every trick he knew to evade Beren's grasp. Unfortunately, Beren had been conditioning every bit as much as Grayden, and he matched him pace for pace.

Then, somewhere off in the direction of Grayden's team's base, a bell rang, and Grayden stopped.

Beren tackled him, knocking him to the ground in a flying leap. "You're captured!" he roared.

"Too late," Grayden laughed, sitting up. "My team just got your flag back to our base."

Beren paused and rose to his feet, his head cocked to one side. As the ringing tones of the bell reached his ears he frowned and shook his head. "I can't believe I fell for that. Who were you working with?"

"Hans," Grayden admitted. "Though we didn't plan it out beforehand."

"Of course." Beren reached down and helped Grayden up. "Well, your team won, but you had to sacrifice yourself."

"You didn't catch me until after the bell rang," Grayden protested.

"In a real scenario, that wouldn't matter," Beren said, his tone serious.

"Ah, don't be such a sore loser," Grayden teased.

"I'm not," Beren replied, no hint of defensiveness in his expression. "But in real combat, the enemy won't stop just because we achieve our objective. They'll make us battle our way back out, too."

Grayden sobered. "You're right. I wasn't thinking about combat, I was just trying to win the game. But out there it won't be a game."

"No."

Together, they hiked to the rendezvous point where both teams were supposed to assemble for their scores.

"Red team wins," Argond read out, to a great cheer from Grayden's team. "Though they suffered far heavier losses than blue team, including the capture or death of their first lieutenant." This brought an end to the cheering. Argond continued, "But since the point of this exercise was simply to achieve the mission objective, blue team will be washing up after supper tonight." He paused. "Along with every dead or captured member of red team. Dead and captured members of red team, you will also do ladder sprints to the top of Black River Hill and back before dinner."

A mixture of laughter and groans met this statement.

"It's more dangerous to get killed in training than by the Igyeum soldiers," one of Grayden's "dead" teammates joked. "At least the Igyeum will leave you alone after they kill you."

The men around them laughed and they headed back to their barracks for the little bit of free time they had each day for cleaning up, writing letters home, or just resting, while Grayden and the rest of their captured or dead teammates began the long series of sprints and jogs up the winding road to the top of the five-mile incline of Black River Hill.

Within a few strides, Grayden had fallen into the easy rhythm of the run. Though he was tired from the game, his body had grown accustomed to running. While his feet pounded against the grass, he let his thoughts drift. He regretted the loss of free time. He had already sent letters to Seren and his parents this sennight. He hoped they were doing well. He had even written a few notes to Hunter and Burke, and one to Ailwen. He had not sent the letter to Ailwen, however. He pushed his body into a sprint up to the front of the line when his turn came, pushing thoughts of Ailwen from his mind as well. Instead, he forced himself to focus on the run and the training and the battles to come.

The exercise helped clear his mind, and by the time they returned to camp he was blissfully tired, thoughts of home expunged from his heart. He entered the barracks and sat on the end of his bunk, tugging at his boots.

"Hey, Grayden," Shep shouted from his own bunk in a teasing voice. "How's that love letter coming along? You ready to send it yet?"

Grayden made a face and tossed a boot at the man, missing him by a wide margin. Jerky grinned and brought the boot over, dropping it to the floor before seating himself on the bunk across from Grayden.

"You should, you know," Shep said in a conversational tone.

"I should what?" Grayden asked.

"Send her the letter."

"I can't."

"Why not? Because you never spoke up about how you felt before you left?"

Grayden glanced up at the man swiftly. "Yeah, that's some of it."

"And you're afraid she doesn't feel the same? Maybe she's already moved on and married someone else while you've been gone?"

Grayden shrugged.

Shep's eyes narrowed. "Or maybe you're afraid that if you write to her she might decide to wait for you. That she might be hurt if you don't come home."

Squeezing his eyes shut and ignoring the pain lancing through his heart, Grayden tossed himself backward onto his bed. "Go bother someone else, Shep."

Grayden dozed for a while until the bell rang for supper. He joined the others in the mess hall, feeling tired and unsettled. He ate his food without really tasting it, and went through the motions of clearing the table and washing the dishes, but his thoughts were far away over the mountains. He found he couldn't join in with the banter of the losing team or his fallen teammates. When someone splashed dirty water at him, he barely noticed.

Once they finished cleaning up, they joined the others in their evening session of jumping off the platforms and learning how to fall in the dark. Captain Argond strode around barking orders at them and reminding them that they would most likely be making any jump they were assigned in the dark, so they needed to be able to hit the ground properly even if they couldn't see it.

"I know you are supposed to have some free time before lights out," Captain Argond said before he dismissed them, "but tonight you will spend it packing."

This announcement pulled Grayden out of his homesick stupor. Packing meant something different was happening tomorrow.

"Now that you have been here long enough to become

acquainted with the basics, you are ready to start learning how to use your skysails in real jumps."

A thrill of excitement surged through Grayden, banishing the last remnants of his melancholy.

"Tomorrow morning we will begin a new exercise. Black Dragons, be ready to leave camp one hour before dawn. Make sure that you have rations packed for all three meals; you can get them at the mess hall. You do not need your full armor and weapons tomorrow, but you will need your regular packs and your skysails, so make sure to check your own and two others this evening before lights out. Dismissed!"

———

GRAYDEN WOKE IN DARKNESS. Grabbing up the gear that he had meticulously packed the night before, he pulled on his boots and left the barracks with the rest of his company. The morning air had a playful sort of bite to it, the kind that held the promise of snow in the near future.

Captain Argond barked the order to move out and they marched away from Attatoire, following him toward the Telseren Grade. Grayden marched near Beren, Shep, and Hans, but they did not converse much. His nose and cheeks soon felt stiff with cold, though the rest of his body quickly grew warm due to the marching. It wasn't until the sun began to rise that anyone broke the silence.

"Where do you think we're going?" Hans asked.

"Seems like we're heading up into the mountains," Beren replied.

"But what for?" Hans pressed.

"I guess we'll find out when we get there," Shep said, a teasing grin on his face.

Grayden chuckled, but didn't join in. Hans was too trusting and he never seemed to understand the joke when someone teased him. Grayden had decided fairly quickly that as much as he enjoyed a good laugh, there was no real enjoyment to be had in giving Hans a hard time.

They marched through the morning, climbing higher and higher into the mountains. The terrain grew steeper, but not so steep that they had to do any actual climbing. The Telseren Grade was different from the Randeau Mountains, not so full of jagged, craggy peaks. And while they weren't as big or as tall as the Greyklasp Mountains which were perpetually topped with snow, the slopes of the Telseren Grade were respectably tall and steep. This close to winter, the tallest peaks already boasted their own shining caps of white. The defenders barely paused for breakfast, pulling their rations out and eating them as they marched.

And still they climbed. The path wound back and forth up the mountain, taking them up into the rocky crags, their feet sinking down into the snow. Around midday, Grayden glanced back the way they had come and found that the camp had grown small and faint, though it was still visible. An hour later, they were nearing the top of the mountain, and the hike began to grow more difficult as the snow lay thicker on the mountain, impeding their progress.

They reached the summit around midday. Panting a little from the effort of the climb, Grayden dug some rations out of his pack. As he ate, he looked around. They stood on a long, wide ridge that overlooked the entire plain below them. The side of the ridge they had just climbed sloped up gently, while the far side actually curved in on itself, resembling a wave of stone. At one end of the ridge, Grayden could now see a tall wooden structure. He studied it, wondering at its purpose.

He did not have to wonder for long.

Captain Argond ordered them to gather around the base of the structure, then sent his Sergeant Major up to the top.

"You will climb up to the top, and allow Sergeant Major Larson to affix the slider to your skysail. On his signal, you will then run as fast as you can to the end of the gangplank and jump. The slider will pull your skysail open, and you will use everything you have learned to land in the valley below. Anyone who does not jump will fail and be sent back to the command he was pulled away from."

The defenders shifted slightly. It was one thing to learn in a classroom about techniques for falling through the air and hanging from an open skysail learning how to maneuver the handles in order to navigate a drop, but to be asked to willingly fling oneself from the top of a mountain suddenly made everything they had been doing seem terrifyingly real. Grayden grinned.

"Permission to go first, sir," he shouted.

Argond's lips twitched slightly and Grayden thought he saw a glimmer of approval in the man's bright blue eyes.

"Permission granted, First Lieutenant Ormond."

"How far is the drop, Captain?" Flint, one of the men in Grayden's platoon, asked.

"Between five and six thousand feet, trooper," Captain Argond said. "This is approximately the height at which you should be deploying your skysail, which is why we've rigged up the hook to do it for you on this first jump. Later, you will learn how to use an altimeter to determine when to open your own skysail, but we wanted to make the first jump as simple as possible."

Grayden pulled on his fur-lined leather helmet and fastened the chin strap. Then he adjusted the protective goggles over his eyes before stepping up to the ladder. He climbed hand over hand, pulling himself up to the platform. At the top, he gripped the railing and looked down. A more perfect location for this exercise could not exist. The gangplank stuck out far enough to give the jumpers a good distance from the side of the mountain, and there was very little between their location here at the summit and the gentle rolling valley below. The only thing better would have been if the cliff faced the camp so that they wouldn't have to hike around the mountain to get back.

He nodded to Larson, who clipped a double-hook-clasp to

the pull-ring of his skysail, which he then belted to another rope. Larson raised his hand and nodded back.

Grayden didn't pause for even a second to think about what he did next. Taking a deep breath, he grabbed the handrails on either side of the gangplank and pushed himself forward, racing down the length of wood at a dead run. He reached the end of the plank and leaped off the end with all the strength in his legs, his only goal to push himself as far away from the cliffside as possible.

There was a single, prolonged space between heartbeats as he soared out over the valley and stared down at the vast amount of space between himself and the ground. His stomach lurched as he began to fall, and then the line attached to his skysail gave a jerk that sent his heart up into his throat before the silk fabric deployed and caught the breeze, arresting his fall and actually thrusting him slightly higher into the sky before sending him into a gentle descent.

Grayden gripped the leather handles attached to his sail and used them to maneuver himself toward the center of the valley, aiming for a grassy knoll. Now that he was no longer free-falling, he found himself able to enjoy the descent and the view surrounding him. The mountains gleamed in the afternoon sunshine. A flock of small birds circled below him, unconcerned by his approach. He drifted lazily through the air, circling lower and lower. Above him, he heard shouts and whoops of laughter and knew that the other men were experiencing their own jumps for the first time.

His feet thudded into the ground hard and he instinctively threw his body sideways, falling the way that he had practiced thousands of times over the past three lunats. A gust of wind caught at his skysail and pulled him backwards across the ground for several yards before he was able to regain control and start winding up the lines, pulling the sail toward him to refold and stuff back into its pack. Back at camp, he knew, he and the others would carefully repack their sails for the next jump. A rush of exhilaration flooded through him and he let out a wild whoop and turned to watch the other men drifting down to join him in the valley.

It took an eternity for the others to make their way to the ground, and Grayden chafed as he watched them, envious of their flight and aching to jump again. Beren landed first, followed by Shep, Jerky, and then Hans. They all landed safely and carefully gathered up their skysails before joining Grayden on the far side of the valley to watch the others in their company landing.

"That was incredible," Hans burst out as he came within earshot, the most animated Grayden had ever seen him.

"I know!" Grayden yelled back. "I can't wait to do it again."

Hans shook his head, grinning broadly. "No. I mean, yes, the jump was great. But I meant you."

Grayden stared at him. "What about me?"

"You didn't holler out or anything," Hans said, beaming at him. "First one up the tower, and you just ran right off the edge and fell without a sound."

Grayden laughed a little. "Really?"

"Yeah." Hans' expression was earnest.

"It's true," Shep confirmed. He pretended to wipe a tear from the corner of his eye. "It was almost inspiring."

Grayden and the others laughed. Hans glared at Shep.

"I thought it was inspiring," Hans insisted.

"Sure, kid. Whatever you say." Shep reached over and thumped him gently on the top of his head.

Hans folded his arms and glowered, but had the good sense to be quiet, though Grayden heard him muttering under his breath for a few more minutes as the sky slowly filled with large, dark sails.

11

Marik surveyed the Longnight Feast set before him on the massive oak table. He was still not entirely comfortable being a guest in the home of these kind people, but he appreciated their hospitality while he healed from his injuries and waited for Wynn to finish repairing the Hawk. Four more lunats had flown by, the golden autumnal days passing in a haze of sweetness and descending into the frigid gray of winter. The physical injuries had long since healed, though Marik would have argued that the mental anguish of waiting on the Hawk's rebuild and worrying about Raisa was worse than the broken bones.

Once his body had healed, it had taken a long time to regain his strength, but the Adelfrieds had been determined to get him back to full health. First, there had been long walks along the riverbank with Cathrine. Then she had encouraged him to help her in the kitchen. He had told stories to the children in Cathrine's school and overseen their contests of skill. Eventually, Drengur had asked for his assistance chopping firewood, and Keene had mentioned he might need an extra hand in the forge, and soon Marik's body was stronger than it had ever been before. Well, mostly, he admitted to himself. His leg would never be completely the same. He couldn't quite get rid of the slight limp, and the spots where the bone had broken ached whenever a storm approached, but at least he could manage to walk and even run under his own power and without a cane.

The work on the Hawk was taking longer than expected, and now that the deep snows had begun to fall the building and restoring project had stalled.

There had been grim discussions, of late. Marik had gone over his experience with the Igyeum's new weapon many times, and Lord Adelfried and his wife would soon be leaving for Dalton to converse with Duke Langston about the deteriorating state of Ondoura since the death of Regeont Roshana and the subsequent discovery of Lord Elan's role as her murderer. And while Thorben Adelfried had received a letter from Ericole Niveya assuring him that Elan would no longer trouble anybody, this did little to resolve the political storm brewing over the hole in Ondoura's leadership, to say nothing of the Igyeum forces now marching deeper and deeper into Telmondir and taking over Ondouran cities.

Longnight Feast approached, and once it had passed, Wynn, Daegan, Keene, and Molly would be heading to the Oreworks in Dalton where they would oversee the work of those who would build their creations.

Marik was pulled from his thoughts as the rest of the family began arriving, stamping snow from their boots as they entered the house and joined him at the table for the evening meal. He glanced up as Cathrine came in. She held a dripping, squirming Hubert in her arms. She laughed at his antics, her head thrown back, her thick dark braid over one shoulder, slightly tousled and wispy, stray curls escaping their bonds to dance about her face, evidence of Hubert's vehement loathing of baths. Her dress also bore scars of battle: the skirt spattered with wet spots and sleeves that were soaked through. She ushered Hubert up to his room and returned a few minutes later with a slightly drier version of her youngest brother, and herself in a fresh dress.

Hubert crawled up onto the bench next to Marik and tugged

on his sleeve. "Uncle Markik! Uncle Markik! Uncle Dalmir and me and Cassrin built a snow fort! After supper, you wanna come see it?"

Cathrine eased onto the bench across from Marik and gave a gentle smile. "It might be too dark after supper, Hubert," she cautioned.

Marik noticed a spot of dried mud still on her cheek and concealed a grin. He looked at the crestfallen Hubert.

"If we eat fast, I'll bet I can come see your fort before the light fades too much," he said. Like Dalmir, he had developed a bit of a soft spot for the youngest Adelfried with his love of building things, his hatred of baths, and his winsome smiles and spontaneous hugs and demands to be tossed in the air.

Hubert clapped his hands together and settled himself on his knees so he could reach the table better. When everyone was assembled, Lord Adelfried said a word of thanks for the food and then everyone began filling their plates.

Marik helped Hubert dish up and cut his food, and then he joined in the clamor and camaraderie as he loaded his own plate. Before he settled back onto the bench, he gazed about, drinking in the moment. The Adelfrieds did not employ servants, though they were wealthy enough. Beyond a part-time cook, the family generally took care of their own needs. No butler came to pour the wine. No servers stood in the wings with plates of food. The whole family would pitch in later to wash the dishes. There was passing of trays along the table, and elbows jostling each other while laughter and conversation reigned supreme.

It was very different from the more austere, sedate memories from Marik's own childhood. His past looked bleak and colorless in comparison. There had been an iron-fast rule of silence at the table, and little in the way of affection, even from his mother. What the Adelfrieds had: this was what family should be—this boisterous cacophony of kindness and working together and caring. Perhaps if this had been his experience... A pang shot through him and he sat in silent contemplation, his plate of food forgotten.

Cathrine caught his eye and gave him a puzzled glance, but he shook his head and forced a smile. He had no desire to dwell on the memories of his past, so he pointed at his own cheek and winked. Her fingers went automatically to her face. At the discovery of the dried mud there, her cheeks darkened and she quickly excused herself from the table, hurrying to the washroom. When she returned, the dirt was gone, and he noticed that her braid had been tidied up, as well.

He grinned and took a bite. She was worth being on the ground for, he decided, though he kept this thought to himself. Thorben Adelfried might be grateful for his information and his service, but though he had been accepted into their home and cared for with kindness through his convalescence, Marik was aware of the great social chasm between himself and the Chieftain's daughter. And yet that had not prevented them from becoming friends. He, the recovering invalid, she, the only one not constantly busy with preparations for war. She, the teacher and her mother's helper, always with her hands full of children or food, always with a quick smile, welcoming a chance to simply sit and talk with him in between her chores, listening to his stories of adventure with rapt attention, and reading him stories from her family's vast library, re-awakening Marik's long-forgotten love of books. They had both been lonely, and so they had turned to each other for companionship.

Marik missed his crew. Oleck, Shaesta, and Mouse had taken the Oddhaven out just a sennight after dropping him off at the Adelfrieds', sent on an errand from Thorben. When the crew returned, they had seemed eager for more work, and Thorben had been happy to oblige, giving them assignments, keeping them busy, and paying them well. Marik's leg had continued to heal, but slowly, and he had been forced to stay behind. He understood why they wanted to keep busy, and had seen their discomfort around the normal bustle of the happy house, but he missed them. Now that his leg was on the mend, he yearned for the open sky once more, but he had forced himself to wait, hoping that Wynn would be able to deliver on his promise.

His thoughts of Wynn made him turn to glance at the man in question, sitting between Ioan and Molly. Marik tried to catch his eye until Molly finally had to nudge him to get his attention. Wynn looked up at Marik.

"How are the repairs coming?" Marik asked.

Wynn stared at him, eyes wide, his fork hovering in front of his mouth. The noise of various conversations droned around him and someone burst into loud laughter that turned into a coughing fit.

"Wynn?" Marik grew concerned at the man's lack of response. "The Hawk? Are the repairs coming along well?" Wynn continued to stare at him, not speaking, and a cold knot began to grow in the pit of Marik's stomach. Wynn's unresponsiveness could only mean one thing: after all his efforts the Hawk was unsalvageable and the kid was too frightened to tell him. Marik stared down at his plate, but his stomach was clenched so tightly, he knew he couldn't eat another bite. Having lost his appetite completely, he untangled himself from the bench, wishing for the first time that the Adelfrieds would just use chairs around their dining table like normal, civilized folk, and stumbled away. He had no destination in mind, just a need to depart, to get away, to run from the truth that sliced through him like an axe cleaving him in two.

His beloved Hawk would never fly again.

Shrugging into his heavy coat, Marik raced outside, taking deep, gulping breaths of the frosty evening air. The wet snow seeped through worn spots on his old boots. He barely noticed.

Oh, there would be other ships. His friends would assure him of that. Adelfried himself would probably commission a new one and give it to him in gratitude for the information he had brought about the Igyeum's new weapons. But he could not imagine his life without the Hawk. She had been his home for so many years, more of a home than anything else he had ever experienced. What few nostalgic memories he had of his childhood were overshadowed and dwarfed by the betrayal he had suffered from those who were supposed to protect him.

Sold into the Igyeum's army as a way to boost the status of his father's merchant trade, Marik had gone quietly at his parents' behest. He had even spent a short while feeling proud of his crisp uniform and the training at which he excelled. He had swiftly risen in the ranks.

But then he had seen what the Igyeum truly stood for. He had watched silently as the soldiers marched roughshod over their own people, silencing their cries and stealing their livelihoods, forcing them to work for the good of the Ar'Mol, never to enjoy the fruits of their own labors. He had seen villages starving while they harvested plentiful crops and sent all but a minute fraction of it to the capital. And then had come the day when he had watched Raisa's father hanged for an offense he did not commit, for an offense against himself that he would have preferred to forgive.

That had been the beginning of the end for him. He had looked for a way to escape, but had feared the consequences of being caught trying to desert.

Then had come the day when his own battalion marched through Enzhou, his hometown. A handful of citizens there had risen up in rebellion against the Ar'Mol, and Marik and his battalion had been sent to quell the threat.

He remembered the hard look in his commander's eyes as he thrust the blazing torch into Marik's hand. Uncomprehending, he had stared at this man he had once admired.

* * *

"Burn it down," the man ordered.

"Burn what?" Marik heard his own voice ask.

"The whole town."

"But..." He stared at the houses, standing in neat rows along cobbled streets. Enzhou was not a small village, it bordered on being a city. "We have only found evidence of a few malcontents here, surely there is no need to burn down the entire town?"

"We must let the blood to stop the disease," his commanding officer said, his voice stern.

Marik stared at the town he had grown up in. He had no love for it, but the people here did not deserve to lose everything because of a few dissenters. He stood there, the torch in his hand, frozen and confused, a rising anger at this injustice in a long line of injustices he had been forced to witness.

"Will you do as you are ordered or not, Captain?"

Shaking his head, he stepped away. "I will not," he murmured. He opened his hand to let the torch drop from suddenly nerveless fingers.

"I will do it!" a familiar voice shouted. He felt himself shoved from behind, the torch snatched from his hand before it could drop harmlessly to a puddle on the ground. Marik watched in horror as the tall figure of his father took the torch and used it to light the walls of the nearest house on fire. A family ran from the building screaming and coughing, the mother carrying a little one in her arms.

Soon, Enzhou was ablaze, its inhabitants standing outside watching their entire world turn to ash.

* * *

His vision darkened and he slipped on a patch of icy ground. Struggling to remain upright, Marik shook away the dark memories. He had left the Ar'Mol's service that night. A deserter, he had wandered for a time, homeless and bereft, constantly looking over his shoulder, sure he would hear the tromp of soldiers' boots coming after him.

Then he had found the Hawk. She had been so much more than just a ship—she was the freedom he had craved, the escape he had needed. She had given him the sky, and nothing could ever recapture that sensation, not any other ship, certainly. He stumbled down the path in the direction of the yard where he knew Wynn had been trying to effect his repairs. Even if she would never fly again, even if she was to be chopped up into scrap wood, he wanted to see her one last time, to stand on her ruined decks, to say goodbye.

As he crested the slight hill and looked down into the yard, he came to an abrupt halt, disbelief washing through him. The Hawk floated lightly alongside the dock they had constructed for her. Marik's confused eyes hungrily traced her sleek lines, picking out every shining detail. Her hull glistened as though polished, and her trim sails were folded neatly against her sides; they looked a bit different, but were still dyed with his signature color of deep maroon. His sharp gaze spotted a few other adjustments here and there as she bobbed slightly in the air: a U-shaped line of vents along the stern, and some smaller ones that seemed to be folded under her trim sails were the most obvious differences, but he could also tell that the shape of her hull had been altered and her mainmast was shorter than it had been.

Chewing thoughtfully on the inside of one cheek, Marik strode the rest of the way down into the yard. He slowly climbed the stairs of the dock, gripped the boarding rope and easily swung over, his boots thumping slightly as he landed on the brand-new decking. The ship fairly sparkled. His ears were filled with the gentle hum of the engines, not as loud as he remembered, but every bit as musical. If his airship had been a person, he was certain she would have winked at him.

Wonderingly, he climbed the steps to the steerage and stood at the wheel, staring down at the contraption Wynn had assembled there. New levers and knobs had been affixed to the area around the wheel, and he had no idea what they all did, but the main thing was that the ship itself looked to be complete. Different, but still his own, beautiful Hawk. He frowned. Then why...

Before he could even complete his thought, he heard footsteps pounding up the stairs, and looked up in time to see Wynn swing over and land on the deck. The young man looked up and grinned at him.

"She looks brand-new!" Marik called. "You had me worried for a minute there."

"Sorry about that," Wynn apologized. He climbed up to stand next to Marik. "Sometimes... with all the noise at dinner... I have a hard time processing." He gave a helpless shrug. "I didn't mean to scare you."

Marik forced a chuckle. "I thought you were trying to figure out how to tell me that she couldn't be fixed."

Wynn's eyes widened. "That's why you ran off." He lowered his head and scuffed the toe of his boot against the decking. Then he looked up, his eyes sparkling. "You want to give her a try? I have a few more tweaks I need to make, but she's almost finished, and seeing her in action would help with figuring out what final adjustments are necessary."

Marik wanted to jump in the air and holler like a small boy. Instead, he allowed a lopsided grin to spread across his face.

"Sure, kid. Let's take her up."

12

It did not take long for Wynn to give Marik a quick rundown of the new controls at the helm of the Valdeun Hawk. Marik pressed forward the control that extended the trim sails, and frowned as he noticed that they were over double the length they had always been. They appeared to be made out of a different material, as well.

Wynn smiled at the trim sails. "She still needs cynders to get off the ground, but those will keep you from falling out of the sky should something happen to the engine," he said proudly.

Marik nodded. Sure, kid, he thought. Like that's possible.

He leaned over the side. The vents he had observed from the ground could be seen now, extending down the length of the trim sails, and Marik wondered about their function. He shrugged it off, making a mental note to ask Wynn about it once they were airborne. A shiver of anticipation and a slight tingle of apprehension revolved around one another like twin snakes in Marik's stomach, churning as he placed his hand on the new lift lever. It had been four lunats since he had been in the air, and while he craved the open sky, he also couldn't deny the trickle of fear dripping down his back or the vivid scenes of his last flight pummeling his memory with unwanted images. Before he could change his mind, Wynn had released the mooring lines and raised a hand from the deck before making his way back to the ladder leading up to the wheel.

"She might be a touch more sensitive than you remember," Wynn cautioned, clipping a safety line to his belt. "I know you didn't want me to make too many alterations, and I think you'll find that the ship itself is as close to her original construction as possible. But the controls"—Wynn gave an excited grin—"well, you told me I could play with them. I think you'll like what I came up with."

Marik gave a tight nod and eased the lift lever up, as gently as he would lift a newborn baby. The Hawk fairly leapt into the air, nearly driving them both to their knees. Wynn clutched at the railing, his knuckles turning white as they gripped the balustrade. The Hawk itself shot into the sky, a sky as blue as the dress Cathrine had been wearing earlier. Marik shook away the distracting image and grimly set about easing off the controls until the airship had leveled out.

"How did that feel?" Wynn asked.

"Like I got left behind at the starting gate in a horse race," Marik laughed. "She's a mite touchy."

"I can adjust that," Wynn assured him. "Though I'm afraid with the new engine she's always going to be a bit more sensitive than she was. Think you can get used to it?"

"Aye," Marik said. "It's just a matter of learning the controls. If you can calm it down a little, that would be a big help."

"Can you try taking her forward?"

Marik touched the control lightly and the airship sped forward with surprising alacrity. Despite the incredible speed with which she responded, Marik was not taken unawares this time. He gripped the wheel, his heart soaring. All fear dropped away as he reveled in the freedom of the sky. The wind against his face, the openness of the horizon, the moon so close he could touch it, the sound of the sails crinkling in the air were all blissfully familiar and beloved. Joy filled him with its tingling, heady fragrance of freedom. He adjusted the wheel, turning the Hawk into a semi-circle, then turned again, circling back the other way in a giant lazy, figure-eight. Mirth welled up within him and bubbled over. He was filled with light, a light that threatened to explode from his chest.

"Good." Wynn's voice barely registered in his joy. He held up a pocket chronometer and Marik resisted the urge to tease. Molly had built the device and given it to Wynn as a present, and everybody in the Adelfried's house had noticed that Wynn sometimes seemed to invent reasons to use it. "Now, I'd like to try something. Get her into position over Adelfried's house, point her at that mountain"—Wynn indicated the mountain in question—"then ease into the throttle until you've reached the maximum speed possible. I'll tell you when to stop. I want to see how fast she can go. I've already paced it out on the ground and made some signs I'll be able to see from up here in the moonlight."

Marik quickly complied, bringing the airship into position. He waited for Wynn's signal, transported suddenly back in time to the excitement of a foot race with his younger brother. His hands quivered, hovering above the controls, and his heart sped up, thundering in his ears. His calves ached, trembling, shouting at him to stretch them, to move, to run.

"Go!" Wynn shouted, and Marik's hand gripped the throttle, pushing it forward. Even in his excitement, his hands were sure and steady on the controls. He did not simply mash the throttle forward, but eased it smoothly to the end of its track until it could go no farther.

The Hawk responded eagerly, bursting forward with a speed Marik had never before experienced. The wind slammed into him, almost driving him backwards. It lashed his face with stinging force that made his eyes water. They sped through the air for what felt like no time at all, and then Wynn was shouting, but he could barely make out his words above the sudden gale. He caught the gist, however, and pulled the throttle back, easing the airship to a gentle, gliding stop where she hovered in the air.

Wynn stared down at his pocket chronometer, his forehead so furrowed that his eyebrows had almost joined together. He leaned over the railing, staring at the ground, then popped back up, shaking his head. A strange tightness filled Marik's throat as he waited. He felt that their flight had been fast, faster than anything he had experienced, but Wynn's reaction confused him and he found himself replaying the memory of the wind on his face over in his mind. Had he imagined the thrill of the speed? The painfulness of the wind? Had it all been wishful thinking? Maybe they had actually been flying at unexpectedly slow speeds, maybe the Hawk had just been too broken to put back together and would never be the same, no matter what anyone did.

Then Wynn leaped in the air and let out a cry that sounded more like a scream to Marik's apprehensive ears.

"What is it? What's wrong?" Marik asked.

Wynn turned in a circle, his fist pumping into the air. "I did it! We did it!" He leaned down and kissed the balustrade. "You beautiful, beautiful machine!" He grabbed Marik's hand and pumped it enthusiastically.

Marik stared at him, a bit perplexed. "Are you going to tell me what you are shouting about?"

Wynn stopped dancing about. "Do you have any idea how fast this ship can fly now? Any idea? Wait... how fast was she before the crash?"

Marik considered. "Oleck and I calculated it out once. I think our top speed was thirty-five knots; why?"

"Because you just managed fifty-eight knots!" Wynn all but shouted. "I marked out spots on the ground earlier so I could arrange the test. And I think I can get that even better with a few adjustments."

"Fifty-eight..." Marik's head spun. "I thought that felt fast." He grinned then sobered. "But if we're going to be traveling at those kinds of speeds, the crew and I are going to need something to protect our eyes."

"Agreed. I was a bit worried for a second there about what

might happen if a bug got in my eye. I should have thought of that before I had you try, but I wasn't sure I had eked that much power out of the engines. Everything I've done has been theoretical until now."

"You've done a fantastic job, Wynn."

"Thanks. Now, turn off the engine."

"Excuse me?"

"Turn off the engine. It's the last test."

Marik stared at the young man. Wynn, noticing that Marik had not moved, looked up.

"Is something wrong?" he asked.

There was no saliva in Marik's mouth. A powerful thirst overwhelmed him, accompanied by a desire to set his feet on solid ground, a desire he had never before experienced.

"Are you insane?" Marik rasped.

"Of course not." Wynn looked confused. "This is the last test, I need to see how it works. Please turn the engine off."

"We'll fall."

"Not if I've done my job correctly."

"Look, kid, I appreciate all you've done for me, for the Hawk... but there is no way in the deep world I am turning off a perfectly functional engine when we're five thousand feet above the ground."

Wynn stared at him. "You don't trust me?" Now he sounded hurt.

"It's not a matter of trusting you, kid. You seem like you know what you're doing. What you've managed here"—Marik gestured at the airship—"it's incredible, but what you're asking me to do..."

"Twice now, your airship has fallen out of the sky," Wynn pointed out in a no-nonsense tone. "The first time, you had Dalmir aboard to save you. The second time nearly killed you. Since it appears that you tend to crash airships at a somewhat alarming rate, I worked hard to insert features into my repairs to help mitigate your recklessness, and I want to see how well they work."

"My recklessness? My own crew mates betraying me and an Igyeum captain pursuing me with an insane weapon are somehow my fault?" Marik retorted.

"Nobody forced you to become a pirate." Wynn did not say it like an accusation. It was merely a statement of fact.

"That's where you're wrong, lad," Marik said grimly. "I'm probably going to regret this... but if I do, at least it won't be for very long." With a terrible tingling that started at the base of his throat and then plummeted to the bottom of his stomach and rested there, Marik jammed his hand down on the lever that controlled the flow of power from the cynders, cutting them off. He waited for that dreadful moment, the rush of air, the sensation of his stomach dropping out from under him, that glorious, terrifying instant of weightlessness that would begin as soon as the airship began to plummet.

It didn't come.

The Hawk drifted in a slow descent, and Marik found that he could still control their direction as they glided noiselessly through the air in a lazy downward spiral.

Wynn punched his fist in the air. "It worked!"

Marik stared at him. "It worked? You mean you weren't sure?"

"I wasn't one hundred percent certain, that's why I asked you to help me test the feature."

For a moment, Marik couldn't speak. A hundred retorts and accusations flitted through his mind, but he settled for, "How did you manage it?"

Wynn began talking about the length and structure of the wings, the materials he had used to rebuild the ship, something about thermal winds, and other technical details. Marik did not understand all of it, but he gathered that the gist was that Wynn had made the ship light enough and the wings large enough that in the event of a power-failure, the Hawk had the capability to glide gently to the ground instead of simply falling out of the sky.

"Might still be a bit of a bumpy landing, depending on the terrain," Wynn admitted. "So I wouldn't use it unless you're forced to... You can turn the cynders back on, now." Wynn glanced up. "I need to get back to the forge: Dalmir said he might need my help with the aton. We can do some more tests tomorrow if you'd like."

"I would like that very much." Marik grinned and powered up the engine once more, turning the nose of his airship back in the direction of Adelfried's docks. Then he looked down at the young man standing next to him. "Thank you," he said simply.

Wynn's face flushed and he ducked his head. "Thanks for letting me make a few changes," he replied.

"After this?" Marik chuckled. "Feel free to change anything you want. Any idea you get... you go for it." He paused. "In fact... would you like to come with me in the spring when we go after Raisa?"

Wynn's face lit up, but then his brow furrowed. "Thank you for the offer, Captain, I'm honored. But Daegan, Keene, Molly, and I are heading to Dalton tomorrow."

"Dalton, eh?"

"The Oreworks." Wynn's voice took on an eagerness. "We're to oversee the production of the Trackless, as well as the hand cannons, and my skiffs."

"And Molly's going, too?" Marik grinned at him.

"Of course, she's Daegan's apprentice, too," Wynn said, then he seemed to catch Marik's grin and he flushed slightly. "I'd go with Daegan and Keene even if Molly wasn't going," he mumbled.

"But her being there doesn't hurt, I'll bet." Marik winked.

Wynn chuckled. "No, it doesn't hurt."

13

———

Dalmir trudged through the snow on the path leading from the Adelfrieds' home to the forge. He had put this off as long as he could, but he had made a promise. Longnight Feast had ended, and with it came the duty he had been avoiding. After dinner, he had spent an hour telling stories to Hubert, Gereon, and Gustaf, Beren's three youngest brothers, after which he had gone for a walk along the river, just enjoying the brisk cold of the wintry air. When the Valdeun Hawk skimmed overhead and descended to settle back into its moorings, Dalmir knew it was time.

A heavy sensation, like a hand pressing down on his spine, crushing him toward the ground, weighed on him. His feet dragged as he climbed the path back to the forge so that by the time he entered Keene's domain the others were already waiting, even Wynn, who had come all the way from the docks. Frieda sat on a low table. Her head swiveled toward him as he entered.

"We thought you might have changed your mind," Daegan said.

"I wish I could," Dalmir replied. He approached the aton, who stared at him with her impassive face. "But I did promise."

"Why do you resist this?" Frieda asked.

"Why do you want to know? You cannot possibly care. Nor can you feel curiosity," Dalmir replied, unable to keep the bitterness out of his tone.

"You are right, I cannot care. But I was built to assist humans, and my... processes are defined by logic. I am able to discern that your behavior is illogical. This is a discrepancy that I do not understand... you might say it... confounds me."

Dalmir sighed. "I don't know that I can explain it in a way that you would understand. And I don't know that it will matter anyway. If this goes as it should, you won't be awake anymore."

"This is true. But perhaps it would help you... if you tried. Helping you is my primary function, after all."

Dalmir scowled. Then a sudden thought occurred to him. "Why are you still functioning at all?" The others stared at him and he continued. "The orb is Mulemo's, isn't it?"

"You are correct."

"Then why are you still functioning? The Maleians have all been relocated far from here."

Frieda was silent for a moment, then she pointed. "That one's blood calls to the orb and keeps it singing."

Dalmir looked where she was pointing and his eyes fell on Daegan's apprentice. His eyebrows shot up as he took in her reddish-brown curls, deeply tanned skin, and smattering of freckles. "Truly? She doesn't look Maleian."

"What do looks... matter?" Frieda asked.

"Never mind."

"Why is it pointing at me?" Molly asked.

"Forgive me, Molly, was it?" Dalmir said.

"Yes."

"You may find this question personal, but... you don't by any chance have Maleian ancestors?"

Molly's expression turned troubled. Her eyes darted from one face to another. Hesitantly, she gave a slow nod. "My mother is Maleian. My father is Dalman, but he thinks there might be some

Pallan in his own heritage, as well, though he's never been able to confirm it."

"Interesting." Dalmir studied her for a long moment.

"How could you know that?" Molly asked.

"What does this have to do with anything?" Daegan demanded, his voice grumpy. "Are we retrieving the power source from this machine or not? If we are not, I have other work to do."

"If you don't want to do this..." Wynn began, but Dalmir waved a hand and he fell silent.

"The orbs cannot activate on their own," Dalmir explained, certain things beginning to click together for him. "They've always needed their creator to bring them to life. But now, it seems that humans with ties to the region each orb hails from have the ability to awaken the orbs and use their power. I'm still not sure why or how this happened, but it has. Frieda was able to stay activated so long as the Maleians she protected in Chasm survived. Now, she remains awake because of Molly's Maleian heritage."

"Intriguing," Daegan breathed.

"This does not... answer the question... of why you do not wish to remove Mulemo's orb," Frieda said.

"I don't know if I understand it, myself," Dalmir began. "Frieda, you have given me back a piece of my two brothers, fragments of them I thought I had lost forever. I do not wish to let that go. What is more, you bear the face of Tel's wife: Lerilei. To remove the orb that powers you feels like... well, it will almost be like watching her die a second time."

"That is illogical," Frieda replied. "Removing the orb will not kill me, but merely cause me to sleep. Also, I am not Lerilei. A person cannot die twice."

"I told you that I wouldn't be able to make you understand." Dalmir sighed.

"Is it possible to fashion a new power source for you, like the ones that power the airships?" Wynn asked.

Frieda turned to him. "No," she replied. "Telsume and

Mulemo were careful to make certain only an orb could... cause me to function. The Esteemed Archidian knew this, that is why she brought me Mulemo's orb when she brought the villagers to Chasm."

Wynn and Daegan stared at the aton blankly. Dalmir ground his teeth in frustration. Emotions he would have rather kept contained simmered to the surface of his thoughts.

"You have insisted since the beginning that I remove the orb from your power core, but you have never explained why. Can you at least tell me that? Why can I not simply leave the orb in your care?" Dalmir asked.

The aton tilted its head to one side, its movements at once jerky and jarringly human. For a moment, the only sounds were those of the tilt-hammer and the gears clicking within Frieda's frame.

"It was part of... my instructions... from the Archidian when she activated me," Frieda said at last. "Along with a message for you."

"What message?"

"She has the information you need... to defeat Uun. You must... call out to her."

"You are just telling me this now?" Dalmir took a step forward, his hands clenching. "Why have you kept this information from me for the past four lunats?"

"I was instructed... not to reveal this until you made the decision to remove the orb," the aton replied. "However... over the past four lunats of observing you, I have come to realize that you will not make that decision without... assistance. I do not have all the answers you seek, but I do know three things for certain: you must retrieve the orb that powers me, you need to know what the Archidian knows, and she cannot come to you unless you call her."

"She cannot come unless I—" Dalmir stopped. The world stopped. Everything went still and silent. Even the relentless pounding of the tilt-hammer was drowned out by the overwhelming rush of comprehension that suddenly pressed in on him from all sides. The pressure of it drove him to his knees. His body filled with light and cold and the edges of his vision darkened. Through the fog descending upon him, he could hear a clamor of voices, but he could not make out individual words. All else fell away in a single, joyous revelation: He had never been abandoned.

"Dalmir? Dalmir?" Daegan's gruff voice cut through the haze and Dalmir blinked as the man's hand came down upon his shoulder.

"Fine. I'm fine," he assured them. "Frieda, thank you. If there is another way to revive your functions, we will find it."

The aton's expressionless face stared at him. It was empty, and for the first time, Dalmir could see past the picture of Lerilei that Telsume had painted on her features to the machine within. There was no creative thought, no emotion, no soul inside this mechanical marvel. It was just a picture that reminded him of everything he had lost. The emotions and humanity were his alone to bear. For a moment, he envied the machine before him: she would never feel loss or grief or love or hope, those gifts had been reserved for his own kind. Not even with the power of the orbs could the most marvelous facsimile attain them. What would it be like, to feel nothing? Dalmir pondered the question for a brief moment, then took a deep breath.

"Let us begin," he said, a new resolve tightening within his chest, a resolve that was bolstered by something he had given up looking for long ago... hope. He turned to Wynn. "Start with that plate."

Wynn worked carefully, following Dalmir's instructions as they opened the chest-plate of the aton. Daegan and Molly stood nearby, carefully documenting each piece as they removed it and placing them in order so that the machine could be put back together at a later date. Dalmir noted that the young man turned each piece over in his hands, studying it briefly from every angle before laying it aside.

"The designer of this machine certainly wasn't taking any chances," Daegan commented at one point.

"What do you mean, sir?" Molly asked.

"Putting the power source so deep inside the aton. Look at all this shielding," Daegan explained, picking up one of the plates. "It seems most of this wondrous creation was designed simply to protect the orb."

"What I still don't understand is why," Dalmir grunted, working on a particularly stubborn bolt. "Wynn, I need a different size wrench."

"Why what?" Wynn handed him the correct tool.

"Why Tel built her," Dalmir explained, grunting a bit as he pushed down on the wrench. The bolt came loose. He paused, twisting his mouth to one side. "Actually, there are a lot of things I don't understand. It appears that Tel was keeping many secrets. I had no idea he had designed his tower to descend underground. I never saw him use the atons as guards, that has to have been Mulemo's idea—they worked together often—but it is hard to fathom how they managed to keep all of this a secret. The barrier they set up inside the tower that nullified my power also seemed more like a Mulemo idea than one of Tel's. But Frieda... she's all Tel. It's just strange, almost like he knew something bad was coming."

"If he knew, why couldn't he guard against it?" Wynn asked.

"Maybe he didn't know," Dalmir amended. "Maybe he just had a feeling, or a suspicion. Or maybe he tried and simply failed. It's obvious he did not know whom to trust. It appears that he only let Mulemo and Shiori in on the secret."

"Who's Shiori?" Molly asked.

Dalmir's eyes grew distant and his hands fell still. The pounding of the tilt-hammer filled the silence.

Dalmir shook himself. "She is the Archidian that Frieda spoke of just now. I do not know how to explain her... she..."

"Is she like you?" Daegan asked, removing another bolt.

"Yes. No. Sort of." Dalmir bent over and carefully pried up a thin sheet of metal. "Ah! There it is!"

They all leaned forward and peered inside. They could now see the spherical gemstone. Dark gray in color, the orb shimmered with a light of its own, a mesmerizing, swirling light. Wynn leaned over it for a long moment as though studying every aspect of its surface.

With deft precision, Dalmir used the long, thin tongs to pluck the orb from its resting place. The aton stiffened as her gears stopped turning.

"Fascinating," Daegan murmured, wiping his glasses.

Molly stared at the small gemstone, her eyes wide. "I can hear it."

Dalmir's eyes widened and he turned to the girl in surprise. "Hear it? What is it saying?"

Molly shook her head. "I'm not sure. It's not words, really, just a sort of sound."

Dalmir hesitated a moment, then held the orb out to Molly. She stared up at him.

"It's all right," Dalmir assured her. "It won't harm you in any way. I have been wanting to get more information about how Uun has managed to use our brothers' orbs, but I have had little time to experiment. When my brothers died, I believed their power died with them. It never occurred to me that others might be able to use what they had left behind."

"I don't understand." Molly's voice became small and uncertain.

Dalmir wished he could explain, but how could he explain something he still didn't understand himself? "I am not good at explaining. It has been so many years since I even spoke to another person, and even after over a year out of my tower I find I am out of practice. It is a long story, and one I am not prepared to relive just at the moment. Suffice to say that each of these orbs holds a portion of power. This power was bestowed upon them by seven different... wizards... I suppose you could call us, for lack of a more accurate description. We were brothers, the seven of us, cursed to bear the weight of a great wrong we committed—a crime that deprived the entire world of knowledge it should have kept. Centuries ago, five of my brothers were murdered by Uun, leaving behind their orbs. The gemstones lay silent for centuries, and I, their guardian, believed them to be nothing more than empty trinkets, painful reminders of the family I had lost. But then, one day, a young man climbed into my tower. A tower which he should not have been able to even experience curiosity about—much less a desire to climb up and investigate, mind you. He tumbled into my room and set my own orb ablaze with light."

"Grayden," Wynn supplied.

"That's right. I did have the chance later to let him experiment with the orb, but that time was quite short." Dalmir nodded, thankful for Wynn's interjection; it helped him focus on the more recent history that was not so painful. "This did something that had not happened in so long, I barely understood what was happening: it piqued my curiosity. How was this possible? I had to find out what was happening in the world. And here we are, over a year later. And my questions only led to more questions." Dalmir pointed at the orb. "I saw indications of my brothers' power at work in the world, but I could not understand how this could be. But now, I think I begin to understand."

Molly stared at him, wide-eyed, the orb still held tentatively in her hand. "Understand what?"

"My brothers and I, we realized the world was too big for us to watch over it from a single location, and as we each had our own interests, we needed space from one another. We spread out and each settled in a different region of the world, shepherding the people around us, guiding them to the knowledge and education they needed as we each saw fit. Except for Uun... he secluded himself in the Whispering Wood and refused to allow anyone to settle in his region."

"He must have been fierce. Nobody goes there even now," Wynn said.

"Yes, well, that is partially my fault," Dalmir admitted. "I set strong barriers in place when I imprisoned him in his tower. I thought they would be enough to keep even the most curious away, but as with everything else, I made a serious error in judgment.

"But it appears that my brothers left something of themselves behind after all. The descendants of the people in each of their regions have the ability to create an attunement to the orb left behind. The strength of these connections seems to vary, but it is clear that some are capable of using the power stored in the gemstones. Uun obviously figured this out. I have seen evidence of Palte's and Avaleun's orbs in both the cynders and the works of the madman you battled in the mountains." He nodded to Wynn. "The Maleians kept Mulemo's orb here activated for generations on the wrong side of the world, and now Molly, with her Maleian bloodlines, also has a bond to it." Dalmir gave Molly a small smile. "If you are willing, I would like to see if you can focus its power."

Molly glanced around. Wynn nodded encouragingly at her, his expression eager and envious at the same time.

"All right," she said. "What do I do?"

"Let's start with something simple. See if you can make it glow," Dalmir said. "Just focus on the orb and the idea of light."

Molly's brow furrowed. "Like a wish?"

"If that helps," Dalmir replied.

Molly stared at the orb for a long moment. Nothing happened. Molly squeezed her eyes shut, the muscles in her face growing tense. The orb remained dark. At length, Molly opened her eyes and regretfully offered the small jewel back to Dalmir.

"I'm sorry," she said. "I can hear it, but it's faint, like music that's so far away you can't really pick out the tune, even though you think it might be a familiar one."

Dalmir accepted the orb back. "Like I said, the connection strength seems to vary." He sat quietly for a moment, his eyes narrowed. He laid a hand on the empty husk of the aton, one finger tapping gently on its frame. "I hate to drag anyone from

Frieda's settlement back into this conflict; they have already been through so much."

"What about the durven?" Wynn asked. "They're Maleian, technically."

Dalmir brightened visibly. "Of course! I don't know why I didn't think of it sooner. Thank you, Wynn."

14

Raisa awoke to water dripping through the thin fabric of her tent onto her face. The pattering sound of rain filled the tiny space and she groaned, pulling her sparse blanket up around her shoulders. Who would have ever believed it could rain so much in the middle of the desert? It was growing apparent that the Weald did not obey any normal seasonal rules. Lorcan had claimed credit for the existence of this massive forested oasis more than once. Could he have affected the weather in some way, as well? She didn't know. She supposed it didn't matter, though; she had long ago lost track of time. How many lunats had passed since she had descended into this misery of existence? Besides the fact that some days it rained and some days the sun shone, the weather did not vary much and there was no way to know if it were midwinter or midsummer or somewhere in between.

The opening to her tent flapped wildly, interrupting her musings. "Captain Virtanen's orders, you're to come to the training grounds now."

Raisa suppressed another groan and sat up, her head pushing against the top of the tent that would have already been too small for her before Lorcan's tampering. Her body ached as she crawled out of the cramped space, her bare feet squelching into the wet sand until they met something sharp, a rock or tree root perhaps. She winced. Not for the first time, she longed for her boots, though she had to admit they would have been useless in most of her training. The soldier gave her a resentful glare and marched off toward the mess tent. She watched him go. His orders to come alert her of the summons had probably interrupted his breakfast. Raisa could no longer remember breakfast.

Taking a deep breath to steel herself against another torturous day, Raisa propelled herself into a steady lope through the dripping trees to the training grounds. Virtanen stood waiting for her, whip in hand, cruel smirk on his lips. She hated him with the fury of a hurricane, but she was powerless to touch him. Her heart sank as he came into view. He was not alone.

Three men stood behind Captain Virtanen. One of them was Lorcan, his appearance bedraggled and soaked through, but he seemed unconcerned by the rain. This did not surprise Raisa. Over the past lunats, she had observed that the madman was impervious to weather; it wasn't that it didn't affect him, he just never seemed to notice. Standing next to him was the Ar'Molon —second-in-command of all the Igyeum, though many whispered that he was the true power behind the Ar'Mol's throne—a large, steel-ribbed rainshade held over his head, protecting him from the wetness that drizzled down from above. Raisa maintained a careful indifference, keeping her gaze from lingering on the Ar'Molon so that she could not be accused of staring, but her heightened eyesight noted that he was impeccably dry. Not a single drop of water had sullied even the cuffs of his neatly pressed trousers. An alarm went off in Raisa's head, informing her that no rainshade was that effective. The third man was darker than the others, his features jutting from his face in sharp, strong angles under a thick, neatly combed thatch of black hair. He was shorter than the Ar'Molon, but every bit as tall and broad as Captain Virtanen, and something about his stance told Raisa he could hold his own in a fight. Even though she avoided allowing her gaze to linger on any of the newcomers—she did not wish for any of them to notice her scrutiny—she found herself studying the third man's face. Then he raised his head and met her gaze, his eyes catching hers and holding them captive for a long moment until she forced herself to look away, focusing again on Virtanen as she came to stand before him.

"Today you have an audience." Virtanen smirked. "I expect your performance to be faultless as you show the Ar'Molon just what you are capable of this morning. He has invested rather a lot into you, and I do not want him to be disappointed in his new asset. Do you understand?"

Raisa nodded mutely. In other words, she should in no way make Virtanen look bad. Hate seethed through her.

"Very well. Same course as yesterday," Virtanen muttered. Then he raised his voice. "Ar'Molon, gentlemen, I present Subject Two Forty-Seven for your observation. I hope you are pleased with the results."

Raisa stood for a moment frozen in place, her eyes on the ground. Inside, she wanted to be sick. She had never thought about what it meant when Virtanen referred to her as "Two-Four-Seven" before, but now she wondered: had there been two hundred forty-six others before her? Two hundred forty-six prisoners subjected to Lorcan's terrifying experiments, the starvation, the training, all of it? Were there two hundred forty-six people like her? Or were they failed experiments? Hadn't Lorcan called her the first? She had thought he meant she was his first experiment... but then she had met Olin and now she questioned everything Lorcan had ever said. Was she merely the latest in a long line of tortured subjects? And if so, what had become of the rest of them? Had they been successfully trained into submission? Were they—with heightened strength and speed and aim like herself— even now marching alongside the soldiers of the Ar'Mol? Or were they like Olin, hiding from the world and their maker while working desperately to create some semblance of a normal life for themselves? No, they couldn't all be like Olin, Lorcan was confused by his existence. But then what? She knew there had been other attempts, Lorcan muttered obsessively about his "fail-ures." She had assumed it simply meant that his experiments hadn't worked. But what if it was worse than that? The thought she had avoided for lunats seized her mind between its terrifying jaws: what if they had all died? Then what made her different? Or was she different at all? Perhaps she wasn't truly the "success" Lorcan gloated about. If she was the first success, then what would become of her when her training was complete? She felt like she was drowning, sinking into the earth as it swallowed her whole, the solid walls of dirt pressing against her chest, cutting off her ability to breathe. Her absolute helplessness overwhelmed her.

"Two-Four-Seven!" Virtanen's sharp command pierced through her panic. "Begin!"

Raisa darted forward instantly, instincts and training taking over her muscles. She knew from lunats of experience that even a heartbeat's delay would cause her to feel the sharp sting of the whip on her back, and so she obeyed without thought. As she ran to the first obstacle, she allowed the wind on her face to sweep away the turbulent worries and questions, clearing them from her mind. For now, all that mattered was the task before her.

"Raisa." She chanted to herself as she ran, the mantra of her own name the one thing that had kept her sane throughout Virta-nen's training, the only thing that kept her from accepting being relegated to a number. "My name is Raisa. Pirate. Navigator. Voice of reason. I belong on the Valdeun Hawk with my captain. His name is Marik. My name is Raisa. Pirate. Navigator..." She leaped up to grasp the handles on the first obstacle and hurled herself over the fifteen-foot-high wall, barely noticing how effort-less it had become. Her feet thudded solidly onto the ground on the other side and she flung her body into the horizontal netting and clambered through it, bare feet treading lightly on the familiar ropes, skimming across without a thought. She was unaware of the tears streaming down her face, unaware of the terrible aching in her heart. She could only focus on the task at hand until its completion.

She finished the course and felt a thrill sweep through her. She knew she had beaten her best time. Of course, even the smallest glimmer of approval would be too much to hope for from Virtanen, but perhaps...

Raisa turned and saw three soldiers advancing upon her. So, the exercise wasn't over. She crouched in the center of the clearing, waiting. The men all bore staves, while she herself was unarmed. Not that she was at a disadvantage; Virtanen had trained her well. And with her added abilities she needed no weapons.

Together, the three soldiers charged at her, coming at her from different sides. This was a tactic they had been working on perfecting, making it much more difficult for her. It was easier if she could face them one at a time, but when they worked together she found herself struggling. The only consolation was that they tended to get in each other's way at times, which often gave her the opening she needed to escape the attack.

She just had time to take a breath before they reached her. Two staves swept at her body, while a third jabbed at her face like a javelin. Raisa managed to throw herself backwards and avoid taking a blow to the face, but the other staves thudded squarely into her side and legs. She landed heavily on her back, the breath exploding from her lungs in a painful shock. She lay there, struggling for air, trying desperately to regain control of her body. A stave crashed into her midsection, expelling what little breath she had recovered back out through her lips. The corners of her vision began to go dark. Desperately, she lashed out with one leg and felt her wild kick connect with something solid. Distantly, she heard a grunt and a thud as one of her attackers crashed to the ground nearby. From the darkening edges of her peripheral vision, another stave swung toward her head. Raisa blocked it with her forearm. Usually, she would have attempted to catch it and yank her attacker off-balance, but she was still struggling to breathe.

Rolling swiftly to one side, she pulled herself along the ground, digging her elbows into the sandy earth and crawling in the direction of the trees. Behind her, she heard footfalls and she lunged to one side as the stave crashed into the ground right where her back had been but a moment before. With grim determination, Raisa sucked in a mouthful of air and pushed herself to her feet. Her vision swam even as she lowered her head and barreled into the side of the man holding the stave. She knocked him from his feet and landed a punch across his jawbone. Pain exploded through the knuckles of her hand, reverberating up her forearm, but she ignored it, grasping hold of the stave and whirling to face the other two combatants.

Now armed, she made short work of the second attacker, parrying his first blow and tapping him lightly on the side of the head, just hard enough to send him unconscious. He slumped to the ground next to his companion. Then she turned and watched the third soldier warily.

Something tapped on her subconscious. It was faint, like far-off music, but so intensely familiar it startled her and for a moment she turned her head to stare in the direction she thought it was coming from. Her eyes met those of the young man who had arrived with the Ar'Molon. He returned her stare, his own face expressionless, his dark eyes vacant, as though he were not truly returning her gaze, but merely looking through her.

A loud crack sounded in her ears as a sudden pain exploded across the back of her skull. In the moments before unconsciousness took her, Raisa realized that she had allowed herself to be distracted from the fight, though she was still at a loss to explain what had taken her attention and held it so insistently. Darkness closed over her.

A moment later, she woke to a firm tapping on her cheek and she stared up into the greenish-yellow eyes of Lorcan. A triumphant grin spread across his face.

"That's my good daughter," he said. "Wake up, now. No time to rest. No, you have more to do today."

Groaning, Raisa pushed herself to a sitting position and

gingerly touched her fingers to the sore spot on her head. Her fingers came away sticky with blood and she growled.

"What was that?" she asked.

Lorcan smiled a knowing smile. "Not for you to know. No. But for me! Aha! My moment of triumph has come. All these years, all these long years of failing and failing, and finally, finally I have prevailed. The patient shall prevail, you know. Oh, yes. It just takes time. And sacrifice. Many have sacrificed. But not in vain. No! Now I know it was not in vain!"

Raisa closed her eyes, wishing he would stop talking. His babbling made even less sense than usual, and the splitting, throbbing ache in her head made it impossible for her to focus on his words or parse through them for whatever he was driving at this time.

Taking a deep breath, she rose to her feet, swaying slightly. But to show weakness or ask to leave would let them know she was not completely theirs, so instead she took a few more long breaths, keeping her eyes fixed on the ground to prevent them from reading any emotion in her expression.

"What would you have me do now, Master?"

Lorcan clapped his hands. "See? See how obedient she is?"

The Ar'Molon approached, rainshade still held in one hand. Raisa's stomach flipped upside down as he stood before her, regarding her in silence. The man exuded a presence that made her want to bow before him, but she resisted the urge.

"She appears to be obedient, but how can you be sure?" His voice was deep and rich. "Two-Four-Seven, look at me."

Raisa lifted her eyes to his face. She had never before been so close to the man. In their two previous meetings, he had been standing in the shadows or hovering behind the Ar'Mol's throne, and so she was not prepared for the distinct resemblance he bore to Dalmir. His features were not quite as sharp and defined, his shoulders were broader, and she would have bet he was a few inches taller, but those brilliant blue eyes, that mouth—even behind the soft, short, brown beard streaked with gray—were the same. Her eyes widened involuntarily in surprise.

"I do not think you are the obedient servant you pretend to be," he whispered. "You try to hide it, but you are clearly the master of your own thoughts."

Raisa did not respond.

"Tell me, Two-Four-Seven, why did you look so surprised just now?" Uun asked, raising his voice so the others could hear the question.

Raisa's heart raced. If she refused to answer, she would prove his guess correct. But she did not know what the repercussions of telling the truth might be. Dalmir was her friend, and she had no wish to betray him, or his relationship to her and Marik's crew. Uun watched her, a mocking tilt to the corner of his mouth.

"I have never seen my lord so clearly before," Raisa replied. "You resemble someone else I have met."

"Dalmir." Uun nodded. His expression was pleasant, but his voice held a sneer. "I am sure he has told you many nasty stories about me, all of them untrue, of course. And how is my dear little brother?"

"He was well last time I saw him."

"I see he has already told you of our relationship. Does it shock you?"

Raisa shook her head mutely.

"And where exactly did you last see dear Dalmir?"

"Telsuma."

"Ah." Uun nodded sagely. "Not recently, then. Unless you are hiding something from me?" He leaned closer, gazing into her eyes, then he rocked back on his heels. "No? Interesting. I wonder..." He stroked his beard thoughtfully with his free hand. "I wonder what your reaction would be were I to tell you that one of my officers chased a small airship out of Malei on the same night you were moved to the Weald?"

Raisa's heart lurched at this sudden and unexpected turn of the conversation.

Uun raised an eyebrow. "I believe they were attempting a rescue. Yours, perhaps? Yes. A small airship full of thieving pirates. The cowards fled toward the Whispering Wood. Almost escaped, but my men used our new weapon on their airship and destroyed it. I'm told the ship went down in pieces, scattered across the Wood beyond repair."

It wasn't Marik. Her thoughts spun on this new information. It couldn't be Marik. He was still out there, still looking for her. Any day now they would swoop in with some elaborate plan and rescue her and she would leave this place forever.

"You used to be part of a crew on a small airship, didn't you? I believe my men said the name of the airship they brought down was the Valdeun Hawk. Not friends of yours, I hope? Oh dear, have I upset you?"

Raisa's mind reeled, spinning away from the terrible words, the terrible truth she saw in his eyes, the calm assurance there that this was not a bluff, but truth—horrible truth. Her heart shrieked an intense denial and a chasm opened within her chest, sucking everything that made her Raisa inside until nothing of herself remained in the Weald. Her body only stood before him as the Ar'Molon raised his eyes to study the reaction his words had wrought, but there was nothing for him to see. Raisa's eyes stared back at him, her face expressionless, her body unmoving, while her spirit tumbled into a bottomless abyss. Rain poured onto her head, plastering her hair to her shoulders and dripping down her face. She did not feel it. She could no longer feel anything.

Uun tilted his head and the smirk faded from his lips. He turned to Lorcan. "You may well have succeeded. I will want to see her in action again tomorrow. And we will continue the other tests, as well."

Lorcan's face contorted with glee. "Very good, my lord. Yes. We will do more tests tomorrow. As my lord commands."

The men left the clearing but Raisa remained where she stood, the rain beating down on her head and shoulders. Even if they had spoken the words of dismissal, she did not know if she could have moved. Her heart shriveled within her. Oleck. Marik. Mouse. Shaesta. Their names pounded through her mind in a steady rhythm of anguish. She felt their loss more keenly than any tortures she had endured in this place, more than any torment Lorcan had subjected her to.

"Two-Four-Seven!" Virtanen's voice sliced painfully through her numb state. "Dismissed! Return to your quarters."

Mechanically, Raisa obeyed. Her body moved, her feet propelling her across the clearing and down the sandy knoll to her tent. Her spirit huddled deep inside, hiding in a dark corner where no one could find it, not even her. Stiffly, she bent and crawled through the flap, her muscles complaining against the harsh training of the past few days, but the pain registered only distantly. Once inside, Raisa found she did not possess the strength even to lift a waterskin to her lips. Instead, she collapsed atop her thin blanket and lay there, face down, her head throbbing with agony that had nothing to do with the blow she had received in the sparring match.

15

Wynn's first glimpse of the Oreworks did not disappoint. The flight to Dalton had been cold and miserable—the Edrian gusts and turbulent clouds full of snow had given them a rough ride—but the Oreworks was as warm as it was enormous. Everywhere he looked, men and women were hard at work, laboring over machines, forges, and tables. Metal clanked and scraped as the people fashioned pieces together and assembled the creations that he and Daegan had mostly only seen on paper.

Daegan took him by the arm and bustled him around, introducing him to artificineers and workers whose names Wynn forgot a second or two after they were uttered. The clang and clamor of the Oreworks surrounded him and embraced him in its cacophony, but he found that it didn't bother him. Every sound had its place here; every noise had its purpose, and all were driving together to build the tools that Telmondir would soon need for its very survival.

A small hand slipped into his own and he glanced over at Molly, who gave him an encouraging smile.

"It's a little overwhelming," she said.

"A little," he agreed. "But not as bad as Daegan's workroom."

"Nothing is as bad as Daegan's workroom," she agreed.

They shared a laugh and followed Daegan as he eagerly wove his way through the factory.

"Daegan!" A burly man stepped away from a work table and clasped the white-haired man by the hand. "Come to check up on us? Are you finally going to get your own hands dirty in the war effort?"

"Plenty dirty already," Daegan assured him. "I want to introduce you to my newest protégé, Wynn Drexel."

"The man who designed the drexelock?" The large man's dark eyes brightened and he stretched his hand out to Wynn. "Pleased to meet you. You'll find you have quite a few fans around here."

"The drexelock?" Wynn asked, confused.

"Your hand cannons," the man said. "I hope you don't mind, that's what we've begun calling them. It rolls off the tongue nicely, and gives you credit."

Wynn had never been so horrified in all his life. "You named them after me?"

"You're the designer." The man smiled, clapping him on the back. "Seemed only right. And the way everything kind of comes together, well, one of my lads pointed out how it resembles a locking mechanism. It's just something the boys came up with. We understand if you had a different name you prefer. There weren't none on the schematics."

"No..." Wynn mumbled. "I hadn't named it."

Molly's hand tightened around his. "It's a good name," she said.

"We won't keep you," Daegan said. "I want to get over to see how they're coming with the skiffs."

"You mean the aerowynns?" The man grinned at them. "Those are in the building next door. This one didn't have doors big enough to fit them through once they were assembled."

"Aerowynns?" In spite of himself, Wynn couldn't keep the grin from spreading across his face. "Is that what they're calling them?"

"If we manage to come through this war in one piece, you're going to have quite the legacy," the big man chuckled.

"I guess," Wynn said, his head spinning. It was all too much to take in. He followed Daegan to the doors at the back of the building, Molly's hand still clutched tightly in his own. They burst through the doors and crossed the snow-swept courtyard to a smaller building with much larger, barn-style sliding doors. Even the short crossing had Wynn's fingers cramping with the cold, and the warmth inside was a welcome relief.

Rows of skiffs in various stages of completion greeted them, along with a quieter buzz of activity. It appeared that this building was dedicated solely to the construction of the aerowynns—Wynn couldn't help but smile at the thought of these sturdy crafts sharing his name. They were every bit as beautiful as he had hoped.

Then Daegan was introducing him to the overseer of the group, a short woman with medium-toned skin and blonde hair pulled back in a long braid, though a frizz of hairs framed her face like a halo of straw. She looked to be in her forties, and she took a moment to wipe the grease from her hands on her coarse coveralls before taking Wynn's hand and shaking it heartily.

"Tess," she introduced herself, repeating the name Daegan had said. "Just in case you need it again." She grinned at him. "I'll bet he took you on the full tour before bringing you here. How many names did he throw at you?"

"I'm not sure," Wynn admitted. "Too many."

"Sounds like our Daegan." Tess smirked. "He sent word ahead, said you might want to work in our department. We could use the extra hands, if you're interested? They want to be putting pilots into these things for test flights as early as Tella, and that's not a lot of time. Just about a lunat away. Think you're up to the task?"

"I would like nothing more," Wynn said.

The woman's face creased into a wide smile. "Good. Daegan can show you to your quarters. There will be coveralls for you there. Come on back whenever you feel settled. If you need some time to recover from your flight here, then I'll see you in the morning."

"No, ma'am," Wynn replied. "I'm ready to start now. Haven't you heard? There's a war going on out there."

Tess's eyes sparkled and she glanced up at Daegan. "You were right, I'm going to get on just fine with this one."

16

Although he had intended to go immediately to the durven, in the wee hours of darkness after Longnight Feast, winter snows descended on Telsuma with a vengeance that kept everyone inside and close to the house for two full sennights. The lunat of Darkthen faded and a new moon rose on Edrian while they huddled together around the hearth for warmth and comfort as the blizzard raged around them.

But today, the early morning sun glittered brightly on the crystalline blanket covering the world, and Dalmir had braved the deep drifts to visit the durven's new home. He approached the entrance to the abandoned mine shaft and nodded politely to the durven standing outside who gave him a respectful nod in return as Dalmir ducked into the tunnel. He had still been recovering from his injury when Marik returned from the Igyeum with these Maleian refugees, but upon waking he had heard the entire tale. Intrigued by the mystery of the durven, Dalmir had sought them out once he had felt up to leaving the house. They were reclusive and wary, but over the lunats, Dalmir had gained Hrafn's trust and formed a friendship with the man. They enjoyed lengthy conversations together and Dalmir had learned much about the situation in the Igyeum. Despite living underground, the durven had kept themselves informed of the goings-on in the empire above them. The rest of Hrafn's people had kept themselves scarce during his visits, but Dalmir understood their caution and the past that prompted it and took no offense.

As he navigated the now-familiar paths to the meeting chamber where Hrafn spent most of his days listening to his people and guiding them with his wisdom, Dalmir marveled at how much of a change had already been wrought on the tunnels. The walls were polished like that of pebbles on the beach worn to a silky smoothness, and they gleamed with leftover veins of silver and blue embedded within, veins revealed by the mining, yet too little and fragile to remove from the walls. These tunnels were swiftly becoming more than just caves, they were dwelling places, filled with beauty and light despite being underground.

"Dalmir! What brings you to visit my humble village on this fine day?" Hrafn rose and strode to greet him.

"Hrafn, my friend." Dalmir bowed his head. "Your people have made incredible progress since I last visited."

Hrafn's eyes shone in the light of the lanterns mounted along the walls. "They are diligent, even in the face of the losses we have suffered so recently. And, of course, with the blizzard raging outside there was little else to do. I think the work helps my people move on; it gives them focus, building a new home."

"You must miss your old home."

Hrafn heaved a sigh. "These tunnels are adequate to our needs, but they are nothing like our home in Malei. The tunnels there are... well, it is difficult to convey their beauty with mere words. And yet, there is no comparison to knowing that our children will be safe here: to not have to hide ourselves away... that is a prize beyond cost. A home can be rebuilt. A people cannot. We left many behind to an unknown fate in Malei. Perhaps someday the world will change enough to allow us to return there, but for now, we are enjoying the security we have found here in Telsuma, which is a beautiful land as well, though much colder than we are used to."

Dalmir nodded. "I hope you live to see that day when you can return in peace to your first home."

"I hope for that as well. But I am also content to set down new roots. But enough about our plight." Hrafn gestured for Dalmir to sit. "What brings you here? I can tell by the look in your eyes, something important has occurred. Tell me of it."

Dalmir clasped his fingers together, wondering how to begin. Sudden apprehension filled him. This people had been altered beyond recognition by a madman carrying one of his brothers' orbs. They had lost their families, their home, and been forced to go into hiding. Even the new generation bore their share of emotional scars because of Lorcan's actions. Why had he ever thought asking for their help with Mulemo's orb was a good idea?

"No." Dalmir shook his head. "Nothing of import. I simply wished to visit with you some more."

Hrafn's eyes flicked across Dalmir's face with such intensity he imagined he could feel the durven's gaze brushing his skin. Dalmir flinched.

Hrafn rose to his feet and crossed his arms with a scowl. "Why are you lying to me, friend?"

Dalmir took a deep breath. "You see to my very heart, as usual. I do carry with me a burden, a burden you or one of your people might help to ease. And yet when I consider all you have already been through, I find myself reluctant to ask anything more of you."

"Ask. If it is in my power to grant your request, I will not refuse you," Hrafn encouraged him.

Dalmir rubbed a hand across his mouth. Quickly, he outlined the story of Frieda and finding his brother's orb within her framework. He released a sad little sigh and held out the swirling gray orb. "I hate to ask, but I fear that if I do not learn how to make use of my brothers' orbs the way that Uun has, we will lose this war. If that happens, there will be no more safety for any of us. This orb belonged to Mulemo, the founder of Malei. I thought that since your people are of Maleian descent, perhaps one or more of you might be able to work with me to learn how to wield its power."

Hrafn did not recoil or flinch at the sight of the orb. He gazed into the swirling gray gem as it lay glittering in Dalmir's outstretched palm. Then he stood, brushing his hands on his pants. "Indeed, I can hear its song, but I cannot answer its call, for my people need me here to lead them."

"I understand." Dalmir tucked the orb away and rose. "Forgive me, I understand how painful this must be for you."

"Where are you going?" Hrafn's voice rasped, startling Dalmir.

"You said..."

"I said I could not answer the call. But there may be one among my people who might help you. In fact, I am fairly certain that I know of one who would jump at the chance." Hrafn made a gesture and out of the corner of his eye Dalmir saw a figure dart down one of the side passages. "My friend." Hrafn's ruined voice grew soft. "Did you think I would equate you with the monster that destroyed my village and changed my people? I blame only Lorcan for what we have endured. Not the orb he used, not your brother who created it in the first place, and certainly not you. I blame only the madman, and the Ar'Molon who encouraged him along the way."

"You sent for us?" A lighter new voice rasped from one of the many doorways in the central chamber.

Two female durven stepped into the chamber, both short in stature, even for durven. But both exuded confidence. The women entered the room with no hint of hesitation. As they stepped into the light, Dalmir saw that they were mirror images of each other, one older and the other quite young, but clearly related. As they drew closer, Dalmir read such sorrow in the older woman's eyes that it took his breath away. Both wore their dark hair in thick braids that glinted with bits of crystal and metallic beads. The younger one's gray skin almost seemed to sparkle faintly in the lantern light, and she shot him an eager grin as she entered the room.

"My wife, Nando." Hrafn indicated the older woman and now Dalmir could see a few threads of gray in her hair. "And Emilee, our daughter." Hrafn gestured to Dalmir. "This is Dalmir, the man I was telling you about. He has come to ask for our aid in a matter of great importance."

Dalmir sat down once more. "How much did Hrafn tell you about me?" he asked the two women.

"That you are one of the seven wizards who created the great towers, and that you are the one who held the Ar'Molon imprisoned for so many years, keeping the world safe from his fell touch," Emilee recited.

"Then you know what this is?" Dalmir held out the orb once more.

Nando grimaced, but nodded slowly. However, Emilee leaned over his hand, curiosity filling her features as she studied the jewel intently. "It is one of the seven orbs of power. We know of these, because it was such a one that allowed the madman Lorcan to alter our people and turn us into what we are now."

"I am sorry," Dalmir whispered.

"Why?" Emilee looked up at him, her glittering eyes gazing directly into his own. Unlike her mother's, Emilee's gaze held no hint of sorrow. She read his face and then glanced briefly at her parents before meeting Dalmir's gaze once more with a slight shrug. "I was not alive when it happened. I did not lose anyone that I loved. I am durven. I have always been durven. I am proud of my heritage and cannot imagine being anything else. The Elders, my father and mother among them, sometimes miss what they lost, but it has been many years even for them. The pain has eased, and we have come to accept, even embrace, what was wrought. We have been given many gifts." She squinted at him. "You are sorry because of the sadness you perceive in my parents, and perhaps even in myself, but it is not what you think. We are not sad because we are durven. We mourn for those who were left behind in Malei. One of them was my brother, Olin."

Dalmir nodded. "I understand. I, too, have lost loved ones."

Emilee pursed her lips. "I can see the truth of that in your eyes. My father says you need help. What can I do?"

"I need to know if you can use this orb, if you can make it do anything."

"Why?" She squinted at him.

"I don't know!" The words exploded from his mouth, frustration at his own helplessness and ignorance bubbling to the surface of his thoughts. He stood and whirled away from her, his heart hammering in his ears in an agony of embarrassment for his outburst. He took several long, deep breaths until he regained control of his emotions. Turning back to the young woman, he knelt on the ground so that they were on the same level. She gazed at him steadily, appearing calm and unruffled in the face of his sudden explosion. Inwardly he marveled at her composure. Lowering his voice, he confided, "I have a glimmering of an idea that this is important, a key to defeating Uun, but it is hazy and unclear." He shrugged. "I feel like I am stumbling around in the dark. I know there is something I must do, but I do not know what it is. I am lost, and I am tired. So much has been asked of me, and I do not know if I have anything more to give. What am I supposed to do? Shiori! What am I supposed to do?" He gasped and bowed his head. "Shiori..." he whispered.

His sleeve moved as a presence knelt beside him. Emilee laid her small hand within his own, her fingers resting against the orb.

"Tell me what to do," she whispered.

Dalmir placed the orb into Emilee's hand. "Concentrate."

Emilee stared down at the gray gemstone, her brows knitting together. After a long moment, she glanced up. "I don't think anything is happening. Should I try something else?"

Dalmir regarded her for a moment. "To be honest, I'm not entirely certain. The whole idea of this is still new to me, as well." At her forlorn expression, he gave her an encouraging smile.

"Don't worry. We'll learn together. Let's try something simple." He drew his own orb out and focused on it. The power within it flared to life, illuminating the gem and sending out a gentle blue glow. "See if you can make yours do the same."

Emilee brought the stone up to her face until it almost touched the end of her nose. Her lips pursed slightly and her eyes narrowed to slits. A moment passed. Then another.

The durven girl squeezed her eyes shut. "I'm sorry."

"There is nothing to be sorry about. Perhaps you are trying too hard. When you concentrate, what do you get from the orb? Can you feel it or hear it in any way?"

"I hear a faint sound, like far-off music or the sound of a nearby stream I can't quite see."

"And how does it make you feel?"

"It makes me miss our home in Malei. A river ran past the Sentinel Door where I was usually posted when I drew guard duty. It was one of my favorite assignments because it was so peaceful, I had time to think. Often I would just sit inside the door and listen to the river burbling and wonder what it was saying and whether or not I'd ever get to travel along it and discover where it went." A wistful note entered her voice. "I never dreamed I'd travel so far..."

The stone in her hand began to pulse with a gentle light. Gray mist swirled inside and Emilee stared at it, the corners of her mouth curving up in fascinated wonder.

Dalmir shook his head in awe. "Even knowing it was possible, I still can't quite believe it," he breathed. "Talk to me, tell me what is happening."

"I can feel it... like a string attached to my thoughts," Emilee whispered, her voice filling with awe. "The connection is fragile, like a spiderweb."

"The connection will grow stronger with time."

"How strong?" Emilee asked.

"I don't know for sure," Dalmir replied. "But you might be able to do some very powerful things."

"Will I have to travel with you when you leave Telsuma?" Emilee asked.

Nando's sharp intake of breath made Dalmir consider his words carefully. "Yes," he replied. "Though I fear the weather will keep me here a while longer. For now, I would simply leave the orb with you to practice, and I can come visit and teach you how to use it."

Emilee's eyes shone like the sparkling snow outside. "I accept the challenge." She wrapped her fingers around the gray gem and closed her eyes. The orb pulsed with a gray light that grew until it filled the whole room. Emilee opened her eyes and smiled, her face beautiful in the light she had created.

"When the time comes, I will travel with you, Old One," she said. "And I will help you as I can."

"Thank you," Dalmir whispered. "I was not sure what to do next."

Hrafn's expression grew wistful. "Do not lose heart. Even in the darkness, there is beauty to be found. None know that better than I." He gazed at his wife, a fond smile on his lips.

"Will you begin teaching me now?" Emilee asked.

"I will," Dalmir replied.

17

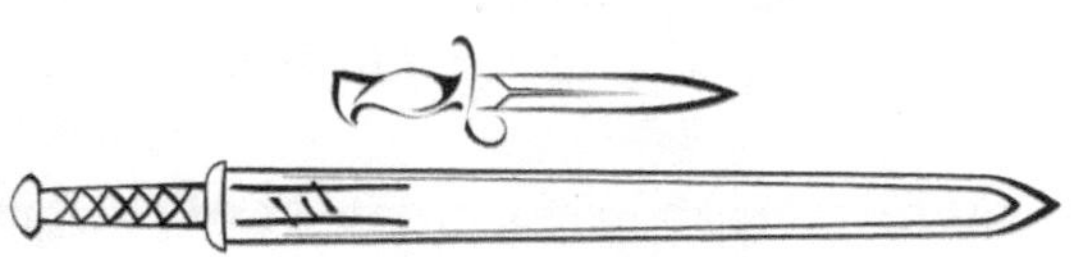

Beren leaped off the deck of the airship and fell through the air, those first few heart-pounding seconds flooding his senses and bringing every sensation into sharp relief. The cold wind numbed his cheeks, the only exposed part of his skin available. His ears filled with the sound of rushing air through his helmet. The round goggles framed the world below in dark circles and he spotted his target, the cargo cruiser just below him. He checked his wrist, reading the altimeter, watching the needle as it moved swiftly to the red line. Now the thumping of his heart and the sound of his own breathing blocked out even the wind.

Just a little longer.

The needle touched the red line and Beren yanked on the cord that would open his sail. That all-too familiar tearing sound that always made his blood freeze filled his ears, but a few seconds later he felt himself jerked upwards just before his fall slowed considerably. He took a deep breath and looked up, glimpsing the reassuring black sail now filled with air above his head.

Beren turned his attention back to the airship below him. This would be his first attempt landing on the deck of another airship. They had been working on hitting targets on the ground, but this would be harder. Although the craft would not be actively moving, it was impossible to keep an airship completely immobile while aloft.

He adjusted the handles of his sail, aiming himself at the deck of the ship. Landing on the deck without getting caught up in the sails would be the most difficult part. When they jumped onto enemy ships, they would not want to have to cut themselves out of their lines and climb through the rigging to get to their foes. Of course, they would also be jumping at night, when they had darkness to cover their approach, though that could be a liability, as well.

He was just hovering above the mainmast when a gust of wind caught his skysail and sent him soaring away from the airship. Beren struggled with the ropes, straining his muscles against the wind. Grunting with the effort, he used every trick he had acquired over the many jumps he had already made, but it was too late. By the time he made it back to the airship, he had descended too far and already hung well below the deck. Another blast of wind caught him and sent him shooting beneath the airship, and for one gasping, terrified second Beren thought his skysail would catch on the trim sail of the airship. He envisioned the skysail tearing apart on the side mast and himself plummeting to the ground with nothing to slow his descent.

Then he heard a sound like a loud whisper as the top of his skysail just brushed against the belly of the airship and he was clear, floating gently to the ground far below. When he reached the ground, he made his way back to the staging area, where he found Grayden and the other members of their patrols waiting to go back up on the next airship. He raised his eyebrows, but they all shook their heads.

"I missed, too," he confessed. "For a minute I thought my skysail was going to catch on a trim mast and tear."

"At least you would have had your backup," Grayden said.

"You know, in that moment, I completely forgot it was there," Beren replied. "I just started seeing visions of myself hitting the ground from a thousand feet up."

"I have those visions every night after a new jump," Shep said. "Can't fall asleep, I just keep seeing all the things that could have gone wrong every time I close my eyes. Stupid, really. None of it happened."

"It happens to all of us," Grayden assured him.

"Form ranks!" Captain Argond's order drifted to their ears and the defenders moved to obey. The captain glowered as he marched back and forth before them. "Not one landing," he barked. "I am disappointed in the Black Dragons' performance. Repack your skysails and get ready to go again. We do it until we get it right."

Beren glanced sideways and met Grayden's eyes, seeing his own bewilderment reflected on his friend's face. Not one? Not one in the whole company of two hundred fifty men? It hadn't even been that windy. He would have expected at least one to hit their mark. Their company was already making a name for themselves when it came to their precision landing inside ground targets. Beren felt his forehead furrowing in thought as he contemplated the problem.

The next several days found the Black Dragons struggling as they made jump after jump, missing their targets every time. Only Jerky came close to landing on the deck of an airship, which he accomplished by getting his skysail caught on the mizzenmast. He ended up swinging from the yardarm waiting for the crew of the airship to untangle him and deliver him safely to the deck. By the end of the sennight, the entire company fell into their bunks in discouraged frustration.

"Think they've given us an impossible task?" Jerky asked one evening.

"Maybe," Shep replied. "Could be no one's ever done it. I mean, if they had, wouldn't the commanders be parading their example about in front of us? Maybe this is all an experiment to see if it's possible."

"There has to be a way to achieve the goal," Grayden said,

lying back on his pillow, hands folded behind his head. "I just can't quite figure out what it is."

Beren nodded wearily. "Maybe we'll get it tomorrow." He closed his eyes and let his weariness overwhelm him.

The next morning, Captain Argond awaited them at breakfast. "Today, we will try something different," he informed them. "I think we need a new perspective on this problem. Half of you will crew the airship targets, while the other half will attempt to jump onto them. Those of you crewing the airships, I want you to take note of everything you see from your comrades and see if you can figure out a way around this problem. The ability to jump directly onto enemy airships could mean the difference in the war. You've all read the reports on the Igyeum's new weapons. As we train here, our intelligence agents have informed us that our enemies are retrofitting their airships to equip them with these new cynderblasts. We do not have that kind of weaponry at our own disposal, and so we need an option for taking their ships out while they are airborne. That is where you come in. So eat up, suit up, and be outside in fifteen minutes for your morning assignments."

Beren shoveled the rest of his food into his mouth and rushed with the others to retrieve his equipment. A new burst of optimism filled him.

"Captain," he said as he passed by Argond. "I shall not fail you today."

Argond nodded at him, but said nothing.

Grayden, overhearing the promise, clasped Beren by the shoulders. "I believe you."

When they reached the snow-covered field, Argond and the other captains split each company in half under the watchful eye of Major Semiv. Beren was assigned with the half of the company going up in the jumpships first, while Grayden and the other half were assigned to man the target airships.

"You will each get three jumps, and then we'll rotate duties," Major Semiv explained to the officers.

They climbed aboard their assigned vessels and soared into the morning sky. On the horizon, the sun rose in flame-colored glory, promising more warmth than it actually gave. Although farther south in Ondoura, flowers were probably already starting to bloom, here in the northern mountains separating Ondoura from Dalma, winter still held full sway. The brilliant blue skies and the golden sunshine only served to accentuate the bitter cold and the sparkling white landscape that stretched in every direction. Edrian's winter bite lingered, making these flights and jumps all the more miserable. Beren had always prided himself on his ability to handle the cold. Being Telsuman meant enduring long winters. But at home he had fur-lined coats and mittens and his mother's cooking and the warm hearth inside to look forward to. Here in the open air of an airship, he only had a long, freezing fall through bitter winds and a cold landing in wet snow ahead. Trying not to think about how cold he was, Beren strode over to the opening in the railing, ready to lead his half of the Black Dragons in their first jump of the day.

The first two jumps were abject failures. Beren managed to get near the target on the first jump, but not close enough to even touch the airship, and the second time he missed by a wide margin. Frustration filled him as he stood waiting for the jumpship to land and retrieve him and the rest of the company. In his mind, he replayed the previous jumps in his head, turning them over and over in his thoughts to see what he might have done better.

"Son, are you all right?" Captain Argond's voice interrupted his thoughts as Beren waited to go back up for his final jump.

"Sir." Beren clenched his fists at his sides. "I swear to you that I will not fail this time."

Several minutes later, he stood at the railing as the jumpship attained the necessary altitude above the target ship. Beren adjusted the shoulder straps of his pack and stared down at the airship positioned well below them. The height no longer bothered him. After so many jumps, he now took the sensation of falling hundreds of feet as a matter of course. It was just part of his day.

He waited for the signal to let him know they had reached the correct altitude, and checked the altimeter strapped to his own wrist to make sure it was still working. He adjusted the leather strap so he could read the altimeter better. The needle inside the little glass face hovered around the dark numbers reading ten thousand, and he nodded. The airship below should be maintaining a height around two thousand feet above the ground, which would give him three thousand feet of falling before he should open his skysail. He adjusted his helmet, pulled the goggles down over his eyes, and caught the fluttering of the red flag.

Taking a deep breath, Beren used the railing to propel himself into the open sky. The air rushed past him as he angled his body toward the airship below. He checked his wrist and saw that he was nearing the moment he should release his skysail.

Closer.

Closer.

He allowed himself to get much closer to the airship than he had on any previous attempt. When only a few meters separated him and the airship, he pulled the cord and felt the sudden jerk as the skysail deployed above him, slowing his descent. Glancing up, he saw more skysails opening around and above him as the rest of the first platoon joined him in the air.

Using the handles to guide his path, Beren lined his feet up with the open deck of the airship he was supposed to land on. A gust of wind caught him. Gritting his teeth and hauling on the handles, he navigated through the gust. He descended, drawing nearer and nearer his target. Using every bit of expertise he had gained the past lunat, Beren steered himself around the masts of the airship. He could see the men below, their heads tilted back as they watched him. He dropped even lower, the deck now so close he could almost touch it.

His boots thumped onto the wooden planks.

A cheer rose around him and Beren raised his hands in

triumph, only to feel himself suddenly yanked backwards. Struggling against the sudden updraft and doing everything in his power to remain on board the airship as the skysail dragged him across the deck, Beren's hands caught at the railing. He struggled to hang on, the skysail shaking him this way and that, battering him against the side of the ship. With a tremendous cracking sound, an entire segment of railing came off in his hands and he soared away from the airship once more.

He twisted his body, trying to regain control of the skysail, but it had caught another errant gust, and now he was too close to the airship to compensate or adjust. A moment later he had lost too much altitude to try again and had to resign himself to another failure.

On the ground, Captain Argond waved a greeting. He met his commanding officer's eyes and sighed, shoulders slumping.

"I'm sorry," he muttered. "I failed."

Captain Argond gave him a funny look, then strode over to him. "Son," he said, his tone serious but his eyes sparkling with mischief, "I don't think it was you that failed." He tapped the forgotten piece of railing that Beren was still holding.

Beren stared down at the railing for a moment, then allowed himself a slight chuckle as he tossed it to one side.

A few of the other men in Beren's platoon managed to get their feet on the deck as Beren had, only to have their skysails drag them back into the air. As they took their places on the airships to allow the other half of the company their turn, Beren could feel the frustration in the air mounting like a tangible thing. He yanked on a rope, adjusting a trim sail to help hold the airship steady in their assigned position. He glanced up at the jumpship high above them. The sun had grown warm, despite the snow glistening on the ground far below.

The first of the second wave of jumpers leaped into the sky over their heads and Beren watched as the man came hurtling toward the airship. The man came nearer and nearer, and Beren wondered if his altimeter was working. Surely he should have deployed his skysail by now?

But the man continued to plummet with no skysail in sight. A knot twisted in Beren's gut as he watched the man fall toward him, getting closer and closer.

"Deploy!" he suddenly heard himself shouting. "Deploy!" He heard the word echoed by the other members of his company. All eyes were fixed on the jumper.

Impossibly close to the top of the airship, the skysail suddenly blossomed from the man's pack, arresting his fall. Beren heaved a sigh of relief, but then his eyes widened once more as he watched the man maneuver toward the top of the mainmast. He was coming down faster than normal due to the late deployment of the skysail. His feet now nearly touched the top of the mast. Beren wanted to shout to the other man to veer away from the mast, afraid he would get tangled in the rigging. But just as he opened his mouth to shout a warning, something glinted in the bright midday sunlight, a flash of silver in the man's hand.

Before Beren could blink, the man slashed his hand above his head, severing the lines connecting him to his skysail. The sail flapped wildly, collapsing in on itself and then flying away like a runaway bedsheet escaping a clothesline. Beren stared as the man hit the mainsail, the dagger in his hand catching in the canvas and slowing his descent considerably until he reached the yardarm and caught the great timber with one hand. With another slicing motion, he had severed a length of rope and now swung cleanly down to the deck where he stood before Beren, an ear-to-ear grin on his face.

"Grayden!" Beren shouted. "What was that?"

"I think it's the only way," Grayden replied, glancing up at the now slightly battered sail above them. "The skysail lets us make the jump, but once we get close to the target airship it just gets in the way."

An incredulous laugh burst out of Beren before he even knew it was there. He punched his friend in the shoulder a little harder than usual and shook his head. "First, you get excited about jumping off an airship whose engine is working perfectly, and then you choose to cut yourself out of the only thing keeping you from plummeting to your death. There has to be a better way."

Grayden nodded, his expression serious. "Yes, I want to talk to Major Semiv about that. We need some sort of clasp on our harnesses that would allow us to release them quickly. Otherwise, I don't think landing on enemy airships is a viable strategy." Grayden turned to the other men who had come up to congratulate him on his successful landing. Even the captain of the airship came forward to offer congratulations, seemingly unconcerned by the tear Grayden had made in one of his sails.

Beren stared at his friend. "I meant a better way than dropping our skysails," he muttered to himself.

18

A lunat passed while Dalmir worked with Emilee, teaching her to use the power of the orb. Outside the tunnels, Edrian's icy winds blew themselves out and faded, followed by the deep—but warmer—snows of Tella. Inside the tunnels, the durven were excellent hosts, providing Dalmir with a room of his own to sleep in as well as food and refreshment throughout his visit. At the end of each day, Dalmir's head spun and his joints ached from being hunched down to the young durven's eye-level, but he ignored his body's complaints and focused on the task at hand. Each day, Emilee grew more adept at commanding Mulemo's orb. As Tella's snows piled up, they took their experiments outside where Emilee turned the orb upon the abundant elements, building and carving immense sculptures of snow and ice outside the tunnels.

"Good," Dalmir congratulated her. "Mulemo loved to work with the elements. He had a great sense of mischief, as well."

Emilee grinned. "I can tell. The crafting is always easier when I'm trying to be extra clever or tricky."

"You have acquired the skill of commanding the orb better than I expected," Dalmir praised her. "There is little left for me to teach you."

Emilee's face fell and she held the orb out to him. "You're leaving, then?"

Dalmir nodded, but he reached out to her open hand and gently curled her fingers around the orb. "I must search for the other orbs," he said. "Are you ready to travel with me?"

A dazzling smile burst across Emilee's face. "I am!"

"Then pack your things. Marik is eager to leave as soon as the final adjustments to the Hawk are finished."

"I will be ready when you call, Old One."

Dalmir grimaced at the nickname she insisted on using. "That is good. Until then, Youngling."

Emilee's eyebrow quirked up in amused outrage. A moment later, a wall of snow curled up over his head and crashed down over him in an icy flurry of powder.

Or it would have, had Dalmir not expected it.

With a wave of his hand, he froze the snow in place, a high, beautiful arc like a frozen ocean wave. He flicked a finger and a perfect snowball formed from the end of the curl and flew through the air, turning into a puff of powder just before it could burst across Emilee's face.

The young durven blinked at him in confusion. "What happened? I wasn't fast enough to stop it," she told him.

Dalmir grinned. "Just be glad I don't have the same sense of humor as my older brother. He would have dumped the entire wave down the back of your shirt. Keep practicing." He gave her a bow and turned to hike back up to the Adelfrieds' home. It was long past time to begin planning his next course of action.

Despite Emilee's cheer and playfulness that brightened his times of teaching her how to use the orb, Dalmir's mood sank back into darkness as he left the durven's new home. He trudged slowly through the slushy mud of the path in the evening glow. He did not turn off at the house, however, but instead continued following the footpath down toward the river. He was not yet ready to face the exuberance of the children or the tender hospitality of Lord and Lady Adelfried. He was a caterpillar, struggling within its chrysalis, knowledge and transformation tantalizingly close and yet achingly beyond his grasp. There was so much he still did not understand. He did not know what his next step should be, and the paucity of his own understanding chafed at his spirit.

Before Uun's betrayal, Dalmir had never found the responsibility placed upon himself and his brothers to be a curse, though he knew Uun had often expressed irritation with it, referring to their gifts as their "punishment." But Dalmir had not felt that way. He had always counted it a privilege: shepherding his people, building the Universities for them and filling those shelves and rooms with the knowledge he and his brothers had deprived the world of with their carelessness. It was a tremendous responsibility, but they had all done their part cheerfully, grateful to be allowed to work toward a solution to the problem they had caused.

All except Uun: Uun, who had been the true culprit behind severing the ties of the original Library from their world; Uun, who had refused to become a shepherd of any group of people, instead preferring to spend his days in the isolation of his tower. They had all believed him repentant. Dalmir himself had even fancied that Uun's actions sprang forth from a piercing guilt, that perhaps he deemed himself unworthy of having students. In their charity, they had missed the warning signs of bitterness, fury, and hatred festering in their brother's heart.

The sun began to settle itself down behind the mountains, its final rays of farewell casting a halo of golden light on the snow capping the tallest trees in a breathtaking display of beauty that contrasted sharply with Dalmir's dark thoughts. He veered off the main road and made his way down to the river-bank through the deep snow. The edges of the river were frozen, though the middle still rippled along, deep and dark.

The music of the water mesmerized him and he stood in the fading twilight watching the water flow, noting where it sped up and slowed down. With a sigh, he bent down and tossed a pebble into the water. He wished he knew what he was supposed to be doing. How could he hope to stand against the might and power Uun had amassed? Inwardly, he cursed himself for a fool. Even as he and his brothers had missed the signs heralding Uun's betrayal, he had been blind to everything since. How could he have missed realizing that Uun had found a way to wriggle free from his prison? How had he not seen that Uun was at work in the world once more? Why had it taken Grayden climbing in through his tower window to wake him from his stupor?

Frieda had said he needed to call Shiori. Could it be that simple? He had tried since they retrieved the orb from the aton, though he had to admit his attempts had been half-hearted. He desperately wanted to see her, but a part of him quailed at the thought of facing her. How could he? How could he not?

"Shiori..." He mumbled her name brokenly. "We parted in anger—I'm sorry. I wish you could be here to help guide me once more." Frieda's final encouragement whispered in his thoughts, and hope ignited once more. "Shiori? Shiori!" He called out her name again, his voice echoing across the water, and again until his throat grew tight with overuse. Only silence replied to his calls.

Disheartened, Dalmir stood in the gathering gloom, his toes growing cold. He no longer knew where to turn. Centuries of grief and guilt pressed down upon him, threatening to crush him with their weight. With a desperate whimper, he sank to the ground, broken.

His knees hit the frozen pebbles at the edge of the river; with a gasp of pain Dalmir's head snapped back. As his eyes turned to the heavens, he caught a glimpse of a star falling through the sky, a sparkling tail like that of a majestic kite trailing after it. A pang pierced him through like a hot iron driving itself deep into his soul. He had long since turned his back on the Builder; surely

Emrithos would never again turn his ear to Dalmir's plea. He knew himself to be abandoned. And yet...

"Emrithos." A childlike hope welled up in his chest as Dalmir breathed the name he had refused to speak for over nine hundred years. Tears gathered in his eyes as shame gathered in his heart. Awkwardly, Dalmir bowed his head and began to pray for the first time in a millennium. "Emrithos, forgive me. I broke the trust you placed in me. I failed in my task. I was negligent of my duties. I allowed my brother's bitterness to creep into my own heart, and I believed his lies. I believed you had turned your back on me, forgotten me, cast me aside. Doubt and anger filled me and I blamed you for my brothers' deaths, for leaving me all alone. I began to regard your gift as a curse, your command as a weight around my neck, and I sought to rid myself of both. I was wrong. I know that. I admit it. But these people should not be punished for my failings, they should not have to suffer under Uun's twisted vision of how the world should be. I will do anything you ask of me, even if it means sacrificing my own life, just please... show me the way?"

The air stilled. In that dusky haze before the absolute dark of nighttime, the world seemed to hold its breath. Even the river slowed in its happy babbling, the water smoothing to a glassy serenity. A peace settled on his heart, replacing the weight he had borne for so long. Forgiveness. Could it be?

"It's about time." The sober, yet lilting timbre of the voice that pierced the silence filled Dalmir's entire being with light. Rising to his feet, he whirled to face the speaker, tears filling his eyes and spilling down his face in unashamed abandon. She was everything he remembered: her youthful face framed by long, silver hair that fell to her waist, rippling gently in a slight breeze that touched nothing but her. Her full lips were pressed together in a silent line he could not read—disapproval, if he had to guess —but for the moment, it was enough that she was there, that she was real. He would gladly accept her disapproval if it meant she came with it. He stared, drinking in the narrow, oval shape of her face, her olive-toned skin, the way she held her hands together, fingers fiddling with the long, loose sleeves of her midnight-blue dress, the only outward sign that she was not as composed internally as she appeared.

"Shiori." A million thoughts collided within his mind at once, emotions he had no name for welled up, choking off all the words he wanted to say, all the words he had held within him for so many years.

"Dalmir."

"Why did you stay away?" he stammered, then flinched. Of all the things he could have begun with, why that?

She gave him a long, level look. "You know why I could not come to you before."

His gaze dropped to the ground and his soul shriveled. Of course. Shiori was a faithful servant of Emri, upon whom he had turned his back. Of course she would not come to him while he neglected his duties and refused to acknowledge their master. That this fact had never occurred to him in all the long years of loneliness made heat burn beneath his skin. Suddenly he wanted to shout all the things he had thought about in those dark, empty days in his tower. He wanted her to know the pain he had felt, to feel the razor slice of abandonment and desolation he had endured. The words sprang to his lips, full of hurt and fire.

But then his glance caught the look in her dark, slanted eyes, and in that fleeting moment he glimpsed the shimmer of tears and an expression of aching grief and loneliness he understood all too well.

The angry words died on his tongue.

Instead, he held out his hand. "My dear friend..." The stinging prickle behind his eyes made him pause as he fought back the rush of emotion contained within those three simple words. "I have missed you."

For the space of an endless breath she stood motionless. Then, in a rush, she reached out, clutching his hand as though afraid it would be withdrawn. And now as she drew closer, he could see that her lips were pressed together not in disapproval, but to prevent them from trembling.

Dalmir pulled her toward him into an embrace and she buried her face in his chest.

"Forgive me, Shiori," he whispered into her silver hair.

"All is forgiven," she whispered back.

They stood there in the gathering darkness for a long while, until at last, Shiori pulled away. "It is good to see you again," she said. "But I am not here just to visit."

"Of course." Dalmir bit out the words, releasing her from his arms. He half-turned away from her, averting his gaze to the river.

"Dalmir." She placed a hand on his arm and he resisted the urge to shrug it off.

"I'm lost, Shiori."

"I know."

"I wanted to end it." The confession rushed out of him in a burst of breath. "I tried to end it."

"I know." At the catch in her voice Dalmir raised his head and looked at her in surprise.

"You know?"

She nodded and stepped closer to him. In the quiet, she began to hum, faintly at first, and then stronger and louder until he could make out the simple tune. A shock coursed through him.

"The little sparrow... that day... it landed on my windowsill. Poor thing, it was nearly frozen. I thought the sudden cold-snap had surprised it, that it had found the warmth of my tower by chance... it wasn't chance, was it?"

Shiori shook her head. "No. It was a gift from Emri."

"That little bird... it saved my life."

"And you saved its."

"It stayed with me through the winter, and in the spring, just before it flew away, it sang me that song." Dalmir shook his head in wonder at the memory.

"I am truly sorry for all you have suffered."

"It wasn't your fault. It wasn't His fault, either. I see that, now."

"Dalmir." She peered up at him. "It is important that you know this: it wasn't your fault, either."

Now the tears did come. They poured down Dalmir's face in an unstoppable flood. He sank to the snowy ground, his body wracked with sobs he had held in for far too many years.

"Then why?" he gasped out between the sobs. "Why? I don't understand. I don't... I don't understand."

She did not respond, but merely knelt in the snow next to him, her hand on his back, its comforting warmth a balm of healing to his wounded soul. Her own warm tears fell on his neck, her grief somehow helping to assuage his own.

After a long while, Dalmir's tears ran out. He scooped up a handful of snow, using it to wash his face. The icy shock acted as a restorative and he sat back on his heels, heedless of the wetness that had seeped through the legs of his pants.

"I have missed you," he said, a wistful smile playing about his mouth.

"And I you." Shiori put an arm around him and laid her head on his shoulder.

"I have been running away for so long," Dalmir whispered. "I'm not sure I remember how to follow."

"You have returned now. That is what matters."

"I have much to atone for. So much..."

Shiori pushed away from him. "That is not how Emri works, and you know it."

"But..."

"Do not go back into the pit from which He drew you." Her voice held a gentle rebuke. Then her eyes softened. "There is such a thing as forgiveness, Dalmir. There has to be, else we would all be lost."

Dalmir accepted this and let it wash over him. "What do I do next?"

"It is imperative that you gather the seven orbs of your brothers," Shiori said. "Without them, you will never defeat Uun or prevent his success."

Dalmir frowned, rising to his feet, lifting her with him. "Why are the orbs so important?"

"When Emrithos gifted the seven of you with your power and immortality, he safeguarded each of you against the others. The only way that any one of you could be overpowered or destroyed was through the use of all seven of your gifts."

Dalmir furrowed his brow. "Then... how did Uun..." He trailed off, realization dawning.

"Whose idea was it to create the orbs?" Shiori asked.

"Uun's," Dalmir breathed. "And it was his suggestion that we weave our power together, and that he hold it, guiding us in what he promised would be our greatest achievement." Dalmir stared at the woman standing next to him, cold horror twisting in his gut. "Everything he did, everything he said..." He stopped, unable to say it out loud. "I wish I could say I didn't believe it." He sighed, then clenched one fist. "I have three of the orbs. My own, Edoran's, and Mulemo's."

Shiori's smile challenged the beauty of the stars. "You found Mulemo's!"

Dalmir nodded. "It wasn't easy. Tel, Mulemo, and you made sure of that. Whose idea was it to use the atons as guardians?"

Shiori chuckled. "Mulemo's. But I think you already knew that. The reflective enchantment in the tower was his, as well."

"I should have known. That almost killed me."

"Killed you?" Her eyes widened in alarm. "What do you mean?"

Dalmir's mouth quirked into a smug grin. "So, you aren't watching all the time. Yes, a young man shot me with an arrow. Can't blame him, he was trying to protect his home. But it made me think: perhaps if I could draw Uun there...?"

Shiori shook her head. "It won't work. You wouldn't have died, even if you'd stayed, though it might have kept you asleep for a few centuries."

"Ah. Well, we can call that plan B, then."

Shiori grinned suddenly. "I've missed you."

"Will you come up to the house? I can introduce you to my friends and together we can craft a plan."

"I wish I could." Shiori gave him a regretful look. "But Emri has other tasks for me at present. I will return as soon as I can."

Dalmir nodded. "Before you go, can you tell me anything about where I should begin in collecting the other orbs?"

Shiori considered. "Uun has Palte's and Avaleun's orbs."

"I had guessed that much," Dalmir said.

Shiori smiled gently at him. "They are well-protected for now. It would be dangerous to try to take them. He also possesses Tel's orb, which resides in the Ar'Mol's scepter. Uun is frustrated that he has found no one to wield it, though everyone who enters the Ar'Mol's presence is required to touch the scepter." She made a pleased sound in her throat. "He does not realize the trick played upon him by the twins. You could attempt to retrieve it, but at the moment, it is safe enough from his use. If you want my advice it would be this: Uun does not have his own orb; that is the one you should search for next."

"How could he not have it? I left it right there in his tower, where he could see it but not touch it. Cruel of me perhaps, but I just assumed..."

"He doesn't have it. And he doesn't know where it is."

"Do you?"

Shiori shook her head. "I wish I did. All I know is that Uun has been searching for it a long time..." Her expression grew strained. "I must go now. I will return when I can."

He clutched at her hand, wishing he could keep her with him, but despite all his yearning, her form faded, as though dissolving from existence. Dalmir was used to the way she came and went, but it still made him uneasy, watching her disappear like that, feeling the pressure of her hand in his fade away. Shiori's powers were like his own, and yet unlike. He still did not quite understand how she traveled between worlds, nor where she went when she disappeared. They had been friends for centuries, but she had remained cryptic when it came to details about herself and her home. Even after so much time, he still knew very little about her and her people, or how she had come to be the custodian of the Great Library that he and his brothers had destroyed.

When she was gone, Dalmir turned purposefully and strode up the path to the house. He had a clear direction now: a calling and a path to follow. It was time to get back to work.

19

Raisa's days fell into an even more predictable monotony. Every day, Uun, Lorcan, and the aloof stranger stood on the outskirts, watching her. The distracting music continued to plague her at irregular intervals as she sparred and went through the obstacle course. Even though she tried to tune it out, she could not help but turn slightly in the direction she felt it tugging at her every time. She worried that her distraction would gain her reprimands and questions she could not answer, but the few times she caught a glimpse of the Ar'Molon or Lorcan when she turned her head to focus on the faint tune, trying to place its familiar sound, she thought she saw delight in their faces. Was the sound coming from them, then? But how? And why? Did they want her to hear it? Were they testing her? To what end? Was this the next step in their plot to turn her into their puppet? Having turned her body into their tool, were they now after her mind as well? She tried in vain to pretend it didn't bother her. Perhaps they wanted her to seek it out. But she had no idea how to go about finding it, and so she continued to focus on the tasks before her that she could accomplish.

One morning, as she finished her solo run, she heard the music and felt its faint tug. It was the first time she had heard it when she was not training before her audience. For a moment, she considered ignoring it. If she did not return to her tent, she might get in trouble. However, the music sang to her softly, urgently, and more clearly than she had ever heard it before; curiosity overwhelmed her and Raisa's feet turned away from her normal path and veered up the hill. Falling into an easy stride, she loped along, letting the music guide her. Away from the prying, calculating eyes of Ar'Molon Uun and the madman and their nameless, silent companion, Raisa allowed herself to focus on the sound for the first time. The more she drew her thoughts around it, the louder and clearer the melody became, and the more sure she was of the direction it was calling her.

In more or less a straight line, she plunged through the trees, which were not as thick on this side of the Weald, until she came to the very southern edge of the oasis. A stretch of flat sand dipped down below her, sparkling like a great, brown sea in the morning sunlight. Raisa paused, listening intently. The music was not calling her out into the desert, but she did feel it pulling her slightly to the east. She turned and saw a large tree with enormous roots billowing up into the air. Cautiously, she approached, eyeing it warily for signs of movement. She had no interest in tangling with one of Lorcan's creations. However, as she approached, the tree remained still, and when she put a hand tentatively on the bark and it remained stationary, she let out a quick sigh of relief. The baumen gave her the shivers, and she had no desire to encounter one outside of Lorcan's influence. The creatures only listened to him, if it could be called listening.

With a little hop, she hefted herself up onto the root. Sidling up to the massive trunk, Raisa peered around it. She half-expected to see someone sitting there playing a flute, but there was no one. The music faded, and Raisa found that even if she turned her entire focus inward she could no longer hear its melody. With a self-deprecating laugh, she slid down into a little depression of the roots and sat there, staring out at the desert. The sun continued to rise over the sand, its heat growing in intensity with every passing moment. Raisa stretched her arms to the sunshine, welcoming its warmth. She had always preferred colder temperatures before, but since Lorcan's meddling, she found that the warmer the air got, the more invigorated she felt.

"What are you doing here?"

The voice startled her and she leaped to her feet, balancing on the root in a defensive crouch, one hand pressed against the tree. She looked down and saw the speaker: the dark-haired man who had arrived with Uun and stood silent and watchful at his side during her training sessions.

"I sometimes come watch the sun rise," she lied.

His eyes flicked to the horizon. "Sun rose hours ago. Shouldn't you be in your tent waiting for your orders like a good pet?"

Raisa's hackles rose, but she tried to hide her irritation. "I was informed by Captain Virtanen that there would be no training today."

"I see." The man sounded as though he really did see, and the understanding in his tone caught her off guard.

"What are you doing out here?" she demanded, trying to turn the conversation away from herself. She did not wish to answer any more questions.

To her delight, the man's expression turned uncomfortable. "I wanted to do a little exploring... but..." He paused and grimaced. "I'm afraid I've gotten a bit lost." He glanced away from her and something about his stance told her he was lying.

"I can show you the way back to camp," Raisa offered. Part of her wanted to pry, but another part of her couldn't help but feel empathy for him. She understood the need for secrecy. Perhaps he did not wish to be in Uun's service, perhaps he was every bit as much of a prisoner as she. For all the times he had stood at Uun's side in the clearing, he had never uttered a single word.

"Thank you." His shoulders relaxed.

Raisa swung down from the root and landed on the ground quietly. "Camp is this way." She pointed and began walking. The man fell into step beside her. "Who are you, anyway?" Raisa asked after they had walked for a little ways.

"I am the Shipwright," he replied.

Raisa eyed him, wondering if he was mocking her. "That doesn't tell me who you are."

"It doesn't?" He looked surprised. "It should."

"Why should it? It isn't a name, it's a title."

The man shrugged. "It's who I am."

"You don't have a name?"

"Not that I can remember."

"I'm sorry," Raisa said, her own sincerity startling her.

The man looked at her askance. "You are? Why?"

Raisa's thoughts stuttered. "I... It just seems sad to me, not having a name."

"Does it? I suppose it would, to you." He gave her a tiny smile. "I have never noticed its lack before."

"Are you the Ar'Molon's manservant?" Raisa could not keep her curiosity in check.

The Shipwright shrugged and kicked at the ground as they walked. "I suppose you could say that." He fell silent for a moment. The sunlight filtered down through the green canopy, speckling the forest floor in spots of greenish-gold. "They work you hard," he commented. "I didn't realize the training for soldiers was so brutal."

"I'm not a typical soldier," Raisa said without thinking.

"No," the Shipwright replied thoughtfully, "I suppose you aren't."

"Have you worked for the Ar'Molon for long?" She didn't know why she suddenly felt the need to talk. This man worked in the service of the monster, and yet, she could not help but notice the air of sorrow in his stance, the depth of thoughtfulness in his eyes, the gentleness of his movements. She wanted to hate him, but found hatred beyond her grasp. Besides, she had gone for so long without the benefit of conversation or companionship with anyone other than the madman, she had not realized how hungry she was for both.

"A few years," he replied.

Raisa determined to stop asking questions. As much as she wanted to hear a kind word, she couldn't risk trying to befriend this man. He might be just as trapped as she, or he might be a monster like his masters. He could have come or been sent merely to pretend friendship and steal any secrets she might have left. That thought sent a tendril of cold snaking down her spine, cutting off her desire to talk as effectively as a gag.

They continued to walk through the trees. Raisa took the most direct route back to the camp, and yet the distance seemed interminable. Surely she hadn't walked so far earlier that morning?

"You were a pirate before."

The man's interruption of the silence startled her. For a moment, she did not know how to reply. The tears from before rose up once again, threatening to betray her heart. With a colossal effort, she quashed the emotions and turned to regard the Shipwright.

"Yes."

"What was it like?"

"Thrilling." Her voice came out in a tone of dry sarcasm.

He stared at her, seeming crestfallen. "No, I mean... what I meant was..." He fumbled about as though trying to find the right words. "What was it like, being part of a crew?"

Raisa's anger dissipated like fog before a sunny day. "It was nice," she said, her words abrupt but her tone soft. "It was like being a part of something bigger than myself. I knew they had my back, and I had theirs. It was nice, not being alone."

"I wish I knew what that was like," the man whispered. He gave her a sad sort of smile, then pointed. "There's the camp. I should get back before they miss me. You should, too." He gave her a meaningful stare, then jogged away in the opposite direction from her tent.

Raisa watched him go, her heart pattering strangely. What did it all mean? Was he as unwilling a servant as she? Or was this some terrible sort of test to see if they had gotten into her head, to discover if they controlled her completely? Lorcan was obsessed with control, he had made no secret of that. Raisa had spent lunats trying to convince him that he controlled more than he actually did. She was meticulous about following his orders, never stepping out of line unless he left a reasonable gap in the words he used. When he was around, she did everything she could to radiate deference, even pretending to care what he thought of her. Thankfully, Lorcan was not as meticulous or careful about his orders as she was about following them.

However, something about the Shipwright had caught her off guard. If he had been sent to spy on her thoughts, to unbalance her with the tantalizing promise of friendship, then she feared he had succeeded. She had been far less careful than normal. Berating herself for a fool, Raisa made her way back to her tent. In her mind, she went over the entire conversation over and over again. By the time she reached her quarters, she had convinced herself that she had not said anything too damaging to her act.

"Two-Four-Seven!" The voice rang out, arresting her before she could duck inside her tent.

Raisa straightened, snapping to attention. "Yes, sir!"

"Report to the training arena," Captain Virtanen shouted. "The Ar'Molon wishes to see how you fare against his elite warriors."

Raisa groaned internally, but kept her face impassive. Her stomach complained that she had not eaten or drunk anything and she regretted her long run with an intense ache. There was nothing she could do about it now, though, so she obediently turned and jogged to the clearing. So much for the promised day off.

Uun, Lorcan, and the Shipwright were already assembled when she arrived. Several men in loose, dark clothing stood nearby. None of them appeared armed, but Raisa assumed they could hide quite a few weapons inside those robes. If experience had taught her nothing else during her lunats in the Weald, it had taught her this: anything that appeared to be a fair fight was probably a trick.

"These are my Kotai warriors," the Ar'Molon said with obvious pride. Raisa forced herself not to react externally, but inside shock coursed through her.

The Kotai? She had believed they were nothing more than a myth. Surely these couldn't be the assassins spoken of in hushed whispers? She had grown up hearing stories of the Kotai as chilling tales around the campfire. She and her childhood friends had told each other Kotai stories in an attempt to scare each other, and it had usually worked.

The leader of the Kotai bowed his head to her silently in a gesture of respect. Raisa returned the bow, partially to hide her face and give herself a moment to compose herself in the face of childhood nightmares unexpectedly stepping out into daylight.

"Ready, and begin." Captain Virtanen's voice rang out across the clearing and this time Raisa did not wait for her opponents to attack, but rather she sprang immediately at the leader.

Halfway through her leap, the music swelled to life in her mind. The intensity of it nearly blinded her. Instead of landing a solid blow, she missed completely and fell to the ground. She hit her shoulder painfully and rolled instinctively just as a dagger flashed through the air where she had been but a moment before. Instead of lodging itself in her stomach, the dagger sliced neatly through the skin of her upper arm, so cleanly she barely felt it, but when she glanced down she saw a thin line of blood.

"Your mistake," she said, grinning at the assassin and dropping into a defensive stance.

Before she could make another move, however, Raisa realized something had gone terribly wrong. The cut on her arm throbbed and burned, and her legs wobbled, refusing to support her weight. Her head swam as she fell with a thud onto the ground. Nausea washed over her in wave after wave, and all the while her arm pulsed with a searing heat. Had she been able to look down at it, she was sure she would have found the wound blackening and curling at the edges before drifting away in seared flakes of ash.

Voices clamored above her, but she could not focus on them and did not know who was speaking. Fragments of the conversation drifted to her ears, but they were garbled and confused and she did not comprehend their meaning.

"Roald! ... specifically instructed... untainted knives! I don't... killing my... determine... her skills... use to you."

"Forgive me, Master, I was sure... cleaned all... poison... blades."

"... good thing... orb... blow could... killed her." Lorcan's voice was soft and the most familiar. Her hatred of his smooth, insane voice seemed to work to combat the pain.

"What is happening?" Uun demanded.

"... her body... expelling... poison."

"... she live?"

"Perhaps. Some trees... capability... defense... Only time..."

"I demand... why there was poison... traitor in our midst."

The voices faded as Raisa drifted into a sea of blackness shot through with ripples of red. No rest awaited her within that sea, only spasms of pain which followed her into unconsciousness and caused her muscles to loosen and contract with waves of agony.

———

RAISA HAD no idea how long she floated in between life and death. Pain assaulted her on every side and she found no relief in the shadowy hinterland of oblivion. She could neither speak nor move; her limbs were heavy as stones. After a while, a gnawing ache in her belly joined ranks with the fire radiating in swirls around her arm. A low groaning filled her ears and she was vaguely aware that the sound emanated from her own lips.

Moments of relief flitted between hours of anguish. A coolness on her brow, a trickle of water droplets down her throat, a gentle dabbing at the wound on her arm, the soothing sound of someone humming a gentle melody that broke through her fevered nightmares sometimes interrupted the pain, but only for brief flickers, melting snowflakes of comfort that dissipated as quickly as they arrived. Raisa lay encased in the stone tomb of her own body, unable to move or even cry out. And through the darkness, the drums of regret boomed steadily, reminding her that everyone she had ever cared for was gone. Mouse, with his cocky little grin but earnest eyes, Shaesta, with her carefree spirit and kind heart, Oleck... her big brother, her protector, her friend... they were all dead. Marik... even in her darkest nightmares, her mind shied away from dwelling on that particular loss... but her traitorous heart whispered that the last thing he had known from her was scorn and recriminations. He had been her savior. And she had spat in his face. In the darkness of her thoughts, she wept for him most of all, and for the harsh way they had parted.

A cool cloth patted her face, and Raisa opened her eyes. All was darkness. For a moment, she panicked, thinking she was blind. With a frightened gasp, she sat up, the sudden movement shooting golden sparks across her vision before the blackness pressed in on her once more.

"Shh, shh, hush now. You're going to be weak for a while until we can get some food into you. Lie back down."

The voice sounded vaguely familiar, but Raisa's head throbbed too much for her to place it. She obeyed, easing herself back down.

"Why can't I see?" she asked, fearful of the answer.

"It's night, and I didn't want to light a candle."

So she might not be blind. The thought filled her with relief. "Why not?"

"Because I'm not supposed to be here. The Ar'Molon wished to see if your resilience could beat the poison, and he doesn't want anything to interfere with his test."

Raisa let her eyelids fall shut. "You've come before, though. I've heard your voice." Her throat caught on the words and she could not say more. She wanted to ask for water, but she could not force sound through her lips. She did manage to emit a dry, rasping cough.

A waterskin touched her lips and blessedly cool water streamed over her tongue. It was too much, her throat could not handle it and she began to choke, drowning in the life-giving substance.

Gentle hands turned her head to the side so the water could dribble out from between her lips.

"I'm sorry, that was too much all at once, I should have been more careful. That is all I can do for now. I will be back tomorrow evening, and if you are feeling up to it, perhaps I can bring you a little broth. It will help you regain some of the strength you've lost." The figure disappeared through the tent flap and Raisa caught a brief glimmer of stars before the flap fell shut and darkness enfolded her once again.

"Thank you," Raisa whispered, but it was too late and her whisper was too soft.

20

Marik strode up the muddy hill to the Adelfrieds' house, a spring in his step. Winter had come to an end, and now they could set sail to find Raisa.

Marik gave a wondering shake of his head as he thought about all that Wynn had done. With all the changes, he was amazed at how the airship still handled exactly as he remembered. It was a work of art, what Wynn had accomplished, a truly impressive feat.

Hubert was waiting for him, bouncing on his toes as Marik came up the walk. Cathrine stood behind him, a rueful smile on her face.

"He won't go to bed until he shows you his loose tooth," she explained.

Marik knelt before the boy. "You have a loose tooth?"

Hubert nodded importantly. "My first one!" He grinned broadly and poked his finger into his mouth, moving the tooth back and forth.

"That's amazing, buddy," Marik congratulated him. "Your first loose tooth!"

To his astonishment, Hubert's face crumpled and two tears slid down his cheeks.

"Whoa." Marik glanced up at Cathrine, but she looked as

nonplussed as he felt as Hubert flung himself into Marik's arms. "What's wrong, little guy?"

"My tooth is wiggly," Hubert sobbed.

Marik had never felt so helpless or confused in his life. "I know," he said, patting the little boy's back awkwardly. "I thought you were excited about that."

"But it's my favorite tooth," Hubert wailed. "I don't want to lose my favorite tooth!"

"You have a favorite tooth?" Marik was treading water far over his head now. He leaned back and looked into the child's face. "Can you show me your favorite tooth?"

Hubert's tears intensified. "All of them are my favorite!"

The last thing he should do at this moment was laugh, Marik knew. To hide his smile, he pulled the child close to his chest and rose with Hubert in his arms. "Hmm, I have an idea," Marik said, grinning over Hubert's head at Cathrine, who looked as if she were about to melt into a puddle over her little brother. Certain that logic and reason had no place in the current conversation, Marik opted for distraction instead. In one smooth motion, he swung the little boy over his shoulder and onto his back. "Hang on!" Marik roared. "It's time for a leythan ride!" The boy clasped his hands tightly around Marik's neck with a hiccuping little giggle as the pirate reared back, his arms pawing at the air. "Whoa! This leythan is a wild one!" Marik shouted. "You'll have to be a pretty good rider if you want to tame him!"

He bolted away, ignoring Cathrine's protests as the little boy's laughter filled his ear. Marik galloped around the yard, his boots squelching in the thawing mud until Cathrine finally caught up with them.

"Uh-oh!" Marik hollered. "The leythan wrangler found us!"

"Run away, run away, Uncle Markik!" Hubert shouted, nearly deafening Marik on one side with his exuberant mispronunciations. "Don't let Cassrin catch us!"

But the look in Cathrine's eye told Marik he had pushed bedtime as far as it would go. After a few swift swerves and dodges that made Hubert shriek hysterically straight into Marik's eardrums, Marik turned and loped slowly back toward the house, swinging the little boy down just inside the doorway. "Time for bed, you wild leythan rider," he said, tousling the boy's fuzzy dark head fondly.

Hubert groaned and his shoulders slumped forward.

"No arguments," Cathrine said, her tone stern.

Hubert heaved a deeply wounded-sounding sigh. "Very well, Cassrin." He stood up a bit straighter, but continued to shuffle his way back to the house.

Cathrine gave a shake of her head and followed him. "Come on, I'll tuck you in."

Hubert perked up. "And sing a song?"

"Only if you hurry."

Complaints forgotten, the little boy bounded into the house and disappeared. Marik couldn't help but chuckle at the child's antics. He crossed the garden and sat down on a bench swing that stood at the top of the hill and looked down across the river valley below. He leaned his head back and watched as the stars winked into existence in the depths of the sky, a sky that once more belonged to him.

He might have dozed a little, because a sudden presence on the swing next to him startled him. Marik jumped and blinked the sleep from his eyes before he recognized Cathrine's gentle smile.

"Hubert asleep, then?" he asked.

"Headed there," she replied. She tilted her head back and gazed up at the sky. "The stars are beautiful tonight."

"I was just thinking that," Marik agreed. "Then I fell asleep."

Cathrine giggled, a mirth-filled sound that hung in the air like silver bells.

"Wynn has worked a marvel with the Hawk," Marik said. "It's finally getting warm enough to take you for that flight I promised a while back."

In the darkness he could just make out her smile. "Now? By starlight?"

"Why not?" Marik replied. "I've gotten a good handle on the new controls and everything is working smoothly. As long as we don't try anything fancy, it should be safe."

They sauntered down the hill to the docks. Cathrine paused to admire the airship, commenting on how pretty it was.

"That she is," Marik replied, a twinge of pride in his chest that ached a little. So many of the changes were Wynn's. Despite his delight at the repairs, he felt as though he could no longer truly claim the airship as his own.

Pushing away these more melancholy thoughts, Marik led Cathrine up the steps and helped her board. She landed on the deck with a graceful thud of her high-heeled boots, then waited for him to join her. Marik eyed the ladder leading up to the steerage.

"The best view is from up there." He pointed. "But in that dress..."

Cathrine did not let him finish. Hiking up her long, full skirts, she easily climbed the ladder. "Come show me what all these levers do," she called down.

Marik grinned, enjoying her adventurous spirit, and raced up the ladder to join her. He helped her clip on the safety line and handed her a pair of goggles. A few minutes later, the Valdeun Hawk lifted gracefully out of her dock and rose into the night sky. Cathrine gasped, spinning around, her head thrown back. Her long skirt swished and Marik grinned, spinning the wheel so the airship lurched to one side, throwing Cathrine off-balance. With a yelp, she tumbled sideways, but Marik caught her in his free arm. "Steady there."

"You did that on purpose!" she accused.

"What in the vast sky makes you think me capable of such an ungentlemanly gesture?" He tightened his arm around her slightly, pretending for a moment that he could ever belong in her life. It was just a wild dream, though. She was a princess and he was a pirate. Nothing could induce him to leave the sky, and he respected her too much to ask her to abandon her home and family for him. He saw how much she loved her younger siblings, and the school that she managed. He could offer her nothing like what she deserved.

"Pirate." Cathrine jabbed a finger at his chest, her chin tilted up, eyes flashing.

Marik squinted down at her, tilting his head to one side. "You might have a point." He released her and turned back to the wheel, making no effort to conceal his grin.

"She's truly beautiful," Cathrine said softly. "Thank you for showing me." Her fingers found his and wound through them.

Startled, Marik coughed, and stiffened, his thoughts whirling into an agony of what if and impossible. Clearly, he had gone too far in his pretending. He stared toward the prow of the airship, suddenly uncomfortable. Something down in the valley caught his eye.

"Look"—he let go of her hand with a surge of relief and pointed before firmly gripping the wheel with both hands— "wylfen. If we don't startle them, we might get to hear them sing."

Slowly, he circled the Hawk above the pack. The lead wylfen raised its head and loosed its mournful cry into the air. The others in the pack joined in, their song filling the sky with its haunting melody. Marik grinned. "That's something, isn't it?"

She nodded, keeping her eyes averted from him.

He frowned. "Cathrine? Are you all right?"

"This has been lovely." She glanced up at him quickly, then back down at the wylfen. "But I should be getting back home. It is getting late, and I have to teach in the morning."

"Oh," Marik replied, feeling inexplicably crestfallen. Had he offended her? He didn't see how he could have done so, but her change in behavior indicated that she was angry with him. "Very well." He adjusted the controls and navigated his way back to the dock, settling the Hawk gently in her moorings.

Cathrine descended the ladder after Marik, but her foot caught in her dress and she fumbled for a moment, nearly falling to the deck. Marik reached up to steady her, but she stiffened, pulling away from him. He backed away, confused and a little hurt by her sudden coldness. She made it the rest of the way down the ladder without incident. Marik held out his hand to help her over the railing, but she ignored him. Taking hold of the rope, Cathrine swung herself over, landing heavily on the platform of the dock, where she swayed for a moment and he once again feared that she would fall, but she put out a hand to steady herself on the railing. Without a backward glance, she descended the stairs and marched quickly up the path toward the house.

Marik jogged after her, wondering what he had done to offend her. He caught up to her just as she reached the door.

"Cathrine," he began.

"Good night, sir," she said in a strangely formal tone, without turning to look at him. "Thank you for taking me flying, your Hawk is lovely." She made as if to go inside, but Marik caught her arm, halting her mid-stride.

"Cathrine, what's wrong? Why are you upset?"

She turned to him, eyes flashing. "I am not upset. Good night, sir."

Marik took a step back, startled by her sudden wrath. She shook her hand free of his and entered the house, slamming the door in his face.

Uncertain about what to do next, he stood on the porch and tried to puzzle out what had just happened.

"Marik?"

Marik turned at the sound of Dalmir's voice. The man joined him on the porch, a heavy weariness about each step he took.

"Rough evening?" Marik asked.

"Aye, but a good one," Dalmir replied. "What are you doing?"

"I'm not certain," Marik replied, at a loss for how to explain. He had grown accustomed to sailing through life. It wasn't always easy, being a pirate, but rarely did his skill and bravado fail him so utterly as to leave him at a complete loss for words.

"Seems you've had a rough evening yourself," Dalmir said, eyeing him. "Want to talk about it?"

"No."

"Good. I'm exhausted." Dalmir opened the door. The lantern-light spilled through the doorway and out onto the ground, a warm and welcoming sight. He stepped through, then paused. "You turning in for the night?"

Marik hesitated. He did not want to go inside after having the door slammed in his face. But he did not want to sleep outside, either. The answer presented itself quietly in the back of his mind and he made a decision. "Yes," he replied. "But not here. The accommodations here are nice, but it's time for me to get used to sleeping in a ship's bunk again."

"Ah. Well, good night then."

Marik nodded and the door closed on the light, cutting him off from its comforting aura of home and hearth. The pirate stood in the darkness, contemplating the house for a long moment, his heart aching with a longing for something he couldn't quite identify. Then he spun on his heel and strode back down the hill. The Valdeun Hawk awaited him, bobbing in her moorings to welcome him home.

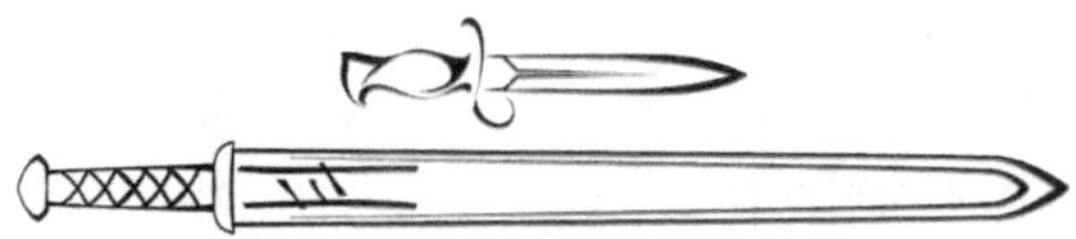

21

Grayden stood in the slushy mud of the now-familiar training field with the rest of the Skyborne. It was the first time in six lunats that they had all been summoned as a single division, and he wondered what it meant. He hoped it signaled the end of their training. What news they had heard from the front lines of Ondoura had not been encouraging. The Igyeum forces continued to advance beyond the border, swallowing up villages and causing Telmondir citizens to flee from their ruined homes. He stamped his feet to warm them. The snow had mostly melted, but the sun's light still brought little warmth in these late final days of winter. He caught snatches of conversation from those standing around him.

"What do you think, my friend?" Beren asked in a low voice.

Grayden shrugged. "An all-division run up the mountain?" he joked.

Beren snorted quietly. "Let us hope not."

At that moment, the major strode out of the main building. The ranks of men parted for him as though on command and all voices fell silent. The commander of the Skyborne division climbed up onto the nearest platform and looked out over the assembly.

"Akkad has fallen," Major Semiv began without preamble.

Grayden's stomach clenched as though someone had punched him. Akkad? Surely not. He and Beren had been at the Southern Command's forward operating base in Akkad not six lunats ago before moving on to the front lines. How could the Igyeum army have moved so far beyond the border? A rumble of low mutters surrounded him as the other defenders contemplated this news.

Major Semiv continued. "The Southern Command is not going to allow them to keep the city, of course. The time has come for the Skyborne to enter the war."

A shout rose up from the ranks. Grayden joined in, raising his voice with the others.

"We fully intend to push the Igyeum forces back across the border, but in order to do that, we have to cut them off from their forward operating base and their supply lines. Each company will receive specific orders shortly. This is the moment you have been training for, men. This is the moment the Skyborne division has to prove the great experiment that has brought us to this base. Many of you have expressed frustration with how many lunats you have had to spend here, and I sense an eagerness in all of you to get down to the business of fighting our enemy and chasing them from our lands. That business is about to begin. You are ready to deliver the stunning blow that will alter the course of this war. I am proud to lead you men into this battle. We will fight hard and we will look after one another. That is all!"

Grayden turned to see a tight grin on Beren's face.

"Finally," Beren said.

Grayden fell into step beside his friend as they strode to the Black Dragon barracks. Once they reached the long, low building, Shep, Jerky, and Hans found them. These had become an insepa-rable trio within Arta Platoon, and Grayden found himself relying on them to keep him apprised of any potential problems inside his command. The men were more likely to talk to one of them than come to their commanding officer, and he was grateful for how easily these three had fallen into their supportive roles.

"About time, right?" Shep said. "I wonder what our assignment will be?"

"I just hope it's not air support," Jerky replied. "I don't want to be stuck on an airship while the other companies get to jump into the enemy camp."

"I doubt Major Semiv plans to lead us into a supporting role," Grayden said.

"Attention on deck!" a voice shouted and every man scrambled to stand at attention near the foot of his bed as Captain Argond appeared in the doorway.

The man raised a hand. "At your ease," he said. "I have our orders here."

"Sir," Hans said, "will we be in the first wave or is Black Dragon slated for air support?"

Argond gave him a tight grin. "We are in the first wave. In fact, we just got news that a small company of Igyeum soldiers has broken off from their main push and is making their way along the Ondouran border in this direction. Black Dragon Company has been assigned the very first mission of stopping them before we join the Southern Command at their new forward operating base in Pentua. It will be our job to carry out our orders to subdue and contain this splinter group swiftly and prove to Command that the Skyborne initiative is worthwhile."

The men raised a cheer at this news, but Argond held up a hand. "No time to celebrate. Get yourselves suited up and meet me at the jumpship in fifteen minutes."

Grayden and the rest of the company moved swiftly to gear up. They checked over each other's skysail packs, shrugged into their leather jackets, wrapped the long silk scarves around their necks, helped each other into the new harnesses with their easy-release buckles, and pulled on helmets and goggles before buckling on their swords and other weaponry. Grayden strapped on his altimeter, buckling the soft leather strap snugly around his wrist so he could see the readout easily.

Outside, it had begun to rain the freezing rain of early spring. Pulling his scarf up higher around his face and hunching his shoulders, Grayden and the others splashed their way across the muddy yard to where the jumpship waited. Captain Argond was already aboard, standing at the top of the gangway and helping direct the men as they arrived. By the time the airship launched itself into the air the deck was slick with half-frozen puddles and Grayden's boots slipped on the sodden boards as he made his way down through the hatch into the hold where he and the others huddled together in an attempt to hoard some warmth. The airship jerked beneath him and his boots slipped. Grayden felt himself losing his balance and grabbed wildly for a handhold. The back of his hand and wrist smacked into the wall with a thump and a cracking sound that made his head spin. Arms caught him from behind, steadying him and preventing him from falling to the floor.

He looked back and saw that Shep and Beren had each caught one of his arms.

"You all right?" Beren asked. "That sounded painful."

Grayden shook out his hand, clenching and unclenching his fingers. It did not hurt as much as he felt it should from the sound it had made. "Seems to be in working order," he said. "Must have sounded worse than it was." He frowned. "Doesn't hurt, anyway."

"That's good," Beren said.

They ducked into the hold and grasped the straps that hung from the ceiling, offering stability in case the airship made any more sudden maneuvers.

"Be careful as you go, men," Captain Argond warned once everyone had assembled. "With the deck as slippery as it is, make sure you have your footing before you jump. We don't need any accidents this close to our deployment. Remember, our brothers at the front are counting on us to finish this job swiftly and then join them with our support."

This pronouncement was met with solemn nods. There had been three accidents during the past six lunats of training. One man had died when his skysail failed to deploy. Nobody was sure why he had not used his backup sail, though the general assumption was that the man had panicked and forgotten he had one, an easy mistake to make while falling thousands of feet through the air. Another man in Leythan Company had broken his arm. The final injury had been a man named Kent in Black Dragon Company. He had suffered a laceration across his face from a loose bit of rigging. The injury had landed him in the troop sychstal for two sennights while it healed. That he had not lost the eye was still a marvel to the rest of the company. Even as he thought of this, Grayden glimpsed the man in question across the hold and gave him a tight grin; Kent nodded in acknowledgment, the puckered scar still red and freshly healed stretching from his chin to his hairline.

They were still surrounded by the wet, gray mist of clouds when the signal came. But this did not worry Grayden. Their jumps generally started in or above the clouds, and jumping blind had become second-nature to the Skyborne.

His turn came. Adjusting his goggles over his eyes, Grayden threw himself into the air and plummeted down through the thick clouds. Stinging particles of mist bit at the small amounts of unprotected skin on his face and for a moment he simply closed his eyes, enjoying the sensation of falling, the wind roaring in his ears. He counted slowly to ten, mouthing the numbers, then opened his eyes. The low-hanging clouds still surrounded him; he could not see the ground yet. Still counting, he checked his altimeter. The needle swung wildly back and forth, and Grayden's heart lurched as he realized that the device had broken. In his mind, he heard the ringing crack of his wrist against the boards of the wall and the lack of pain; the altimeter must have taken the brunt of the blow. Panic coursed through him, but his lips continued to move, counting the passing seconds.

Eleven.

Twelve.

Grayden strained his eyes, trying in vain to pierce the murky clouds, trying desperately to glimpse the ground below and gauge how far he had to go.

Thirteen.

Fourteen.

He could hear his heart pounding in his ears. Should he risk waiting for a break in the clouds? But he had no idea how low they were. What if he had already passed the safe zone? Now he wished he had stayed above deck on the jumpship so that he could have observed where the cloud cover began. If he hadn't gone below, his altimeter would probably still be working.

Fifteen.

Cursing himself for choosing comfort over keeping himself alert and carefully observing his environment, Grayden's heart thudded. He needed to make a decision.

Sixteen.

Better to deploy too early than too late, he reckoned. Even if the wind blew him far off course and caused him to miss the battle, at least he would survive. He might not be able to reach his platoon in time to be part of the mission, but at least he could join them eventually. If he hit the ground without his skysail, that would be his end.

Seventeen.

With a mighty tug, Grayden pulled the cord that loosed his skysail. His ears filled with the blessed sound of silk unfurling and flapping as it caught the wind and immediately arrested his descent. His racing heart began to calm as he felt himself floating lightly. The wind caught his skysail and he used his anchor ropes to maneuver himself lower and lower in the sky, taking long, lazy circles to keep his speed under control. Since he still could not see the ground, he had no desire to hit it too fast; a mistake like that could result in two broken legs. As he came through the final layer of clouds, he blinked through the steady rain and saw the rolling forest close below and knew that he had made the right decision. He glanced around, and glimpsed other skysails drifting through the air nearby and breathed a sigh of relief. He would not miss the battle after all.

22

"Good morning, Hubert," Marik said to the little boy as he entered the dining room the next morning. Sleeping in his own bunk had helped clear his head, and put a little bit more perspective on the events of the evening before.

"Good morning, Uncle Markik."

"Smells like breakfast," Marik commented.

Hubert nodded, not taking his eyes off the pile of plates clutched tightly in his small hands. "Cassrin said soon."

"Your sister in the kitchen?"

"Yup."

"Thanks, Hubert. You're doing a good job with those plates."

The little boy grinned and kept working at setting the table. Marik strode past him into the kitchen.

A blast of warmth hit him as he entered the room. The great, black-iron wood-fire stove stood against the exterior wall to his right and heat radiated from it in hazy shimmers. The walls of the kitchen were lined with low cabinets covered by wooden countertops polished to a smooth shine and waxed to make them easier to clean. The cream-colored plaster walls above the countertops were adorned with hanging pots and pans and all manner of utensils.

The rich aroma of baking bread and smoked ham filled the air and Marik stood at the doorway for a moment, memories of childhood playing unbidden through his thoughts. He remembered his family's cook, Gertie, a tall, wiry woman with snow-white hair and a kind smile. She had always had a treat for him whenever he found his way to the kitchen. A roll, a pastry, a slice of cheese, sometimes a bowl of hot, buttered vegetables, or even just a tall glass of fresh, cold milk from the cellar. Gertie had an uncanny knack for knowing when he might visit the kitchens, and she was always ready with a snack or a story. She had taught him how to cook and her sympathetic ear had been the one he turned to most often when he was troubled or wanting advice. Unbidden, he was struck with a vision of the last time he had seen her, standing in the doorway of the kitchen, the flames around her leaping up to blacken the walls... his mind slammed the door of memory shut with a hasty bang.

Cathrine, in her everyday blue calico dress, bustled about the kitchen, completely oblivious to Marik's presence. She stopped at one of the counters to slice a large block of cream-colored cheese, the knife thudding firmly onto the countertop. She laid the slices out on a tray, then turned to the stove and stirred the large skillet full of eggs, scrambling them efficiently. She opened the oven door and slid in the long-handled paddle, pulling out four large, round, brown loaves of dark bread. Cathrine deposited these on another tray.

Marik moved toward her. "May I help you?"

Despite his efforts to keep his voice low and gentle, she startled a bit at his question. Her eyes darted to his face and then swiftly back to her work. He watched as she wiped her hands on her apron, then pressed the back of her wrist to her forehead for a moment. Was it his imagination, or did her face grow darker beneath the flush from the heat of the oven?

"Oh! Marik," she said. "Yes. You can carry in this." She wrapped the handle of the skillet in her apron and shoved it at him.

He backed away, hands up. "Can I get something to shield my hands? That looks hot."

Her cheeks definitely grew darker this time, and she quickly grabbed a rag from the countertop and tossed it to him. He used it and accepted the skillet of eggs.

"Of course," she said. Turning back to the counter she spoke over her shoulder in a tone of studied nonchalance. "If you want to come back for the bread and cheese, I'll just... I'll just fill these bowls with preserves." The glass bowls clinked together as she pulled a stack of them from the shelf.

"I can do that." Marik took the skillet out to the dining room and placed it on the table. More of Cathrine's younger siblings were already assembling, pulling mugs and silverware from the dresser in the hall to lay on the table alongside the plates Hubert had already situated.

Marik made two more trips to the kitchen, one for the bread and cheese and another for the large, sliced ham. Cathrine was busily spooning various spreads into the glass bowls with an earnest will that appeared to be consuming all of her focus. The rest of the family and guests had arrived and were finding their places at the table.

After a moment of waiting, Marik strode back through the door and nearly ran into Cathrine, balancing the heavy tray filled with glass bowls of sparkling jams and jellies. She stumbled backwards and he lifted the tray from her grasp easily with one hand, then steadied her with the other. He grinned down at her.

"Fifteen spreads? Do you really think we'll need that many?"

He expected her to laugh with him, enjoying the humor of trying to anticipate the tastes of a large family and a house full of guests, but instead she stiffened. "If you have nothing but criticism to offer, you are welcome to find your own breakfast." She reached out to reclaim the tray.

Marik frowned, raising the tray out of her reach. "Cathrine, what is going on?"

"Nothing," she snapped, curtailing her own efforts to snatch the tray.

"That isn't true. If there wasn't something bothering you, then why didn't you laugh? Why did you slam the door in my face last night? Why can you barely look at me this morning? If I've done something to offend you..."

Cathrine let out a sharp, bitter laugh. "You!" She clamped her lips tightly together. Glaring daggers, she lifted her chin. "Fine, if you want to put the spreads on the table so badly, then go right ahead." She sniffed imperiously and swept past him into the dining room.

Marik followed, careful not to let the bowls rattle together too much. He set the tray down and took a seat. With so many already at the table, he found himself squeezed between Drengur and Conrad, Beren's second and third brothers. They jostled him as they reached to begin passing the food, heaping their own plates with mountainous servings and peppering him with questions about his airship and when he would take them flying now that the weather had turned nice. Marik managed to rescue a few eggs, some cheese, and a slice of brown bread for his own plate all while giving noncommittal answers to the two young men, who seemed to take his lack of enthusiasm to mean a resounding "yes!" Marik chuckled and tried to catch Cathrine's eye to share the humor of the situation, but she had managed to place herself at a spot at the far end of the table and was in a deep conversation with her mother.

Marik sighed and spread his slice of bread with butter and one of the jams, not bothering to take note of which flavor it was. He took a bite. Tartness exploded in his mouth in an unexpected way. He lifted his mug and took a quick drink of milk, then peered down at his bread. The orange jam smiled up at him, coating the dark bread with unassuming innocence.

Orange was not his favorite flavor.

As surreptitiously as possible, he used his knife to scrape the offending preserves off his bread, then craned his neck to look over the various options and frowned. All of the bowls appeared to hold the same citrusy spread. He was about to ask Conrad if there were any other flavors at the other end of the table, when Drengur's voice rose above the general hum of conversation.

"Hey, sis, no options this morning?"

Cathrine glanced at him archly. "Whatever do you mean?"

"There's fifteen bowls of preserves on the table and all of them are orange-flavored."

"Of course there are options," Cathrine replied primly. "You can decide either to have orange jam or not."

The older boys erupted into raucous laughter at Drengur's discomfiture, and Marik was glad he had not said anything. As he frowned down at his breakfast, his mind flashed back to their first meeting at the Arxis. He had told her he would rather eat canvas than orange jam. For a moment his heart beat a little faster at the realization that she had remembered such an innocuous moment, but just as quickly, his appetite fled. Clearly this dig was meant for him, though he still did not know why.

Breakfast ended and Marik volunteered to clear the table and wash the dishes. Cathrine politely told him it was unnecessary, but the rest of her siblings shouted their thanks and made a hasty exit, leaving the two of them alone.

Instead of trying to talk, Marik piled up the dishes and took them to the kitchen, where he set them on the counter and turned the crank to open the steam-boiler that would allow hot water to flow into the large sink. As the steaming water poured out of the spigot, Marik could not help but marvel. Hot water at one's beck and call was a luxury he had rarely encountered, and it was a daily reminder that while Lord Adelfried and his family did not put on fancy airs, they were on par with the nobility of the Igyeum. Even with his own family's wealth, Marik's childhood home had never had running water within the house, let alone a steam-boiler that could deliver heated water directly to one's desired destination.

When the sink was full, Marik began scrubbing away at the dishes with a clean cloth and soap. He handed the clean dishes silently to Cathrine and she rinsed and dried each dish carefully. At times, he could feel her eyes upon him, but he kept his own gaze strictly on the dishes. If she did not wish to tell him what was on her mind, that was her choice, and he respected it. He wished she would tell him, but he would not push her.

The stack of dishes shrank as they worked together in a silence that began to feel moderately less frigid. As Marik handed Cathrine the last dish, their eyes met. She grimaced and looked down swiftly, but Marik reached out and placed a gentle finger under her chin.

"Cathrine," he whispered, "what is wrong? Something is wrong, my friend, and I fear it is my fault. Please talk to me."

"It's not your fault," she whispered back, hoarsely. "It's nobody's fault but mine." She shrugged her shoulders and turned her head, studiously rinsing the final dish and drying it with her apron as carefully as though it were made of fine crystal and not just tin. She set it down gently and then leaned her elbows against the counter, placing her face in her hands. "I'm so embarrassed," she said in a muffled voice.

"What reason do you have to be embarrassed?" Marik was mystified.

She raised her head and stared at him, her expression filled with disbelief. "For last night."

"What? You mean for slamming the door in my face?" Marik waved a hand. "It's forgotten."

"Um. No. Well, yes, I am sorry about slamming the door in your face. I should not have done that." Cathrine winced.

Marik tilted his head, scrutinizing her. She still refused to meet his gaze, but by the way her voice was trembling, he could tell she was near tears.

"You don't have to tell me," he said quietly, feeling more confused than ever. "It obviously is important to you, but if you don't want to tell me, that's fine."

Tears spilled down her face. "I'm sorry." She closed her eyes. "I... last night was so perfect and beautiful... getting to fly on your

Valdeun Hawk, and the stars, and the wylfen singing... I just, I got carried away. I thought maybe you felt... but you... um... forget it, I was just being silly." The words tumbled from her mouth in a rush.

Marik stared at her, struggling to comprehend her meaning. She glanced up at him and seemed to understand his confusion.

"When... when I..." She paused, pressing her lips together and closing her eyes. Her words came out then in a rush of speed that left Marik reeling as he tried to make sense of them. "I tried to hold your hand. You obviously didn't want me to—perhaps somebody else already holds your heart, I never asked, perhaps I should have. No, I definitely should have. Or perhaps you simply don't feel the way I do. Either way, it was presumptuous and unladylike of me, and you have my deepest apologies, sir. I have shamed myself and embarrassed myself and I am sorry and I just wish I could take it all back."

Marik's eyes widened as a wild hope fluttered in his chest. His heart careened up into his throat, choking him from any ability to speak words. Sternly, he reminded himself of all the reasons why he was wrong for her.

"Ah," he finally managed. "That." He paused, uncertain what to say next.

She shrugged one shoulder. "It was silly. I'm sorry for acting angry with you. I was embarrassed, I felt a fool. I shouldn't have taken it out on you."

"Cathrine." Marik took her hands in his and lowered his head to look directly into her eyes. He could get lost in those eyes. Quietly, he spoke aloud the words he had oft-repeated to himself of late. "You are kind and gentle, and you have a spark of fun about you that is infectious. Any man would be a fool not to wish for you to favor him. I have enjoyed our friendship these past lunats. But you are a princess here, and I—I am just a pirate. I care for you deeply, but you must know that I will never give up the sky, and I could not ask anyone to give up a life such as the one you have." He shifted slightly, not sure what else to say, wishing he could say very different words, but knowing that such a wish must always be in vain.

"I understand." She smiled faintly and then extricated her hands from his grasp. She paused at the door. "When you do rescue Raisa, make sure she knows how lucky she is." A tinge of something mocking and despairing filled her tone. Then she slipped through the door and disappeared.

Marik frowned, not entirely certain what she meant by that. Strangely disheartened, he tapped his fingers on the countertop. Glancing up through the window, he saw a lumbering airship descending toward the docks, and his spirits lightened. His crew had returned from their latest mission. He took a deep breath, the weather had turned, it was time to rescue their missing crewmate. And while they traveled, maybe Oleck could explain to him why women were so complicated.

———

LATER THAT EVENING, when the Oddhaven had been unloaded and everyone had gathered around the table once more, Dalmir looked about the beautiful home he knew he must now leave. Lanterns set along the dining room table flickered gently, casting the entire room in a friendly glow. The curtains rustled as Nadia closed the windows that had been flung open all day to let in the warm spring breezes. A somewhat subdued Cathrine set plates with lingonberry cardamom cake before each person. Dalmir smiled at her as she set his down last and then took a seat on the bench next to him. He took a small bite and was instantly transported to another place and time as the sweetness of the cardamom mixed together with the hint of tartness from the lingonberries, all nicely accented by the sliced almonds sprinkled on top. Closing his eyes, Dalmir could see again his brother Telsume, his huge frame leaning backward in his chair with Lerilei admonishing him for being a bad example for their daughter.

"Do you like it?" Cathrine's anxious whisper broke into Dalmir's reverie, pulling him back to the present.

He nodded, swallowing past the sudden lump in his throat. "Very much," he whispered back hoarsely, blinking away the sudden moisture in his eyes and trying to focus on the meeting.

Ioan, Oleck, and Mouse sat along one side of the table. Marik and Shaesta sat along the other side along with himself and Cathrine. Thorben sat at the head of the table and Nadia was just taking her place at the other end.

"There is much to discuss," Thorben began. "Several of our guests have approached me today, not that I can say I am surprised. Now that Malla has arrived the weather is turning far more spring-like, and there is less danger of the sudden wintry storms here in the mountains. With Wynn's help, the Hawk is fully flight-ready and Captain Marik believes it is time to leave us."

"Captain, are you certain about this?" Oleck's voice rumbled with a note of concern. "You got pretty banged up in the crash..."

"I'm not an invalid, Oleck," Marik replied calmly. "All my broken and cracked bones are sound once more. And Wynn has done wonders with the Hawk. She's flying better than ever, you won't believe it. We should call her the Phoenix; Wynn is a wizard, a true wizard." He wished the young man could be there to hear him say it; he'd be sure to let him know when next they met again. But Wynn had left lunats ago with Daegan and the others and Marik was certain that the Dalton Oreworks were now running far more smoothly than they ever had before.

Oleck's mouth quirked sideways. "Well, I can't say it won't be nice to fly a real airship again. The Oddhaven has more pluck than you'd guess, but she bobs about in the air like a drunken goose. Besides, Raisa's waited long enough."

Marik's expression hardened. "Yes, that she has."

"Captain..." Oleck's voice held a note of caution. "You know we can't be sure..."

"We have to try, Oleck." Marik's voice was almost too soft to hear. "I can't give up until I know. She's part of my crew, and she's been a captive far too long as it is."

Oleck nodded. "We all feel the same, Captain."

Marik looked around at his small crew, meeting their gazes one at a time. "All of you?"

Shaesta and Mouse nodded.

"All of us, Cap'n," Mouse volunteered.

"Not that we're all that big a group," Oleck muttered. "Do any of us even have an inkling of where to begin our search?"

"I might be able to help you there," Thorben volunteered. "I have recently received some troubling reports about Igyeum troop movements up into Palla. I thought you might want to begin your search there."

"Whereabouts in Palla?" Shaesta asked.

Thorben grimaced. "I didn't get as many details as I would have liked. But it sounds like they've been sighted traveling north-west away from Melar."

"Not much up in that region besides a few roving groups of bardani," Oleck grunted. "Mostly just desert for hundreds of miles. Why would they be sending their troops up there?"

"That's the question," Thorben agreed. "One that we would like to know the answer to. Even if you don't find your missing crew member, there's pay in it for you to go investigate on our behalf."

"It's a place to start, anyway," Marik said. "But Oleck is right, the four of us don't make much of a crew. We can handle the Hawk just fine, but I'd prefer to have a few more swords along."

"I will accompany you," Ioan spoke up swiftly. Then he hesitated. "Uncle, if I may have your leave? I know that the defenders need me..."

"Ioan, you are still recovering from your own ordeal," Nadia argued.

"It's been nearly a year, Aunt Nadia," Ioan said quietly. "If I haven't healed yet, I never will." He glanced at Thorben once again. "But I am still on leave from my regiment."

Thorben nodded slowly. "I anticipated this. I wrote to your commanding officer a few sennights ago requesting that you be allowed to remain here for a special assignment from the Council. His answer just arrived this morning. He agreed."

Ioan's posture relaxed slightly. "I'm with you, then, Captain," he said to Marik.

"Glad to have you aboard," Marik replied.

Dalmir cleared his throat. "I would like to accompany you on this mission as well, Captain. Though I do not know where Raisa is being held, I can be of assistance in the rescue once we find her."

Marik grinned. "I know from experience how helpful you can be," he said. "To be honest, if you hadn't volunteered I was planning to ask."

Dalmir gave him a solemn nod, knowing how much it had cost the man to admit that. "Then, once we rescue Raisa, may I request your assistance, Captain?"

"Anything," Marik replied.

"I have learned how to defeat Uun," Dalmir said, drawing a series of gasps from around the table. "But it requires the use of all seven orbs."

"You already have three of them, right?" Nadia asked.

Dalmir nodded. "Yes. And Uun has three."

"And the seventh?" Cathrine asked quietly.

"The seventh has been lost for many years," Dalmir said. "We must find it before Uun does. Once we have it, we can figure out a way to retrieve the other three. I have asked Emilee to come along with us as well."

"Hrafn and Nando's daughter?" Marik looked a little disturbed. "Why?"

"She has an affinity for one of the orbs," Dalmir replied. "And I invited her to come with us when we leave so that I can teach her more about wielding its power to help me defeat Uun."

"I see," Marik replied. His brow remained furrowed, but he did not raise any arguments.

"When do we leave?" Dalmir asked.

"I'd like to be off as early as possible," Marik replied. "I've been stocking the ship with supplies for the past sennight, anticipating the weather turning and Oleck and the others getting back. Is dawn tomorrow too soon for anyone?"

"We just need to move our own things over from the Oddhaven," Shaesta said.

"I can be ready anytime," Ioan added.

"I have very little I need to bring along," Dalmir said. "I will let Emilee know to meet us then."

"Excellent," Marik said, pushing himself up from the table. "Then we leave at dawn."

23

Days passed in a fevered, pain-filled blur. The second time she woke, Raisa managed to drag her prone body into the trees, where she tried to clean herself a bit with leaves and then just lay there beneath the boughs, soaking in the comforting presence of the trees. When she finally returned to her tent, she found it had been moved several paces, and someone had left her a clean blanket and a fresh set of clothes.

The stranger continued to come every night, bringing her water, broth, and words of kindness and comfort. By the third day, he added soft bread and diced vegetables to the food he brought. Raisa could sit up by herself now, though her muscles still felt limp and weak like yards of cotton cloth hanging from a dress form. She still did not know the identity of the kind stranger, for he only came at night, and she suspected he had a cloth covering his face, for even with her enhanced vision in the darkness she could make out no features, and his voice sounded muffled, though its familiarity tickled at the edges of her mind.

Slowly, she felt her body healing.

A sennight after her first memory of waking, Lorcan appeared at the doorway of her tent. She pushed herself up to a sitting position and blinked at him. His face split into a beaming smile.

"Ah! So you are awake, my Raisa, my daughter. You have beaten the poison after all. They all said you would die. The Kotai poison is strong and swift, but you fought back, a hard fight, but a fight it was and you won. I am pleased. Yes, pleased."

Raisa frowned at him, wondering at his words of fighting. Had he been the stranger tending to her in her illness? Her mind balked at the very idea. It could not have been him. Surely she would have recognized him! Besides, she did not believe he could have concealed his madness for so long, nor been so caring. Nothing of tenderness or compassion existed within the madman. What did he care if she lived or died, anyway? She was nothing to him, an experiment, a test, that was all. His false words of "father" and "daughter" rang ludicrously of deceit. She longed to shout these words at him, but—due to the nourishment she had been receiving from her mysterious benefactor—she was strong enough to swallow the angry diatribe and feign weakness.

"Water," she begged, making sure her voice rasped in a low whisper. "Please, Father."

His eyes brightened and he came to her, roughly cradling her head in his hands and lifting the waterskin to her parched lips. She swallowed, grateful that she could do so without choking. When she had drunk her fill, she closed her eyes.

"Hungry," she whispered.

"I will bring you food, my child," Lorcan replied.

"What happened to me?"

"Do you remember fighting the Kotai—the assassins, Lord Uun's men, his elite? He wished to see how you fared against them, yes, and you fared well. But one of them forgot to clean his blade thoroughly. Clumsy oaf! Elite!" Lorcan let out a loud snort of disdain. "Still stained with sparrack root—the blade. You were poisoned. Poisoned! We did not know if you would survive. Such a waste that would have been." Lorcan brightened. "But you have survived. And you will be stronger for it." He patted her cheek as one would pat a beloved pet. "I must inform the Ar'Molon of your recovery. We must get you strong. The tests are almost over."

Then he was gone.

Raisa lay there, working her muscles one at a time, beginning the long work of building up the strength she had lost, wondering what he had meant by "the tests are almost over." They contained a ring of finality, a note of fearful, impending judgment. What did they have planned for her? Or was she simply a disposable prototype, something to test and see if it worked before discarding her and perfecting their technique on someone more trustworthy, more loyal?

With sudden clarity, Raisa sat up. The Kotai were Uun's elite. Why would he bring them here? Why would he care to test their skills against hers? Unless it was all just a test, not for her, but for them: to see what they might gain if they volunteered to become like her. A chill shuddered through her and she wrapped her arms around her knees. Why would they bother with a soldier they could never fully trust if they had loyal volunteers? For an elite group of assassins, of course her skills and enhanced abilities would seem tempting. But then what would become of her?

She did not need to search hard to figure out the answer. Her speed, strength, agility, and endurance had all been measured, and now they knew she was resistant to even the deadliest of poisons. They could not have many tests left, and when they had discovered all they needed to know, she would no longer be a necessary part of the equation. She needed to escape, and soon, before they decided she had outlived her usefulness.

24

———

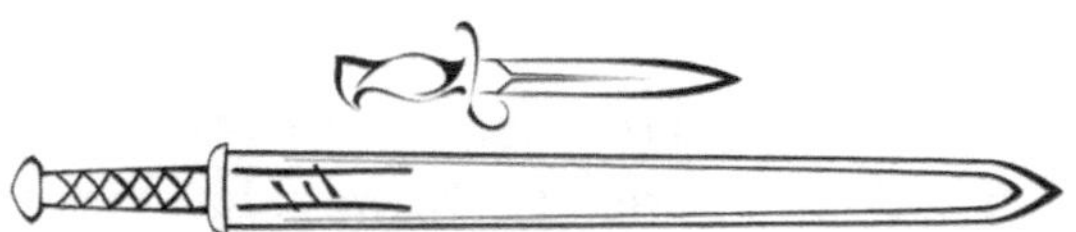

As the last of the jumpship fleet landed and the Black Dragons disembarked, their boots squelching in the muddy field, a squad of men greeted them at the outskirts of Pentua, their leader an older man with golden triple triangles pinned to his collar.

Captain Argond saluted as he drew closer. "General Travenn. The final company of the Gray Malkyns are here reporting for duty."

The general saluted back. "Captain. Welcome to Pentua. I heard of your successful mission on your way here. Congratulations. Are your men all assembled?"

"Assembled and ready for anything, sir."

Travenn's eyes roved over the ranks and Beren thought he saw a slight curl of the man's lip. "Your troops are in shabby disarray, Captain. What do you have to say for yourself?"

Beren's fists clenched. Their company had just spent the entire day crammed inside the jumpship, after taking out a rogue encampment of Igyeum forces that had slipped past the border guards. How could the man expect them to be ready for any kind of inspection after that?

"Our uniforms might be a little rumpled, General," Argond

replied evenly. "But you will find our bowstrings dry, our blades sharp, and our wits keen."

Travenn stared at him for a long moment, his dark eyes boring into Argond's. The captain did not flinch, he merely met the other's gaze with stoic assurance. After a long moment, Travenn nodded.

"Very well. You will follow us back into Pentua where the rest of your division is waiting. Instruct your men to march in orderly formation. We have set up temporary barracks for you all. It isn't much, but my intelligence assures me that you won't be here long."

"That's what I like to hear," Argond replied. "My men are eager to get at the enemy and start pushing them out of Telmondir."

General Travenn's jaw tightened, but he did not comment. Instead, he marched with perfect precision across the field and onto the road leading into Pentua, a city bustling with defenders. This was no walled city as Akkad had been. Though a sizable city in its own right, Pentua had no fortifications, no defensible merits. If the Igyeum forces had already taken Akkad, they would have no trouble walking right into Pentua. Hopefully, the Gray Malkyns could do their job and arrest the Igyeum's heretofore unchecked assault on Ondoura. Travenn did not lead them into the city itself, but rather took them around the outskirts where large temporary shelters had been set up.

"Your men will bunk here," he said. "I will send over my aide with a duty roster for you. Everyone here pulls their weight helping fortify the town and assisting the people who live here."

Beren heard a rumble of discontent that cut off as the general's sharp eye fell on them.

"I'll leave you to get settled in," Travenn said. Turning on his heel, the general strode away.

As one, the men hefted their supplies and entered the various barracks while Argond headed over to the command tent to check in with Major Semiv. Beren ducked beneath the low-hanging canvas doorway after his own platoon and glanced around looking for an open bunk.

"Might as well have given us pallets of straw," Trinh muttered, tossing his bedroll over a faded and lumpy looking mattress. "Would have been more comfortable."

"Travenn's men are all quartered comfortably in the city," Cole grumbled. "And we get a drafty tent in a muddy field."

"You can't blame them, though," Beren said. "They've been here fighting. In their eyes, we're the lucky ones."

"Doesn't make it right," Trinh said.

"No," Beren agreed. "But it does make it understandable."

The other men offered him a shrug, and he turned away to make his own bed. They might not appreciate his logic, but they couldn't argue with it. Besides, they wouldn't be here long. The new Command Hearth here in Pentua was merely a brief stop before they received their formal mission assignment, which could come any day. All they needed was for their spies to confirm the location of the Igyeum's supply lines and forward operating base. There was no need to get comfortable here; they wouldn't be around long enough for it to matter.

As if to mock his optimistic thoughts, the following days dragged by with a slowness that grated on Beren's nerves. Every day that passed was like an open wound being prodded by a needle. They fell into a maddening routine of mundane tasks punctuated by derisive comments from General Travenn aimed their way. He found fault with everything. The man could find a grain of sand out of place at a beach. He criticized the Gray Malkyns' uniforms. He inspected their tents at all hours, demanding their bunks be perfect. He stalked through their camp and ordered the men to do menial tasks for the slightest infraction.

"I'd not put it past him to make us iron the canvas covering the barracks," Grayden joked one day at lunch.

"Hush!" Shep glared at him. "Don't give him any ideas!"

This caused several of the men to chuckle, a sound of merriment that was cut abruptly short when the subject of the joke suddenly appeared in the doorway of the mess tent. He glanced around briefly, and then disappeared, leaving behind a far more subdued group of men, who focused their entire attention on eating their meal.

The actual fighting had not reached Pentua, so other than the disapproving presence of General Travenn and his constant list of demeaning assignments, their days were not unpleasant. Here in the southern reaches of Ondoura, spring arrived earlier than it did in the mountains near Dalma, and so the weather held more than a hint of warmth in these early days of Malla. In the fields around the city, early flowers were beginning to spring up here and there, adding welcome splashes of color to the otherwise dreary scenery.

In addition to the duties from General Travenn, the Black Dragons spent their days drilling and sparring. They routinely went up in the jumpship, flew south over Doran Harbor, and practiced jumping with their skysails onto various sailing ships docked offshore for just such a purpose. As first lieutenants, Beren and Grayden each had charge of a platoon, and found themselves having to work harder and harder to keep their men's morale up. The longer the war dragged on without them, the more the men seemed eager to make dangerous decisions during their daily training sessions.

"They need to let us do our job," Grayden said, keeping his voice low as he and Beren made their evening rounds one night. It would not do for the men to hear them sounding discontent.

"Words of truth," Beren agreed. "But we wait for the scouts and their report."

"Why train us to do all this if they won't let us into the war?" Grayden asked.

"These tactics have never been tried before," Beren reminded him. "Figuring out how to deploy us to the best effect cannot be a simple task."

"That's probably true," Grayden allowed, rolling his shoulders and swinging his arms. "But I hate just sitting here. Every day we see men coming back from the front injured or rotating for a rest, and we're just sitting here in safety. The rest of the Southern Command... well... the men have heard them making some comments."

"Their comments don't mean anything," Beren replied evenly, pushing down his own irritation. "You and I, we've been on the front lines. How would we have felt?"

Grayden nodded. "That's what I told Shep, but he's kind of a loose sail-string. I'm worried he's going to start picking fights."

"Well, he's in your platoon and it's your job to keep an eye out and see that he doesn't. I've had to do the same in my own platoon."

"I know," Grayden said. He paused. "It's just... there's a part of me that thinks there should be someone around here to keep me from picking fights right alongside him."

"That's my job."

The two men whirled and looked right into the grim face of Captain Argond. They stared at him as he walked up behind them and Beren wondered how long he had been listening.

Argond cut his eyes sideways and then his stern face relaxed into a grim smile as he fell into step between them. "And Major Semiv's job is to hold me back from joining in."

Beren blinked.

Grayden let out a low chortle of laughter. "Well said, sir."

Argond glanced at them both, then slapped them each on the shoulder. "We'll get through this, lads," he said. "Together. The command structure is there for a reason. You help up the men below you and lean into the ones above. That's how we stay sane. That's how we stay accountable. That's why we are stronger together. Remember that."

"Yes, sir," they echoed back.

"Good evening, then," Argond said, veering away from them and ducking into his own tent.

Beren shared an incredulous look with Grayden. "That was..."

"Yeah."

They both laughed, but quietly, and continued on their evening rounds.

———

THE NEXT MORNING, a small, unmarked airship settled down onto one of the makeshift docks. The men all muttered about what it might mean, casting inquisitive glances at the arrival as they went about their duties. But it wasn't until mid-afternoon that Major Semiv called the ranking officers into a meeting in the mess.

"Men, this is Sergeant Major Brinns," Semiv introduced the stocky defender they had seen disembarking earlier that day. "He is here to bring us our orders."

Brinns nodded at the men, his expression sober. "Men. I know you have been waiting for this report for far longer than you would have preferred. But now your waiting is over. Just this morning, the Igyeum soldiers in the Whispering Wood received a shipment of cynders and supplies, along with more troops. We knew they would be getting reinforcements soon; their forces have spread thinly as they have besieged and taken Baktan, Akkad, Ergan, and are now getting ready to surge forward to attempt routing us from Pentua, as well. It's the perfect time for us to use our new tactics and send the Skyborne to stop the new attack before it has a chance to begin."

Beren listened intently as the man continued to speak, detailing the assignment he had brought them. Later, he would go over the paper copies again and again, committing every last detail to memory so that he could make good decisions in the field. As he listened, Beren's heart surged in his chest.

Later that evening, as they began gathering up their gear and packing their bags, Beren caught Grayden's eye.

"You once asked me why I was at the Academy," Beren said.

His friend eyed him. "I remember that conversation. You avoided answering."

"It was for this mission," Beren said.

Grayden gave him a strange look. "You couldn't have known about all this..."

"Not this mission specifically," Beren said quickly, forestalling his friend's argument. "I didn't know about the Skyborne until we got to Attatoire. I meant... this work, missions like this. Doing work that protects Telmondir, that protects our families, our people."

Grayden's expression turned sober. "Me too," he said simply.

25

Grime dripped from Raisa's body as she pushed herself, sprinting up the gentle slope, her movements fluid and graceful as they had never been before Lorcan's tampering. The waiting observers came into view and she dug deep into the reservoirs of her strength, putting on another burst of speed. Then she was across the line Virtanen had drawn on the ground and she stood before them, panting slightly from so much exertion so soon after her brush with death.

"How do you feel, Two-Four-Seven?" Virtanen shouted at her.

"Ready for battle, sir!" she declared.

"Who are your enemies?" he barked.

"The enemies of the Igyeum, sir!"

"What do we do to our enemies, Two-Four-Seven?"

"We destroy them, sir!"

"Demonstrate!"

Raisa dropped into a crouch as a sword swept through the air where her head had been but a moment before. Whirling, Raisa faced her opponent, an older soldier who stared at her with a look of startled surprise written across his face. Raisa did not give him time to recover. He had a weapon, she did not. She could not afford to let any advantage slip through her fingers. She rushed the man, throwing her shoulder sharply into his stomach and bowling him over. He stumbled backwards, but did not lose his balance completely. Pain exploded in her side and Raisa sprang away, one hand pressed to her torso where the man's dagger had pierced her skin. She snarled, berating herself for not noticing the off-hand weapon.

Warily now, Raisa circled her opponent, her eyes scanning him for any more hidden advantages. This time, it was the soldier who attacked first. Raisa fended him off, darting back from the sword thrust. With the speed of a pouncing grymstalker, she spun on her heel, coming around in a full circle and catching the man's wrist before he could ready himself for another strike. She held his wrist firmly in her strong hand, squeezing until he dropped the sword. Then she trapped his other hand under his forearm, forcing him to turn his hand inward, pressing the dagger toward his chest. He fought her, but the struggle was futile. She saw the desperate panic in his eyes as the dagger's point inched closer and closer to his skin. Now its tip rested against his thin shirt. His eyes widened and he struggled to throw himself backward, to release himself from her iron grasp, but Raisa clenched her fingers ever tighter. Inside the cage that was her mind, she screamed to stop, but she knew she couldn't. Not if she was to prove to them that they controlled her completely, and so she ignored the part of herself they hadn't been able to touch and maintained the pressure. The tip of the dagger pierced the man's skin and a bright drop of blood blossomed up from the wound.

"Enough!" Virtanen's voice rang out across the clearing and Raisa froze, her stomach twisting with equal parts rage and relief.

"Release him."

Raisa opened her hands immediately and the soldier stumbled backward, shouting incoherent, furious words at his captain. Virtanen barked back at him, assuring the man that he had been in no danger. The shouting continued back and forth for a moment, but Raisa did not bother to listen to any of it. She knew what came next, and she needed every second of respite the shouting match afforded her in order to prepare herself.

"Two-Four-Seven!" Virtanen's voice sliced through the air and Raisa straightened. "Stand!"

The whistle of the whip was her only warning before pain exploded across her back, but Raisa dared not allow herself to so much as blink at the punishment. The whip cracked again and again. Raisa stood immobile beneath every lash. The first time she had been instructed to bear this punishment, she had worried there would be no skin left on her back at all. To her surprise, she later found that the alterations had made even her skin tougher than it had been before. Not only was it harder to pierce or slice, but it had an uncanny new ability to heal more swiftly. That didn't mean the lash hurt any less, however.

"Hold!" Uun's voice rang out across the clearing and Virtanen's weapon fell mercifully silent. "I've seen enough," the Ar'Molon said. He nodded to Lorcan. "You have done well with this one. I had my doubts. As you know, most of your creations have failed to deliver what you promised. Oh"—he held up a hand, forestalling Lorcan's defensive retort—"they have their uses. They are not complete disappointments. But this one..." He came over and circled Raisa, eyeing her critically. "This one might just be the answer we've been searching for all these years." He nodded abruptly. "Yes, you may continue this experiment. The rest of the prisoners are at your disposal."

Raisa's heart shriveled. The other prisoners had been left alone for so long, she had hoped—foolishly, of course—that they were to be used for manual labor or perhaps ransomed. In the deepest corner of her heart, she knew she had not truly believed that to be the case, but at the very least, she had hoped for a little more time. As long as she had breath, she could not allow the madman to do to anyone else what he had done to her. But she was at a loss. What could she do? She could not even save herself. How could she save the cage full of prisoners who hated her and thought her a traitor?

The Ar'Molon had stopped in his circuit around her, and now stood with his back to her, talking to Virtanen, discussing the next level of her training. He stood completely at ease, her presence entirely forgotten even as he formed her destiny. Raisa gritted her teeth, wishing she could strike out at him in some way. Then she paused. Perhaps this moment was the one she had been waiting for. She could break the man's neck in less than a heartbeat. He would never see her coming. He stood tantalizingly close. It would take only a single swift motion. They would kill her immediately, of course, but perhaps it would be worth it to rid the world of this monster. In her conversations with Lorcan, Raisa had quickly come to understand that Lord Uun was the true power behind the Igyeum; he was connected to the orbs in some mysterious way and, like Dalmir, he possessed some great power of his own. Bring him down, and the Igyeum itself might topple.

Her arms held at her sides, she stretched her fingers, flexing them, preparing to strike, when suddenly, out of the corner of her eye, she caught a flicker of movement. Freezing, keeping her head down in humble submission, she turned slightly and raised her gaze to focus on the source of the movement. The Shipwright now held her entire attention. There was a desperate warning in the depths of his dark eyes, and he gave a tiny shake of his head before turning slightly and tilting his head as though he were deeply invested in the conversation between Uun and Virtanen.

Raisa frowned, but relaxed. She did not know why he had given her the warning, but it was enough to divert her from following through on her chosen course of action. She could not know for certain whether or not the man was a friend. That he traveled with Uun and worked for him was more than enough evidence that he was not, and yet why else would he have warned her? And how could he have known what she was preparing to do?

"Very good," Virtanen was saying. "Two-Four-Seven, dismissed!"

Raisa strode out of the clearing without a backward glance. At first she headed to her tent, until she realized that the captain had not given her a directive as he usually did. With a rebellious curl of her lip, Raisa changed direction and walked straight to the lake, following the shoreline into the trees. Leaping into the air, she caught a branch and pushed herself up into the canopy. Her steps light and sure, Raisa ran along the branches, stepping easily from one tree to the next, heading deeper and deeper into the Weald following the tiny rivulet of a stream that twisted and turned below. Finally, she made her way back to the ground, dropping to the earth and standing beside the stream. Glancing about to be certain she had not been followed, she scrambled beneath the enormous roots that hid the source of the lake, a large spring in a strange, otherworldly cavern created by the twisted, knotty roots. Not quite underground, not quite above it, the spring was something she had happened upon quite by accident the first time Virtanen had neglected to give her a direct order when he dismissed her from training.

She retreated to this haven whenever she could. She never stayed long. Enough soldiers patrolled the huge forest that if her absence was noticed, they would find her soon enough and she wanted to keep this place secret. But she could slip away from time to time and spend a few minutes, perhaps an hour, alone. She might have that long now. Lorcan would be preoccupied with reporting to his master for the moment, and with permission to continue his experiments he might not think of her again for days. She shuddered and sank down on the ground next to the spring. Cupping her hands, she washed away the muck in the stream, then she drank from the spring that fed it, soothing her parched lips and aching throat. Her head throbbed, so she curled up on the ground and closed her eyes. The burbling sound of the water soothed her turbulent thoughts and she allowed herself to drift gently between waking and sleeping, never daring to cross the border into true sleep, another newfound skill this new form had granted her.

"This is lovely."

The voice did not startle her as much as the realization that she had heard no one approach. Raisa was on her feet in an instant, her body crouched low to the ground, her muscles taut and ready to spring at the least provocation.

The Shipwright poked his head through the roots and caught sight of her defensive stance. He grimaced and retreated, his hands in the air. "I mean you no harm, Raisa."

"You again."

"I did not mean to startle you," the man said. "I am glad to see you feeling better."

"What do you want? Are you spying on me for the Ar'Molon? I have done nothing wrong." The words spilled out of her and she immediately wished she could take them back. A good weapon would not react so defensively. She bowed her head submissively. "Does my master wish for my return?"

"You can drop the act with me, Raisa." He poked his head back into the cavern and gave an apologetic smile. "You can relax. I'm not here to hurt you. I just wanted to talk. I didn't know how I would manage it back in the camp, but then I saw you in the treetops and I realized that this might be my only chance." He raised his hands. "I bring no weapons to your haven."

Raisa did not relax a single muscle. She knew well that the absence of a weapon meant nothing in this place. "What did you want to talk about?"

"Escaping."

She blinked. "Excuse me?"

"You heard me correctly." The man coughed. "May I come in? These roots are rather uncomfortable."

"No. Good."

"Very well." He sighed. His face disappeared from view for a moment. She heard him muttering something, then he reappeared.

"There is no escape." Raisa could not keep the bitterness out of her voice.

"There might be, if we work together."

"This could still be a trap of some kind."

"To what end?"

"I don't know. I don't know anything anymore. I've been imprisoned, beaten, forced to train as a weapon for the enemy I hate, my very being has been altered, changed. Look at me! I'm barely human anymore!" Raisa's voice rose in a wail. "How can there ever be any escape for me? Even if I managed to leave the Weald, I still wouldn't be free. I'll never be free." Her voice sank to a hopeless whisper.

"Don't you want to try? Or do you prefer to be Virtanen's obedient leythan and Lorcan's pet?"

Raisa glared at the man. "Do you have a plan?"

"Parts of one."

Irritation flooded through her. "I've heard that before. Part of a plan is worse than no plan at all."

"That's why I need you." The Shipwright grinned.

"Oh, really? And what makes you think I can help you? You know nothing about me. I could be terrible at planning things."

"True." He gave a thoughtful nod. "But I don't think so. You've managed to rebel quietly in spite of Lorcan and Virtanen's best attempts to gain your obedience, but you've also been careful not to allow them even a hint of suspicion. You follow their orders to the letter, and from what I saw today, you only break free when you can identify a loophole in their directives. Am I close?"

Raisa shifted uncomfortably.

The Shipwright grinned. "I am, aren't I? You don't have to say anything, you don't even have to trust me. Well, you might need to trust me, but I know I can't force that. Trust has to be earned, and I've done little to earn yours. Unfortunately, trust also requires time, but that's something we don't have much of."

"Why not?" The question burst forth before Raisa could stop it.

"Because the Ar'Molon has ordered the time-table to be accelerated. Now that he's seen you survive poison and make a full recovery, I think he is eager to move forward. Unless you want to spend the coming war on the front lines trying not to kill your friends, I think you might find that it's in your best interests to work with me."

"What makes you think I have any friends?"

"Don't pretend to be stupid, it's embarrassing. Everyone knows your story by now, how you were a member of the most notorious pirate crew in the skies."

Raisa's lips twitched. "My captain would like to think so, but I'm afraid we weren't that famous. Our anonymity was one of our greatest strengths."

"And it was, until the Valdeun Hawk was shot down over the Whispering Wood. Suddenly, your names are on everyone's lips. Or at least, the late Captain Marik's is. Besides, I was there when Uun told you about your airship going down. You did a good job hiding it, but I kept watching after Uun turned away. You have friends, or at least you did, and I'm willing to bet there are others still out there you care about."

Raisa had thought herself prepared for anything. She had spent lunats building up her armor, laying the bricks and mortar around her mind and heart, protecting them from anything her enemies might throw at her. But the pain of having Uun's taunt about the Hawk going down confirmed sliced through everything she had built to protect herself.

"No..." she breathed, then again, "Oh, no. Oh no! No!" Red washed across her vision as sorrow mingled with rage. With uncanny swiftness, she leapt at the man, her fingers outstretched like claws. He reared back away from her just in time and her hand raked harmlessly against the rough bark of the roots. "How dare you use my crew in an attempt to manipulate me into helping you! How dare you!"

"I... I'm sorry," he gasped.

"You're a monster!" Raisa screamed. "All of you are monsters! I will never work with you! I will never..." Great sobs welled up within her, choking off her words. Pressure mounted at her temples and pain tore at her insides as the all-too familiar sensation of fresh grief suffused her.

"I'm sorry I didn't tell you more gently. I should have realized you believed the Ar'Molon was lying," the Shipwright said, his voice soft. "It makes sense that you thought that. I didn't mean to... no wonder you kept your pain hidden so well. I know it hurts now, but think for a moment. What would have happened had Lorcan or Virtanen or Uun used this information as a weapon? If they had found a way to confirm it as I just did, your reaction would have destroyed every advantage you have built. It would have given you away completely."

Raisa knelt in the dirt, her shoulders heaving as she wept for her crew. Her family. Now that Marik was dead, he could have no objections to her using the hated word. The Shipwright remained silent and still, letting her mourn. When her tears of the moment were spent, Raisa ground her teeth together. She raised her head.

"I am sorry for your loss," the Shipwright whispered.

"The Igyeum has taken everything from me," she growled.

"I know."

"I had to be careful before. But now... now I have nothing left to lose." She regarded him for a long moment. "You said you had parts of a plan?"

The Shipwright nodded.

"Very well. Tell me. Maybe I can fill in the gaps."

26

Raisa listened to the Shipwright's plan, her emotions a mix of excitement and trepidation. If he could deliver what he promised, it might just work. However, there was one problem.

"What about the others?" she asked.

He stared at her blankly. "What others?"

"The other prisoners, the ones Lorcan intends to... to alter"—she spat the word—"now that he's proved it can work."

"I'm sorry." The Shipwright shook his head. "There's no way we can take them with us. I don't think you understand just how small the vessel is that I'm talking about."

Raisa's stubborn streak flared. "I'm not leaving them."

"What do you care about them? I'm told they hate you as much as you hate Lorcan."

"They are prisoners here, the same as me. It's not their fault they can't see through the mask I wear. That's the whole point!" Raisa said, exasperated. "I promised myself I would do what I could to help them. I won't leave them here."

"You're going to have to. Either that, or you'll have to stay here with them. We cannot take them all with us. We can't take any of them with us."

Raisa stared at him. "You say it's small. Just how much room is on this airship of yours?"

The Shipwright glanced away. "It's..." He sighed. "It's not really an airship."

"I knew it." Raisa threw her hands in the air. "If you don't really have an airship, then we don't really have a plan, not even parts of one. We don't have any chance of escaping at all." She paused, shooting him a withering glare. "They're going to be missing me soon; I have to get back to my tent." She made her way toward the exit.

"Wait! You don't understand. I have a vessel. It's an experimental vehicle, and it flies—well, it hovers—but it's very small, meant for one pilot. We can fit two... maybe a third... but that's it. Any more and she won't fly."

"A third?" Raisa paused. Perhaps she couldn't save everyone. But one would be better than nobody.

"What are you thinking?" The Shipwright eyed her warily.

"My... brother."

The Shipwright blinked at her. "The one Lorcan keeps in a cave?"

Raisa nodded.

"Can you get him out?"

"I think so."

"Is he really your brother?" the Shipwright asked, his tone more curious than accusatory.

Raisa ignored the question. "How long do you think we have?"

"A sennight at the most."

"Four days, then, to be safe. We leave in four days. We meet right here, at dusk after my training." Raisa made up her mind abruptly. "I have to get back." She pushed her way through the roots and scampered up a tree to the long, widespread boughs. Nimbly, she raced through the thick canopy, her footsteps swift and sure until she made it back to the outskirts of camp. The sun was still high in the sky, and the activity in the camp made it clear that she had not been missed. She found her other hiding spot, a hollow in the top of one of the largest trees near camp, and settled into it. Raisa had enlarged the hollow a bit at a time over the past lunats—using the knife she had managed to steal off of one of the soldiers' belts—she had scraped away the rough edges until the opening was just the right size for her to sit in. She had even carved out a little pocket inside the hollow where she kept various items and extra food whenever she could find it. She deposited another handful of nuts into the pocket and pondered the Shipwright's shaky plan. They would need more supplies, which would be difficult to obtain. So far, she had kept her thievery to tiny items no one would miss, but for their escape to be successful, she would need to be bolder, more daring. And she needed to speak with Olin again. Raisa sighed. That meant speaking to Lorcan.

Reluctantly, she eased out of her comfortable hollow and clambered down the tree's great trunk. With confident strides, she crossed the camp and returned to her tent. Nobody took any notice of her return. Except for the prisoners in the cage, who glowered and hissed at her. She ignored them, ducking into her tent where she curled up and waited, counting the minutes as they ticked slowly by. When she felt enough time had passed, she poked her head out. Sure enough, the soldiers on duty had dispersed and the new shift had arrived. Raisa approached the nearest soldier.

"Can you tell me where Lorcan is?" she asked.

The soldier eyed her with a mixture of distaste and indifference, but no suspicion. It was not an unusual request. He shrugged. "Haven't seen him today, I just got here. Go look for him yourself."

Raisa accepted the order that gave her permission to roam about the camp freely without allowing herself to reveal the satisfied smirk she felt inside. Instead, she turned and shuffled away, doing her best to appear reluctant and defeated.

She took her time searching for Lorcan, but she eventually

found him in his workshop, a large tent with open sides lined with tables. The madman was absorbed in arranging various vials and jars on one of the tables. Another table held a strange device that resembled a chronometer in many ways, but Raisa knew it had nothing to do with telling time. The madman looked up as she approached.

"I do not have time for games today," he snapped. "I have work, important work to do. The Lord Uun has finally seen what I am capable of, and he has given me permission... permission!"

"Forgive me, Father," Raisa said, keeping her voice meek. "I do not mean to interrupt your important work. I was just hoping that perhaps you would take me to speak with my brother again."

Lorcan paused and set down the vial he had been holding. "You wish to speak with your brother?" His eyes darted back and forth and he licked his lips, a swift motion that reminded her of a lizard. She could almost see him weighing the worth of her request against the work he was so excited about. "Why?"

"I thought I might persuade him to speak with you."

"Well..." He drew the word out as though caressing it. "Well, perhaps I could take a short break. Just a short one. I would like for my children to speak to one another, get acquainted. Yes. Perhaps. Just let me complete this measurement, and then I can take you."

Raisa gave him a small smile and took a seat on a nearby stump. Lorcan finished pouring the vial of liquid into a beaker and then puttered about his workshop, straightening his tools and instruments. He tinkered for a moment with the gears on the machine, then turned, wiping his hands fastidiously on a rag.

"Come, we will go see your brother." He strode off into the trees, not waiting to see if Raisa would follow. It irked her that he could feel so certain of her obedience, but she rose and trotted after him, reminding herself that it was only for a few more days. Escape was near.

They arrived once more at the overgrown cave, and Lorcan

waved the emerald orb across the entrance, causing the roots to pull apart, revealing an opening.

"I only have a few minutes," Lorcan said. "But you go in and speak with him. He does not wish to see me." The madman's face flashed with anger, then smoothed to its accustomed, placid expression. "I understand. He is angry and confused. You will explain to him what he needs to do, and then he will tell his father everything."

Raisa nodded solemnly as if the madman's words made sense to her, then she stepped through the web of roots and entered the cave.

She felt her way carefully along the tunnel-like entrance, until she reached the main chamber, where she stood for a long moment waiting for her eyes to adjust to the darkness.

"Olin? Olin!" she called out in a low whisper, not seeing him anywhere in the cave. "Are you in here?"

Nothing but silence greeted her, and Raisa began to panic. Perhaps Olin had figured out a way to escape all on his own. If that was true, then she had just called attention to his absence. The soldiers would be sent out to scour the area, and her own escape would become impossible.

"Olin!"

A movement and a loud snore from the other side of the chamber drew her attention and she breathed a sigh of relief as she made out the shape of the sleeping Olin. She strode over and knelt beside him, shaking him awake. He sat up instantly.

"I'll smash your head with a rock!" he exclaimed loudly.

"Shh!" Raisa put her hand over his mouth, then leaped back with a cry. "You bit me!"

"Raisa?"

"Of course it's Raisa," she replied, wringing her finger irritably. "Who did you think it was?"

"I wasn't exactly thinking," Olin muttered. "I was sleeping."

"I apologize for intruding on your rest, but I have something important to tell you, and I don't have a lot of time." Lowering her voice to a whisper, she swiftly told him about the Shipwright and outlined the plan they had fashioned. "I want you to come with us."

"How do you know you can trust this Shipwright?" Olin asked, his tone suspicious.

"I don't... not really," Raisa admitted. "But he seems to be risking a lot to plan this escape with me."

Olin eyed her, his expression skeptical. "But this Shipwright works for the Ar'Molon himself, just like the madman. Nothing good can come from trusting him."

"And nothing good can come from staying here. Lorcan has been given permission to begin altering the other prisoners. What's to stop him from experimenting on you next?"

"He can't do anything more to me than what he's already done."

"Are you certain?"

Olin frowned up at her. Then his shoulders slumped. "Very well. What do I need to do?"

"You need to come out and speak with Lorcan."

Olin reared back as though she had struck him and he glared fiercely. "Never! I will never speak to that evil lunatic!"

"Then you'll rot in this cavern until he decides he can improve on his mistake," Raisa shot back.

Olin's mouth worked soundlessly for a long moment. "How did you find out?"

"Not too hard to guess, actually," Raisa said, forcing her voice into a gentler tone. "He's obsessed with figuring out how your alterations happened. He's certain you are one of his experiments, probably one he believed failed at the time, but he has no idea which one. It's driving him mad." She paused, then amended, "Well... madder. I'm guessing you could tell him exactly what he wants to know, but you won't, because it would enable him to hurt more people, and you don't want that. So we need to figure out a story that will satisfy him, but won't give him the ability to ruin any more lives."

"Why do I need to talk to him at all?"

"Because I can't open the door to this cave without Lorcan," Raisa explained. "Which means you are going to have to pretend to want to work with him so that he will give you a little bit more freedom."

Olin heaved a sigh. "You'd better have a fantastic story. If he figures out I'm lying to him..."

"I know. Don't worry." Raisa shot him a quick grin. "I've got just the story."

———

RAISA EXITED the cave where Lorcan waited impatiently. He did not move as she stepped across the entrance, but watched her through slitted eyes. A flicker of trepidation fluttered through her. Could he have heard the conversation all the way out here? If he could, all was lost. Raisa eyed him back, assessing his stance, his expression. No, she decided. He was naturally suspicious—paranoid, even—but if he knew what she and Olin were plotting, he would have called Uun already.

"Father." She bowed her head, doing her best to maintain her customary level of reluctant deference. It would not aid her plans if she started acting too respectful, that would just spark his paranoia. Keeping him placated meant maintaining an extreme level of balance.

"My daughter." He continued to eye her askance.

Raisa's heart beat faster, but she pretended her usual lack of concern. "My brother is stubborn." She curled her lip.

Lorcan's shoulders lowered slightly. "I feared as much." His voice lost a little of its suspicion. "Did you make no progress with him? You were in there longer than I expected."

"He wanted to throw me out." Raisa pressed her lips together. "But I insisted he listen first."

"And?"

"I persuaded him to speak with you. He's not happy about it, but I think if you explain things to him, he might see reason."

Lorcan rubbed his hands together, all suspicion fading into an excited gleam. "Ah, ah! I knew you were my favorite. Yes." His lips stretched in a terrible grin. "My favorite, my good, good daughter. I will speak with him. When does he wish to speak with me?"

"I think it should be soon," Raisa said. "Maybe even now. It would not be good to allow him time to change his mind. Like I said, he is stubborn."

"I will speak with him now." Lorcan stepped up to the entrance of the cave, then paused. He leaned toward her. "That's my good daughter. You may go and wash yourself in the lake, and then you may tell the guards that I instruct them to give you two portions of meat and bread for supper."

Doing her best to repress the shudder that coursed through her, Raisa bowed her head once more. "Thank you, Father."

Lorcan disappeared into the cavern, and Raisa headed back to camp. The next part of the plan was up to Olin. There was no more she could do for him. But the extra rations would be helpful for their escape. She only hoped she could smuggle away enough food to get them across the Plains. There was a spring in her step as she returned to the lake, though she did her best to suppress it by the time she came into view of the guards.

She informed the nearest guard of Lorcan's orders, and received her extra rations gratefully. Then she returned to her tent to begin the next stages of her plan. In her tent, she quickly arranged the few things she had managed to collect over the past few lunats. With the rations she had just received she had four joints of dried meat, three cakes of hardtack, a few handfuls of dried berries, and an entire pocketful of nuts. If she included the ones she had squirreled away in her hollow, maybe three pockets-full. She also had a dagger in the hollow, as well as a small shard of broken mirror, a blanket, a small coil of rope perhaps two or three paces long, and a waterskin. Perhaps she could take the tent. She hated to leave such a useful item behind, but it would be hard to deconstruct and carry away so she tallied it in the "maybe" category.

"We need two more waterskins and more food," she muttered.

Those items would be the hardest things to get. But she had a few more days. She reminded herself that she had had the opportunity to snag a waterskin in the past, but had refrained since such an item would soon be missed, and she did not want to endure the punishment that would come her way if they found it in her possession. Besides, even if they hadn't found it, she might ultimately be blamed and punished, as she was a convenient target.

A rustle behind her made her whirl around. She stared into the Shipwright's face, astonishment and outrage warring within her.

"What are you doing?" she snarled at him. "Do you want to hang a sign outside telling them we're plotting together?"

"I had to take the risk," he replied, his tone low. "We're out of time."

"What?" Her thoughts were taking longer than usual to catch up with the words being flung at her. "What do you mean? You said Uun would stay a sennight at the least."

"I was wrong. He's leaving in the morning. And I'm supposed to go with him. If we're going to escape, it has to be tonight."

The weight of a cynder settled in the pit of her stomach. "We can't possibly," she protested weakly, gesturing at the items she had assembled. "We don't have nearly enough of what we need to survive crossing the Plains. We need more food and water. Even in this skiff of yours, we won't be able to travel as swiftly as an airship. It will take us several days to cross the sands and reach civilization, and even then we won't have any money to pay for more food."

"I can get food and water, and I have a little money," he said. "But if you want to bring your friend along, then we have to get him out of his cave tonight. Is that possible?"

"It might be. I don't know." Raisa's thoughts whirled. "I set things in motion, but Lorcan is unpredictable in the best of times, and paranoid. Olin's sudden change of heart might make him more suspicious." She blinked. "Speaking of suspicious, you can't stay here."

"What?"

"GET OUT!" she shouted, pushing him through the door. The Shipwright stumbled backwards, his face alight with stunned surprise as he toppled through the flap of the tent and landed on the ground. "You can't come in here and order me about! I report only to Lorcan or Captain Virtanen, and you have shown me no proof you come from either of them!" She stood at the entrance of her tent, hands on her hips, glaring down at him.

Alerted by the sudden ruckus, two of the guards took a few running steps their direction, then paused as they saw what was happening. Raisa turned to the closest one. "This man tried to turn me into his personal servant!" she fumed. "I demand that you report him to Lorcan immediately!"

The Shipwright stared up at her with such a look of hurt that Raisa found she couldn't look at him. There was no way to assure him that she was not betraying him, or that he would be fine, that all she was hurting was his pride.

The soldier she was shouting at continued to approach, but he was now laughing. Ignoring her, he reached down and helped the Shipwright to his feet.

"Easy does it there, friend," the soldier said, grinning broadly. "You should know that one's off-limits."

The Shipwright spluttered incoherent protests, his face reddening.

The soldier slapped him on the back. "Can't blame you for trying though."

The Shipwright bent over, dusting off his knees for a moment. When he straightened, he appeared to have regained his composure.

"Quite," he said stiffly. Then he turned on his heel and strode away without a backward glance.

Raisa slunk back into her tent, hoping he had understood, but not certain about anything. She swiftly gathered up the few items she had assembled, tying them into a bundle inside her threadbare blanket and shoved it into a corner, trying to make it look like nothing more than a wadded up rag. She then seated herself on the ground, resisting the urge to leave her tent and pace. Everything in her screamed that she must act, but there was nothing more she could do while it was still daylight; she must wait for the cover of darkness before anything more could be accomplished.

She drifted within the boundaries of her newly discovered half-sleep for a couple of hours while she waited for the sun to set. Outside the tent, she could hear the soldiers talking, discussing their assignments, complaining about the food, speculating about when they would begin the invasion of Telmondir. Several groups of soldiers' voices blended in a jumble. Had she been fully awake, she might have been able to listen for specific voices and eavesdrop on a single conversation, but in this state she could not focus her attention so acutely.

A piercing scream yanked her out of her rest. Raisa's eyes flew open, her body already in motion, leaping through the doorway of her tent, her muscles taut and ready to defend herself before she was even fully awake.

A commotion near the cage drew her attention and Raisa peered through the gathering gloom of twilight, her improved sight picking out each detail.

A group of four soldiers stood at the cage. The door was open. Two of the soldiers wrestled with a weakly struggling woman. She wailed and thrashed against them as they pulled her from the cage. Raisa's heart sank. She knew she could not help the woman, or any of the others, but she wanted to with every fiber of her being. Perhaps this woman was the mother of the child that Raisa herself had pushed through the bars into the safety of Marik's arms. As she watched the woman struggling, Raisa wondered what had become of the child. She hoped she was safe, somewhere far away from the Igyeum. One of the soldiers clubbed the woman on the back of the head and she went limp as they half-carried, half-dragged her away. The remaining soldiers slammed the cage door shut and the other prisoners huddled on the far side, their eyes wide and scared.

Had it been a mercy, giving them her extra food? Perhaps if they were weaker, they would not survive Lorcan's experiments. Raisa winced, wondering if her kindness had only prolonged their suffering. She turned and watched the light fading from above the treetops. She could not think of them now. Escape was within her grasp. Focusing on those she could not help would only distract her.

As darkness suffused the camp, Raisa took her bundle and snuck out to the tree line. Moving quickly, she trotted down to the fire where she joined the soldiers in the mess line. The other soldiers elbowed their way in front of her. By the time it was her turn, the only thing left in the stew pot were blackened flakes of tough gristle that had burned to the bottom of the big cauldron. The cook scraped a few of these out and set them in her bowl, then dumped a few crumbled pieces of leftover hardtack on top with a mirthless grin. Raisa accepted the food meekly, grateful to get anything at all. Some evenings, not even that much was left.

She ladled water into her tin cup and drank thirstily, downing the water in two gulps. She was always thirsty these days, it seemed. Quickly, before anyone noticed, she ladled a second cupful and hastened away from the mess line, making her way deeper into the forest with long, purposeful strides. Glancing over her shoulder, Raisa snatched up her bundle and leaped up into the branches of the nearest tree, scurrying stealthily from branch to branch until she reached her hollow. She nestled herself into the space, hiding from the view of those below, and settled in to wait for the soldiers to fall asleep.

27

Dalmir stared down at the mountains of Telsuma falling away swiftly beneath their passing. The cold air on his face invigorated him, but the fleeing landscape had a soporific effect. He leaned against the railing of the airship and let his mind drift, not pausing too long on any particular problem, rather merely brushing them gently with his thoughts.

"You look like a man with rather a lot on his mind," Marik said, coming over to stand next to him. "What's troubling you?"

"I've just been pondering the problem of Uun's orb," Dalmir admitted. "I can't figure out why Uun doesn't have his own orb."

"How do you know he doesn't have it?" Marik asked.

"Because Shiori told me he doesn't have it."

"And who is Shiori?" Marik asked.

"An old friend," Dalmir said evasively. He had no wish to get entangled in a discussion of the past at the moment. "Someone I trust."

"All right." Marik leaned his forearms on the railing. "But what's the big mystery? Several of the other orbs made their way across the world. One of them sat in Aubri Niveya's necklace, and another one was powering that aton under the mountain for a couple hundred years. Why is it surprising that Uun's orb disappeared?"

Dalmir shook his head. "The other orbs were in the wall outside the tower. I put them there as memorials to my fallen brothers. But Uun's... I put it in his prison with him."

Marik shuddered. "That room where we found the girl?"

Dalmir nodded. "Uun saw me do it. It was spiteful of me, I admit, putting it there where he could see but not reach or touch it."

"So... then..."

"It must have happened before Uun broke out," Dalmir said. "Someone climbed up into that tower room, walked past a man in chains, stole the orb right in front of him, and left."

Marik grinned. "Sounds like a pirate."

Dalmir gave a rueful shake of his head. "Even guessing at what happened, it doesn't tell us where the orb ended up or why Uun can't find it."

"If Uun has been looking for it, he may have left a trail," Marik suggested.

Dalmir eyed him, wondering what the pirate was thinking. "It's possible."

"And maybe Raisa will have heard something. She's been a prisoner all this time."

Dalmir doubted that Raisa would have managed to glean any useful information from her captors. In fact, it would be a miracle if she were even still alive, but he did not say these things. Before he could say anything at all, Ioan and Oleck came over to stand with them. Marik stepped to one side to make room for them.

"Shaesta wanted a turn at the wheel," Oleck said. "She likes the new controls."

Marik grinned. "I can't blame her."

"Oleck and I were just talking," Ioan said. "Uncle Thorben's intel seemed a little bit vague."

Oleck nodded. "Captain, do you have any ideas where to start looking besides just flying back and forth over all of Palla looking for Igyeum troops?"

"The Plains of Temna are a barren desert. There aren't a lot of places they could hide any large number of soldiers," Marik replied. "But the bardani have managed to carve out a life for themselves there, traveling the sands in search of water and food. If the Ar'Mol is hiding troops in Palla, then the bardani will know about it. I know where a few of their watering holes are. We can stop at one and barter for information."

"If the bardani travel so much, can we be sure to find them at a watering hole?" Dalmir asked.

"Their travels are fairly predictable," Marik replied. "They can't stray too far from water out there. The Plains of Temna are harsh and unforgiving."

"Only madmen can survive there," Oleck added.

"The bardani aren't madmen," Marik said, shooting Oleck a frown.

"I didn't mean them," Oleck muttered. "Just... anyone else."

"What about a madman with the ability to control plants?" Ioan asked, his voice soft.

Marik waved a hand, dismissing the suggestion, but Dalmir rubbed his chin thoughtfully.

"Perhaps, but to what end?" Dalmir asked.

Marik rolled his eyes. "Don't tell me you think this madman you told me about, Lorcan, is growing trees out in the desert. Why in the endless skies would he do that?"

"I don't know," Dalmir admitted. "I'm not a strategist, but Uun is."

"The Plains could be the perfect place to hide an army," Ioan said in a low voice. "The Igyeum has already made deep incursions into Ondoura. If Uun wanted to have reserve troops ready to launch to the front lines in airships, he would want them somewhere Telmondir couldn't keep a close eye on them. Where better than a place nobody would think to look, even the people of his own empire?"

Marik turned thoughtful now. "There's something to what you're suggesting," he admitted. Curiosity glinted in his eyes. "But to hide that many men in the desert, the Ar'Mol would need a lot of space and water for all those men. Can this Lorcan find water with his powers?"

Dalmir frowned. "I don't know the extent of his abilities, but I would guess not. His powers appear to be over plants and animals."

"If they found a small oasis, they might be able to expand it, though," Ioan said. "Or if they set up next to a river, they could redirect some of it to their own use."

"Well, the Plains of Temna are the only lead we have," Marik said. "And if any kind of forest has suddenly grown up in the region recently, the bardani will surely have heard of it and be able to point us in the right direction."

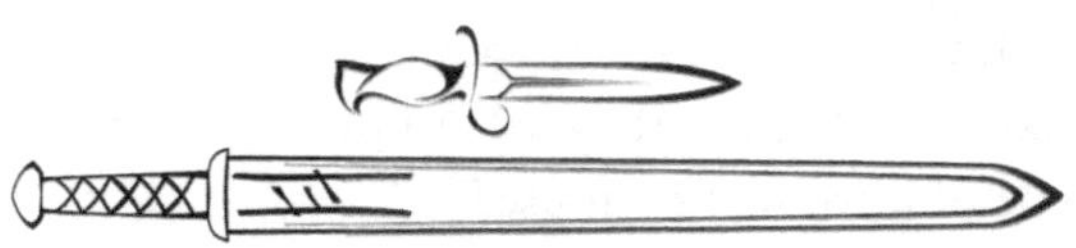

Grayden climbed aboard the jumpship, feeling his way along the railing. The late moonrise this night would offer them the perfect conditions for their first real mission. He glanced around at the shadowy figures of the men on the ship, the rest of Black Dragon Company, and felt a surge of pride to be standing among them. They were about to do something nobody had ever done before. The culmination of all their training over the past nine lunats had led them to this moment, this mission. He patted his front pocket, feeling the reassuring crinkle of his father's note and promised himself that if this mission went well, he would finally read it.

At long last, he felt the ship beneath him shudder as the silent engines powered up and the vessel gently lifted off the ground. He marveled once again at how such an unlovely beast of a machine could move with such grace.

The hours passed in an anxious stillness of waiting. The ship rumbled beneath his feet, passing like a wraith just below the patchy clouds.

The men around him shifted slightly, some of them standing, some of them sitting. The wind riffled through his hair and caressed his face, cool tendrils of air brushing past his skin and calming him. It was eerie, flying so long on a ship filled with so many defenders in such silence. The need for their secrecy did not allow for the exchange of words, or even much moving about, for the tromp of feet thudding across the deck could be enough to give the enemy a slight warning. And so they flew in utter quiet, the darkness filled only with the sound of breathing.

Finally, the airship slowed, hovering high above the drop location. Grayden peered out over the rail and could see the faint black shapes of the other jumpships carrying the rest of their regiment. Captain Argond gave no orders, made no signal, lit no lantern. He merely stood for a set of heartbeats at the opening in the railing and then plummeted over the side. The rest of the Black Dragons crept softly to the sides of the airship and in orderly fashion followed his example. Within seconds, the sky had filled with the dark smudges of skysails, drifting about like low-hanging clouds. Waiting in line, Grayden checked his new altimeter, but he could barely see the white face or make out the black needle. He would have to count his way down and hope he deployed his skysail at the right moment. At least this time he could see the ground.

At last it was his turn. As he had done a hundred times before, Grayden confidently stepped over the side of the ship and dropped through the empty air.

He was thankful for his mishap on their last jump at Atta-toire, because Captain Argond had insisted that all the men practice counting as they fell so they knew when to open their skysails even if something happened to their altimeters. He wondered if anyone would have realized that they wouldn't be able to read the small devices in the dark? Maybe Wynn could figure a way around that problem someday.

A handful of heartbeats later, with his skysail deployed, Grayden watched the dark ground race toward him. He frowned, puzzled. It seemed to be approaching faster than usual.

Too late, he realized that what he was seeing was not the ground, but the tops of the trees that filled the Whispering Wood.

Too late, he yanked on the handles attached to his skysail, scanning the ground frantically for a nearby clearing, trying to steer himself to a better landing zone. But it was a vain attempt.

A moment later, he crashed through the branches. Abandoning the handles and any attempt to steer, Grayden threw his arms up to protect his face. Branches swept past him as he flew through them with bruising force. He was suddenly grateful for the heavy wool pants and the leather jacket he had complained about so often throughout the last two lunats as the hot, early summer of Ondoura had descended upon them in full force. Without their protection, he was sure his clothing and the skin beneath it would have been flayed from his bones.

His fall was arrested by a painful jerk on his harness. Looking up, he confirmed what he already knew: his skysail had caught fast in the branches. Now to figure out how to extricate himself from his sail and still reach the ground safely. His hand groped at his hip for his knife. He could easily cut himself free of the harness, or use the quick-release feature, but the fall from here would probably break his legs. No, he had to be patient and figure this out.

Grayden swung gently, his mind racing. Captain Argond had warned them that they would face situations like this. What had he advised? Follow the training. He didn't need the best solution, just a solution. Suddenly, he knew. He would not extricate himself from the sail and harness, rather, they would be his means of escape from the tree.

Reaching up, Grayden gripped the long lines of his skysail and hauled himself up hand over hand. It was arduous work, but eventually he reached a branch sturdy enough to accept his weight, where he took a moment to rest. Then he pulled out his knife and sawed through the cords, releasing himself from the tangled skysail. Tying the cords together with secure knots, Grayden looped the cord around a branch and slowly worked his way down the tree. It wasn't pretty, but it got him back to the battlefield and that was all he was hoping for.

He stepped back and looked up, marveling at the fact that he had reached the ground at all, let alone safely. Perhaps the Builder that Dalmir had mentioned really did exist and was watching out for him.

Rubbing at the painful knots that had formed in his neck, Grayden checked his compass, holding it up to a shaft of moonlight until he could read it clearly. Determining his course, he drew his sword and loped through the forest in search of the rest of his company and the enemy's base. He wondered how many other Skyborne had been caught in branches after their jump. While they had practiced jumping into forests in their training, none had been so thickly populated with trees as this one, and they had often been aiming for a large clearing, not just randomly jumping into the center of the woods. He hoped they had all made it safely to the ground as he had. An idle thought crossed Grayden's mind. Had the Igyeum chosen this location for that very reason? Could they know about the Skyborne? Had they just jumped into a trap?

A sudden rustle in the bushes to his left arrested his progress. Crouching into a fighting stance, Grayden aimed his sword at the sound, but he relaxed as he heard the whispered password of "Gray."

"Malkyns," he replied with the counter word, sheathing his sword. "Who's that?"

"Kent." The man emerged from behind the bushes, a crossbow held loosely in his hands. "I'm glad to see you, First Lieutenant. I've been wandering around down here for an hour and I can't find anyone."

"The trees were a bigger obstacle than I expected," Grayden said. "Did you have any trouble getting to the ground?"

Kent shook his head soberly. "I managed to come down in a bit of a clearing. But I saw one of ours hanging from a tree back there and he wasn't moving."

"Do you know who it was?"

Kent shook his head. "I couldn't climb up to cut him down, either."

A pang shot through Grayden at the thought of one of their men meeting his death before even getting to the battle, hanging ingloriously in this dark forest. He clamped down on the thought, shutting it away. Right now, he needed to focus on the mission objectives. There would be time to mourn later.

Or he would be dead.

"Come on, then," he said. "The Igyeum camp should be that way. The rest of the regiment will be closing in on the enemy base. We need to find Captain Argond."

Kent nodded and fell into step next to him. They crept silently through the woods, keeping their eyes and ears alert for any sounds that might indicate other soldiers, be they friend or foe. But for a long while, they heard nothing other than the sighing of the leaves rustling gently in the night breeze. The trees grew thickly together here in the forest, which slowed their progress but kept them hidden. Centuries of superstition and terror of the wood had allowed it to grow wild and unruly, a true, untamed wilderness.

Finally, Grayden caught sight of a glimmer of light up ahead, too near the ground to be anything other than the glow of a campfire. He pointed it out to Kent, who nodded and hefted his loaded crossbow to signal that he was ready.

As they drew closer to the orange glimmer, the underbrush grew thinner. Here, the Igyeum forces had been hard at work, clearing out the rotting logs and tangling thorns, making space for their camp.

Grayden paused as they reached the open space, an idea hovering on the edges of his thoughts. "I'd like to angle to the south a bit more," he whispered. "Even if it makes our trek harder, I don't want to risk being heard."

Kent nodded amiably.

"Keep a sharp eye," Grayden added.

Together, they crept around the outskirts of the camp, staying well away. They made good time, traveling in a wide arc around the distant campfire, keeping it always on their left. They had gone about a mile when Grayden heard a noise up ahead that froze the blood in his veins. Footsteps! Gesturing to Kent, he darted behind a tree. Kent joined him, their backs pressed up against the bark.

"Ours?" Kent whispered.

"I don't know," Grayden replied.

The footsteps drew nearer.

"Gray!" Grayden hissed.

There was a pause. Grayden glanced at Kent and gripped the hilt of his sword. Kent raised his crossbow.

"Malkyns," came the whispered reply.

Grayden felt his muscles release, and he poked his head around the tree. "Jerky?" he asked, recognizing the stocky frame. "That you?"

"Lieutenant?" Jerky replied. "Yeah, it's me. Where've you been?"

"Got in an argument with a tree on the way down," Grayden offered, the last of his tension leaching out of him. "Took me a while to convince it to see things my way."

"You're lucky." Jerky's voice held a subdued note. "We lost some good men to the trees."

Grayden sobered. "How many?"

Jerky shook his head. "We don't have an exact number yet, and some are still straggling in, but estimates are around a hundred."

"So many." Grayden felt his heart sink. Against the five thousand in their regiment, he knew it was what the commanders would consider an acceptable loss, but the mere thought of a hundred men already gone staggered him. How could they have lost that many men before the fighting even started? Horror coursed through him. "Beren?"

Jerky pointed back over his shoulder. "I'll take you to him. He's with Captain Argond at the road. They'll be glad to see the two of you."

"You found the road?" Grayden asked, relieved to hear that his friend was not among those hanging in the dark forest.

"Yeah. Pretty fancy path they've cut and trampled, but we're setting up roadblocks and barricades to fall back to." Jerky beckoned for them to join him.

"Any activity yet?" Kent asked, jogging behind their guide.

Jerky peered at him without pausing. "You're with Wylfen Company, right? No, we haven't encountered any Igyeum soldiers. They're keeping their patrols pretty tight around their camp, and we've been careful. Won't be able to hide much longer, though. Captain wants us to attack before we lose the cover of darkness."

They had reached the road. "Hey, Shep, Beren, look who I found wandering around the forest," Jerky called out in a low voice as they approached two familiar figures stacking a large log on a growing structure.

Beren's teeth glinted. "About time you showed up."

"I see you managed to avoid most of the work," Shep added.

"You seem to have things well handled," Grayden shot back, grinning in relief at seeing his friends.

"Quiet down," a whispered order cut through the night. "Ah, Grayden, good to see you're still with us." Captain Argond appeared, his hooded lantern held up to illuminate Kent's face. "And who is this?"

"Kent, sir," Grayden said. "From Wylfen Company."

"Wylfen." Argond's voice grew strained. "Your commanding officer will be happy to see you. Your company suffered the heaviest losses on the way down."

"Do you know anything about Teps or Brady?" Kent asked.

Argond paused, and Kent's shoulders slumped.

"I'm sorry, son," Argond replied, his voice gentle. "They didn't make it."

"I'm sorry," Grayden whispered, putting a hand on the other man's shoulder.

Kent's jaw tightened. "We knew the risks we were signing up for. I just never figured they wouldn't even make it into battle."

"It's a hard thing," Argond said. "I'll take you over to the other road; we rearranged the assignments a bit since Wylfen's numbers were the most affected. Grayden, you help out here for now. Most of our men are accounted for, so the coordinated offensive against the camp takes place at dawn as planned."

29

The moon hung over the Weald. Raisa winced. It was not an ideal time to be fleeing into the darkness. Though only half full, the silvery light of the first quarter moon shone down like a beacon and would highlight their movements should they be spotted. However, Raisa could not afford to wait until midnight for moon-set. Instead, she waited until most of the soldiers had bedded down for the night. Then she crept out of her hiding place. With swift, steady hands, she retrieved the few items she had stashed in the hollow and added them to her bundle, keeping only her knife at the ready.

She slipped down from her perch and crossed through the tightly woven canopy to the rendezvous point. The Shipwright had already arrived and stood waiting. He had a large bundle on his back, and he handed Raisa a full waterskin, which she accepted gratefully.

"Did you get the tent?" Raisa asked.

He nodded and hefted the bundle on his back. He did not mention the scene she had made earlier. "This is more than I wanted to carry. Are you sure we need all these things?"

"If you want to survive our escape," Raisa replied. "The Plains are unforgiving and harsh. We need to be prepared for the crossing."

"If you say so," the Shipwright said. "Where's the third member of our party?"

"We will have to go fetch him. He doesn't know the wood the way I do."

"Lead on, then. We don't have much time."

Together they plunged through the forest. Raisa stepped lightly and silently, one with the trees. The Shipwright tried, but she winced as he brushed against branches and stepped on leaves that crunched beneath his boots. The noise he made sounded deafening to her ears, but the Weald remained still and sleeping.

Finally, they reached the entrance to Olin's cave and Raisa's heart fell. The roots were still tightly crisscrossed before the entrance. Her worst fears were realized. Olin had not been able to convince Lorcan of his sincerity in a single afternoon.

"Olin!" She pressed her mouth up to a narrow crack between the roots, trying to keep her voice as quiet as possible. "Olin!"

Footsteps sounded in the depths of the cavern.

"Raisa?" He was there, on the other side of the impenetrable barrier.

"What happened?" she asked. "Why is the cavern still blocked?"

"I'm sorry, Raisa." Olin's voice was low. "I couldn't do it. I couldn't stand there in the presence of the man who hurt my parents and pretend to work with him. I tried, I really did, but I just couldn't force myself to say the words I needed to say. If I had spoken, I would have poured out every atrocity at his feet, and then he would have known what happened and, worse, he would have known how to do it again. I can't allow that, not even in exchange for my own freedom. You understand, don't you?"

"But if you stay here, he will eventually force it from you anyway," Raisa whispered mournfully. "He will destroy you until you have lost every last shred of who you were before, and then you will be his. You will be happy and thankful to work for him.

We have to get you out of there!" She began prying at the roots with her strong fingers, but to no avail.

"Leave me," Olin said, his voice low and resigned.

"No!" Raisa insisted. "We will get this door open. Shipwright, help me!"

The Shipwright merely stood there, arms at his sides.

Raisa paused and stared wildly up at him. "Aren't you going to help me?"

"What can I do?"

"Use a knife? Help me pull these vines away? Do something!" Pressure began to coalesce in her temples.

"There's no time!"

"Then what are we even doing here?" Raisa demanded, oblivious to the way her voice was growing louder and drifting through the trees. "Are you telling me I can't save any of them: the prisoners, that woman, Olin? What use is any of it? Even if we escape, we'll probably die in the desert."

"We can escape," the Shipwright said, his voice low. "Perhaps if we escape, we can send aid to them. We can tell the forces in Telmondir where the Weald is located and they might even be able to stop the war before it truly starts. Uun has only sent troops to a few locations as of yet. His main force is still here, with the army Lorcan has promised to build him."

The pressure within her head throbbed, threatening to overwhelm her, and Raisa leaned her forehead against a large root, tears leaking from the corners of her eyes. The life circulating through the roots pulsed against her face, calming her. The trees overhead whispered to her with gentle susurrations, strengthening her resolve and giving her the glimmer of an insane idea. Gritting her teeth, she lifted her head and swiped angrily at her face, ridding herself of any evidence of weakness.

"No!" she said. "I am not going to just give up."

"We don't have time..." the Shipwright warned.

"Let me just try once," Raisa pleaded. "If it doesn't work, we will go."

"Very well." The Shipwright stepped back.

Closing her eyes, Raisa reached out and grasped hold of the roots with her hands. This time, instead of trying to tear them apart, she focused instead on asking them to move aside. She wasn't sure she could communicate with plants. It wasn't like she had ever heard them use words, but she felt suddenly quite certain that she could convey an idea to the trees whose roots even now formed the barrier in her way. After all, she had seen them move by the power of Lorcan's orb.

For a long moment, all was still. Even the leaves ceased their rustling. The Shipwright shifted his weight anxiously, clearly nervous and impatient, but Raisa did not allow him to distract her. With everything she had, she formed a picture in her mind of the roots moving aside, freeing the entrance of the cave, and allowing Olin safe passage through. She pictured a young seedling struggling to poke up through the detritus of the previous autumnal leaves and thatch, and then pictured herself, a gardener, kneeling down to clear away the obstacles in its path so it could grow straight and true. A soft humming filled her entire being and the song slipped out from between her lips. The melody came to her unbidden, a strong, ancient melody she did not recognize, and yet it felt achingly familiar. It reminded her of her father's arms: wrapped around her, keeping her safe. It brought to her long-forgotten memories of her mother's smile, bending over her cradle and murmuring words of love and peace. It was a song of strength and home and all of her most precious experiences deeply rooted within her heart, weaving together to make her into who she was.

The Shipwright's sudden intake of breath made her open her eyes. With shock coursing through her, even as the power of the tree-song still thrummed through her veins, she saw that the roots had gently drawn aside, revealing Olin standing in the cave, his mouth hanging open in astonishment. With one swift motion, he stepped across the threshold, as though worried the roots might swing back together at any moment. The three of them stood together in silence in the moonlight.

"What just happened?" Olin asked.

"Ask her." The Shipwright gestured at Raisa.

Olin glanced up at her but Raisa shook her head wordlessly. She could no more explain what had just transpired than she could explain what prompted a mother's love, or how the potential for an entire oak tree could fit inside a tiny acorn.

Olin shrugged and hefted his own small bundle. "Now what?"

The Shipwright grinned, his teeth shining and white in his dark face. "Now we escape the Weald. Follow me."

They followed the Shipwright as he led them through the forest. Raisa's heart stopped every time a branch moved in the wind, but no signs of pursuit appeared, and the three companions made their way to the edge of the Weald without incident.

They emerged from the trees and Olin let out a small gasp as he took in the endless sea of sand and rolling dunes for the first time.

"How are we supposed to get across that without being caught?" he asked gruffly. "I thought you said you had a plan." He scowled accusingly at Raisa.

The Shipwright dug about in the undergrowth, pulling back branches and long vines. "I could use some help," he called in an exasperated tone.

Raisa and Olin hastened to help him clear away the covering foliage. When they had extracted the item from its hiding place, Raisa could not help but stare.

"This doesn't make me feel any better about our chances," Olin groused.

Raisa had to agree with the sentiment. From the Shipwright's description, she had been expecting something at least a bit bigger. The contraption before them looked to be little more than a long bench attached to a set of sails. A thin wall rose up in the front with a steering mechanism attached. She watched, speechless, as the Shipwright unfolded the tall sail and set the mast and cross-piece in their fittings. Her thoughts whirled. Had this all been an elaborate ruse? A test of her loyalty to the madman?

"I see why you said we couldn't take many with us," Raisa bit out, placing her hands on her hips. "Are you sure it will carry any of us?"

"It will carry the three of us away from this place, I assure you."

Raisa was about to issue a retort when her ears caught a faint sound. She paused to listen, thinking it might just be another false alarm. But as she strained to identify the noise, her heart began to pound more swiftly. It was not a normal sound of the Weald, and it was getting closer.

"We have to leave, now!"

The Shipwright turned to her. "Why the sudden rush?"

"They've discovered our absence," Raisa replied. "Something is coming in our direction, fast."

"Just about finished." The Shipwright's hands moved swiftly, adjusting the sail and pulling out another large swath of fabric and affixing it to the base of the bench-like platform with three sets of handles sticking up at regular intervals. "Done! Get on."

Raisa and Olin stared at him.

The man made an exasperated sound. "Like this!" He climbed aboard, straddling the bench as though riding a horse and gripping the steering levers.

Olin clambered up behind him, his much shorter legs swinging in the space above the boards that ran along the base of the bench on either side. Something large crashed through the trees toward them, and Olin looked back, his face pale in the moonlight. Raisa leaped into the last spot on the contraption. A low buzzing sound filled the air around her and the vessel lifted off the ground as the large thing pursuing them burst out of the Weald. Raisa looked back and gasped.

"No!"

A bauman, one of Lorcan's "generals," as he called them. She had not seen any of them in action, but she was already familiar with their abilities; Lorcan had boasted endlessly about them. They were men he had fused with trees. Given the ability to walk and move like people, but completely mindless, they were perfect soldiers, though they were not very good generals, despite what Lorcan called them. They could not speak or command units, nor could they truly think for themselves. However, once they were set upon a task, they would never abandon it. The human soldiers spoke of them in shuddering whispers of disgust and fear.

A leafy vine shot out at them and wrapped around the back end of the skimmer, halting their flight with a nausea-inducing lurch. Olin yelped and nearly toppled from his seat, but Raisa managed to grab a fistful of his shirt and wrestle him back into place.

"If that thing doesn't let go..." the Shipwright hollered over his shoulder.

He did not have to finish the statement. Raisa knew what would happen to them all. "Wait for my signal!" she shouted, then flipped herself backward, caught herself on her hands and threw her body into the air, twisting as she went so that she landed on her feet on the vine clinging to their vessel, facing the general. She stared at it, her stomach roiling as she tried not to think about the man trapped inside. He was gone, whoever he had been, but knowing that did not help her feel any better.

Whipping out her dagger, Raisa dug it into the bark of the vine at her feet. The creature did not flinch. With swift movements, she began sawing at the vine. The bauman lashed out at her with another snaking tendril, but she dove out of its way, slithering farther down the vine. Swinging herself around and back up, she continued to work at the gash she had created. The dagger was dull and the vine was tough. The creature jerked backward, nearly toppling Raisa from her perch. The knife nearly slipped from her grasp, but she tightened her grip around the hilt, even as her body swung away from her target. She clung on desperately with one hand; she was not terribly high up, but a fall would most likely result in a broken bone, especially if the bauman stepped on her once she got to the ground. With a monumental effort, she swung herself back up on top of the vine. Her fingers scrabbled in the moonlight for the place where she had been working; she did not want to have to start over. For a moment, she worried that she would not find it, and then her fingers felt the ragged edges of the gash. She fitted the blade into the spot and began sawing once more. She worked away, using all the strength she possessed. Suddenly, the vine bent beneath her weight. Terror coursed through her and she flung herself forward just as the weak spot she had created snapped. She hurtled through the air, her fingers stretching, grasping for the back of the skimmer. She missed. Her body began to plummet, falling toward the sand.

Something caught her arm, and her fall halted. Her body dangled in the air as her mind raced to catch up with what had happened. She looked up and saw the silhouette of Olin hanging over her, his hands wrapped around her wrist; above him, the Shipwright strained, one arm locked around Olin's waist, the other still gripping the tiny vessel's control lever.

"I got her!" Olin called.

"Good man!" the Shipwright replied. "Can you pull her up?"

With much effort, they got Raisa up onto the skimmer all the while speeding farther and farther away from the oasis. Raisa pulled herself onto her seat and glanced back. The diminishing figure of the bauman stood on the dunes, looking forlorn. A pang of pity flitted through her consciousness, but she dismissed it. There was nothing she could do for him. She winced. That was quickly becoming her mantra, and she hated it. Hated herself for it. The helplessness of her predicament threatened to drown her. It was a foreign sensation, this utter inability to enact any sort of change over her own circumstances, let alone anyone else's. It surprised her to realize just how used to freedom she had been.

Freedom.

That was what being part of Marik's crew had granted her.

She missed it. But there was more to it than that. She missed the crew. The good-natured banter, the thrill of each heist, the open horizon surrounding her whenever they took the Hawk up. Her eyes stung as memories of camaraderie and laughter filled her thoughts. She wished she could speak with them once more, tell them what they had meant to her.

"Where to?" the Shipwright hollered.

Raisa tilted her head back and studied the stars. She sighted the one she was searching for and pointed. "West, and a little south!"

The Shipwright nodded and turned the little vessel along the heading she had given him.

To herself, Raisa whispered, "I'm going home." Something lonely and forlorn seemed to curl up within her chest, and she squeezed her eyes shut against the tears that threatened to over-whelm her.

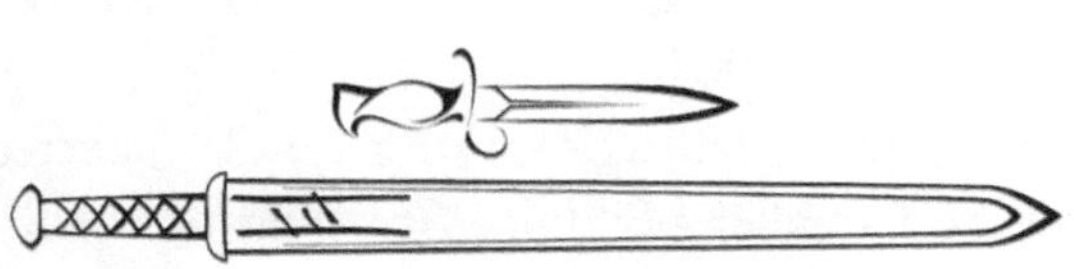

30

Beren knelt at the edge of the clearing as the sky lost a shade of darkness. Somewhere beyond the trees behind them, the sun must be approaching the horizon, the first breaths of dawn emanating into the heavens. The orders had come through the ranks to get into position, and now he waited, his body tense, his massive sword hilt gripped in both hands. Arta and Vector Platoons had been ordered to the north road to help support Wylfen Company's part of the attack. To his right and to his left, the men of Vector Platoon, his platoon, waited alongside him, and he could see that their muscles were also taut and coiled. This was what they had trained for. They were ready.

High overhead, a series of whistling arrows sailed through the sky, giving the signal to attack.

Silent as grymstalkers, Beren and his men burst through the tree-line on either side of the road. An Igyeum soldier stared at them, eyes wide with shock, and then he fell to the ground, cut down by the sweep of a sword before he had a chance to raise the alarm.

Around him, the defenders advanced along the road. To the left stood a row of buildings that looked to be some sort of supply sheds. Beren caught the eye of his highest ranking script.

"Trinh, take your men and clear those buildings. Be quick, careful, and quiet."

"Yes, sir." Trinh and several others peeled away from their formation.

"Stan, take a patrol across the clearing and check the other side. Seems quiet for now, but there might be other guards making rounds."

Stan nodded once, jerked his head at the men behind him, and took off across the glade.

To their right, the faint gleam of a candle flickered through the window of a smaller building. Creeping to the door, Beren listened for a moment before bursting through. The soldier inside half-rose from the chair, a sleepy, confused expression on his face. Beren hesitated for half a second, unwilling to strike down an unarmed man.

In that heartbeat, the soldier raised a crossbow from beneath the table and fired. Beren's left arm went numb and he stared in disbelief at the shaft that had suddenly blossomed from his shoulder. He didn't have time to contemplate what had just happened, however, because the soldier had tossed away the crossbow and now rushed him, a blade glinting in the candle-light. Beren barely parried the attack. The man kept coming, his dagger flashing with swift strokes. Beren backed away, unable to use his great sword to any effect in the cramped quarters. His back thumped against the wall and he felt a second of panic as he realized he had angled back too far to the left and missed the door.

Someone burst inside the guardhouse. A thump sounded and Beren's attacker crumpled to the floor. In a bit of a daze, Beren glanced up and recognized Badger. He gave the other a nod and stumbled out of the now-empty guardhouse. The sound of clashing swords reached his ears, but it came from the other end of the camp. Here, all was still. But now the sky had turned a pale blue, and the massive structure before him could be clearly seen.

"What is that?" he whispered.

"There are no other guards at this end of the camp, sir," Badger reported, emerging from the guardhouse at his side.

Beren glanced down. "Thank you, Badger. Have Trinh and the others finished checking out those sheds?"

"Not yet, sir; want me to go help them?"

Beren shook his head. "No, but can you help me get this arrow out of my shoulder?"

He saw the man's eyes widen as he suddenly noticed the crossbow bolt sticking out of his commander's arm. "If you could kneel down, maybe, sir."

Beren gave a hoarse chuckle and sank to his knees. He was used to being taller than most men, but Badger barely cleared five feet with his short hair sticking straight up. The man was fearless, though, and had proven himself a fierce opponent in sparring matches during training, which had earned him his nickname.

"It's gone all the way through, sir, so that's good news," Badger said. "If I break off the end"—there was a snapping noise and Beren gritted his teeth at the sudden spike of pain—"there we go. Now let me just bind it up." He pulled a length of bandage out of his pack and wound it around Beren's shoulder. "You should get one of the doctors to do this properly."

"I will," Beren said. "But that will do for now, thanks." He shrugged his injured shoulder experimentally and winced. It hurt, but not enough to slow him down.

"Beren," a familiar voice called out, and then Grayden trotted over. He took in the bandage and the broken arrow now lying on the ground in a single glance. "Are you well?"

"Well enough," Beren said. "Have we figured out what that is?" He nodded at the enormous construction of iron-banded beams and support pillars in front of them. It spanned the width of the clearing.

Grayden grimaced. "I was about to ask you the same thing. If I didn't know any better, I'd say it's an airship dock."

"There's no airship in the world big enough to land on that," Badger retorted. "It has to be a thousand feet long!"

"That we've seen," Beren countered. "Who knows what the Igyeum has been doing on their side of the world? My father and the Council have suspected them of preparing for war for years. What if they really have built something that big?"

"Can you imagine the power it would take to keep it airborne?" Grayden breathed.

A shout came from the far side of the clearing. Beren and Grayden shared a glance and then dashed beyond the mighty structure above to find a deadly fight raging with a squad of Igyeum soldiers. They joined in, and were soon fighting for their lives in a swift, furious battle.

Minutes passed, or perhaps hours, Beren had no way to tell. The field around him lay strewn with the bodies of friend and foe. After accounting for his men, Beren looked for Grayden, only to find him standing motionless before what looked to be a cattle stockade. Grayden turned and pointed, and Beren saw instead of cattle, thousands and thousands of gaunt, hopeless faces staring back at him through the fencing.

"What is this?" Beren asked.

A woman stepped forward. "We are slaves of the Igyeum."

"They must be from Akkad and Baktan," Stan muttered.

"Not enough people in both those cities combined to make up this group," Badger countered.

"Some of us are," the woman replied steadily. "But most of us are Igyeum citizens."

"Igyeum citi...?" Beren stared, his mind stuttering over this simple pronouncement. A hundred questions tumbled over each other in his thoughts, but the only one that made its way into the air was, "Why?"

The woman considered the question and then replied, "No, it would not be obvious to you. You are fighting the Ar'Mol to keep your freedom. He has already taken ours."

"We can provide you with food and medical attention," Beren began. "Just..."

"Just let us out of here," she interrupted.

"Of course. Stand back." Beren hefted his sword and when the prisoners had all moved back a ways, he brought it down with a mighty blow on the timbers, splitting them through in a single swing.

Once they were out, Beren sheathed his sword and turned back to the camp, trying to match up what he could see with his memory of the map they had studied. From the far side of the camp, the sounds of battle informed him that the rest of their regiment had encountered far more resistance than they.

"Over there," Grayden said.

"Yes," Beren agreed. "I was just..."

"Sir!" Trinh's voice drifted over to him and Beren could see his sergeant running toward him. His movements were odd as though laboring under a heavy weight.

"Sergeant," Beren greeted him. "Are you injured?"

"I'm fine, sir," Trinh said, pausing to catch his breath. He raised his hands and displayed a glowing yellow cynder. "We found these in the last of the abandoned buildings."

"Our intel must be correct: they're getting ready to bring in more troops and airships," Grayden muttered.

The other men of both platoons gathered round, staring at the gleaming object.

"I've never seen one out in the open," a soldier commented.

Jerky stepped back from the circle, a thoughtful expression on his earnest face. "You know... I've been told those things are dangerous."

"Dangerous, how?" Trinh scoffed.

"My uncle is an artificineer in Telsuma," Jerky replied. "He says he's seen one explode."

Trinh's eyes narrowed. "What made it explode?"

"It got dropped," Jerky said.

Trinh brought his other hand up to stabilize the cynder, suddenly holding it far more carefully. "Oh really? And you're sure he wasn't just sending you up the rigging with a blindfold on?"

"No joke," Jerky insisted. "One of the artificineers lost his leg in the explosion."

"They can't be that fragile," Grayden argued. "We saw an airship crash into the mountains, it didn't explode, and it had to have had at least three of those things on board."

"They aren't fragile," Jerky said.

"But you just said..." Trinh shouted.

Jerky held up his hands. "There's a little more to it. You ever wonder why these things are wrapped in leather for shipment? Or packed in crates full of straw?"

Shep made a face. "I've never given two seconds of thought to how a cynder is transported."

"Most people don't," Jerky agreed. "But that's how they're packed. See, the thing is, you can drop one from a pretty good height and nothing will happen. Maybe even throw it pretty hard against a wall, and it can survive. But if the outside surface gets scratched deep enough, then even a little bump is enough to set them off."

Beren stared at the cynder, mulling over Jerky's words. "Give it here."

Taking the cynder, he drew his knife and carefully scored the circumference with the blade. Then he raised the glowing cylinder and threw it toward the tree-line with all his strength. A massive boom shook the clearing and a shower of dirt and bits of tree flew through the air.

"That'll do it," he muttered. "Tell the others to grab a few more out of that storage shed and then follow me."

"What are we doing, Lieutenant?" Badger asked.

"We're going to finish taking this camp," Beren said. He did not look behind him to see who was following; he knew they all were.

He led them across a large, muddy field and then they wove their way through a line of trees. By the time they reached the other side, Beren's plan had solidified. Here they found a set of more permanent structures surrounding a neatly manicured parade ground with banners at each corner and draping every building. In the center stood a magnificent flag waving above all others, bearing the image of the Ar'Mol. To their left was an open-walled barn with the smells and sounds of animals emanating from beneath the thatched roof. On the far side of this, they could now see the rest of their regiment engaged in furious battle in what looked like a miniature city made of tents.

"Badger and Stan, you saw what I did to the cynder?"

They nodded.

"Take a team each and secure the tower back there." Beren pointed at the high tower they had passed a few seconds before. "We need to get eyes up high to see where everyone is. Take a few of the cynders with you, and if you see an easy target, see what you can do. But only if you can be sure of only hurting the enemy."

Badger grinned. "I can think of a target that might work."

They left to carry out Beren's command.

"Grayden, we need a diversion." Beren turned to his friend.

Grayden gave him a grin. "Way ahead of you. Hand me one of those cynders. Squad Seven, on me! The rest of you, report to Lieutenant Adelfried here until I get back." He nodded firmly at Beren. "My men are yours."

Crouching low, Grayden and fifteen of his men headed into the barn. Beren watched him go, then turned to the rest of the waiting defenders. "We head the other way and wait for Grayden's signal."

"What's the signal?" Cole asked.

"It's Lieutenant Ormond," Dirk joked. "Could be anything, but you know we won't miss it!"

A quiet chuckle rippled through the men and Beren fought to keep his laughter from showing. During training, Grayden and his platoon had earned their reputation for quick and unconventional thinking in the middle of stressful situations. He had no idea what Grayden was about to do, but he knew it would be both effective and impossible to ignore. In the meantime, they needed to get into position to make best use of whatever Grayden had in store.

They made their way to the south-west corner of the command building, where they crouched beneath a window opening. Around the corner, he saw a squad of Skyborne behind an overturned wagon; they were pinned down by arrows raining into their ranks from somewhere overhead, cut off from the rest of their platoon. Frowning, Beren tried to gauge the trajectory of the bolts, when he suddenly realized that they were coming from the roof of the building he and his men were currently hiding behind. He raised himself up and glanced through the window. Nothing moved in the gloom within, but arrows continued to fire rapidly at their soldiers. Probably more than two archers up there then, possibly as many as five, judging by the number of bolts being fired.

Ducking back down, he got the attention of one of his men. "Pass me a cynder," he whispered. "And on my shout, get ready to run through that line of trees on the other side of the road."

Trying not to think too hard about what he was doing or how dangerous it might be, Beren carefully dug the blade of his dagger down the long sides of the cynder, repeating his earlier action. Then he waited.

He did not have to wait long. From the direction of the barn came an echoing roar as if hundreds of leythan had all been terri-fied out of their minds. He heard the snap and crunch of boards being shattered by the force of the great beasts and then he heard the stampeding sound of mighty hooves and he knew that Gray-den's distraction was well underway. Men began shouting, and a leythan raced past, its lumbering body moving faster than seemed possible for such a large creature.

"NOW!" Beren shouted. His men darted away from the building and across the road. As soon as they were clear, he hurled his cynder through the window with all his considerable strength and raced after them.

He felt the sound of the explosion like a heavy drumbeat in

the center of his chest, and then a wave of heat and debris slammed into his back, pushing him through the line of trees. He turned to look behind him and saw a sizable pile of rubble where the wall of the building had once stood. The roof had collapsed and he could see the bodies of the archers who had been perched on top of the building lying in the debris. Even knowing what destruction was coming, Beren felt his eyes widen in stunned disbelief.

Through the trees, he saw the squad the archers had been harrying rise to their feet, their faces pale in the morning light as they stared at the half-fallen command center. More leythan came barreling across the courtyard, swerving around the fallen building. The battleground devolved swiftly into chaos. Beren and both platoons now raced into the fray, joining the rest of the Gray Malkyns.

Around him, he heard shouts and knew that men were fighting and dying, but he kept his focus on the battle before him. He strode toward the enemy, sword at the ready.

The skimmer was not very comfortable with all three of them sitting on it. Clinging to it might have been a more accurate description, Raisa thought in irritation. The tiny craft had been damaged in the fight with the bauman, and it lurched its way over the windswept sand dunes like a faithful leythan lumbering along as best it could with two broken legs. Raisa sighed. At least it lumbered silently.

Raisa's entire body ached and she longed to stop their flight and walk. However, she kept her teeth clamped shut, knowing it was a foolish request, and tried to be grateful for the little skimmer and the speed with which it carried them across the desert. Raisa had more than one reason for keeping her teeth clenched tightly together: the night air was frigid, and the wind bit through her thin clothes with needle sharp teeth. She wished she had managed to squirrel away a cloak, but wishes would not keep her warm. Olin and the Shipwright appeared unaffected by the chill, and Raisa comforted herself with the thought that come noon the next day she would be yearning for the cool of the night once more.

Throughout the night they fled. The fear of looking over their shoulders and seeing pursuit pushed them to keep going, even as weariness also hunted them. The moon had long since set, and the only light now was that of the stars, but a haze of thin, wispy clouds dulled even their brilliance. Raisa was grateful for the cover of night that kept them from being easily spotted, but it made it harder to stay awake. Her thoughts grew sluggish and her eyelids became heavier and heavier. She struggled to keep them open, often jerking herself upright on the uncomfortable seat, but eventually, even the numbing cold could no longer keep her alert. Afraid that if she drifted off to sleep she might fall from her perch, she raised frozen fingers and—reaching past Olin, whose chin kept drooping to his chest—tapped the Shipwright on the shoulder.

"We need to land," she shouted over the wind. "We need rest!"

He nodded in response and angled the skimmer to the ground, settling it to rest in the sand at the base of a large dune. Raisa swung herself stiffly off the seat and nearly collapsed as her muscles protested against being moved and stretched for the first time in hours. Her back hurt and her entire body complained as she pushed herself upright and forced herself to walk around in a small circle, swinging her arms to get the circulation going. It was a bit warmer now that they were out of the wind, but Raisa was still concerned about the temperature.

"We need to get some sleep, but I'm worried about the cold."

"We have a tent and blankets," the Shipwright replied.

"The blankets are not warm enough, not meant for these kinds of temperatures," Raisa pointed out.

"We could start a fire," the Shipwright began, doubtfully.

"With what?" Raisa asked. "And even if we could find something to burn, the fire would instantly become a beacon to anyone searching for us. No, a fire is not the answer."

"What do you propose?" the Shipwright asked. "Should we keep going? Once we get to civilization..."

"It will take us days to cross the desert," Raisa said. "And we can't go that long without sleep."

"I might have a solution," Olin offered. "I'm not supposed to do this in front of outsiders, but it's preferable to freezing to death, and the two of you are my allies." He stepped up to the dune and reached out his hands, immersing them in the sand.

Raisa and the Shipwright watched in astonishment as the sand rippled away from Olin's touch, slowly at first and then faster and faster. Minutes stretched into an hour, and Olin walked slowly forward, the sand moving away from him until he had a good-sized cave hollowed out of the hill. He lowered his hands and swayed slightly. The Shipwright moved forward swiftly, catching hold of the durven's shoulders and steadying him.

"All right?" the Shipwright asked.

Olin nodded, perspiration glinting faintly in large droplets on his small face. "Yes," he rasped. "I'm used to working with a group, and never so big a project all at once. But sand is easier to work with than other earth." Raisa brought him a waterskin and he took several long draughts before he handed it back. "Thank you," he said, his voice weary.

"How did you do that?" Raisa asked, touching the side of the cavern, marveling at how firmly the sand was now packed.

Olin shrugged. "All my people can do it. Like I said, we usually conserve our strength and work more slowly." He swayed again, his eyes closing. "I might have overdone it a bit..."

"We need to get him lying down," the Shipwright said.

Raisa hurried to the skimmer and retrieved a blanket. She returned and the Shipwright held up a finger to his lips. Olin let out a gentle snore and Raisa grinned back as they worked together to ease their companion into the cave and tucked the blanket tightly around him.

"Help me push the skimmer inside the entrance?" the Ship-wright asked. "It wouldn't do to leave it out there like a flag for anyone to notice."

It only took a few minutes for them to move the skimmer inside and set up the rest of their meager camp. It was warmer inside the sand cave, and Raisa wrapped her blanket around her shoulders, sitting down with her back to one wall. Weariness overwhelmed her and yet she found herself reluctant to sleep.

"Want to take a walk?" the Shipwright asked. "Just to check behind us for any sign of pursuit?"

Raisa rose to her feet, feeling a deep sense of gratitude. "Yes, please."

They left the cave and climbed up the sand dune. Nothing stirred in the blackness. Raisa strained her eyes, scanning the darkness for several minutes. Nothing appeared. No silhouettes of armored airships or walking trees threatened their escape.

"Any signs of pursuit?" the Shipwright asked.

"None that I can see," Raisa replied.

"Good," the Shipwright said.

They stood together for a moment as more clouds rolled in, cloaking the sky. Raisa wrapped her arms around herself, shivering.

"Let's get back inside," the Shipwright said.

Trying to keep her teeth from chattering, Raisa nodded and they descended the dune and ducked back into the cavern. Raisa sank to the ground and pulled her blanket up around her chin.

"I think we should take turns keeping watch," the Shipwright said.

"That's a good idea," Raisa replied wearily. She began to uncurl from her spot, but a hand on her shoulder stopped her.

"I'm fairly alert still, and you need to get warm," the Shipwright said, his voice kind. "I'll take the first watch."

Fighting against the weights that seemed to have attached themselves to her eyelids, Raisa nodded. "Wake me at four bells."

The Shipwright chuckled as he pulled an elaborate chronometer from his pocket and held it close to his face. The hands on the device gleamed an eerie sort of green. "We're not aboard a ship, you know. You could just say in three hours." He paused. "How do you know what time it is, anyway?"

Raisa gave a low laugh. "Just a knack I've always had. I can't explain it, but it comes in handy when you're a pirate."

"I'll bet. Three hours it is, then."

———

AT FIRST, Raisa was not sure exactly what had awakened her. She and the others had taken turns keeping watch throughout the night and into the next day, having decided that they needed some extra rest and that it would be safer to travel by night. Outside the cave, the sun was setting; the sky was awash with gold and purple. She stood and stretched, rolling her neck. Sleeping on sand might seem like a good idea, but the hard lumps and mounds did not yield as much as one might assume.

Only after she had cleared her body and mind of the sleep that clung to her did Raisa notice the music. The light notes rang with familiarity in her mind and she glanced about, suddenly fearful. She had only ever heard that music in Lorcan's presence. Had he found them already? But there had been no shout of warning from outside—surely if Lorcan were near the others would have alerted her.

A clinking sound at the cavern's entrance drew her attention and she crawled forward to find the Shipwright lying beneath the skimmer, tinkering with the engine. Raisa frowned and glanced toward the cave's entrance, where Olin sat guard. She crawled over to him.

"Morning," she said.

He nodded, his eyes on the horizon.

"Olin, now that we're away..." Raisa began, then paused. She had no right to pry into things he might want to keep private.

He turned his strange eyes on her and she felt her face growing warm under his scrutiny. She looked down at the sand. "Never mind," she muttered.

"You can ask your question," he said simply.

Raisa found she couldn't meet his gaze. She made a helpless gesture at the cavern Olin had created for them the night before, then let her hands fall into her lap.

"You wish to know more about my people and what Lorcan did?" he asked.

"Yes," Raisa replied softly. "I can't help but be curious."

"It is similar to yours," Olin said, his voice soft. "With you, he melded human and tree. With the durven, he attempted to meld humans with leythan. All the adults he tried the experiment on died, but the children... they survived, though that knowledge was hidden from Lorcan. My parents were two of those children; I am of the second generation and was born durven. We gained the leythan abilities to see in the dark, our skin is tougher and we withstand extreme temperatures better than most humans, and we gained a power to work with earth that none of us really understands. My people have remained hidden underground in Malei for decades, but we tried to help Captain Marik free you. That was when I got captured."

Raisa felt a twinge of guilt at that. The durven had been brought to Lorcan's attention because of her. "I'm sorry," she whispered.

Olin shrugged. "I was careless."

The music with no discernible origin surged again, interrupting their conversation, and Raisa scanned the area, searching for the source.

"Almost time to get moving again," Olin commented.

"Have you seen anything moving out there?" Raisa asked, wondering if he could also hear the phantom music.

Olin shook his head. "All's quiet."

Raisa frowned, puzzled. The faint music still rang in her ears, a warning that Lorcan was nearby. "I'm going up the dune to get a better look," she said. "Tell the Shipwright to be ready to go as soon as I get back."

Without waiting for an answer, Raisa climbed up the dune, her hands and feet digging into the sun-warmed sand. Once she reached the top she stared about in every direction, but no airship could be seen in the cloudless sky, and no sign of troops appeared on the ground. And yet the eerie music rang insistently inside her skull. Frustrated, she slid back down the dune to join her companions.

"Anything?" Olin asked.

Raisa shook her head. From where he lay beneath the skimmer, she could hear the Shipwright humming faintly, a slightly repetitious few bars of a vaguely familiar song. She scooted over to him and ducked down to ask if he had noticed anything out of the ordinary... and froze.

In one hand, the Shipwright held a small, round gem that gleamed with a yellow-orange light, the same color as the cynders she had changed so many times in the Valdeun Hawk. The music swelled to a crescendo in her mind; recognition mingled with fury and panic and she stumbled backwards, away from the skimmer.

"Raisa?" Olin's voice seemed to be coming from a long way off. "What's wrong?"

She couldn't answer. She could only back away, her head shaking in a quiet, stunned denial. The music in her mind abruptly stopped as the Shipwright slid himself out from under the skimmer and sat up.

"Got it," the Shipwright said, wiping his hands on his pants and rising. There were smudges of grease on his face and fingers, and no sign of the golden orb. For a moment, Raisa wondered if she had imagined the whole thing. The Shipwright glanced over at her. "Ah, you're awake, goo... Raisa? What's wrong?"

"Nothing." She gave a little jerk of her head toward the horizon. "Time to go."

The Shipwright stared at her for a long moment, and then his shoulders slumped. He reached inside his pocket and drew out the gleaming jewel. "You saw this."

Raisa's fingers tightened around the hilt of her dagger and she glanced down, surprised to find it in her hand. She didn't remember drawing it.

"You don't have to be afraid of me, Raisa," the Shipwright said.

"How can you say that?" Raisa demanded.

"Have I done anything to make you doubt me?"

"Raisa." Olin's calm voice came from behind her. "He helped us escape."

"Who are you?" Raisa demanded, ignoring Olin.

"I told you. I am the Shipwright," he replied. Sorrow filled his eyes as he gazed at her over the orb.

"That tells me nothing. You say it like I should understand, but I don't."

"I design airships. That's why they call me the Shipwright. Not the first ones, of course, those belong to my predecessor. I like to think I've made some improvements on his creations, though." He straightened up a little, his voice filling with professional pride.

"Are you like Lorcan, then?"

"No!" He shook his head emphatically. "I am nothing like that madman. I'll tell you a little something I learned about him, though. Did you know that he started out by testing his experiments on himself? He sought to give himself eternal life, instead he drove himself mad. The stories about that one..." The Shipwright shuddered. "You don't want to know. There's just enough of his original genius left that the Ar'Molon tolerates him, which should tell you something, as Lord Uun is not known for his patience, and he's put up with Lorcan for nearly a hundred years now."

"He found the key to eternal life then?" Raisa asked, putting as much sneering disbelief into her tone as she could.

"No." The Shipwright shrugged. "Not eternal life. He has managed to extend his lifespan, but at what cost?"

"And you are different how?"

"I've only been working for the Ar'Molon for fifteen years."

"Only." Raisa snorted.

"It's a far cry from a hundred!"

Raisa shrugged.

"I didn't really understand what I was signing up for. I was young, ambitious, and when someone as powerful as the

Ar'Molon offers you a job, you don't exactly bite your thumb at it. At first, it was normal things, working on schematics, solving equations, that sort of thing. But then one day, Uun brought me the orb." The Shipwright closed his fingers over it, but light still spilled out between the gaps. "My predecessor, the man who designed the first airships, had died in his sleep, and Uun wanted to see if I had the ability to use his orb. I have to admit, it was exciting, learning to use its powers. I had a strong affinity for it." He licked his lips. "I didn't see the truth of what I was doing until it was far too late. I thought I was helping the world, building safer, more efficient engines for the airships. Please believe me when I tell you I've been trapped every bit as much as you. When the Ar'Molon told me about you, I hoped to be included in the voyage to see your abilities firsthand, but when I first saw you, I despaired. It seemed Lorcan had finally done all that he promised —he had created the perfect soldier, not just in body, but in mind, as well. I believed he controlled you. But then Uun stood before you; I saw the hatred in your eyes, I saw the way your fingers twitched, I saw everything, and I knew! I knew because I recognized everything you were feeling, it was like looking into a reflection of my soul. I knew they hadn't broken you as much as they thought. You were clever, letting them believe they'd won. Letting them think they had the upper hand, and all the while plotting your escape, your revenge. I can't tell you how much hope that brought me, seeing your resistance. Of course, Uun couldn't see it; his arrogance often keeps him from noticing how he is truly regarded."

Raisa's heartbeat calmed slightly at his words.

"I believe him," Olin said simply. "Besides, he showed me the orb before he started working on the skimmer."

Raisa lowered her dagger reluctantly, then slid it back into the sheath at her belt.

The Shipwright let out a soft breath and returned the orb to his pocket. Then he stuck out his hand. "Davin."

Raisa glanced up, startled. "What?"

"I lied when I said I didn't remember. Davin was my name before I became Uun's shipwright. I would like to be that man again."

Olin stepped forward first, shaking Davin's hand. "Pleased to meet you, Davin." The durven nodded. "It is a good name."

"Thank you." The Shipwright—now Davin—looked at Raisa questioningly.

She gave a stiff nod, trying to move past the unpleasant shock of seeing him with an orb. Dalmir had an orb. Clearly, the power within the gems could be used for good as well as evil. She reminded herself that Davin had risked everything to free her and Olin from the Weald.

Davin gestured at the skimmer. "Shall we? The sun is down and it is best if we do not linger."

"I'm ready to be quit of this desert," Olin announced, clumping across the sand and boarding the skimmer. "Besides, we need food and water, lots of water with the way that one drinks." He jerked a thumb at Raisa.

She grimaced. She had been conserving water as best she could, but her mouth and throat remained in a state of permanent discomfort and dryness. Even now, her lips cracked painfully as soon as she moved them. At the mention of water, the thirst that had been her constant companion since Lorcan's experiment threatened to overwhelm her, but she determined to say nothing. This weakness could be overcome, just like any other. Raisa hopped on the back of the skimmer, and the Shipwright—Davin —climbed into his spot at the strange contraption that served as the steering mechanism. He gripped the long bar and used his foot to kick a lever forward. With a lurch, the skimmer leaped into the sky in eerie silence. Raisa could not help but feel a glimmer of awe. Even the Hawk's engines hummed a little. This sort of silence was a pirate's dream.

32

Roald stretched first his fingers, then his arms. He rolled his shoulders a few times and turned his face experimentally, the back of his head rubbing against the hard board upon which he lay. The day had passed in a blur of excruciating pain, but now he emerged from the haze and for the first time since the madman's process had begun, he did not hurt. His muscles were weak, and his mouth and throat were parched, but the pain was gone.

"Water," he croaked.

He sensed the approach of someone, and then the Ar'Molon's face came into view above him. "How are you feeling?" There was no concern in the question, just calculated curiosity.

"Thirsty," Roald whispered. "And weak."

"The thirst appears to be an ongoing side-effect of the transformation," Uun informed him. "The weakness should fade in a few hours. Can you sit up yet?"

Roald struggled to push himself up off the hard bed, managing to get himself upright without assistance. Uun then handed him a small cup of water. Roald gulped it down and looked hopefully at his master, but Uun shook his head.

"Lorcan says too much water at first is not optimal."

Roald wilted, lowering himself back down. His body ached for more water, and he wished he had not drunk what he had been given so swiftly. Then a thought occurred to him. "My men? How are they faring?"

"They appear to be adjusting as well as you," Uun replied. "Though most of them are still unconscious, since you insisted on being first. Really, Roald." He shook his head with a disapproving frown on his lips. "Was that a truly necessary risk?"

"It was," Roald replied, his voice even. "I could not ask my men to undergo the process unless I was willing to go first."

"Such loyalty is to be commended. Even if it was foolish." Uun's tone was dry.

"What some call foolish, others might call heroic." Roald was aghast at his rash words. Before, he would never have dared contradict the Ar'Molon so openly. But now he felt different. Powerful. He knew that the madman's experiment would alter his body, giving him the strength of the trees, as well as other benefits such as speed and endurance, but had it also altered the very essence of who he was? He wondered what punishment would befall him for speaking so bluntly. He shivered, the coldness of the air suddenly filled with menace and warning.

Uun's soft chuckle filled his ears, chilling him. "It is good to see you have regained some of your spark. A good tool can be difficult to replace."

"What about Two-Four-Seven?" Roald asked, trying to clear the fog that clung to his mind. "Has she been found?"

Uun's smile turned fierce. "Not yet."

"I wish you had let us hunt her down."

"Perhaps it was short-sighted on my part to decline your offer," Uun replied. "But you have a much more important mission to complete: your primary mission. The breakthrough that Lorcan made with Two-Four-Seven is the key we have been searching for. You and your men are too important to the cause to send you out on such a paltry errand. Do not worry, she will not get far. There is nowhere for her to go. The desert is assurance enough that we will either soon catch up to her, or we will find her remains once she runs out of food and water. She cannot hope to cross the Plains on foot."

"What if she is not on foot?" Roald asked, struggling to prop himself up on one elbow. He looked around for a blanket. Why was it so cold?

Uun stared at him. "What are you implying?"

"If she stole an airship…"

"All of our airships are accounted for. No, she must be on foot. Lorcan says that one of his generals took damage, but the bauman could not describe what happened." Uun's lip curled in disgust. "Useless creatures."

Roald nodded. "Then she will not get far."

"Rest now. I will inform Lorcan that his first patient is recovering well."

Uun departed, leaving Roald alone with his thoughts. He tried to obey his master's order, he even closed his eyes and sought sleep, but his mind rebelled at the idea of returning to unconsciousness so soon upon waking. A tingling sensation flowed down his arms and legs, as though the blood in his veins had been dammed up while he slept and now, suddenly, the flow was released to circulate through his body once more. Energized, he pushed himself up. The motion came with far less effort this time. Cautiously, he swung his legs off the table. Keeping his hands on the edge of the table, Roald lowered himself to the floor and stood. He swayed a little, his head spinning with the transition, but after a moment, the dizziness faded and he stood solidly on his own two feet. He took a tentative step, and then another, crossing the room. At the door, he paused. He had been instructed to rest. Curiosity and restlessness consumed him, and he pushed the door open, stepping out into bright daylight. He blinked as he came out of the temporary building that had been assembled for Lorcan's needs. His bare feet sank into the warm sand, and the sun caressed his head and shoulders, chasing away the strange coldness that gripped him.

A soldier passed by, caught sight of him, paused, and then hurried on. Roald frowned. Stumbling a little, he wound his way to the tent that had been provided for him. Once inside, he fumbled through his things for the mirror he kept on hand in case he needed to send signals to his crew still aboard his airship and studied himself in its reflective surface. The horror of looking into a mirror and barely recognizing himself consumed him and the nausea of standing for the first time returned with a force he was unprepared to combat. The edges of his vision grew dark and the tent spun out of control around him.

"Roald?" Uun's voice barked outside his tent.

With trembling hands, Roald put the mirror down. Closing his eyes, he took a deep breath, then he rose and exited his tent.

"Yes, Ar'Molon Uun?" he asked. He tried to keep his voice steady, but as he stood before his master, he encountered another shock, as he suddenly realized that he was looking down at the man who had always been taller than him.

"I ordered you to rest." Uun frowned up at him. "One of the soldiers saw you up and around and came directly to me, he said you did not look well, and I have to agree."

"Sir." Roald swallowed. "Forgive me. After you left, I felt restless and I thought I was up for a short walk. I should have listened to you. It appears I have overtaxed myself. I would like to lie down, but I do not wish to go back to that room." He barely contained a shudder. "May I stay in my own tent? It is more comfortable than that board."

Uun scowled. "It is easier for Lorcan to observe your recovery if you stay in his laboratory."

"I will return there when I wake," Roald said quickly.

"Very well. But only for such a loyal servant would I make this concession. Make sure you report back to the laboratory as soon as you are rested."

"Yes, sir."

Uun turned to leave. Roald knew he should let him go, should stay quiet, but once again, he could not contain the words that tumbled out of his mouth. They sprang to his lips with an intensity and desperation that frightened him.

"Sir? What am I?"

Uun glanced over his shoulder, a strange light in his eyes. "You are whatever I wish you to be."

Roald swallowed again, the scant saliva in his mouth burning like sandpaper on the inside of his throat. The need for water consumed him, but he knew better than to go down to the lake. To do so would be seen as defiance and disloyalty, and he had seen firsthand the merciless way in which those attributes were punished. Instead, he retreated into his tent and lay on his blanket. The welcome heat of the sun beat down on his tent, warming him through. He worked his shoulders into the ground, trying to rearrange the sand into a more pleasing shape beneath him, to no avail. Eventually, thirst and weariness overpowered him and his eyes fluttered shut.

———

"ROALD!" Uun's furious voice reverberated throughout the laboratory as he burst through the flimsy door, slamming it open.

"Yes, my lord?" Roald said, standing at attention and wondering what had happened that could make his master lose control of his so carefully kept emotions. He had woken from his rest feeling almost back to his normal energy levels and had reported to Lorcan straightaway. Roald did not like being the subject of the madman's scrutiny, but he endured it, knowing that the trials he was currently undergoing were nothing more than a means to an end: the power to complete the mission he and his crew had been assigned. So many others had failed to bring the Ar'Molon his lost orb—the prize he sought so fervently—but Roald had promised himself that he would be the one to find the precious object and deliver it to his master, no matter what the cost.

"It turns out I need you and your crew to hunt down the prisoners, after all. Are you up to the task?" Uun glared at Lorcan. "Are they ready?"

Lorcan's head listed to one side. "Another day of rest would be better, especially for the others. This one... this one could be ready."

"I need them all ready now." Uun's face contorted with rage.

"Perhaps... can you give me an hour?" Lorcan wheedled.

"You have thirty minutes." Uun spun on his heel.

"My lord," Roald began. Uun paused, glancing at him over his shoulder. "Why the sudden urgency for my crew?"

Uun's face darkened. "I have just discovered that our escaped prisoner had help. Her disappearance now goes beyond mere inconvenience. There is treachery at work," he snarled. "The Shipwright has disappeared, along with another prisoner Lorcan had in his custody. I can only assume my Shipwright helped both of them get away, though to what end, I do not understand."

Roald's head throbbed with anger at the idea of such blatant disloyalty. He gave a solemn nod. "My men and I will bring them back, my lord."

"It turns out your hunch may have been correct."

"My lord?" Roald blinked, trying to remember what his hunch had been.

"They may not be on foot. It seems that one of the sentries saw the Shipwright riding a tiny airship earlier on the day of escape. He told me he was testing a new weapon in the desert, which is why I did not question his absence. But now it grows obvious that I have been deceived!" Spittle flew out of Uun's mouth and his eyes burned. "I must return to Melar. When you find them, bring them to me there."

"Did he take his orb?" Roald asked.

"Yes," Uun snarled.

Roald smiled. "How fortuitous."

Uun narrowed his eyes at him questioningly, and Roald basked in the sweet taste of triumph hovering above his head, tantalizingly close—he could taste the succulent juice already—all he had to do was reach out and take it.

"This will be an excellent test for my men," he explained. "To see if the transformation was worth the pain. If we can sense his orb, we should be able to track the traitor with ease and bring him back. Do you want him alive or dead?"

"Alive," Uun spat, "so that I can rip him limb from limb."

33

The wind rushed past Marik's face and he couldn't help but laugh at the sheer freedom and speed of flying. He swung from the netting on the side of the Valdeun Hawk's hull, his arm through a rope, and his safety line securely attached to his harness. He leaned away from the hull, his free arm outstretched, glorying in the thrill of an endeavor that never grew old. The wing above him sheltered him from the blazing sun overhead.

"Cap'n? You see anything?" Oleck called from above.

Marik sobered and returned to scanning the ground for signs of encampments below. Nothing marred the surface of the desert; the dunes rolled gently in uninterrupted, rigid waves. Only the wind moved across that barren expanse.

"Not yet!" he hollered back up to his first mate.

Oleck's head disappeared from sight and Marik continued to scan the ground. It had taken a lot of arguing to decide exactly how high they should fly. Marik had argued that being too high would mean they might more easily miss signs of where Raisa was being kept prisoner, but Oleck and Shaesta had reminded him that if they flew too low, they would be more easily spotted. His riding in the netting was the compromise. He could see better if he didn't have to crane over the side, and the crow's nest only took him farther from the thing he needed to be able to see.

Movement stirred at the periphery of his vision. A line of small, dark specks crawled across the sand. Marik let go of the netting while simultaneously using his feet to push himself away from the hull and forward, out from under the wing. For one moment of mingled terror and thrill he hung suspended in the air, then the safety line caught on the ingenious mechanism he had asked Wynn to create and began to pull him up. In a series of jumps, Marik belayed up the side of the ship, his final push flinging him into the air above the railing. He landed on the deck with a hearty thump and grinned as he unclipped his safety line.

"Captain?" Shaesta stood at the wheel.

"Movement to port," Marik said. "Looks like a caravan."

"Should we investigate?" Shaesta asked.

"Yes. I don't think it's the Igyeum, but if we're lucky enough to have found one of the bardani tribes then they might be able to give us better information about where to continue our search."

Shaesta nodded and turned the wheel, veering in the direction Marik indicated. A few moments later, they had descended enough that Marik could make out the individuals within the caravan. He waved a blue flag over the side, indicating a desire for a friendly exchange of information or goods. The caravan halted and tiny figures rushed about. Eventually, a blue flag was waved in return.

Shaesta lowered the airship until it hung close enough to the ground that Marik could descend the rope ladder lowered over the side. Dalmir followed, while the others stayed aboard the airship, not wanting to overwhelm the caravan.

Marik's boots hit the ground. A middle-aged woman approached, the blue flag in one hand, a rod in the other. Her long, white tunic rippled around her as she moved across the sand to stand before Marik, and the tails of the green-and-white wrap upon her head were pulled aside in a symbol of friendship so that Marik could see her face and know her dealings were honest.

Wisps of the bardani's signature bright red hair escaped her headdress and curled around her pale, freckled face.

"Blessing upon your feet," the woman greeted them.

Marik covered one fist with his other hand and brought them to his lips. "And upon your head may the sun's rays be pleasant."

The woman smiled, wrinkles forming at the corners of her hazel eyes. "You have spoken with the bardani before."

"I have traded with your people a time or two," Marik replied.

"For knowledge or goods?"

"Knowledge."

"I see." The woman's eyes narrowed and she glanced up at the airship hovering above them. "Knowledge is precious. It often comes at a high price."

"The knowledge we seek is of a nature that may benefit you to share with us, should you have what we need."

"We do not trade in 'may' and 'perhaps,'" the woman replied. "My people need food, water, clothes, and shelter from the heat of the sun and the chill of the night winds."

"We have a barrel of water we can spare, and rather a lot of good quality leather," Marik said wryly.

The woman's eyes widened at this revelation, a response Marik was sure she had not meant to allow him to see. She covered her reaction swiftly. "Leather might be of interest to some," she said, her voice demure. She beckoned with one hand. "Come, join me in the tents and we shall see if any among us has the knowledge you seek."

They followed the woman to a large tent that the other members of the caravan had assembled while they spoke. Inside, a low table was set with fruit and goblets filled with a dark liquid. Scattered about the table were large pillows decorated with golden braids and tassels.

"Welcome, travelers and traders," the woman said, picking up two goblets and offering one to Marik. He took the presented goblet and stretched it forward, looping arms with the woman.

"I am called Marik," he said. "And by this sign I pledge to be honest in my dealings with you and yours."

"And I am called Lora," she replied. "By this sign I pledge the same."

Together, arms looped, they drank, each from their own goblet. The liquid was rich and cool; it smelled of cloves and tasted of honey and a fruit Marik was not certain he was familiar with.

"Now." Lora unhooked her arm from Marik's and gestured to the pillows scattered around the short table. "Please, my guests, sit. Tell me, what is it you wish to know?"

Marik seated himself on the ground, grabbing a large pillow and resting an elbow on it. Dalmir followed suit.

"This may sound a bit strange," Marik confessed, "but we have heard rumors of a garrison of soldiers here in the Plains. We are searching for any signs of it that we can find. Anything you might be able to tell us would be helpful. Have you or your people seen an increase in airship travel in this area, or have there been any rumors of such a gathering?"

Lora thought quietly for a few minutes. When she again met Marik's gaze, her eyes were troubled.

"There have indeed been more airships passing by overhead," she admitted. "As for a garrison... I have not heard those rumors. It does not make sense to try to station large numbers of men in the wilderness. There is not food and water for entire regiments. What would they live on? Where would they hide from the sun? The soldiers do not know the Plains as we do; they would not survive." She made a dismissive gesture. "I cannot trade for such information that you must surely already know."

Marik leaned forward, pushing himself up higher on his arm. "I was under the impression that it is not usual for a woman to lead a caravan."

Lora's expression settled into a frown. "It is not usual, but neither is it against our custom. When unusual need arises, unusual measures must be taken."

Marik nodded. "I also noticed that most of your caravan is made up of women. Can you tell me what strange circumstances have caused this unusual need?"

"As I have told you, the rumors about increased activity by the Igyeum military in this area are true. This has also resulted in many of our men being forced into the ranks recently. The Igyeum always takes a few of our men each year, but this time was much different. They took all who were over fifteen summers. My husband and son were among those who were taken from us. My husband was the caravan leader, so I was left alone to be strong for our people." Her mouth twisted in an angry snarl that instantly smoothed. "We have met other tribes in the past several lunats who tell the same tale."

"I am sorry," Marik replied. "I did not mean to open a raw wound. I wonder if you could tell me, and this is going to sound very strange, but have you or your people heard any rumors about a new forest anywhere in the Plains?"

Lora's head snapped up. "What did you say?"

Marik glanced down at his goblet, trailing a finger around its rim. "A new forest," he repeated, knowing how mad it sounded, even to his own ears. "Trees where there didn't used to be any, that sort of thing?"

The silence stretched out between them until Marik glanced up. Lora's face had gone even paler, and the hand holding the goblet trembled slightly.

"Lora?" he prompted.

She shook her head and raised her chin imperiously. Her eyes flashed. Her voice rang out loudly within the tent. "I do not know how you have heard this wild tale, but I can assure you, it is false! Now, if you have nothing of value with which to trade other than rumors and fairy stories, I must ask you to leave. My people must move on while the air is still cool and there is yet light." The woman rose, drawing herself to her full height and staring down at them with imperious wrath.

Marik rose and pressed a hand against his fist once more,

bowing his head over them politely. "Forgive us for upsetting you," he said. "We shall send down the barrel of water and three hides as compensation for the precious time we inadvertently caused you to waste. Our humblest apologies."

He backed out of the tent and then turned and strode toward the Hawk. Dalmir followed after him. He could feel the older man's mystified stare on the back of his neck, but he could not afford to stop and explain now. He had traded with the bardani before, and this kind of response could only mean one thing. He reached the rope ladder and hauled himself up, hand over foot. When he got to the deck, he barked orders at Oleck and Mouse to help him get the promised goods into the net so they could lower it over the side. As they did so, Dalmir finished climbing the ladder and pulled himself over the railing.

"That was disappointing," Dalmir muttered.

"Why?" Mouse asked.

"Their leader knows something but chased us away without answering our questions."

"Then why is Cap'n so chipper?" Mouse asked. "And why's he trading like he got exactly what he wanted?"

Dalmir frowned and Marik met his gaze with a grin, but did not stop what he was doing. Together, he and Oleck hoisted the barrel and leather over the side and eased them to the ground. Below, Lora herself walked up to the net as her people removed the goods and hauled them away. The woman stood and watched, one hand resting idly on the rope attached to the net. When the trade was complete, Lora glanced up. Her eyes met Marik's. She gave a single, slow, exaggerated nod, and then she walked away.

Marik grinned as Oleck raised the now-empty net back to the deck of the airship.

"You seem rather cheerful for a man who just got told he was chasing a mirage," Dalmir commented.

Marik laid a finger along the side of his nose. "Oleck, check the net and make sure it's not tangled," was all he said.

Oleck shot him a strange look, but began carefully bundling

up the net. Before he had taken up half of it, he stopped with an exclamation of surprise.

"What's this?"

Marik held out his hand expectantly.

"She sent up a note, Cap'n." Oleck shook his head with a wry chuckle. "You knew this was coming, didn't you?"

"She couldn't say anything where her people might hear," Marik replied. He unfolded the piece of paper and smoothed it between his hands. The note was short:

The uncanny forest you seek lies a hundred miles south-east from here. I do not know what your business is, but your ship looks like the one they call the Hawk. Should you see among the ranks of Igyeum soldiers a man of medium build and dark hair with a scarred cheek... I will not ask you to help him escape, but if you have the ability, please tell him that his Lora waits anxiously for his return. He will help you if he can.

Marik read the note aloud. When he finished, he nodded at Mouse. "Tell Shaesta we have our heading."

The boy scampered off to obey.

"How did you know she would send a message?" Dalmir asked.

"It's not something I can explain," Marik said. "It's just a sort of knack you acquire after a life spent swindling people: you recognize it when you're on the receiving end."

"Why couldn't she just tell us?" Dalmir asked. "Why a hidden note?"

Marik shrugged. "That I don't know. The Igyeum usually leaves the bardani alone—mostly because they're too difficult to go hunting for in the desert. Maybe she's worried about her position as leader? Or maybe there is some dissension among the tribe? She mentioned other tribes, as well; perhaps she fears repercussions for acting against the Igyeum in any way. I don't know. But I don't think we could get a clearer sign that the Ar'Mol is preparing to go to war in earnest."

"Then all the more reason to find the orb quickly," Dalmir said.

"And to free Raisa," Oleck added.

"Right on both counts," Marik nodded. "South-east it is, with all due speed."

———

"TREES!" The shout went up across the Hawk several hours later as a greenish blur appeared on the distant horizon. At the sound of the call, Marik—taking his turn at the wheel—pulled the lift lever and sent the airship into a steep climb into the relative safety of the clouds. Thankfully, the clouds were fairly thick, and the ground was swiftly obscured from view.

"What's the plan, Cap'n?" Mouse inquired, climbing the ladder and poking his head up over the upper deck. His eyes were bright with excitement. "We gonna rescue Raisa tonight?"

"I hope so, Mouse," Marik replied. "But first we have to find a safe place to put down, and then we need to do some scouting and see if we can find out where they are keeping her."

"I can help scout," Mouse said, his voice eager.

"I know you can. But I'm not sure you're the right one to send."

"Why not? I've scouted for you dozens of times. Have I ever been caught?"

Marik shook his head. "No, but..."

Mouse cut him off. "I'm your best scouter. You've said so yourself."

"I'm not sure 'scouter' is a word," Shaesta murmured. The boy shot her an irritated glare.

"Yes, Mouse, but..." Marik tried to interrupt, but the boy kept talking.

"Raisa is my friend, too. She's part of the crew. I gotta do my part to help bring her home. I just got to. I can get in and out without being seen, I promise! You know I move quieter than anyone else, you know I can get into places too small for anyone else. And I'm a good listener. I'll get all kinds of information nobody else would be able to get. Please, Cap'n! Please let me do this!"

"Mouse!" Marik barked, infusing his voice with a hint of the irritation he felt. "I didn't say no, understand? But this is going to be the most dangerous mission we've ever undertaken. More dangerous than stealing the caravan of cynders, more dangerous than that heist on the De'Anan's vault, more difficult than the Stone Barrel Caper, and even more dangerous than rescuing Beren and Wynn from the Niveyan stronghold last year. We have to think about this very carefully and plan it out well. You make some excellent points in your favor, and I will take them into consideration. But you are also going to have to accept whatever my final decision is, understand?"

Mouse's head sank until only his eyes and forehead were visible above the top of the ladder. "Yes, Cap'n."

"Good. Now get back to your duty station," Marik barked. "We have a lot of work to do, and not much time to do it in. We need to find a safe place to descend by nightfall so that some of us can disembark for the scouting mission, and if you don't return to your duties now, your name definitely won't be in consideration for that mission."

"Yes, sir." Mouse retreated down the ladder.

"You're not really going to let him scout, are you?" Shaesta asked, taking over the wheel and giving Marik a worried look.

Marik frowned and stared into the mist. Despite his sharp words to the boy, everything Mouse had said was true. The lad did have a knack for sneaking into places and back out without anyone being the wiser for it. But he hated the idea of sending the youth into hazardous territory without knowing the lay of the land first. They still had no idea how many enemies were assembled in the oasis, or what kinds of weapons they were up against.

For all they knew, every tree in the forest could be one of Lorcan's terrible creations, ready to fight on behalf of their insane master. No, he did not like the prospect of navigating blindly into that ominous wood, but he did not see that there was any other choice.

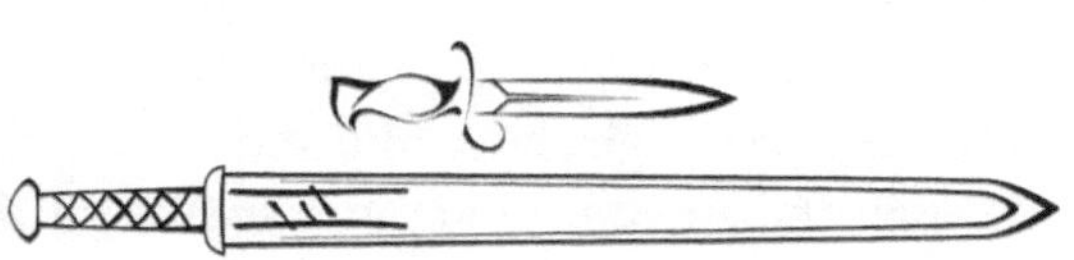

34

Three hundred leythan could spread a fair amount of destruction rather swiftly. The enormous beasts pounded their way through the camp, barely stopping or swerving for anything in their path, be they man, tent, or tree. Grayden's eyes lighted on the malkyn pen next. He shimmied through the gate and looked around. The sleek creatures regarded him with noble stares and he picked out the one he wanted. The sable-furred cat's ear twitched, but otherwise did not move a muscle as Grayden approached; a well-trained beast, it watched him solemnly as he released its tethers and climbed onto its back. Grayden squeezed his legs as he would have had he been riding a horse, and the creature shot forward. In a single, fluid bound, it had cleared the six-foot fence surrounding the pen, and now it raced toward the battle without hesitation. He sliced through the enemy soldiers like an airship cutting through the clouds. Around him, arrows poured down from all sides, but nothing could touch him. The malkyn beneath him serpentined across the field, its great claws lashing out at any of the soldiers who tried to stop him.

A noise like thunder roared to one side and the enormous cat Grayden was riding veered away from a shower of debris with a startled yowling scream. Together, they raced silently through the battle. Grayden's sword flashed from one side to the other, taking down enemy soldiers before they even saw him coming.

A tree exploded at the far northern edge of the battlefield, and the malkyn spooked. It reared up on its hind legs, clawing the air in frantic terror. The creature fell backwards, twisting at the last second and landing on its feet, leaving Grayden sitting on the ground. He shook his head, stunned, wondering where that blast had come from. His thoughts churned slowly. The squad Beren had sent must have reached the top of the tower. He let his eyes travel up to the large deck high above him and saw another projectile hurtle through the air to explode in a shower of dirt, rocks, and grass.

Despite being taken by surprise and outnumbered nearly two-to-one, the Igyeum soldiers rallied around their leaders and the battle raged on. They fought like rabid wylfen. They were a grim, organized force and they handled the strange tactics of the Skyborne regiment with impassive resistance. The defenders had to battle hard for every inch of ground.

The day wore itself out before the fighting finally ended. Strange shadows cast themselves across the clearing and the sun began to sink low in the sky as Grayden felled his current opponent and looked around to find himself alone in the field. The sounds of fighting had ceased. No enemy soldiers could be seen. Wearily, he sank to his knees in the churned mud and let out a deep sigh.

It was there that Beren found him.

Grayden looked up at the touch on his shoulder. "Is it over?"

Beren nodded. "Captain Argond is looking for you."

Grayden pushed himself to his feet and followed his friend. The other defenders were rounding up the frightened animals and creating a semblance of order in the camp that was now theirs.

"Grayden!" Captain Argond came striding over to meet them.

"Sir?" Grayden could barely manage the single word. His whole body ached with weariness.

Argond did not speak, he merely gave a jerk of his head, indicating that Grayden should follow him. Mystified, he forced his legs to obey.

Moments later, he found himself in the still-standing command building. Major Semiv and other officers stood around a large table in the center of the room covered with maps.

Semiv spoke. "Gentlemen, we have completed the first part of our mission. I am proud of each of you and your men. I don't have the final reports, but the camp is ours, though there were many casualties." He looked around. "Who was it pulled that stunt freeing the leythan?"

Grayden felt his stomach lurch, but his father had always taught him to own up to his mistakes, so he stepped forward. "That was me, sir."

"Nice bit of work, young man," Semiv said. "Quick thinking."

Relieved, Grayden allowed himself a modest shrug. "It seemed like an efficient way to throw the enemy off-balance, sir."

"Yes," Semiv mused. "Captain Argond here has told me that you're good at that sort of thinking. I could use some of that right now."

"Sir?"

Argond gestured at the two maps before him. "We have taken the camp and blockaded the roads successfully. Our job is now to hold this position until the rest of our army can punch through the Igyeum occupying force and meet us here."

"What's the problem, sir?"

"Distance and time," Semiv barked, pacing around the room. "The same problem that permeates all warfare. The Igyeum clearly intended to use this camp as their main forward operating base for a massive invasion of Telmondir. Our own army has to march through not one, but two occupied cities standing between us and them at the moment, and we don't have a force big enough to go toe to toe with the entire Igyeum army."

Grayden interrupted. "From what Beren and I saw at the other end of this camp, they're planning on docking a fleet here, and... something else." Semiv whirled and narrowed his eyes in a questioning sort of way. Grayden continued. "You should walk down and see it, sir, it defies description."

"So I hear." Semiv heaved a sigh and returned to his chair. "In your mind, Lieutenant, is there anything we can do to help get our army here faster?" He looked around at the rest of the men standing in the room. "Do any of you have any ideas?"

The men shifted imperceptibly, their expressions turning thoughtful.

Grayden frowned, his mind spiraling through what assets he knew they had at their disposal and comparing them to the problem at hand. What would Wynn do? he wondered. Then he looked up at the major, an idea beginning to form.

"Our men did find a thousand cynders in one of the supply sheds," he said slowly. "And there are six perfectly functional airships docked just across that field. Of course, we'd probably only need one."

Semiv steepled his fingers together in front of his mouth, waiting. "Expound."

"Air support," Grayden said simply. "If we score cynders before we drop them, the impact of dropping them from an airship will make them explode. Our reports agree that few of our own people remain in Baktan or Akkad. I would think that those two cities now qualify as military targets."

Semiv walked to the window, deep in thought. Silence filled the room. Finally, without turning from the window, he spoke. "Lieutenant, our orders are to secure this base and hold it until the Southern Command rejoins us. We also have standing orders to bring any cynders or useful equipment we find to Pentua so they can be used by our own fleet."

Grayden gave a stiff nod. "Understood, sir." So, the major had orders that would not allow the use of the cynders. He wondered if they would get in trouble for the ones they had already wasted.

Semiv rejoined his officers at the center table, his expression troubled as his gaze passed over each of them, then he abruptly dismissed everyone. As Grayden turned to follow the others out of the room, Semiv's voice arrested him. "Argond, Ormond, a moment."

Grayden and Captain Argond waited as the other captains and their aides filed out, the door swinging shut behind them. Grayden resisted the urge to glance questioningly at his captain. Instead, he braced himself for the verbal reprimand he was about to receive.

With his back still to them, Semiv spoke, his voice so soft that Grayden had to strain to hear it. "You will load nine hundred cynders onto one of those airships. Tell First Lieutenant Adelfried to take Vector Platoon and deliver the cynders as ordered to General Travenn at Pentua. As soon as he is done, he and his men are to return here. I want them back here before sundown."

"Yes, sir," Grayden replied.

"Lieutenant Ormond, you will load the remaining cynders onto a second airship. I want you to take Arta Platoon and perform the operation you just outlined for me. You will wait an hour, then follow after Vector. Your orders are to clear a path for our army to reach us more swiftly. Focus on Akkad—that's where the majority of the Igyeum forces are currently deployed—and be back before dawn tomorrow. These orders are yours alone. Understood?"

"Yes, sir," Grayden said, his voice barely above a whisper. "We won't fail you, sir."

"Dismissed," Semiv said, still not turning around.

———

GRAYDEN RELAYED the major's orders to Beren and ordered his own men to help load up the cynders.

"We're leaving behind a hundred cynders," Beren noted. "I thought you said our standing orders..."

Grayden shrugged uncomfortably. He did not like keeping his friend in the dark, but he had his orders. "Who knows?"

Beren peered at him. "What aren't you telling me?"

Grayden gave up on the idea of keeping secrets from Beren. "Orders from Semiv. Can't say more."

Beren's eyebrows shot up, but he did not press the question further. He understood orders: how to give and how to take. His men carried the crates of cynders carefully onto the airship he would be taking to Pentua, securing them safely in the hold. They made short work of the job, and the airship was soon aloft and swiftly growing smaller.

Grayden then ordered his own men to load the remaining crates of cynders onto a second airship.

"What's up, Lieutenant?" Shep asked, as Grayden gathered his platoon onto the deck of the ship.

"Orders. Help me get this ship up inside those clouds and you'll find out more," Grayden said, bounding to the wheel. He gripped the controls eagerly, his heart leaping at the mere thought of piloting an airship again. While skysailing was a thrilling exercise, it still couldn't quite compare to the freedom of standing at the wheel of an airship.

Several hours later, they reached the outskirts of Akkad. In the twilight haze, they risked dipping down below the sparse clouds to inspect their target.

"We're really going to drop cynders on one of our own cities, sir?" Joss asked. Grayden studied him. Though he was the youngest man in the platoon, Joss had proven himself to be a fierce sparring partner, and was one of the few men in Grayden's command who had never balked at leaping off an airship. Now, though, his face seemed strangely pale.

"You heard those prisoners we rescued," Grayden said. "Most of our own people fled when the Igyeum took over. They aren't our cities anymore."

Joss shifted from one foot to the other. "I know, but..."

"We're taking it back, Joss," Grayden said. "We might have to rebuild a little, afterwards, that's all."

Joss nodded.

A pang shot through Grayden. The kid trusted him to make the right decision. He stared down at the city. Obvious military targets only. But from such a distance, how could he be sure? Then he realized what he was seeing and his stomach clenched in horror.

Below, Akkad was already a smoking ruin. Large swaths of blackened trenches had been cut across the town, as if carved by a great butcher knife. Buildings had been reduced to smoking rubble. Streets were marred and pocked with craters. No wonder the people had fled; there was nothing left.

"What..." Words failed. Grayden's lips tightened in numb horror at the scene of devastation that had once been one of Ondoura's largest cities. Here was evidence of the Igyeum's new weapon, clear and unmistakable. He had heard the rumors, but the reality was stark and unforgiving.

Next to him, he heard Joss take a shaky breath through his teeth. "Those prisoners, they said everyone fled the city?" the kid asked.

Grayden nodded, unable to trust his voice just yet.

"They couldn't have," Joss whispered. "How could anyone have survived long enough to flee... that?"

Resolve hardened in Grayden's gut. "Shep, Jerky!"

The two men marched over to stand before him. "Yes, sir?"

"We need to know the most effective place to use the cynders. Care to do a little recon for us?"

The two men exchanged a glance. "We didn't bring our skysails."

"I know," Grayden replied. "But we're in an airship with Igyeum markings, and you're the best fast-ropers I know."

The two men nodded. "Aye. If you get us low enough, we can find a target to your liking."

"When you find it, drop a smoke signal on it, and leg it to that stand of timber," Grayden said. "We'll pick you up after we deploy the cynders."

"THERE'S THE SIGNAL." Joss pointed as a billowing plume of smoke wafted into the sky, a smudge against the growing darkness.

Soldiers scurried around the building in a sudden uproar, trying to determine the source of what they must believe to be a fire. From this high up, the people were indistinct little dots on the ground.

A second plume of smoke began to fill the air and Grayden gave a tight smile. Trust Shep and Jerky to climb a second mountain. They had found a secondary target and marked it. Grayden navigated the airship into a dive, aiming directly for the column of smoke.

"When we're directly above it, drop ten cynders," he shouted. "Hold another ten in reserve for the second target."

His men nodded, readying themselves, holding the cynders aloft. Grayden felt a certain amount of pride in his men as they lined up along the side of the airship. Despite the clear evidence during the battle of the damage they could do, not one of his men had balked at the idea of scoring the cynders or of holding them in their hands once they had been damaged. He swooped through the smoke, and each man dropped his cynder over the side. As soon as they had released all of them, Grayden pulled the ship into a steep climb, not sure how high they would need to be to escape the explosion about to occur. A heartbeat later, the ground beneath them thundered with the force of the cynders, and a fine mist of dirt flew into the air behind them.

Swiftly now, Grayden aimed at the second target, where they repeated the drop. Below, he could hear shouts as the Igyeum soldiers reacted to the sudden destruction that had just fallen on their heads. Grimly, he soared up into the darkening sky above the thin layer of clouds. There he waited, but no airships appeared to challenge them, and so he risked ducking down to the stand of timber where he had told Shep and Jerky to wait.

They hovered over the trees for several minutes, and Grayden's heart hammered in his ears. There was no sign of either of his men. Had they been captured by the enemy? Worse, had they been unable to get clear of the explosions?

"They're not here, Lieutenant," Joss reported, a note of panic in his voice.

"We'll give them a few more minutes," Grayden replied.

"They should've gotten here before us," Joss insisted.

"They had a lot of ground to cover," Grayden said.

Minutes ticked by. Grayden glanced at the ship's chronometer, growing dread writhing in the pit of his stomach.

"How long are we going to wait, sir?" Joss finally asked. "The longer we stay here, the longer we put the whole platoon in danger."

"A few more minutes," Grayden barked, bile rising in his throat at the thought of leaving Shep and Jerky behind.

"Aye, sir," Joss whispered.

He continued to hover above the sparse branches of the trees, straining his eyes as hope trickled away from him like the last drops in an empty waterskin.

"What's that?" Flint pointed.

All eyes focused intently on the spot where Flint was looking. Two shadows slipped quietly and slowly across the field and darted into the trees.

"Do you think...?" Joss breathed.

Grayden lowered the airship as far into the trees as he dared go. A hollow sound rose up into the air, three thumps, a pause, and then a single thump, as if someone were banging a stick against a tree trunk.

"It's them," Grayden said, recognizing the sound. "Lower the harness!"

Ropes were flung over the side of the airship, and a few minutes later Shep and Jerky both tumbled onto the deck in an exhausted heap.

"Might want to get out of here quick, Lieutenant," Jerky gasped. "I think we were followed."

"What took you so long?" Grayden demanded, aiming the airship back into the sky toward the relative protection of the clouds.

"Ran into a patrol of Igyeum soldiers and got conscripted into helping dig some men out from under a building," Shep explained, gulping gratefully at a cup of water someone had gotten for them. "We couldn't just walk away without looking suspicious, but we knew we couldn't stick around for too long—someone was bound to realize that nobody knew who we were."

"Are either of you injured?" Grayden asked.

"Nah," Jerky replied. "Got tangled up in a thorn bush on the way out of town, took Shep a few minutes to cut me out of it."

A sense of relief flooded through Grayden. He had never considered before that having a command of any size might mean that he would have to send men he cared about into danger, had never realized how difficult it would be to have to wait in safety to find out whether or not they would return. "How much damage did we do?" he asked.

Shep's cheerful expression faltered. "Not much," he admitted. "I mean, the cynders exploded like they're supposed to, but they mostly just blew up the ground. I think one of them might have hit a supply shed, but it didn't seem like they lost anything important."

Grayden grimaced.

"We'd have to fly a lot lower if we wanted to hit more precise targets," Jerky added, his mouth twisted into a grimace.

"How much lower?" Grayden asked.

"Low enough that the airship wouldn't be much protection against archers," Jerky admitted. "Or even soldiers determined to board."

Grayden clenched his jaw. They still had eighty cynders in their hold. But the Igyeum troops below had now been alerted to their presence. To fly low enough to be more than a minor annoyance would put his men in danger, with no guarantee of success. The cynders had worked well earlier that day because they had caused chaos and confusion in an active battle. Precision had neither been needed nor wanted. But this... he let out a slow breath. He had to admit that this application of the strategy was far from ideal.

"What do we do now?" Shep asked, as though reading his thoughts.

Everything in him screamed that they could do more. If they could harm the enemy here, they could make retaking Akkad easier for the rest of the army. If they could retake Akkad, they could secure their borders and possibly mount an offensive of their own. Secure borders meant safeguarding their families, all their people from the monster that was the Igyeum. He had only seen a minute fraction of what the Igyeum was capable of, but it was enough to make him determined to fight against it with everything he had.

Even if it meant putting himself in danger.

Even if it meant asking his men to walk into fire.

But they didn't have the right tools for the job. If he asked his men to do this, it wouldn't just be dangerous, it would be suicide; and they might not even achieve their goal. Dawn approached, and Captain Semiv's orders rang in his memory.

Gritting his teeth, Grayden gripped the wheel. "We head back."

"But..." Jerky began, but broke off as he caught the expression on Grayden's face.

"It's not our time, yet," Grayden said. "But we'll get our chance."

"Every man here would volunteer to stay," Shep said in a quiet tone.

"I know," Grayden replied. "And that's why we have to return. I won't lose good men to a hopeless strategy." Reluctantly, he turned the ship and urged it back the way they had come. They would retake Akkad another day.

35

The three fugitives flew through the night, huddling together, thin blankets wrapped around their shoulders in a desperate attempt to keep warm. The skimmer gamely hurtled through the air, swooping silently above the desert sands. No pursuit materialized behind them, which did not help ease the butterflies in Raisa's stomach. The odds that Uun and Lorcan would just let them go were smaller than those of Marik turning down a risky job.

The thought of Marik struck her in the gut and she doubled over, gasping out unexpected sobs that the wind carried away. In all the flurry of their escape, she had not had a chance to truly grieve, but now it consumed her with an overwhelming force. Clinging to the back of a skimmer being piloted by a man she barely knew was not the ideal place or time for mourning, but then, grief was not the sort of thing to stand by waiting for convenience, it just came. Tears leaked from the corners of her eyes and trickled down her face, then blew away, evaporating before they could water the thirsty sand. Hanging on to the stabilizing bar with one hand, Raisa covered her face with the other, unable to stanch the flow of sorrow streaming from her heart.

Dawn broke over the horizon behind them and the sun began

its climb through the sky. As the daylight intensified and gained warmth, Davin angled the skimmer down to one of the larger dunes in the area. As they rounded the side of the dune, however, Raisa hissed through her teeth at the sight of a small caravan resting in the valley. A large, round tent rose up from the desert floor, and she could see a dozen shaggy, long-horned sibirix resting in the shade of the tent, their heads lowered into a long trough of water. She reached forward to warn Davin, but a crowd had emerged from the tent and from the way they pointed and waved she could see that they had already been spotted.

As they descended the dune, Raisa tore a ragged strip from her blanket and worked to wind it around her head and face. She could do nothing about her bare arms and the strange markings on them, but at least she could hide her pointed ears. They landed near the large tent and Davin powered the skimmer down before dismounting. Olin glanced up at Raisa and pulled his blanket over his head like a hood, hiding the greenish-gray hue of his skin in shadow. Raisa's stomach flipped nervously as several bardani women approached.

"Blessing upon your feet," one of them said, her eyes wide and fixed on the strange contraption they had been riding.

"And upon your head may the sun's rays be pleasant," Raisa replied, keeping her voice light. "Forgive us for startling you, we did not intend to intrude upon your morning."

"You certainly caused a rippling of sand. What is this contraption that you ride?"

"It is a skimmer," Davin said, his voice tinged with pride. "Only one of its kind."

"Our leader will wish to speak with you, please come."

Davin gave them a wary look, and Raisa prodded him in the back. "We have to accept," she muttered. "None of them will touch the skimmer; the penalty for thievery among the bardani is harsh. Besides, Olin can stay here and keep an eye on it."

Olin nodded enthusiastically, his eyes darting about. A pang of sympathy shot through Raisa as she realized how exposed he must feel. This was probably the largest group of people he'd ever seen outside his home; even in the Weald he'd been kept in his small cave. The world must feel extremely large to him all of a sudden.

Reluctantly, the Shipwright allowed himself to be propelled forward. In short order, they were ushered inside the tent, where a woman sat in a chair behind a large desk and sipped daintily from a tiny cup. Raisa blinked. She had traded with the bardani before, but none of them had ever drunk tea, or sat in chairs, or had such dark coloring. Most bardani were fair, with red hair and varying shades of green eyes. This woman looked more traditionally Pallan, though not as dark as Shaesta.

"Be welcome," the woman intoned. "My people tell me you arrived on a most unusual airship. Tell me, what brings you to my humble tent?"

"Uh, happenstance, my lady," Davin said. "Mere... happenstance."

The perfectly sculpted eyebrow rose, arching gracefully. "Happenstance."

"What my pilot means to say," Raisa interjected, "is that we have gotten a little lost. Perhaps we could bother you for directions?"

The woman's dark eyes narrowed. "Directions to where?"

Raisa thought quickly. "Which way to Ondoma? And how far?"

"Ondoma?" The woman's tone turned disdainful. "You cannot expect me to believe you would seek out that flea-infested poisoned spring."

"It's not our first choice, but we have business there," Raisa replied, keeping her voice even.

The woman sniffed. "It is approximately two hundred leagues north-west of here."

"I see," Raisa said. "We have truly gotten off course. My thanks."

"Is there anything else I can help you with?"

"I do not believe so," Raisa replied, though she longed to beg for some water. "As I said, we got a little lost."

"You do not wish to trade?"

"My lady, we have nothing to trade with," Raisa admitted humbly. "We have desperate need of everything we carry."

"I see. Yes, my people inform me that your ship does not have room for much in the way of possessions." The woman took a long sip from her tiny cup, then rose, waving a hand magnanimously. "I am being remiss in my duties as hostess for my clan. Please, sit, let me pour you some tea."

"Thank you, kind hostess." Davin gave a flourishing bow and sat down upon one of the pillows. He stared up at the woman's face with rapt attention and Raisa groaned internally. The last thing she wanted was to waste time here. The longer they lingered, the more memorable they became. And since they had nothing valuable enough to trade for silence, it was imperative they take their leave swiftly. Raisa tried to express these thoughts in a fierce glare at her companion, but Davin studiously ignored her. The woman poured tea into two tiny cups, identical to her own, and Raisa reluctantly took the one offered to her; to refuse would be the height of rude behavior, and she could not afford to make an enemy of this woman. She frowned down at the tea, still bothered by its existence here in the midst of a bardani camp, but she drank it anyway, grateful for any kind of liquid.

"My name is Haizea," the woman said as they all sipped the hot tea together. "I am the leader of this caravan in my husband's absence."

"Where is your husband?" Davin asked.

Horrified at his bluntness, Raisa took a large gulp of her tea. She instantly regretted doing so; the hot liquid scalded her tongue and burned as it trickled down her throat. She pushed the tail end of her strip of blanket over her mouth to hide her grimace of pain as she tried to suppress her sputtering gasps in the wake of the unpleasant sensation.

Haizea lowered her eyes demurely. "He has been elevated to

the rank of Koldo and called to serve at the pleasure of the Ar'Mol in the great war against those invaders from Telmondir."

"That is quite the honor," Raisa said, managing to keep the ire out of her voice.

"It is." Haizea smiled beatifically. "But come, we are traders. And to drink tea with guests and then not trade with them is a dishonorable thing, indeed. Surely we have something you could use." She eyed Raisa's head wrap distastefully. "A new turban for you, perhaps? Or food and water for your travels? This location is a regular resting place for our caravans because of the deep well it holds. To offer you life-giving water is no difficult thing for us here."

Davin settled his cup onto the tiny saucer and shrugged regretfully. "As my companion says, we truly have nothing to trade with. While it is true that your caravan possesses a great many things that are beautiful and could ease our travels, and our need for food and water is great, alas, we have nothing of equal worth to offer in return."

"Have you not?" Haizea's eyes glimmered with mirth.

Raisa's heart hammered a warning in her chest at the woman's coy smile directed at Davin. She wanted to shout to warn him, but she bit her tongue. There was no easy way to communicate her reservations to him without being impolite, and she was curious to hear what the woman had in mind.

"I do not believe so, fair lady," Davin said. "But if you think differently, please tell me, and I will see what I can do."

Haizea idly traced the rim of her cup with one long, graceful finger. Then she looked up, fiery desire smoldering in her eyes. "I know you need your small airship to carry you on your journey, but for a single ride upon it, I would gladly trade new clothes and turbans for all of your companions. And if you teach me how to fly it, I will gladly throw in food and water enough for three days."

Raisa narrowed her eyes at the woman. The deal seemed far too good to be true, as well as too easy. She had been to the Plains of Temna with Marik in the Hawk several times, and deals with the bardani were never struck so quickly. The caravan leaders loved haggling, and they rarely ever demonstrated such a visible desire for anything. Raisa drummed her fingers against the sand, wondering what she was missing. She took another tiny sip of her tea. This time it had cooled to a sufficiently pleasant temperature, but unfortunately, due to her hasty gulp from earlier, she could no longer taste the flavor with her scalded tongue. Sighing with regret, Raisa set the cup down and caught Davin's eye.

"May I confer with my companion?" Davin asked.

"As much as you like," Haizea replied.

Davin rose and Raisa followed him to the tent flap.

"What do you think?" he asked.

"I think it seems too easy," Raisa admitted. "I've traded with the bardani before, and they never come right out and say what it is they want."

"I thought she seemed a little eager," Davin replied. "But perhaps she just isn't used to being the leader? It doesn't sound like she's been in this position of authority long."

"True." Raisa crossed her arms. "But all the bardani haggle. It's a cultural point of pride for them. Her position as tribe leader shouldn't change that."

"You traded with them when you were on the Valdeun Hawk?"

Raisa swallowed the painful twinge. "Yes."

"Maybe you saw them haggle so much because you had much to trade? To be bluntly honest, we look like paupers."

"That could be the case," Raisa said slowly, her thoughts awhirl. "But something is off here. Even the tea is wrong."

"I don't know what that means," Davin said. "And I don't trust her either, but we need what she's offering."

Raisa chewed on the inside of her cheek. "You're right. We can't cross the desert without food or water."

"Listen, I'll give her a flying lesson, just the basics. You and Olin stay here and gather up whatever these people are willing to trade, and we'll leave as soon as I get back."

Reluctantly, Raisa nodded. "I can't think of any better plan," she admitted.

Moments later, Raisa watched as Haizea climbed onto the back of the skimmer, her firm, decisive movements belying the tentative expression on her face. Raisa shook her head, unable to push away the niggling sensation of danger.

"What's wrong?" Olin asked.

"I'm not certain," Raisa replied. "I'm just not comfortable with this arrangement."

Olin shrugged. "It appears to work in our favor."

"That's the problem. The bardani usually work extremely hard to make sure all trades err in their favor. It seems to me that we are getting a lot for very little. As Marik would say, 'smells like a sun shower.'"

"A sun shower?"

"It's an expression for times when the sun is out but it suddenly starts raining."

"I thought there needed to be clouds for it to rain." Olin's brow wrinkled in confusion.

Raisa smiled. "There do. But sometimes those clouds are so high up and so thin, that you can't actually see them from the ground. And sometimes there can be a single cloud full of rain on an otherwise sunny day. Marik usually says it when he thinks there's hidden danger somewhere. Or..." She faltered. "I mean... he... he used to say it..." Pain shot through her and her throat tightened as she fought against the prickle of tears.

"Miss? Sir?" a polite voice said from behind them.

Raisa and Olin turned, Raisa instinctively putting a hand to her makeshift turban to ensure it still covered her ears. A young girl with spiraling red curls stared up at them eagerly.

"Yes?" Raisa asked.

"Lady Haizea said I was to take you to my mother's table and let you both choose any clothing you like."

Raisa and Olin followed the girl through the large tent to a place near the edge of the trading area. A young woman sat atop a crate with various clothing hanging on collapsible racks around her, and more crates overflowing with fine cloth of every type and color imaginable. At the sight, Raisa's heart sank at the number of choices before her. She did not enjoy shopping, and none of these garments fit her preferences. She missed her soft breeches and high boots, her long-sleeved shirts and long-tailed jackets that hung around her hips like a skirt. She missed the feel of the wind on her face, the thrill of climbing the rigging of the Hawk, or of completing a successful heist. She missed the security of her rapier swinging against her leg. As she fingered the various long robes and colorful head wraps, she could not help but wonder what the future held for her. Without the Hawk to return to, what would she do? Where could she go?

"May I help you choose?" the woman asked, breaking into Raisa's thoughts.

Raisa smiled in relief and nodded, not trusting herself to speak.

The woman rifled through the various garments and held up a green robe with tan embroidery that decorated the bodice and twined down the long, billowing sleeves. "I think this would fit you well," the woman said. She glanced at Raisa's arms and then swiftly looked away, a flush rising in her pale cheeks.

"It is very beautiful," Raisa said, touching the fabric. Shaesta would approve, she thought. She wondered if the young woman had still been aboard the airship when it went down. For all her bitterness over Shaesta's betrayal, she had been a friend, once. Perhaps she could have been again.

"It would hide your arms, as well. May I ask, what do the markings mean?"

Raisa stared at the woman, uncomprehending. Then she glanced down at her bare arms and felt her cheeks burn with shame and anger. "They don't mean anything," she said, her voice bitter. "I didn't choose them."

"Then you must choose a meaning for them," the woman said. "Else they will haunt you forever."

Flustered and confused, Raisa found herself at a loss for words.

"Here, this head scarf will go nicely with that, and you'll want a sturdy pair of boots for traveling across the sands." The woman thrust the dress and a length of tan fabric into her arms. "You can change in there"—the woman gestured to a small, curtained area —"I will help your friend with his choices."

Dazed, Raisa allowed herself to be ushered behind the curtain where she stood for a moment, her arms full of fabric, wondering if she had fallen into a dream. The cotton cloth was light in her arms and she marveled at its softness, even against her newly toughened skin. All hesitation fled and she changed quickly into the new robe, tying it at the waist with a length of cord the woman had also provided. Artfully, she draped the scarf over her head and wrapped it around her neck a few times so it would stay in place and be available should she need it to block windblown sand from getting into her face. The robe fit her well, and as the woman had said, it hid the markings on her arms and neck. The scarf covered her pointed ears, and shadowed her face, making the fainter lines and swirls there invisible to a passing glance. The new boots were stiff and pinched her toes, but they were better than nothing, so she kept them on. She would break them in soon enough.

Leaving her filthy rags in a pile on the sand—she never wanted to see them again—Raisa stepped out from behind the curtain. The little girl who had come to get her clasped her hands together and smiled.

"You look like a princess," she breathed. "Just like a princess from the stories."

"There are no princesses in real life," Raisa said, but she smiled to soften her words. "But thank you."

A few minutes later, Olin also emerged, completely transformed. His robe was white and unbelted in the men's style, and his head wrap was coiled atop his head with a trailing length wrapped around his face so that only his eyes were visible, glittering darkly from behind the slit of fabric. Raisa had to admit, if she had not known it was him, she would have been unable to identify the durven. Other than his stature, he looked normal.

He stared up at her anxiously, and she nodded, smiling to let him know she approved.

"Thank you," Raisa said to the woman.

"It is my pleasure. My daughter has filled several waterskins and a satchel of food for each of you. It should last you several days."

"Thank you again," Raisa said, taking the proffered items. "The clothing is lovely."

She started to follow Olin back to the place where they had been waiting for the Shipwright, but a tug on her sleeve arrested her mid-stride and she stopped. The woman held her sleeve between her fingers, a frightened look on her face.

"You are in danger," she whispered urgently. "When your friend returns, you must go, as quickly as possible."

"What? Why?"

"Last night, an airship passed overhead. They circled our caravan, and a man descended on a ladder. He spoke with Haizea and told her he was searching for three criminals who had escaped from prison. He described you well. Haizea may be our leader, but she has not always been one of us."

Raisa leaned closer to the woman. "What do you mean?"

"She is not true bardani, though she married our leader. It is a long story, but she does not understand the voiceless law of the Plain. Her mother was Pallan, but she was born and raised in Malei; she is, in many ways, still Maleian, and fiercely proud of her heritage and the Igyeum, as well as extremely loyal to the Ar'Mol. We bardani have always seen ourselves as separate, not part of the Igyeum, not even truly part of Palla, and until recently our scattered, wandering lifestyle and small numbers kept the Ar'Mol from caring about us. Haizea is proud that her husband now fights for the Igyeum. She cannot understand why the rest of us are bitter. My husband and my three sons..." The woman's voice broke. "They have been stolen from me. But Haizea is our leader, so what can we say?"

"Thank you for telling me," Raisa said.

The woman shrugged. "Haizea breaks our law by choosing sides. I am merely doing what I can to balance her wrong."

Raisa bowed her head slightly. "Upon your head may the sun's rays always be pleasant."

"And upon yours." The woman pressed her hand to one fist and bent her head over them.

Raisa walked swiftly to catch up with Olin, who glanced at her out of the corner of his eye when she arrived at his side.

"What was that all about?"

"I was right to be suspicious," Raisa said. "Haizea is trying to delay us here so she can turn us over to the Igyeum." Tea. That was why the tea had struck her as odd. The bardani drank a cool, spiced wine when they made trade negotiations. Never tea.

Olin's eyes widened. "How does she know about us?"

"An airship with people looking for us. Probably Uun's men. As soon as Davin returns, we have to leave."

36

Roald stood at the prow of his airship, his jaw tight as he scanned the ground. Behind them, the sun was just cresting the horizon, casting a sheen of golden light into the darkness, chasing away the night with the same dogged determination that Roald himself felt toward his prey. His own outcome would be similar: just as morning always came, he would find the prisoners and bring them back to his master as he had been commanded. It was inevitable. He, the hunter, now enhanced with the madman's gifts, had never felt stronger. His muscles burned with pent-up energy, yearning to run, to jump, to climb, but he held himself still. Discipline had brought him this far; he would not abandon it now.

One of his men handed him a cup of water; Roald drank it down in a single gulp, his thirst an unquenchable abyss within him, a dryness that could not be assuaged. He hoped Lorcan had been telling the truth when he said the thirst would fade with time. He would always need more water than he had before, but the madman had assured him he would not always feel it so keenly.

"How are you?" he asked the man, handing him the cup back.

"A little off-balance, sir," the man replied.

"It will take some getting used to," Roald replied. "But I believe the benefits will far outweigh the temporary discomfort."

"Yes, sir," the man said, staring at the planking. He looked up at Roald, his bright green eyes determined. "We will find the prisoners and deliver them back to our master."

"Yes," Roald replied. He turned back to scanning the ground, still amazed at his heightened visual acuity. He could see farther and more clearly than he would have previously thought possible, and yet his vision for things that were close to him had not diminished in any way. His hearing was also better, and now that the weakness he had awoken with that first morning had worn off, he felt stronger than he ever had. He wanted to test his new limits, discover his capabilities. He turned back to his crewman and grinned fiercely. "Yes, we will recapture the prisoners and return them to Ar'Molon Uun. And then..." Roald gripped the railing tightly with both hands. "Then we will finally fulfill our primary mission: to find our lord's lost orb and return it to him so that he can at last take his rightful place as ruler of both the Igyeum and Telmondir."

"Sir? Do you really think it possible? The Kotai have served Ar'Molon Uun for so many generations." His subordinate looked at him, a hunger filling his expression. "Will we finally be the ones to bring him the orb?"

"We will," Roald said firmly. He could feel it. The madman's plan had actually worked, and now Roald had the tools he needed to fulfill his primary directive. But first, he needed to deal with a minor annoyance. "Bring me more water," Roald barked. "And you and the others make sure to drink deeply. Quench the thirst if you can. I want every man steady on his feet within the hour. I won't have weakness in my crew. If we are to hunt the prisoners and retrieve what was stolen from our master, there cannot be any room for distraction. Sevalk will finally be found."

"Aye, sir." The man saluted, raising his arm stiffly so that the palm of his right hand hovered a few inches from his right ear.

"And make sure that the weapon is fully charged. We may need it."

"Sir? Do you expect our quarry to put up that much of a fight?"

"Perhaps not, but it is always best to expect the unexpected. That way, you're never surprised. Now go fulfill your duties."

The man accepted this answer, saluted again, and disappeared below. Roald's throat ached, already dry, as though he had been gargling sand from the desert below. His hand strayed to his neck, scratching lightly at his skin. To the gentle brush of his fingers, there was no noticeable difference, but he knew if he pressed harder he would begin to feel the subtle ridges that had developed in the past day, ridges that matched the new, dark lines that covered his body like faded tattoos. He put his hand down and caught a glimpse of the skin on the back of his wrist. For a long moment he stared, studying the way the skin had darkened, tracing the faint swooping lines that were like nothing so much as the pattern of bark on a tree and contemplated the horror of what he had allowed himself to become. With a shudder, he tugged the sleeve down until it met the edge of his gloves. It did no good to regret what could not be undone.

Taking a deep breath, Roald closed his eyes and focused his attention toward the center of his chest. The gentle tugging sensation was so subtle he needed to concentrate in order to even notice it, but when he did, he could feel it clearly, like a gossamer thread tied around one of his ribs and pulling him in a specific direction. To his surprise, he could now feel several threads: seven, to be exact. Each thread hummed a separate musical note in the depths of his thoughts. In his mind's eye, he held the threads across his fingers as his master had taught him, then he let six of them slip from his grasp, focusing only on the one that led to his quarry; for now, that was the only one that mattered. The others, he would attend to later.

Mouse dashed through the trees, scrambling over the enormous, twisted roots. His lungs screamed with every breath, but he could not give them the rest they desired. Berating himself for allowing the soldiers to spot him, Mouse raced across the forest floor, just ahead of his pursuers. Loud footsteps thumped the ground behind him and occasionally the sound of a shout reached his ears. His size gave him a slight advantage in these overgrown woods, but he did not know the terrain as well as the men chasing him did. He leaped over a root but misjudged its height; the obstacle caught his toe and he lost his balance, tumbling to the ground on the other side. He landed on one knee and skidded forward, catching himself on his hands before his chin collided with the dirt. Sitting up, Mouse pressed a hand over his hurt knee and clasped the other hand over his lips to stifle the moan of pain. Lifting his fingers, he saw that the wound on his knee consisted of an angry-looking scrape, but it did not appear to be deep and was not bleeding. He carefully brushed the sand out of it before attempting to stand. The knee ached as he straightened it, but the pain faded as he worked it.

The sounds of pursuit drew closer, and Mouse glanced about, searching for a hiding place. He couldn't stay ahead of them, not without leading them straight to the Hawk, and he would give his last breath before he allowed that to happen. His sharp eyes spotted a small hollow in the ground at the base of a nearby tree where the roots had pulled slightly out of the soil. He did not like the idea of confining himself in a space with no secondary exit, so he hesitated for one loud heartbeat. The impending sound of footsteps tramping close behind made the decision for him and Mouse threw himself toward the tree, closing the distance and dropping to the ground. The opening was a tighter squeeze than he had expected and he found himself stuck, his torso under the tree, his legs sticking out where they could easily be spotted. Panicking, he jerked himself sideways with increasingly frenzied attempts, his arms scrabbling at the opening, trying frantically to dig out the entrance so he could curl up inside.

"I thought I heard something moving over that way." The words floated to his ears from far too close, and Mouse's heart leaped into his throat. With one final, desperate motion he managed to cram himself through the opening.

There was no ground inside the hollow.

Mouse plummeted into darkness.

The unexpectedness of the fall startled him so much that he didn't make a sound as he tumbled into the chasm. He twisted in the air, flailing to catch hold of something solid, but empty air was all that he found. In the darkness he had no idea how deep of a hole he had fallen into, and for the space of a breath he feared that he would go on falling forever. Then he hit the ground hard, his fall stopping as suddenly and unexpectedly as it had begun. He landed on his arm with a painful cracking sound that filled his world with flashes of red and gold. If he had had any breath to spare, he would have screamed.

Mouse lay at the bottom of the hole, gasping and squeezing his eyes shut against the stinging tears that had sprung forth at the impact. For a long moment, he didn't move. He was too afraid to move, his arm felt wrong, and the wrongness of it terrified him.

He could no longer hear sounds of pursuit, but he did not

know if that was because the soldiers had already passed by, or if it was simply because of how far underground he had fallen. After a few minutes, Mouse attempted to move. Cautiously, he pushed himself up with his right hand. When he tried to move his left arm, pain assailed him in a blinding slash of light. His head swam and the darkness turned even blacker around the edges. His breath came in short, frightened gasps, and then he knew no more.

When he came to, Mouse blinked in the darkness, trying to remember where he was and what had happened. He sat up carelessly and agonizing pain sliced through his arm, reminding him fiercely of the events that had transpired before he lost consciousness. With his right hand, he pulled his left arm toward his chest. With his fingers, he carefully felt his way up and down the length of his appendage. To his relief, he did not feel any sharp edges of bone piercing the skin. The arm might be broken, but it was not so badly broken that he needed immediate help.

With a tremendous effort, wincing with every movement, Mouse used his right hand to tug the sleeve from his left arm and twist his shirt slightly until he had managed to position his elbow within the sleeve where it attached to his shoulder, creating a pathetic sort of sling. He needed a physician, but he didn't think he was likely to find one down here, and at least this would keep his arm stabilized and prevent him from being tempted to try using it.

His head swam, but he managed to work his way up to a standing position. Gritting his teeth, he slowly craned his neck, trying to figure out where he was. On unsteady feet, Mouse walked a few experimental paces. A tiny amount of light came through the entrance above and now he could see that he had only fallen a few meters, but with no rope or ladder plus a broken arm, it might as well have been twenty thousand leagues. There was no way he could haul himself back up to the entrance, and there was no hope that anyone from the crew would find this particular tree and come to rescue him. Mouse took a shaky breath. His only hope lay in finding another way out of this chasm, assuming there was another way out.

He had to get back to the Hawk. Marik and the others needed to be told of the things he had learned.

Raisa had escaped!

But she was in danger, and they had to find her before the hunters did. Thankfully, there hadn't been many soldiers tramping about, and this was all vital information that Mouse knew he needed to get to his crew. But how?

Now that his eyes had adjusted to the dim light, he could see that the cavern he had fallen into was larger than he had first thought. He felt his way around the chamber and found that one wall narrowed into a tunnel just big enough for him to crawl through. Wincing because of his injured arm, Mouse navigated his way into the tunnel. He hoped it would lead him somewhere, and not just to a dead end.

38

Raisa paced impatiently, her eyes scanning the horizon for any sight of an airship. She growled lightly under her breath. "Where are they?" she asked for the hundredth time.

This time, Olin jumped up and pointed as the skimmer appeared around the dune in front of them. It whizzed past, slowing a bit, and Raisa tried to calm her racing heart. Every instinct screamed that they had to get away as fast and as far as possible. Haizea's eyes sparkled through the slit in her head wrap as Davin reached around her slim waist to show her which lever would slow the skimmer's pace. They coasted to a stop and Haizea clapped her hands.

"I think I'm ready to try it on my own!" she exclaimed.

Raisa and Olin shared an alarmed look, and Raisa strode forward. "I am pleased you enjoyed your flying lesson, honored leader," Raisa said, putting a firm hand on the lever. "But my companions and I really must be going."

"The lady has quite a knack for the machine," Davin said, jumping off the skimmer and landing on the sand with something like a swagger, except that he stumbled slightly and had to reach out to grip the skimmer's handle. In her mind's eye, Raisa compared his gesture with Marik's easy charisma and winced.

Haizea tugged at her scarf and pouted. "Davin promised he would let me try it on my own."

"Ah, I'm sorry, lady," Davin said. "I didn't realize how late it was getting. My companions and I have to be on our way. But perhaps our paths will cross again."

Haizea hesitated, a strange look in her eye. For a moment, Raisa thought she would try to steal the skimmer, but with both her and Davin's hands on the flier the bardani woman couldn't get away easily. Raisa narrowed her eyes, wondering if Davin had stumbled on purpose, and re-evaluating her uncharitable thoughts from a moment before.

Haizea reluctantly slid off the skimmer, her hand trailing across the seat with a sigh of longing. Then she turned bright eyes on Davin once more. "You still need to pick out some new clothes for our trade to be complete. Come!" Her tone turned to one of command and she swept him along in her wake. He glanced questioningly over his shoulder at Raisa, his own expression full of concern, but she gave him a nod and he relaxed visibly.

Raisa sighed and tugged the skimmer into the shade of the tent. She did not wish to linger in this place for another minute, but she comforted herself with the reminder that Haizea had no way of contacting the Igyeum. All she could do was delay them. The important task had been accomplished: they had kept their ride out of Haizea's clutches.

Davin was only inside the tent for a few minutes. He emerged, dressed in a long gray robe and cream-colored turban with gold trimming. Haizea walked next to him, holding his arm possessively in her own. He said something and she laughed.

"Are you ready?" Raisa asked, climbing onto the skimmer behind Olin.

Haizea clung to the Shipwright's arm. "I wish you could stay longer."

Raisa glanced about, noticing the disapproving glares from those of the tribe who were watching. Haizea's actions were not gaining her any friends among her people.

"We thank you for your hospitality," Davin replied. "But we need to move on. May the sun's rays upon your head be pleasant."

"And on yours," Haizea returned the blessing in a sullen tone.

Davin climbed aboard the skimmer, a bemused expression on his face. In a moment, the vehicle hummed to life and they shot across the desert. The sun had traveled well into the sky by now, and the heat grew steadily in its intensity, but Raisa gritted her teeth and said nothing, wanting to put as much distance as possible between them and the bardani caravan.

"What happened while we were gone?" Davin asked.

Still irritated with Haizea, and in no mood to try to have a conversation in the whipping wind, Raisa did not reply. Davin turned his head and frowned, but then he shrugged and flew on. They had been flying for over an hour, when suddenly Olin started to topple sideways. Raisa gave a shout and reached forward, catching him and pulling him back before he could fall off the skimmer, but his eyes were closed and his skin had turned a pale gray.

"Davin!" Raisa shouted. "We have to land!"

The Shipwright glanced over his shoulder. Upon seeing their companion's distress, he immediately brought the skimmer to a stop next to the closest dune. Together, he and Raisa dragged Olin off the skimmer and laid him on the sand. Raisa patted his cheeks and shouted his name, but Olin did not stir.

"What's wrong with him?" Davin asked, standing over them.

"I don't know," Raisa replied. "Get me some water."

He handed her one of the waterskins and Raisa forced Olin's mouth open and poured some of the liquid between his lips. For a moment, he did not respond, but when he inhaled, water went down his throat and windpipe and he began to choke and cough. Raisa quickly rolled him onto his side and the precious water dripped out of his mouth onto the sand. Next, she poured a little of the water onto his face and neck, and was relieved to see that his color appeared to be darkening back to normal.

"I think he just needed water," she said, taking a drink herself and then offering the waterskin to Davin. "We've been so careful with our water rationing, we forgot to drink anything all morning."

Davin took a long sip, wiped his mouth on the back of his hand, and squatted down next to her. "You want to tell me what all that urgency was about earlier?" His eyes grinned at her from behind his turban. "You weren't jealous, were you?"

Raisa stared at him, dumbfounded. "No! What? I wasn't... I don't..." She realized she was stammering, but the very idea was so inconceivable that she had no words to respond with.

"I'm teasing, Raisa," he said in a low voice. "I know something happened to spook you. Can you tell me what it was? If we're in danger, I'd rather know about it."

Raisa relaxed slightly. "The woman who gave us our clothes told me that Haizea had spoken with the soldiers on an airship that passed by last night. Haizea guessed who we were and was doing everything she could to try to delay us."

"I could tell she was trying to delay us, but I couldn't figure out why. I thought the caravans sort of operated outside the Igyeum."

"They do," Raisa said. "But Haizea isn't from the desert, she is originally from Malei and married into the tribe. She's fiercely proud of the fact that her husband was recently conscripted, and she can't understand why the other women are horrified by what has happened." Raisa glanced at him and took in his suddenly subdued expression. "I'm sorry, but her interest in you was less than sincere."

Davin shrugged and looked away, one finger tracing a pattern in the sand. "I figured," he said in a wry tone.

Before Raisa could say anything more, Olin coughed a little and his eyes fluttered open.

"Olin!" Raisa said.

"What happened?" the durven asked, glancing around in confusion.

"You fell off the skimmer, and we couldn't wake you," Davin

said. "We think you must have gotten too dehydrated." He held out the waterskin and Olin accepted it, taking several long gulps.

"I'm sorry to be a burden," Olin said when he had finished. "I should have been more careful. The sun... I'm not used to it. We've been traveling by night so it hasn't been an issue, but today..."

"Don't think about it." Davin stood abruptly. "This place is as good as any for us to stop. None of us can keep going much longer anyway. It'll be too hot soon. Olin, do you think you have it in you to make us another cave? Raisa and I will help."

Olin nodded and took another long swig of water. "I am feeling much better already."

39

Mouse made his way painfully through the narrow tunnel, his heart sinking with every step he took. He was growing more and more certain that he was not in a tunnel at all, but merely a normal occurrence of empty space beneath a tree whose roots had come loose in a sudden windstorm or other violent weather system. At any moment, he was certain he would find himself at a dead end, far underground, and farther than ever away from any hope of aid.

A few moments later, his worst fears were realized, as his outstretched good hand collided with a solid mass of dirt and knobby roots. The boy's eyes stung with disappointed tears, and panic clawed at his insides. He would never get out, he would die down here, buried alive in what would become his tomb.

With an effort, he turned around. He knew he needed to retrace his steps back to the entrance where he had fallen, but exhaustion consumed him. Perhaps he would just rest for a little while first, then when he had regained a measure of his strength, he would return and see what he could do about his situation. Maybe it was not so dire as he feared, he thought, trying to cheer himself up. Maybe he had misjudged the distance, or might find a friendly network of roots with which he could pull himself out of the hole. Or maybe he hadn't been so far down as he thought. Surely in his panic and pain he had misjudged the impossibility of the situation. Besides, the soldiers who had been chasing him were surely all gone by now, passed on to continue searching the forest, and he could make his way back to the Hawk without being spotted. He had to make it back; Marik needed the information he had discovered. His bottom lip quivered and he bit down on it, hard. Raisa needed him to be brave. He would be brave for her. But first, he would rest for a bit.

Mouse leaned back against the wall of dirt, shifting himself around in an effort to get comfortable. With a suddenness that sent his heart careening against his rib cage, the wall collapsed, and he tumbled backwards, striking his head solidly against the ground. The sudden motion made his arm scream with pain, and he could not keep back the cry that escaped his lips. Terrified that he had been heard, he stayed where he had fallen, squeezing his eyes shut and straining his ears for the sounds of soldiers. He lay there for a long while, feeling sorry for himself and how everything today had gone wrong.

Then, as the pain subsided and his racing heart began to slow, Mouse opened his eyes. The warmth of hope spread through him as he realized what had just happened. The dead-end no longer blocked his path. Pushing himself up painfully, he peered about in the dim light. The opening he had fallen into was not large enough for him to stand in, so he crawled forward, nearly blind in the darkness, to investigate how far his newfound good fortune would take him. After a minute or two of crawling and pushing through the loose dirt and tendrils of roots, Mouse began to realize that the dim light was growing brighter. A moment later, he could tell that there was definitely light coming from up ahead, and another startling discovery was that the tunnel he was now in appeared to have been shaped, dug out by someone. The farther he went, the more convinced he became that the tunnel had been durven work, and his heart leapt. Perhaps a durven was somewhere ahead. At the thought, he slowed. What durven could be here? Was it a traitor? Was he walking into a trap? Or perhaps... had someone been captured when they fled the caves beneath Malei? He frowned. Yes. He remembered Nando and Marik talking about Olin being captured during their first attempt to free Raisa. Mouse had known Olin a little before he left the Deepway to join Marik's crew. Could Olin have been brought here to the Weald with Raisa? Might he be up ahead somewhere? If he was, would Mouse end up imprisoned alongside him? Or might he find a whole enclave of durven? They had left so many behind when they fled...

He paused at that thought. But there was no going back. He knew that in his heart; even if he could lie to himself and pretend that he might be able to go back the way he had come, he knew the truth. He would never be able to pull himself out of the chasm into which he had fallen. There was nothing he could do but go forward. And if he did, maybe they could rescue Olin, or any durven that had been captured, as well as Raisa. With that thought cheering him up, Mouse continued to crawl forward.

The tunnel got larger and larger until Mouse could stand upright within it, and the light grew brighter until Mouse emerged with cautious steps into a small cavern. A pallet of straw sat in one corner, and a stone shelf along one wall held a cup and a dish, as well as a very dirty spoon. It had all the signs of being a prison, but as he glanced about, Mouse saw that he was alone in the cave. His spirits sank and he nearly cried again, until he saw that the entrance to the cave was unblocked. He crept to it and peered out, first one way, then the other, but the entrance was truly unguarded and he could not hear anyone nearby.

Without hesitation now, Mouse darted out of the cavern. He clambered up on top of the cave and looked around, trying to get his bearings. The trees towered over him, but sunlight filtered down through the leaves and he rejoiced in the brilliance and wonder of something as simple as the sun.

Using what he could see of the sun's position in the sky, Mouse determined which direction was north and headed as quickly as he could toward the spot where the Hawk waited, being careful to remain as silent as possible. He raced through the forest, trying to keep his arm steady, but it was beginning to complain with an insistent ache that throbbed with every step.

When he came to the edge of the forest, Mouse glanced about. The soldiers who had been chasing him were still nowhere to be seen and he hoped they had given up the chase. He took several deep breaths, trying to infuse his nerves with iron, for the next part of his escape put him in the most danger. He crept out of the trees, holding his breath as he ran for the nearest dune. He felt keenly how exposed he was against the sand, and how easily his enemies could hide in the trees and fire arrows at him. This was the part of the plan that Marik had argued about the most, but in the end, the captain had to admit that it was better for the airship to stay hidden behind the dunes.

It took Mouse a long time to scale the sand dune—he kept tripping—and by the time he reached the top he was dripping with sweat and his arm hurt so badly he didn't think he could continue another step. He crested the dune and his body rebelled against the torment he had put it through in the past hours. His feet stumbled over one another and his legs locked at the knees mid-stride, sending Mouse toppling down the other side. The only thing he could do was clutch his left arm with his good one and hold it tightly to his chest as he tumbled and rolled and slid down the mountain of sand. He had no idea how long he fell, but when he finally stopped moving, he found that he no longer had the will to go on. He lay there in the sun and let his eyelids flutter closed. He had done his best, and it had not been enough. His last thought before he lost consciousness was how sorry he was that he had let his crew down.

40

It did not take Olin long to hollow out a cave for them. When he finished, they ate some of the food they had gotten from the caravan, and then Olin crawled to one corner and fell asleep, exhausted.

"I'll take the first watch," Davin said to Raisa. "I'll wake you in a few hours."

Raisa nodded and retrieved her blanket. She lay down, closed her eyes, and willed sleep to come. She fell into a fitful doze, filled with dreams of sinister people threatening her.

Raisa woke with a gasp; the hair on the back of her neck prickled and her thoughts whirled over what the bardani woman had told her. If the Ar'Molon had sent an airship after them, it meant that he would not easily give up on recapturing her. And if he had learned of Davin's desertion, it would only heighten his anger and desire to bring them back within his grasp. She knew they had to rest, but she also knew how quickly an airship could travel, and even though Davin had fixed the skimmer, it still couldn't reach speeds any higher than that of a heavy cargo cruiser. The military ships might be bigger and heavier, but they also carried more cynders, which meant more speed. Not as much speed as the Hawk on a good day, Raisa thought, loyally, but still, faster than their skimmer.

Sleep refused to return. Raisa rolled over and studied Davin's silhouette sitting at the entrance to their cave, the sun setting far off on the horizon. He looked as tired as she felt and a twinge of regret twisted in her stomach. With a sigh, she rose and went to sit next to him.

"You stumbled on purpose, didn't you?" she asked.

Davin's head bobbed. "Her flattery was too overt to be real."

"I'm sorry."

His head swung to look at her, his features shadowed. "For what?"

"For not trusting you," Raisa said.

"Forget it," he said. "I wouldn't have trusted me either, in your position."

A long silence hung between them.

"Raisa?"

"Hmm?"

"Do you think I can ever..." Davin paused. "Do you think it's possible to change?"

Raisa blinked. She opened her mouth for a hasty answer and then stopped, thinking hard. His question was not one to be answered lightly. "I think so," she said. "I know someone who did."

"You do?"

"My captain." She whispered the words. "He used to be an Igyeum soldier. He's the reason my father was killed. But he left all that. And even recently... he changed more. Found a purpose."

"You sound like you admire him."

Raisa's mouth quirked to one side. "I've been in love with him since I met him," she offered suddenly, startling herself with the words and mentally kicking herself for saying them out loud.

"He's a lucky fellow," Davin mumbled, grabbing a handful of sand and letting it sift through his fingers.

"Not really. He's dead, after all."

Davin's head shot up and she could almost hear his face turning red. "I didn't think... I just meant... I'm sorr... I just... um... meant that... any man you're in love with would be lucky to have you," he finished the stumbling sentence quietly.

Raisa gave a sorrowful little smile. "Thank you. But it was a young girl's infatuation with everything he represented, really. He always thought of me as a little sister, being quite a few years older, as he was." She chuckled. "He'd have been horrified to know I felt that way. I just wish he knew... how much I admired him. How much he had become family to me. There was... tension between us before he died."

"Oh." Davin turned to look at her. "I'm sorry."

"Don't be. It's my own fault for never saying anything. I always just kept hoping that one day he'd turn around and see me and... know... or something. It's silly. But he shouldn't have died not knowing how much I cared."

"My parents let Uun take me without a single word," Davin said.

"How old were you?"

"Twelve summers."

Raisa grimaced.

"I used to make up stories about how they were plotting to rescue me, how they'd find me and tell me they'd made a mistake, and then we'd run away to Telmondir together." Davin dug his fingers deep into the sand. "Lies I told myself to ease my loneliness, I guess."

"Maybe they didn't have a choice."

"I was the one with no choice!" His tone dripped with venom and his hand clenched into a fist around the sand.

A surge of sympathy filled her. She opened her mouth, but there were no words, no words for that kind of betrayal and pain. In a flash, she was transported back to the night of her father's death.

* * *

A pounding on the door. Furious shouts and thudding feet.

The soldiers outside had been stirred to a boiling rage, and now they wanted blood. Fear, frigid and dizzy, filled her as her father pushed her away from the door.

"Get back, stay inside," her father whispered. "Do not speak. Do not move."

"Papa!" Her own whisper caught in her throat. "Don't leave, don't..."

"My Raisa." His eyes softened and he wrapped his strong arms around her, the last embrace he would ever give her; had he known? Had he gone to his death voluntarily? She believed he had, to save her. "My Raisa, never forget that I love you. Your mother loved you. Be strong, my daughter."

Then he was gone. Forever gone, and his last act had been to take upon himself the punishment that should have been hers. For it had been Raisa, and not her father, who had crept to the stables in the misty, early hours before dawn and unlocked the door, letting Oleck and his friends escape into the night.

* * *

"They should have fought for me." Davin's voice dropped to a miserable whisper. "They could have at least tried."

"You're right." Raisa met his gaze and held it. "You're right," she repeated. "That's what parents are supposed to do."

Davin leaned back against the sand. "How's your arm?"

It took Raisa a moment to understand what he meant, her mind reeling from the sudden change of subject. She pushed her sleeve up and glanced down at her upper arm, where the jagged cut of the assassin's blade had torn through her flesh—how many days ago had that been? Was it only days?—and was now healing, an ugly yellow scab surrounded by a sickly, spreading purplish-red bruise.

"It's healing," she said with a shrug.

"Any pain?"

"Not that I notice."

"Good."

A sudden flash of insight shot through her and Raisa stared, her mouth suddenly dry. "It was you."

He frowned at her.

"When I was poisoned. You tended my wound... but why?"

Davin brushed his hands together, freeing them of the grains of sand sticking to his skin. "I needed you healthy so you could help me escape. Besides, I felt a little guilty."

"Guilty?"

With a surreptitious glance at her, he withdrew the golden orb and held it up. After a moment, Raisa's head began to swim with the now-familiar music emanating from it. She closed her eyes against the sudden wash of dizziness and raised a hand as if she could ward off the sound. The music faded even as the glow did, though the tugging string that now connected her to the orb remained.

"Why can I hear it?"

Davin pressed his lips together. "Because that was the point all along."

"What do you mean?"

"Uun is searching for another one."

"Another orb?"

Davin nodded. "Apparently there were seven, and the one that belonged to him went missing, or was stolen, I've never been entirely clear on what happened to it. But he's been looking for it for a long time. He even has an elite group whose sole purpose is to search for the orb, though sometimes they do other work for him, as well."

"The assassins..." Raisa breathed.

"Yes. They call themselves the Kotai. The members of the group have changed over the years, but their purpose has never altered."

A chill trickled its way down Raisa's spine. "Did he intend to force me to join them? If they had broken my mind, would that have been my fate?"

Davin gave her a quizzical look. "Broken your mind?"

"The torture, the training." A terrible premonition slipped into her thoughts and Raisa paused. "Or did it work, after all? Is this an elaborate game of some kind to show that I can be brought to heel like a well-trained malkyn?" Her throat tightened and panic threatened to strangle her. Her breaths came in short, quick gasps as her worst fears sprang up to torment her. What if they had succeeded in turning her into one of them? She stared wildly at Davin, all her old fears rearing back up. Could she trust him? Or was he another one of her tormentors, sent along to test her obedience? With a snarl, Raisa rose to a crouch, her fingers tightening into claws.

"Raisa..." Davin's face turned pale. "What are you talking about?"

"Don't pretend with me," she hissed. "You don't know what I've been through. You don't know what I've been fighting! They've been trying to turn me into their puppet, their weapon, their obedient soldier."

Davin shook his head. "No... they haven't."

"Lies!" Raisa inhaled sharply, then paused as his words registered. "What?"

"The training? It wasn't because they thought they could control you. You might have gained a measure of Lorcan's trust, but never Uun's. They wanted to see what your limits were. They were measuring your strength, your stamina, trying to see if there were any flaws in Lorcan's design, trying to perfect the experiment before using it on the Kotai." Davin eyed her askance. "You really thought they could control your mind?" His lips quirked up briefly, but then his expression turned serious again; the transition was so swift, Raisa could not tell if she had only imagined it.

"You're laughing at me."

"No... maybe a little."

"All this time..." Raisa slumped back down. "I thought..." She put her head in her hands. "I've been going insane trying to keep my thoughts my own, convinced they were trying to turn me into a better version of Lorcan's baumen."

Davin sobered. "I'm sure he would if he could. Spending any amount of time in Lorcan's constant company would be enough to drive anyone insane. I'm certain your attempts to stay sane were not completely unwarranted. But they didn't need to turn you into their weapon, not when they have men eager to volunteer if Lorcan's process could be proven safe and beneficial."

Fresh understanding struck Raisa with horror and she lifted her head. "The Kotai..."

Davin nodded. "Probably already undergoing the process. Maybe even already on our trail. The other prisoners, too."

"No," Raisa breathed.

Davin gave a sharp nod. "Yes. The Kotai were climbing over each other to be first in line for Lorcan's treatments." He slipped the orb back into its pouch. "Which is why I can't risk using that anymore. If everything went as well as it did with you, they'll be able to track us by it if I use it. Possibly even if I don't. Lorcan wanted to test that, next, but he never got the chance."

"Why?"

"The orb that the Ar'Molon is seeking may not be in the hands of someone who can use it. In that case, the Kotai would not gain much of an advantage in their search. His great hope was that Lorcan's alterations would help the Kotai hear every orb, whether or not it lay dormant."

"Can just anyone use the orbs?" Raisa asked.

"I'm not certain how it works, exactly, but only certain people seem to have the ability to use them... and so far as I know nobody can use more than one."

"You said there were seven of them? How many does Uun have?"

"Only three that I know of. Mine, Lorcan's, and the one the Ar'Mol has in his scepter."

Raisa closed her eyes, remembering her audience with the Ar'Mol, back before everything had gone horribly wrong. "I remember. A dull gray stone affixed just below that curved blade at the top."

"Yes. As far as I know, Uun's never found anyone who can use that one. That's why the Ar'Mol has everyone who enters his presence touch the scepter: they're looking for someone with the affinity for it."

"I wonder why they've never found anyone?"

Davin shrugged. "I don't know, but I do know it's been a nettle under the Ar'Molon's heel for as long as I've been in his employ, probably longer. There are times when I think..."

"What?"

"That even he doesn't quite know what's wrong with it."

Raisa narrowed her eyes. "Is that possible?"

"He's not all-knowing." Davin shrugged. "All I know is that I've seen him staring at it, usually when he thinks nobody's looking... and the expression on his face when he does is one of confusion." He cleared his throat. "I'd like to try something, if you're willing?"

A surge of suspicion welled up in Raisa's chest, replacing the pleasant camaraderie they had built throughout their conversation. And yet memories of the past few days tugged at her heart and indicated a veracity in his words. Why could she not trust him? A memory wormed its way through her mind.

"I heard the music of your orb when I was fighting," she said, trying to keep the accusation out of her tone. She wanted answers, not reprisal. "It distracted me."

Davin's expression clouded. "That's what I felt guilty about."

"You did it on purpose?" Hot betrayal pooled at the base of her throat. "Why?"

"I knew their blades were poisoned. I heard Roald and his men discussing it the night before, and I knew they were planning to kill you if they could. But I also knew they would need it to be a clean kill, that Lorcan and Uun would not allow a killing blow after you were down." He hung his head. "Perhaps I had too little faith in your abilities, but I needed you alive."

She stared at him, wounded. How wounded, she could not yet tell, nor why. Was it because he had seen her as a tool in his own escape? Or that he had thought so little of her fighting prowess? How could she hold either against him when they had not yet known each other? After all, he had tended her wound after, cleaned her tent, and treated her with kindness and dignity.

"If you wish to leave, I can't stop you," he whispered.

"What did you want to try?"

His eyes widened, and Raisa took pleasure in the surprise reflected there.

He uncurled his fingers, revealing the orb once more. "We know you can sense the orb when I use it. But the true test is if you can sense it when it's inactive. If you can't, then we have little to fear. But if you can..." He let the sentence trail off and a hollow formed in the pit of Raisa's stomach. Whatever she could do, the Kotai could match.

"Let me try." Raisa closed her eyes and concentrated, focusing her thoughts on the memory of the music she had heard several times. Silence pounded rhythmically in her temples, matching the cadence of her own heartbeat. She steadied her breathing, focusing on keeping her exhalations soundless. The dry air of the desert enfolded her. The warmth of the sun on her head began to grow uncomfortably hot, the sand coating her skin itched and irritated her, but Raisa forced herself to remain still, straining, listening, seeking the faintest echo of the music of the orb.

As she waited, she grew aware of something she had not noticed before. Not a sound, this sensation did not resemble the music she heard when the orb activated—no, this was a gentle, constant buzzing that raced its way up her spine and burrowed into the center of her chest just below the base of her throat. Curious, and without opening her eyes, Raisa turned slowly away from Davin to her right. The sensation changed; now it felt as though a string had been attached to her chest and was subtly— but insistently—pulling at her, compelling her to move to her left. Without opening her eyes, Raisa rose to her feet and took a few steps out into the desert. The tugging sensation did not alter intensity in any way, but she knew with absolute certainty in exactly which direction Davin sat.

"I am going to count to ten," she said aloud. "Stand up and move somewhere, as quietly as you can."

Davin did not reply. Keeping her eyes closed and plugging her ears, Raisa began counting out loud. When she reached ten, she focused once again on that quiet sensation and slowly turned in a circle until she was certain she was facing the Shipwright. Cautiously, she took a step forward, then another. Again, no alteration in intensity occurred. Another step, and Raisa opened her eyes to find herself standing just a pace away from Davin. He stared at her, his expression troubled.

"You can sense it, then?"

Raisa nodded, her stomach lurching at the implications of her discovery. "It's different than when it's active, though. I don't know how far away it is, just the direction. That's the only one I can sense right now, though I might be able to sense the others now that I know what I'm looking for."

"Then we aren't safe as long as I have the orb."

"What can we do, though? It's not safe to leave it lying around. We can't let Uun reclaim it."

"Then we just have to keep running until we get somewhere safe. Somewhere beyond his reach," Davin said.

"Where?" Raisa asked, hopelessness threatening to overwhelm her.

"Telmondir."

She stared at him for a long moment, then nodded. "I'll wake Olin."

41

———

"Mouse knows what he's about." Marik kept his voice calm, sensing the rising unease in the two remaining members of his crew.

"It's been too long," Oleck insisted, his face darkening behind his beard.

"Someone should go after him," Shaesta added, one hand resting gracefully on her hip, her chin thrust forward defiantly.

Marik kept his eyes on the desert between them and the forest, that massive, impossible forest. He had given Mouse strict instructions not to wander too far inside the tree-line. A body could get lost for sennights in that dark tangle of unnatural foliage. He definitely did not like how close to the ground they were hovering at the moment, though it seemed nobody had yet spotted them. Perhaps the Igyeum camp was much deeper inside the forest. He concealed a shudder that worked its way through him at that prospect, for it meant they were safe from prying eyes, but also that Raisa might be hidden away in the depths of those trees.

"Do you see anything at all, Captain?" Oleck asked.

"Other than the truly creepifying forest out there?" Marik waved a hand. "No, no sign of Mouse, yet... Wait!"

Marik turned his full attention back to the ground, scanning the area for whatever had just flickered in the corner of his vision.

There! A small splotch of darkness on the sand partway down the dune in front of them. He squinted, sure that the splotch had not been there a moment before. It did not move. And yet... Marik did not hesitate. He grabbed a rope, flung it over the side of the airship, and without a sound or word of explanation he jumped over the rail and slid down the rope, his feet thudding to the ground a moment later. A sudden weight on the rope above before he let go informed him of someone following his lead, but he didn't wait, instead he began to run up the dune. The sand gave way beneath his feet, slowing his frantic progress, exacerbating his limp, and mocking his efforts to gain speed. The muscles in his legs and chest screamed at him to stop, but he could not, for as he drew closer to the splotch, he began to make out the small form. His eyes now confirmed what his preternatural sense had already informed him was true: it was the figure of a small boy. Mouse!

A tall, dark figure suddenly surpassed him, and Marik grimaced as Ioan outpaced him and ran nimbly up the dune without any seeming difficulty. The defender reached the splotch in seconds and knelt down. Doggedly, Marik lowered his chin and propelled himself forward, reaching the boy's side several minutes behind the defender. He doubled over, breathing hard, his eyes scanning the familiar features of his cabin boy before glancing up at Ioan, fear clutching at his heart.

"Is he alive?"

Ioan's hands moved deftly across the boy's body, searching for injury. He touched the boy's left arm and Mouse fairly screamed, though his eyes never opened.

"Does that answer your question?" Ioan asked. "He's alive, but I think this arm is broken."

"Can you carry him back to the Hawk?" Marik asked.

Ioan nodded. "Easily. Help me lift him, though. I don't want to jostle that arm any more than we have to."

Marik helped lift the boy, arranging him in Ioan's arms as though Mouse were but a wee babe.

Ioan grunted. "It's a good thing he weighs so little."

"And that you can move across sand with such ease."

Ioan's gaze darted away, and even in the fading light Marik could see the muscle that suddenly began to twitch in Ioan's jaw. Before the other could say anything in response, however, Marik waved a hand. "You get Mouse back to the ship. I'll struggle along behind and catch up with you soon. Tell the others to make ready, we need to get out of here, and quickly."

Ioan nodded and sped off down the dune. A spike of envy pricked at Marik as he watched the ease with which the man moved across the sand, his feet treading so lightly they barely made any impressions at all. Meanwhile, Marik descended the dune in great, jolting steps, the sand giving way beneath his feet. With each step, he could feel granules of sand slipping inside his boots and slithering inside his socks, chafing against his skin.

"By the time I've gotten back to the ship, I'll be bringing the entire desert with me," he growled. Still, he kept his ears alert, but no sounds of pursuit reached him, which he took as a good sign. Whatever had happened to Mouse in that forest, he appeared to have escaped cleanly.

By the time Marik made it back to the airship, Mouse had already been transported to his room belowdecks. He lay in his hammock, his face pale, eyes closed. Shaesta stood on the far side of his hammock, holding a cloth to the boy's forehead.

"Did he say anything?" Marik asked. Ioan shook his head, backing away to make room. Marik knelt at the boy's side. "Mouse?" Marik's voice came out in a strained tone. "Mouse?" His head drooped. "I knew I shouldn't have sent him in there alone. This life is no place for a child."

"It's the life he begged you for," Shaesta murmured from the doorway.

"And in the past year what has it gotten him? Nothing but pain."

Mouse's eyes, glassy with fever, fluttered open. "Cap'n?" he moaned.

Marik bent over the boy. "I'm here, Mouse."

"Heard them talking. They said the prisoner escaped." Mouse paused, breathing hard as though winded. "They're chasing her. The Ar'Molon was here, but he's gone... back to Melar."

"That's good," Marik muttered.

"Sent... assassins after Raisa. They're heading west. We have to find her first!" Mouse's voice grew agitated and he struggled to sit up, a wild look in his eyes. As he moved, he let out a scream of pain and sank back into his hammock. He glanced down and grimaced. "Broke my arm again, Cap'n."

"I saw that." Marik frowned. "You should take better care of yourself. We worry, you know."

Beneath the stern reproach, Mouse beamed. "Aye. I'll do better. Promise..." His eyes closed and his breathing evened out.

"He's worn out, poor little mite," Shaesta said. "I'll watch over him for now." She gave Marik a meaningful glance. "We have to go after Raisa and find her as swiftly as we can. But Captain... Mouse needs a physician to treat his arm or it won't heal properly. From what I can tell, this break is in the same place as the last one. It's beyond my skill to set it. More than that, though, is the fever... it's worrying."

"Understood." Marik strode out of the room, his face grim.

A moment later, they all felt the vibrations of the airship as the cynders flared to life, lifting them out of their hiding place and into the evening sky. The chase had begun.

42

Raisa opened her eyes to darkness. Rolling over, she worked her jaw, opening and closing her mouth a few times, trying to generate enough saliva to swallow. Her dry, chapped lips stung, and her throat begged for water. She fumbled for her waterskin with one hand, the other massaging along her jawline in an effort to rub the fog of sleep from her brain. The cool water eased her parched tongue and helped push away the veil of weariness, but even the blessed liquid could only do so much to atone for the long, cold nights of fleeing and fitful, sweltering days lying in discomfort on the hard, lumpy sand. She had lost track of how long they had been traveling through the Plains, but she harbored a nugget of worry that they had veered off course somewhere. They ought to have reached the edge of the desert already, and yet it still stretched out before them, though the terrain had grown rockier of late, with small cliffs rising up among the dunes. This had stopped Olin from being able to dig caves, and they had been forced to fly around looking for natural shelters where they could hide. Rolling her shoulders, she put the worry out of her mind. Perhaps they weren't traveling as fast as they thought. Davin had been able to make a few repairs to the skimmer, but knowing that they were being pursued by men who could hear the song of his orb made him loath to use it, and Raisa could not blame him. She had no interest in being recaptured.

With a sigh, Raisa shook her companions. Olin, who had dozed off at the entrance of their nook, jolted awake and spent the next few minutes apologizing for sleeping during his watch. Raisa felt that she ought to reprimand him, but she was too weary and thirsty to muster the energy to do so.

Davin waved a hand at the durven. "No harm done," he muttered.

They gathered their few belongings and stepped out of the hollow. The moon had been rising late, and so the darkness of the night was complete. Davin coaxed the skimmer to life, and Raisa eyed it. Was it her imagination, or did the engine's gentle hum seem to stutter? Had it taken a few seconds longer to activate? The skimmer represented their only path to freedom. They could not survive in the Plains if they had to walk the rest of the way, especially if they had veered off course. And yet she could not solve any of their problems with worry. She gazed at the endless expanse of dark rocky outcroppings curving along the horizon in every direction and shuddered at the thought of being lost in this barren rock waste.

"Raisa!" Olin's voice whispered through the darkness.

She turned and studied his silhouette. He hung back a few paces. Respect for the stocky durven filled Raisa. He had no training for traveling in such conditions, and yet he had not uttered a word of complaint throughout their entire ordeal. It struck her suddenly that perhaps he had as little waiting for him as she did. He had worried that he had told Uun and Lorcan too much when they were torturing him. Had the Igyeum found the Deepway as Olin feared? Could Olin be the last of his kind?

"Don't worry about falling asleep on watch," she said kindly. "Davin was right, no harm."

"No." Olin raised an arm and pointed at the sky. "That!"

Above her, the sky was black, devoid of stars. For a moment, she did not understand. Then it struck her. The stars were gone!

They should have been there, dotting the sky with their cool, pale light, but she could not see them. Her exhausted brain struggled to process the information coming from her eyes; no, the stars were not gone, they had been blotted out, blocked by something large... her eyes darted back and forth, catching the starlight around the object, tracing its shape... an airship! A colossal airship soared toward them. Her breath caught in desperation. Had they been spotted? Their figures were so small and the darkness so complete, there was still a chance they hadn't been seen. Her ears caught the soft flutter of movement all around them, and then silhouettes began to descend from the airship; slowly they came down on the ropes they had dropped.

"Davin!" Raisa hissed.

"I see them." He was at her side, his voice soft.

"What do we do?"

"Thank the Builder they haven't used their beam weapon." The Shipwright's whisper in her ear was tense. "They must have been instructed to bring us back alive."

"I won't go back." Raisa brandished her dagger.

"We can't hope to stand against so many."

"The skimmer!" Raisa gasped. "Before they reach the ground. We can outrun them."

"For how long?" Davin's weary tone made Raisa's anger flare.

"For as long as it takes!" The three of them fairly threw themselves onto the little craft. "Go!" she urged.

The Shipwright twisted the throttle and they lifted off the ground and sped across the sand. Behind them, Raisa could hear startled shouts as the assassins realized their quarry had fled.

"We can't outrun them," Davin shouted over the whipping of the wind. "I haven't been able to make the repairs she needs, and our cynder is almost depleted. Besides, we're stuck hovering just a few feet off the ground. This thing can't get any kind of altitude. We're sitting ducks."

"What can we do?" Raisa wanted to punch something, or better yet, run someone through with her rapier. She missed her rapier, the elegance of it, the finesse it required to wield. She had left it on the Hawk when she posed as a merchant in Melar, but the Hawk had crashed into the Whispering Wood, and her rapier had gone down with it; she would never see either again. Her mind raced erratically, searching for a solution. They couldn't outrun their pursuers. They couldn't stand and fight, not with a couple of daggers against an entire crew of assassins—especially if Davin's suspicions were correct and the assassins had been altered in the same way Raisa herself had been. Even with her additional training, she would not be able to defeat them all by herself; after days wandering through the desert, dehydrated, exhausted, and malnourished, she was not exactly in prime condition. Another problem suddenly presented itself, as off to the east, the moon began to rise above the horizon. Soon, its light would illuminate them against the desert floor, making them a much easier target for their pursuers to spot.

"What are we going to do?" Olin asked.

Indecision paralyzed her, surrounding her like bands of iron. Raisa's chest heaved and she could not breathe. "We stand and fight," she growled. "Davin, put our backs to the biggest cliff you can find. We make a stand there."

"Are you sure?" The skimmer lowered slightly, the wind of their passing throwing stinging particles of sand up at their faces.

"What choice do we have?"

Davin's shoulders hunched forward and he leaned over the steering mechanism, angling toward a cluster of dunes and cliffs off to their left. Within moments, they were weaving through a maze-like rocky terrain. The ground dropped out from beneath them and the skimmer plummeted down a steep incline to speed along the floor of a sudden ravine. There was no time to contemplate their surroundings, however. Raisa could feel their pursuers behind them, the silhouette of their ship like the very shadow of death itself following their trail, in no hurry, confident it would catch its prey sooner or later.

"There!" Raisa pointed at an outcropping of rock that jutted from the side of the ravine. "That will give us something to put our backs against, at least."

Davin swung the skimmer into the meager shelter and cut off the power. Together they huddled under the outcropping and waited.

The ravine was too narrow for the enemy airship to maneuver down into, but in the rising moonlight, they soon began to see the figures of their attackers creeping across the dunes and along the ravine floor. Raisa gripped her dagger, the weight of its inadequacy heavy in her hand.

"Steady," she murmured to her companions. "Let them come to us."

A shape flew at them from the side, and Raisa met the attack by crouching down and thrusting her dagger upward. She hit something, and heard a sharp intake of breath. Her attacker lurched back and for a moment she lost him. A heavy blow landed on her shoulder, knocking her sideways. She hit her head on the rocks and lay there gasping, a great ringing filling her ears. She saw the stocky figure of Olin leap past her prone body and saw him swing his small shovel at her attacker's head. The thick, wooden implement made a sickening sound as it connected solidly. Then Olin stood over her, reaching down to pull her to her feet.

"Thanks," she said. She paused and searched the unconscious form until she found the sword he had dropped. She hefted it in her hand. It was heavier than she liked, and the balance wasn't perfect, but it was better than her dagger alone.

"No problem." Olin lunged to one side, swinging his shovel again at an attacker Raisa had missed. The man let out a yell and darted out of range while Raisa stared at the durven in surprise.

His teeth flashed in the darkness. "Didn't I mention I can see in the dark?"

"Right," Raisa replied. "But so can they."

Three more enemies converged on their position. The fugitives fought, but the assassins outnumbered them. The Kotai fought with a skill that even Raisa couldn't match, though she struggled desperately, her sword ringing as it clashed again and again against the blades of her opponents.

She slashed and parried, moving to the edge of the overhang, but never stepping fully out into the ravine, making sure never to leave its safety or her back unprotected. Her opponent pressed his advantage, then seemed to falter, as though distracted. Raisa's blade whipped through the air at his suddenly unprotected side.

"Raisa!" Davin's sudden shout arrested her stroke. She glanced over and saw that one of the Kotai had an arm wrapped around the Shipwright's neck, his sword held across Davin's chest in a threatening position.

"Surrender now, or this one dies," the warrior snarled. "Throw down your weapons or I slit his throat."

Raisa's breath caught. In the soft glow of the moon, she could clearly see the panic on Davin's face and her heart quailed within her breast. She exchanged a look with Olin. The durven hefted his wooden shovel, his face shadowed and grim as he silently let her know he would not go down without a fight.

"No!" a new voice rang through the night. "All the Kotai throw down your weapons, or I run your leader through."

Raisa, her own blade still raised, felt her heart leap into her mouth at the familiarity of the voice shouting commands through the darkness. A painful tingling pressure began to build at the back of her nose and tears sprang to her eyes. That voice! But it couldn't be. It couldn't be... She edged out from beneath the outcropping of rock above her and cut her eyes this way and that until she caught sight of the speaker off to her left. Even with her improved eyesight, she could not make out anything more than his shadowy form at this distance, but he stood in a similar position to the man holding Davin, and she could only assume that he held his sword to the throat of the Kotai leader.

"Marik." She mouthed the name soundlessly, unwilling to believe it, unwilling to hope against hope that her ears were telling her the truth, a truth her heart said could not be. And yet, it was his voice, his stance... a glance up at the sky confirmed that a second airship hovered above them, a smaller, more graceful airship, with a silhouette she would have recognized anywhere.

"Marik!" The name now exploded from her lips in a glad cry, a wrenching sob, an eruption of emotion she could barely understand.

Her outburst went unnoticed, as Marik—it could only be Marik, and yet how could it be? He was dead—prodded his hostage, forcing him to take a few steps forward. From this new angle she could tell that in addition to the sword across his throat, Marik had a dagger pressed between the Kotai's shoulder blades. The man stood stiffly.

"You're supposed to be dead," the man muttered, his voice carrying across the rocks, amplified by the ravine walls.

"Sorry to disappoint you," Marik replied, his tone light. "Tell your man to let his prisoner go."

"No!" Marik's prisoner growled. "Keanin, do not do as he says. Our mission is more important than any of us. Take the Shipwright and the prisoners back to our master."

"But De'Anan Roald..."

"Do what I say!"

"I wouldn't," Marik said, his tone mild.

"Why not?" Roald spat.

Marik made a small gesture and an arrow thumped to the ground between Roald's feet. "Because you and your men are surrounded," Marik replied, his tone a lazy drawl. "And my men have bows, and they're fair shots."

Roald stiffened, and even in the darkness Raisa could see his fury. "More of my men are still aboard my airship," he growled. "If I don't return soon, they will fire the cynderblast into this ravine. You escaped its power before, but I'm sure you haven't forgotten. Here in this enclosed space, none of you will survive."

A tingle of apprehension shivered up Raisa's spine. She remembered the bolt of fiery sunlight all too well. Even now, she could feel the searing heat of its power through the bars of her cage on that night so long ago, the first time Marik had tried to rescue her.

"Your men would sacrifice their leader and comrades?" Marik asked, his tone incredulous.

"For the sake of our mission? Yes. That one"—he indicated Davin—"stole something from our master. We will recover it or die trying."

Davin held up a hand, and the area around him suddenly lit with a bright, golden glow. "What if I give it back?"

"Davin!" Raisa shouted, but he gave a tiny shake of his head.

"What if I hand it over? The orb for my freedom, the orb for all our lives?" Davin asked.

Keanin, his face now illuminated by the soft gleam of the active orb, frowned. "You would simply hand it over?"

"To save my life and my friends? Yes."

"My master wishes to rip you apart," Keanin said.

"And he may still get to do that, but at a later date." Davin attempted a grin, but it wavered.

"De'Anan," Keanin called out, "it's a good deal. The Ar'Molon gets his orb back, and we all go our separate ways. We continue our original mission..."

"Shut your mouth!" Roald barked the order and Keanin's lips clamped shut. The De'Anan stared darkly at Davin. At length, he gave a single, sharp nod. "Very well. I accept your terms."

"Not so fast." Marik's fingers tightened on the hilt of his sword. "How do we know you'll honor the agreement?"

"You have my word."

Marik gave a sharp laugh. "What is that worth? The word of an assassin?"

"This, coming from a pirate," Roald scoffed. "You're not one to be casting stones, dear captain. I may be an assassin, but I am an honorable one. When I give my word, I keep it. From your reputation, I believe you understand honor."

"Perhaps, but I'd like some additional assurance. Have the rest of your men head down the ravine and return to your airship.

Then that Keanin fellow and I will meet in the middle. Davin will hand Keanin the orb, then Keanin will let him go, and I will let you go. Deal?"

"Crude." Roald sniffed. "But effective. You have a deal." The assassin raised a hand. "Kotai! Return to the airship and may you find Sevalk."

"May Sevalk be found." The answer came faintly in response as the rest of Roald's men melted away, backing down the ravine. Raisa watched them go, alert for any sign of treachery.

Once the assassins had begun to climb the ladders lowered from the airship's sides, Marik prodded Roald forward, and Keanin did the same with Davin until they stood only a few paces apart. Marik nodded at Davin. "Go ahead."

Davin opened his hand, holding the orb out.

Keanin gave his captain a questioning glance. Roald bobbed his head, a slight motion, but Keanin's hesitation melted away and he plucked the orb from Davin's open palm. As the Shipwright released the orb, the gem dimmed and faded, throwing them once more into darkness. Raisa blinked, struggling to force her eyes to adjust in the pale moonlight left behind.

There came a sound of rushed steps and a grunt of pain. Raisa's heart hammered against her ribs and she strained her eyes, trying to force them to adjust. A click sounded softly and a pinpoint of light appeared, followed by the glow of a lantern. Marik held the lantern up, and Raisa could see that the exchange had transpired. His sword now rested lazily against his right shoulder, and the dagger had disappeared, replaced by the lantern.

"Until next time, pirate." Roald's voice floated across the ravine as he and his comrade backed away, their gazes fixed on Marik.

"Next time, I kill you." There was no malice in Marik's voice, just a simple statement of fact.

A low chuckle emanated from the assassin. "It is too bad we serve different masters, pirate. In another life, we might have been friends."

Marik's face split into a grin. The lantern light flickering across his features made the expression into an eerie, otherworldly sight. "Perhaps. But you chose the wrong side, assassin." He gave a single nod, and something about the way he did so almost seemed like a bow of respect.

The Kotai leader spun on his heel with military precision and he and his crewman disappeared into the night.

Only then, did Marik turn to look at Raisa. The lantern cast a small ring of light around him and Raisa stared into it, trying to assure herself that this was not a dream.

"Raisa?" He raised the lantern, peering into the darkness surrounding her. It was his voice, his mannerisms, and yet, still Raisa hesitated. He was dead. This must be a dream. Or perhaps a nightmare. Or a trick. As Marik took a step toward her, she recoiled involuntarily, shuddering deeper into the shadows. A hand on her arm made her give a startled gasp and leap to one side, but it was only Olin.

"What's wrong?" Olin asked.

Tears blurred her vision. How could she answer such an innocent question? Everything was wrong, it was all wrong. She was all wrong. And yet, Marik was alive. The impossible, the extraordinary, the only thing she had wanted to be true and the only thing she had not entertained a sliver of hope for now stood mere paces away, and she slouched in the shadows, too petrified to accept the miracle.

"Raisa?" Marik called again, his voice quiet, hesitant. He called her by name. Her name. How long since someone called her by name rather than the hated number? How long since someone had spoken to her in kindness? Someone who knew her and cared?

With a broken sob, Raisa fled from the shadows, intent on flinging herself into his arms, and yet, as she reached him, an unfamiliar shyness clasped its arms around her and made her halt just inside the halo of lantern light. She stared at him, painfully aware of just how much she had changed. She stared directly into his eyes, not having to look up at all to meet his gaze. Her own gaze fell to the ground and she dug the toe of her new boot into the sand.

"Raisa." Marik said her name again. "We thought…"

Whatever he had been about to say was lost as someone collided into her from the side. Her instinct was to lash out at this unexpected attack, but then she caught a whiff of a familiar scent and heard Oleck's booming voice as his arms wrapped around her and raised her up off the ground to twirl her around.

"Raisa!" he bellowed.

She relaxed into his exuberant embrace, allowing a timid smile to creep across her face. As he spun her around and around, chortling and exclaiming his delight at finding and rescuing her, a laugh—such a foreign concept!—welled up within her and escaped in a strangled burst of sound from between her lips. It sounded more like a gasp, or perhaps a sob, but she believed it could have been a laugh, in another life.

"Put her down, Oleck," Marik commanded, but there was mirth in his voice, as well. "Come, we should return to the airship where we can have a proper reunion and have some introductions, as well. Besides, we need to get Mouse to Ferndale."

"What's wrong with Mouse?" Raisa gasped out as Oleck gently placed her on the ground and looped an arm protectively across her shoulders.

"He'll be fine, but he needs a physician to set his broken arm," Marik said. "We'll explain everything on board. But I'd like to get out of here before those assassins decide to try to double-cross us."

Together, they headed toward the rope ladder that swung in the moonlight and led to a home she had thought gone forever. Her traitor heart fluttered with apprehension, and she grimaced, sternly reminding it that this was a moment for joy. But even in the midst of the reunion, she was alert, her soul curling in on itself awaiting the next blow that life would deal her.

43

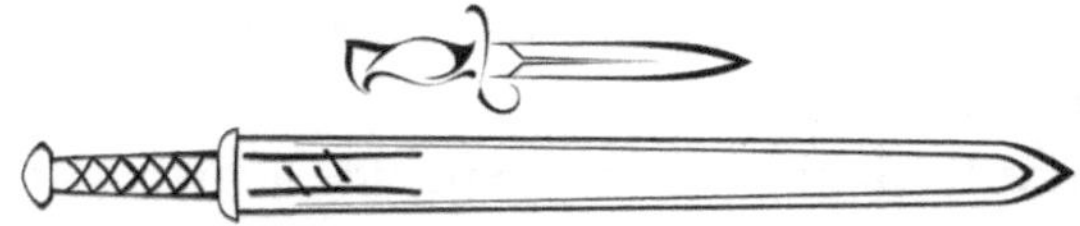

The camp inside the Whispering Wood was a frenzy of activity as the cargo cruiser lowered itself into the dock. Beren watched it settle, wondering what tidings such a messenger might bring. It had been sighted earlier that morning from the tower in the center of the camp, flying the colors of Dalma, and speculations on what its purpose might be had occupied the ranks for the last two hours.

"Think it's your father?" Grayden asked, coming to stand beside him as the airship settled in its moorings and powered down.

Beren shrugged. "He shouldn't have any reason to come here. But it might be a message from Central Command."

"It's a big ship," Grayden commented. "Maybe it's bringing supplies or reinforcements? It can't be just a messenger."

"We will know soon enough," Beren said.

"Oh, come on." Grayden elbowed him. "Aren't you curious?"

"Yes."

Grayden chuckled. "You must have at least a guess."

"No."

Shaking his head, Grayden lapsed into silence. Beren appreciated his friend leaving him alone. How could he explain that speculation felt like so much wasted time? They would learn the purpose of the airship once it landed. They had been waiting for new orders for nearly a lunat, and every defender in the camp was growing restless. Action was needed. There had to be something useful they could be doing. Something more than simply fortifying the base and running resupply missions back and forth between here and Pentua. They had buried their dead, a somber and grueling task. But beyond patrolling and staying alert, there had been little to occupy their hours. Docks were already built and ready for their airships. Boredom was becoming a problem.

The Southern Command was on its way, they had been assured. But their movements were slow. The Telmondir response to the Igyeum incursions had stalled. The unofficial cynder-dropping run that Grayden had commanded had been an abject failure. The Igyeum still had Akkad and Baktan in a stranglehold, and they could not be forced out. Word was that Northern Command was sending regiments down to help in Ondoura. Now that the Skyborne had cut off the Igyeum's supply center here in the Whispering Wood, perhaps progress could be made and they would get new orders. Hopefully.

The gangway was lowered and a tall, pale man stepped through the door. Beren felt Grayden stiffen next to him, and he took a closer look at the new arrival's face. Recognition dawned even as Grayden called out his name.

"Wynn!" Grayden strode across the grass to greet his friend with a back-pounding hug. Beren joined them, grinning his pleasure at seeing their friend once more.

"Welcome to Forest Camp," Beren rumbled, grasping Wynn's forearm.

"What are you doing here?" Grayden asked, grinning from ear to ear. "Couldn't stand being left out of the battle any longer?"

Wynn laughed a little self-consciously. "Yeah. Well, no. I mean..." He shook his head. "There's so much to tell you. When Marshal Freidzen sent for me, I hoped I'd find you here, but I wasn't sure... we don't get a lot of news inside the mountain. I mean, I get some, because of Lord Adelfried, but he doesn't always share with us, but then we traveled to Dalton…" Wynn paused, flustered. "It felt wrong, me sitting in the safety of the Oreworks all this time when I knew the fighting had started in earnest."

"I was teasing," Grayden assured him. "Your work is as important as ours. Probably more."

"So, you're part of the Skyborne?" Wynn asked, glancing between them.

They both nodded, and Wynn's face broke into a broad smile. "I knew you would be. When Lord Adelfried told me about the program, I was sure you both would be. I'm glad. I don't know anyone I'd trust more with…" He trailed off again. "Well, you'll learn about all that. Tell me everything."

They shared stories of working with Niveya in Doran, their training in the mountains, and the battle to take the camp. Grayden detailed the events of his unofficial mission and how badly it had failed. Wynn nodded, his attention seeming to wander at various intervals, but Beren had learned not to be deceived by this habit. Wynn was listening avidly, even if he didn't always appear to be.

"And yourself?" Grayden finally asked.

Wynn fidgeted, his fingers tapping nervously against his thigh. "I've been working on quite a few projects with Daegan and Keene," he said. "One of them is the reason I'm here. There… are changes coming… big ones." He faltered. "I'll be, um, debriefing everyone all at once."

Grayden's eyes widened. "Talking to the whole regiment?"

"The whole division." Wynn nodded, his face turning a little green. "The general will be disembarking later."

Beren and Grayden shared a startled look. "The other regiments are coming here?" Beren asked.

"Yeah," Wynn said. "One regiment came on that ship with me. The others will be here this evening." He glanced around. "Good thing there's plenty of space for everyone."

"Near as we can figure, the Igyeum carved out a camp for an entire division of their army before attacking Ondoura," Grayden said. "And we think they were planning on dropping another division to join them and finish building... those." He waved at the enormous struts across the field. "I can't even imagine anything that big being able to stay in the sky, but... I can't think of anything it could be other than an airship dock."

"You're right," Wynn muttered, eyeing the massive beams. "That's one of the reasons for... well... like I said, you'll find out soon enough."

"So, you're really going to speak to the whole Skyborne division?" Grayden asked. "That's..."

"Close to forty-five thousand men." Wynn grimaced. "I don't want to think about it too much. I tried to convince them to send someone else, but Daegan insisted I was the only one qualified." Wynn caught their curious gazes. "Well, how about you both take me to your command center and I can check in with Major Semiv?"

"Sure," Grayden said, his gaze darting curiously to the airship his friend had arrived on.

Beren wondered how much effort it was taking for Grayden to keep all his questions silent. The three of them fell into step.

"How is my family?" Beren asked.

Wynn's face practically shone as he answered. "They are well, or at least, they were when we left for Dalton," he said, launching into detailed stories about all of Beren's various siblings. Beren soaked in the little glimpse of home that Wynn had brought with him, treasuring every word, until suddenly something Wynn said caught at his attention like a coat snagged on a nail.

"What did you just say about Cathrine and Marik?" he growled.

Wynn stuttered to a stop. "I... I... what?"

"He took her on up in his airship? Alone?" Beren could feel his hands clenching into fists.

"I..." Wynn gulped. "That's what the letter from Drengur said." He shot a terrified look at Grayden, who laughed.

"Beren, Cathrine is a grown woman and fourteen years older than you," Grayden reminded him. "From what you've told me about how she runs her school, I'm pretty sure she can handle even a pirate captain."

Beren glowered darkly. "What is she thinking?" he muttered angrily. "Surely she can't possibly think... He's a pirate!"

"And he's working an honest job for Telmondir," Grayden said. "And from the sound of it, bringing us a good share of important intel at great personal danger and sacrifice to himself."

Beren's thoughts whirled darkly. "She can do better. She's practically a princess."

"The princess and the pirate." Grayden grinned, his eyes twinkling mischievously. "Has a nice ring to it, don't you think?"

Red mist swirled in Beren's vision. "No," he said shortly. "No, I don't." Feeling as if his temper might explode out at someone who didn't deserve it if he continued this line of conversation any longer, he sped up his strides, pulling away from his friends and leading the way to the command building. Perhaps it was unreasonable for him to get so angry at the idea. Grayden was right, Cathrine was a grown woman and could make her own decisions. But the idea that she might choose someone like Marik... it would be like having Ericole Niveya as a brother. Beren ground his teeth together in frustration. He needed to hit something!

———

IT TOOK hours for the various troop ships to land and the men to disembark, but finally the entire division stood in neat ranks in the main field facing the command buildings. The airships had also transported General Severs, the head of the entire Skyborne division, a man Beren had only caught the barest glimpses of during their training. He was a short, broad-shouldered man, with impeccably trimmed steel-gray hair and mustache. General

Severs marched up in front of them, barked an introduction, and then stepped back as Wynn climbed up the steps of the command building to address them. Beren watched him, marveling at the surety of his friend's steps, the determination in his expression as he faced them. Though he still looked a little pale, Wynn did not falter as he began to speak, his voice carried across the crowds by an ingenious device he had brought with him. Wynn had gotten a little carried away trying to explain how it worked, but Beren had understood none of it.

"Men of the Gray Malkyns," Wynn began. "I have been sent to issue your next mission."

Beren felt a ripple of surprise course through him at this pronouncement. Thoughts of his sister and her possible romantic interests fled his mind, replaced by curiosity.

"As you know, the Igyeum fleet has been strangely quiet of late," Wynn continued. "And while some have speculated about this, we now know the true reason. The Igyeum has developed a new weapon. You have all seen the effects of a broken cynder?"

The men nodded.

"The Igyeum has learned a way to harness that power and aim it at their enemies. I have seen the destruction that they can wreak with this weapon. And I have spoken to men who have experienced it firsthand. Our spies have brought us news that our enemy is building a handful of enormous airships and fitting them with these new cynderblast weapons. You've seen the docks here in this camp. Imagine an airship large enough to make it look small, outfitted with a whole row of cynderblasts."

The mood of the defenders shifted perceptibly, as though it were something tangible. Beren stared at Wynn. How could they go up against that kind of weapon?

Wynn was still talking. "I have been working with the finest artificineers in Telmondir, and we've come up with a few things of our own to answer the Igyeum's new firepower." He glanced to the left and nodded, and two men climbed the steps, carrying a large crate between them. Wynn reached into the crate and pulled out a strange looking device made of wood and metal. It had a long, round barrel with a hole in the center of it that flared out at one end. The other end tapered into a narrow handle that looked like it would fit easily into a man's hand. A mechanical lever jutted off one side, and it had a smaller lever that stuck out from the bottom of the barrel and looked like a crossbow trigger.

Wynn held it up. "This is a hand cannon," he said. "Allow me to demonstrate."

He turned to his right, pointed the flared end of the device at a tree, and pulled the small trigger. They heard a slight pop, and then there was a tiny explosion of bark in the center of the tree trunk.

Beren caught his breath.

"As you have already discovered, just scoring a cynder and tossing it at the enemy makes a lot of noise but can be hard to use with precision. We've figured out a way to store the power of a cynder into much smaller objects," Wynn explained. "And the hand cannons allow us to project them in a specific direction. You can't be much farther away from your target than I am to that tree if you want it to explode on impact, though, because some of the cynder power is used to propel the coria out of the hand cannon." He stopped speaking and nodded at someone standing near the front.

Major Semiv stepped up to stand next to Wynn. "Thank you, men. Lieutenant Drexel here assures me that he and the other artificineers have been hard at work on a few other things that the defenders will find useful such as troop carriers that have shielding to protect against the cynderblasts and smaller-form airships. But he is here today to deliver the hand cannons and the coria they use because the Skyborne's next mission will be to jump down into the Igyeum shipyards and disable or destroy as many of these monster airships as possible. You will each be issued one hand cannon, and you will spend the next few sennights learning how to load, aim, and fire them before leaving for the jump. I wish we had more time, but the Igyeum airships may launch at any moment. Crates will be delivered to your barracks and your captains will be in charge of assigning you these new devices and your allotment of coria to use in practice before our mission. Targets are being set up on the east field. You will learn how to use this new weapon with the same speed and excellence that you have shown every day since you arrived at Attatoire."

The men let out a single shout.

"Dismissed!" Major Semiv yelled.

The regiment broke up in an orderly, if somewhat noisy, fashion, everyone heading to their barracks, eager to try this new wonder. But Beren and Grayden hung back, waiting to catch up with Wynn.

They had to wait for a while, because several of the higher ranking officers were chatting with their friend, asking questions about the mechanism. Eventually, they let him go, and he turned to face his friends with a strained look on his face.

"Wynn, that was incredible," Grayden said.

Wynn gave a weak smile. "Thanks. I wish..." He shook his head. "Thanks."

"I am eager to learn how to use this hand cannon," Beren said, gazing at the one still held in Wynn's hand.

Wynn held it out to him. "We can go to the range and practice now, if you'd like. I have a few more in this crate; I can teach you how to use them. I need to get some practice in, as well."

Beren frowned, glancing up from his inspection of the device. "Why?"

Wynn gave a sheepish grin. "Because, ah, I'm going with you on the mission."

Grayden paused, mid-stride. "What?"

"It's true," Wynn said.

"But... you can't..." Grayden started, then paused, turning to Beren. "Tell him, Beren."

Wynn frowned, a look of hurt creeping across his features.

Beren hurried to explain. "It's the skysailing. It takes quite a bit of training to master."

Wynn's expression cleared. "Oh, that. No, I'm not jumping with you. I'll be staying on the carrier. I'm just going along to keep an eye on the hand cannons and deliver you to your jump zone."

"Ah." Grayden nodded. "Forgive me, Wynn. I misunderstood."

Wynn shrugged a shoulder. "You won't catch me jumping off an airship and leaving behind a perfectly good engine. That kind of thing is for crazy people."

Grayden and Beren chuckled. They crossed the lane, came through a line of trees, and found the bales of hay wrapped in burlap with red circles painted on them already lined up in a neat row. Beren watched closely as Wynn showed them how to load the coria into the chamber at the hilt of the hand cannon, how to aim, and how to sight along the barrel to fire.

"Now, we don't want to do too much damage to the targets," Wynn explained, holding the hand cannon out and aiming it at the targets that were set up about fifty paces away. "So we set them up just outside the explosion range of the coria, but still close enough for accuracy. Try to shoot them at anything much farther away than that, you probably won't even hit what you're aiming at unless it's the size of a house." He pulled the trigger and they watched in amazement as the coria punctured the burlap near the center of the red circle. "And that's all there is to it," he said, handing the device back to Beren. "You try."

Beren loaded the coria carefully, just as he had seen Wynn do. Then he aimed, taking his time. He touched the trigger and the handle of the device vibrated and jerked slightly backwards, sending his aim wide. The coria ripped neatly through the corner of the hay bale.

"It's not as easy as you made it look," Beren said ruefully.

"It's hard to describe the kick it gives," Wynn said. "I've found it's better for people to just feel it for themselves. Try again. It gets easier once you know."

Taking aim once more, Beren used both hands on the handle,

as he had seen Wynn do. Ready for the sudden vibration, this time he managed to compensate, and the coria blasted through the outer rim of the red circle. He grinned, pointing the barrel at the ground and glancing at his friends.

"Better," Wynn congratulated him. "You'll probably be as good with that thing as you are with a crossbow by the end of the day."

"My turn," Grayden said, stepping up to the line.

The three men spent a pleasant hour practicing their aim and improving their technique at target practice. The hand cannons were difficult to get used to, and each one seemed to have its own finicky aiming issues. Wynn suggested that they figure out a way to put their names somewhere on the device so that they always shot with the same one.

"Hopefully we can learn how to make them to a more constant standard in the future," Wynn said as they walked back to the barracks. His shoulders suddenly slumped and his expression turned troubled.

"What's wrong?" Grayden asked.

Wynn shrugged. "It's just... I didn't even want to make these things in the first place. When I had the idea, it horrified me. I thought it meant there was something dark in my soul to even be able to conceive of such a device. But now I've not only built them, I'm talking about making more, perfecting them. And the other artificineers... they named them after me."

Grayden fell silent, turning the device over in his hands as they continued walking.

"Do you think the man who invented the crossbow is a monster?" Beren asked. "Or the sword?"

Wynn looked up at him, an expression of surprise flitting across his face. "No."

"How are hand cannons different?" Beren asked.

"I..." Wynn paused, thinking. "They aren't, I guess."

"You've created a weapon," Beren said gently. "We will use it in this war to defend our homes, our families, our people."

"But what about after the war?" Wynn asked. "Hand cannons will still exist, even if the war doesn't."

Beren nodded. "And some will still use them to kill. But some will use them to defend others. And some may use them to feed their families. A hammer can be used to build something, but it can also be used to crack a skull. Does that make the hammer evil? Or the man who invented it?"

"Of course not," Wynn replied swiftly. Then he paused. "Ah." They walked a few more steps before Wynn spoke again. "Thanks, Beren. Molly and Daegan sort of said the same thing when I showed them the design... but... hearing it from you helps."

44

Raisa stood in the silence of her quarters, spent and bewildered. There had been a flurry of joyful but hurried reunion once aboard the airship, but Marik swiftly began barking orders and the deck became a bustle of activity. To Raisa's surprise, Olin had been welcomed with open arms and no introductions needed. A small, female durven had flung herself at him with exclamations of jubilant relief at finding her brother alive, and then he and Davin had been ushered off to a room they would share. Shaesta had kindly commented on Raisa's apparent exhaustion. Now she stood in the confines of her former quarters and an overwhelming sensation of lostness besieged her as she stared around at the familiar and yet wholly foreign surroundings.

The Hawk no longer felt like home. In the exclamations and snatches of welcoming words that had tumbled over her, Raisa had learned that Uun had not lied to her completely. The airship had crashed into the Whispering Wood, much of its contents and parts scattered across the forest floor and left there to rot. And though Marik and Mouse had survived, the Hawk had been smashed beyond recognition. Wynn had done his best to keep the airship true to her original form, but Marik had given him permission to make adjustments. The result, to Raisa's mind, was disorienting in the extreme.

Home.

She was home, and yet, she felt a stranger, an outsider. In the lunats since her captivity, her crew had not frozen in time, there were adventures she knew nothing about, experiences she couldn't fathom, wounds and healing she would never understand. And her own wounds were beyond their comprehension as well. She could see it in their eyes, in the slight hesitations in their words and motions around her, even in these first few short interactions. Raisa wrapped her arms around herself. It did not seem possible that she could feel more alone here than she had in the Weald.

She wanted to pace the room, to return to the deck and demand to be given an assignment, to insist that she was fit for duty, that nothing had changed. But it was a lie. Everything had changed, and exhaustion gripped her firmly, laughing at her feeble desires. With a soft moan, Raisa pulled herself up into her bunk. The bed seemed smaller than she remembered, the space more cramped, though not uncomfortable. It bothered her, until she remembered that she had gained several inches through Lorcan's maniacal mutations. She shifted, burrowing her shoulder blades into the softness of the thin mattress. The comfort of something so simple as a mattress could not be taken for granted, and a sigh of pleasure escaped her lips. She still felt confused and overwhelmed and awkward. She still had no idea if she could ever fit into her old role again. But tonight she slept on a mattress, her head cushioned in the blissful softness of a pillow, and she could get a drink of water whenever she desired. Joy at these simple, yet breathtaking, luxuries pushed back the edges of the darkness that shrouded her soul. Perhaps healing might come, in time.

With these thoughts swirling in her mind, Raisa succumbed to the coziness of her bed and drifted into a deep sleep.

———

Nobody woke Raisa the next morning, and she slept late. Sunlight flickering across her eyelids through the porthole brought her gently out of slumber. Sitting up, she glanced around the empty chamber. The room looked the same as it had when she fell asleep, there was no indication that Shaesta had come in during the night or slept in her own bunk. Puzzled, Raisa hopped out of bed. The cool floorboards on her bare feet sent a shock through her and she smiled at the familiarity of the sensation. She paced to the pitcher, poured herself a drink of water, and gulped it greedily. Next, she opened the cupboard and let her fingers trail along the shelves containing her clothes and belongings, all neatly folded and waiting for her. She marveled at how much had survived the crash and been carefully kept by her crew. Picking out her favorites, Raisa poured water into the basin and found a cloth, using it to clean the grit and sand from her skin as best she could, before tugging a comb through the tangles of her dark hair. When she had finished, she grimaced and promised herself a bath as soon as they landed.

"Oh well." She sighed. "The washbasin is better than nothing."

She got another drink and then began tugging on her clothes, and immediately encountered a problem. She had forgotten to account for her new height, and while her clothes still fit around her, everything was too short. The cuffs of her sleeves hit her arms midway between elbow and wrist, and her trousers ended in a ridiculous fashion just below her knees. With an exasperated sigh, Raisa stomped a foot.

"Looks like I'm going to need new clothes after I've gotten that bath," she muttered. Reluctantly, she returned to the robes that the lady in the caravan had given her. Thankfully, her old boots still fit, and Raisa shoved her feet into them with a snarl, not caring that they looked ridiculous under the robe. Her sore feet twinged with relief as they settled into the soft leather; at least some things hadn't changed.

Next she picked up her rapier, and she couldn't help but grin a little at its familiar feel in her hand. "Hello, old friend. I've missed you," she whispered, buckling it snugly around her waist. This, at least, had not changed. Now she felt a bit more like herself.

A glimmer of her reflection in the mirror hanging on the wall above the washbasin caught her eye. She flinched, jerking her gaze away. In all her preparations, she had avoided allowing herself to even acknowledge the mirror's presence. But now she could not pretend it did not exist, and a morbid curiosity stirred within her, along with a question she could no longer avoid: what did she really look like?

Cautiously, she approached the mirror, glancing at it sideways out of the corner of her eye. When she had reached an appropriate distance, she squeezed her eyes shut and turned to face the mirror squarely. She cracked first one eyelid slowly open, then the other. Her gaze fell upon a reflection of everything she felt: familiar, yet wholly foreign. Her facial features were, for the most part, the same: she still had a slightly rounded chin, a fairly nice nose, and a high forehead. Her dark hair fell in waves about her shoulders, a little longer than it had been before, but otherwise unchanged, though it seemed to have some lighter brown strands that had never been there before. But her eyes, once round and hazel, now stared back at her almond-shaped and green, the deep green of a forest canopy at twilight. Her ears were another noticeable change, the pointed tips of them sticking up through her hair and drawing attention to their strange, leafy shape. Raisa sighed. Maybe Shaesta would have some ideas for how to hide her ears, or—she grinned—knowing Shaesta, she'd be excited about various ways to accentuate them and make them into something beautiful and exotic. Her shoulders drooped. It wasn't her eyes or her ears, or even the four inches she'd grown that stood out the most, though, it was the strange pattern tracing across her skin: the faint whorls and lines that covered her entire body and resembled nothing so much as tree bark. The coloring of her skin even resembled bark now: the grayish-brown hue of the trunk of a towering pine.

Raisa made a face at her reflection, then sighed again. She could no longer put off leaving her room. It was time to face her crew. She craved their company, yet dreaded their questions, their stares, their pity. Anger roiled in her stomach and propelled her to the door. With a hasty motion she grabbed the knob and jerked it open.

A few minutes later, Raisa climbed blinking onto the deck of the airship into the full light of day. Familiar sights and sounds filled her senses and provided a salve for her soul. Wind whipped through her hair, and she tilted her head back, reveling in the feeling of flight. Above her, the perfectly blue sky stretched around her in an enormous, unbroken circle. Oleck stood at the helm, his hands on the wheel, solid and dependable as always. The rigging creaked as someone climbed about in it, attending to various concerns. The sails flapped, and the scent of oils filled her nostrils as she placed a hand on the smooth, oak railing that gleamed like new. It probably was new, she thought sadly, but it was no less beautiful for that. The sounds surrounded her in the comfort of the familiar.

"It is good to see you up and around."

The voice behind her startled her and she spun, her eyes wide as she came face-to-face with Marik. "Captain!" she gasped, then stood silently, not knowing what else to say.

"We thought we'd let you sleep. You've been through a harrowing ordeal. Though Oleck was starting to get worried."

"Worried?"

"Well, you slept all day and through the night. We wanted to wake you and have a big breakfast to welcome you back, but Shaesta said you needed your rest and that a big hubbub might be too overwhelming for your first day."

Her mouth opened and closed mechanically, like a broken cog in a chronometer that causes one of the hands to tick back and forth instead of progressing around the face like it should. Raisa blinked. Could she really have slept that long? Then again, she had been half-starved and sleep-deprived from being on the run. Not to mention the toll lunats of captivity had taken.

Marik smiled, his expression gentle. "It will take some getting used to, being back with us. Take all the time you need. We'll be at our destination soon. In the meantime, if you're hungry there's food in the mess, and water. Davin said you've been thirsty. Ioan says that will decrease a bit in time."

Raisa managed to snap her mouth shut and nod, trying to place the unfamiliar name Marik had just mentioned. She tried to figure out which question to ask first. The most pressing seemed to be her companions in flight from captivity. "Davin?"

"He's told me a little about your escape from the Weald."

"Has he told you who he is?"

"The Shipwright?" Marik's mouth quirked. "Yes, he told us how he used to work for Uun. After that business with the orb, I had to ask a few questions before I could let him rest."

"He's a good man," Raisa murmured.

"He helped you. That's enough for me."

"Where's Olin?"

"In the mess, he just got up a few minutes ago and is catching up with his sister. Ray..." Marik paused and she watched a myriad of unreadable emotions cross his face. "Take your time," he said after a moment. "I know you're going to want to pretend everything can get back to normal right away, but you need to take some time."

She wanted to argue with him, but the words all stuck in her throat. Instead, she simply nodded.

"It's good to have you back," Marik said.

"Who's this Ioan?" She latched on to the unfamiliar name he had said.

Marik hesitated. "I think I'll let him introduce himself."

She frowned.

"He's with Dalmir," Marik explained hurriedly. "A defender."

"Captain..." She hesitated. A thousand thoughts and none

flashed through her mind and she found herself at a loss, not knowing what she wanted to say or ask.

"Yes?" Marik looked at her questioningly, a haunted expression in his eyes.

"Where are we headed?"

Was that relief she saw in his face? Marik's lips relaxed into a half smile. "The Healing House. Mouse needs his arm set, and I'd like the physicians to have a look at you as well."

Concern for Mouse overwhelmed her as she remembered Marik's information from the night before. "Mouse! Is he... can I...?"

"He's in his quarters resting. I'm sure he would love to see you. He's quite the little hero, you know. It was Mouse who found out you had escaped, that the Kotai were chasing you, and which direction we needed to go."

"I will make sure to thank him."

"We also have to talk about all the things Davin has told us about the Ar'Molon's plans, but we'll talk about that after we land and take care of Mouse."

She nodded, then paused. Something he'd said made her give him a quizzical frown. "You said we'd be at Ferndale soon?"

Marik nodded.

"How? I know I slept for a whole day and night, but that journey should have taken at least a sennight."

Marik grinned. "Wynn is the magician behind that answer. After the Hawk crashed a few lunats ago, Wynn put her back together, and he made some improvements while he was at it; one of those improvements nearly doubled our top speed."

Raisa's eyes widened. "Oh," was all she could manage in response to this startling news. "Well... I'll just go... get some breakfast." She turned to go back down the stairs.

"Raisa..."

The anguish in his voice arrested her mid-step.

"I'm sorry." Marik said the words in a rushed mumble.

She frowned at him, confused. "What?"

"I'm sorry," he repeated. "So sorry... that I couldn't get to you sooner."

With those words, the dam in Raisa's heart burst open. Tears flooded her vision. Then Marik held her in his arms, patting the back of her head like she was a small child. She sobbed into his shoulder, letting the emotions she had held in check for lunats consume her. Anguish shook her thin body and exploded from her throat in gulping groans that to her own ears sounded strangely like laughter. Her nose began to close up and she found herself struggling to breathe through the grief that poured from her heart and soaked the fabric of Marik's coat-sleeve.

After a few minutes, she pulled away, sniffling. Humiliation and relief warred inside her and she did her best to wipe the moisture from her face with the backs of her hands, but even though they had stopped flowing, the tears still seemed to multiply, frustrating her efforts to regain any semblance of dignity.

Marik took pity on her and produced a large, wrinkled handkerchief, which she accepted gratefully, keeping her eyes downcast as embarrassment gained the upper hand. How could she have fallen to pieces so completely in front of him? She, who had maintained her composure throughout lunats of captivity and torture, who had not flinched under punishment and starvation, nor allowed a tear to escape from her eyes under the lash of the whip or even in the darkest solitude of her tent at night? Raisa kept her eyes fixed on the floorboards, unable to meet her captain's gaze.

"Raisa."

She couldn't help herself. At the sound of his voice, she looked up. What she saw there shattered her very soul. He looked at her with tender compassion she found difficult to bear. Wrapping her arms around herself, as if by so doing she could hide from his sight or perhaps hold the broken pieces of herself together, she took a shaky breath. "I think I'll go get some breakfast," she repeated.

Marik nodded. Then his eyebrows drew together in puzzlement. "Why didn't you change into your normal clothes? We made sure to put everything back where you left it. We even washed everything."

Heat flooded her cheeks. "Nothing fits anymore," she mumbled.

Marik's eyes widened and then he, too, glanced away, shifting uncomfortably. "I didn't think about that. I'm sorry, I should have. We'll get you some new things when we set down at Ferndale."

Raisa felt up to trying a tentative smile. "That sounds nice."

"Good! Good." Marik nodded firmly. "It's settled then. Look, Ray... I know it's going to be difficult at first. But you're home, and we're glad you're here. Where you belong."

"Thank you," she whispered.

"Go on, get some breakfast before your friends eat everything in the kitchen."

She tried another smile. This time it came more easily. Then she descended the stairs. At the bottom, Raisa paused, a startled thought filling her mind: Marik had not commented once on her changed appearance. With a rising hope filling her, she turned and dashed down the hall to her quarters and stared into the mirror. Her spirit sank. The reflection had not changed. She scowled at her face, hating its strangeness. The scowl faded into a pensive frown. It was not possible that Marik had simply not noticed the difference in her appearance, and yet, in their conversation he had not even seemed to be pretending to ignore it. She replayed their interaction in her mind. True, he had acted apprehensive, but she sensed it had nothing to do with her appearance.

Chewing thoughtfully on the inside of her cheek, Raisa slowly entered the mess. At one of the small tables, she saw three figures. She immediately recognized Olin and Davin, but the third was unfamiliar to her. With a shake of her head, Raisa got herself a bowl of porridge and strode over to the table. When she reached it, the third figure stood and greeted her.

"You must be Raisa," he said, his voice soft and kind.

Raisa nodded and looked up, about to ask his name, but the

words died on her lips as she stared into his face. The man gazed down at her with bright green eyes set deeply beneath heavy dark brows. His wild dark hair was tousled as though he had been standing in a windstorm, but the effect was not unruly or unpleasant. But it was not the squareness of his jaw, the broadness of his shoulders, the pleasantness of his face, or the piercing, intense gaze that caught her attention and made her breath catch. It was the faint pattern of lines etched across the skin of his face, and his strangely pointed ears that mirrored her own that stole all her words. Her lungs struggled to expand, but for a moment she could not take in any air.

"Ioan Petrescu." The stranger extended a hand to her and she clasped it at the wrist, noticing vaguely that the pattern also covered his hand and arm, just as it did her own. And yet, the coloring was different. While her skin had taken on a brownish-gray hue, his was lighter brown and had more reddish tones to it.

"I... ah..." Raisa stammered, trying to wrap her mind around what she was seeing. "Who are you?" Her thoughts whirled, catching up with what she had already heard him say. "Petrescu..." She frowned. "Wasn't that the name of the man the Regeont of Ondoura's daughter married?"

Ioan's teeth gleamed white as he grinned at her. "I'm impressed."

"Don't be," she replied, speaking without thinking. "In our line of work, it's important to know as much as we can about any potential mark." Realizing what she'd just said, she bit her upper lip in horror, but Ioan just chuckled.

"That makes sense. Will you join us? Your friends were just regaling me with the tale of your escape from the Weald. It sounds like you've had a rough time of it."

Raisa eased herself gingerly into the remaining chair at the table across from Davin, with Ioan on her left. She busied herself with her porridge, but continued to sneak glances at Ioan between bites. Her muscles tensed involuntarily and she fought an overwhelming urge to flee the room. His presence explained why her appearance had not fazed Marik. Across the table she caught a glimpse of Davin watching her. When he saw that she had noticed him, he gave her a sly wink. Inexplicably, Raisa felt heat rising in her cheeks and she focused on her breakfast, determined not to stare at Ioan again.

As Davin continued telling the story of their trek across the Plains of Temna, with Olin filling in here and there, the jittery hiccoughing in Raisa's stomach began to quiet. Ioan listened attentively, asking questions intermittently for clarification, but mostly just listening. Her porridge consumed, Raisa could not help herself, but found herself once more studying the man sitting next to her. He was tall, taller than her by several inches. He held himself like a warrior, and the chevrons on his collar named him a defender of notable status. And yet, the pattern on his skin and the tips of his leaf-shaped ears said there was far more to his story than that of a wealthy young man who had joined the army. She wondered what had happened to him. Lost in her musings, she almost didn't notice when Ioan glanced over and caught her staring. A soft light of understanding lit his brilliantly green eyes. For a moment, she felt compelled to speak to him, to ask him to tell her his story, to confide in him. She could sense that he would be compassionate to her tale. His eyes were kind and held a depth of gentleness. She felt her heart flutter a bit.

Suddenly, she was standing, backing away, stumbling in her haste to leave the table. Her companions were looking at her, staring at her as if she were acting strangely. Raisa knew she was acting strangely, but she needed to get away from that intensely green gaze.

"I... Marik said he had something to discuss... you can... I'll just be..." The words would not come, mostly because she had no idea why she was leaving, or what it was she was trying to say. She just knew that she had to get out of the room, away from those eyes that said they understood. Her thoughts conflicted within her, jumbling together in a collision of fear and confusion that she could not sort through.

She fled.

When she reached the hallway, she collapsed against a wall, gulping for breath. The panic subsided, leaving her feeling ashamed and a little silly.

"Raisa?"

The gentle voice startled her and she whirled to see that Ioan had followed her. Her heart careened against her rib cage.

"I didn't mean to startle you," Ioan said. He stood a few feet away, his expression cautious, like that of a shepherd approaching a wounded lamb. "I know everything is difficult and probably frightening right now. But if you ever want to talk, I'm here."

"Frightening?" Raisa gave a scornful laugh. "Why would you say that? I'm home. You want to know what was difficult? Being forced to crawl through mud and leap over walls and spar against men who wanted me dead. Difficult was doing what I could for the other prisoners, even though they despised me. Frightening? After lunats forced to grovel at the feet of a madman, I doubt anything will ever frighten me again. And why would I want to talk to you? How could a stranger understand anything my crew wouldn't?" She spat the words, hurling them like poisoned daggers.

Ioan did not flinch beneath her angry tirade. He merely bowed his head. "Forgive me if I overstepped. I only... well... forgive me." He spoke with such gentleness, it made Raisa's teeth ache. She wanted him to lash back at her, to give her an opponent, to make her hate him the way she hated... her mind clamped down, refusing to continue.

Without another word, she whirled about and stalked down the hall. Tears blinded her, but though the Hawk had been altered in many ways, the halls were still the same. She did not need to be able to see to navigate these familiar passages. Returning to her cabin, she slammed the door and threw herself down on her bunk, her tears soaking the pillow.

45

The airship settled down on the placid pond outside Ferndale. Raisa watched as the longboat was lowered into the water. Oleck handed Mouse gently down to Marik and Dalmir, who laid him carefully in the boat before taking up the oars. Shaesta hesitated at the rail, her expression concerned as she peered into Raisa's face.

"Are you sure you don't want to come into town with me?" she asked.

Raisa forced a smile. "I'd rather not go out looking like this" —she indicated her tattered clothing with a rueful wave of her hand—"no shop owner is going to take me seriously. No. No, you have my new measurements and I trust you to pick out appropriate attire. Maybe..." She hesitated, picking idly at the fingerless gloves covering the patterns on her hands. "A hood? If there's enough left over from what I gave you."

Shaesta's eyes softened. "Any particular color?"

"Whatever goes with the other things you pick out. You've always been better at this than me."

Shaesta reached out and gave her arm a reassuring squeeze. "I'll do my best. Do you want everything in your usual style?"

Raisa nodded firmly. "As much as possible."

"Very well. I'll be back soon." Shaesta disappeared over the side of the airship and the longboat made its way across the lake, pulled by Marik's sweeping oar-strokes that sent ripples out on either side.

Raisa tugged at a lock of her own hair and heaved out a restless sigh. She paced the deck a little, watching as Marik and the others reached the shore and were greeted warmly by the physicians who had come down to see why an airship had landed in their lake. Again. A smile tugged at the corners of her mouth. Apparently this was becoming something of a habit for the crew of the Valdeun Hawk.

"Raisa." The deep voice made her whirl and she looked up into Oleck's familiar face. He smiled at her shyly from behind his bushy beard. "We haven't exactly had a moment to talk about everything," he muttered. "But I wanted you to know... it's good to have you back, kiddo."

Something inside her shattered at his words and she flung herself into his arms, burying her face against his chest. She didn't cry. It wasn't a moment for tears. His arms went around her and he patted her back, comforting her as he always did.

"Captain never gave up on you. None of us did," he said. "I'm sorry it took us so long. We tried, you have to believe that we tried. But then... when the Kotai caught our tail and we had to make a run for it, and the Hawk went down..." Oleck trailed off. She looked up at him.

"Then they really did...? The Hawk really..." She couldn't continue. The evidences of the Hawk's injuries were everywhere she looked in its new trimmings and trappings, but she still had a hard time picturing the airship strewn across the forest floor the way Shaesta had described it.

Oleck nodded. "Worst moments of my life. Cap'n and Mouse were over here, and Shay and I were on a horrible old barge with all the durven, and the Kotai were firing that weapon of theirs. Darkened skies, Raisa, that thing is terrifying. Then Cap got it in his head that he had to protect us, and he did. But he was injured, bad. He's still limping, though he tries to hide it. And the Hawk... well... that's why she looks so different. Wynn fixed her up..." Oleck turned aside and ran a hand along the railing. "She's not quite the same." He grimaced behind his beard, which had grown shaggy. Raisa wondered at that. Usually Oleck kept it meticulously trimmed. "But the lad did a good job, nonetheless. I've been having to relearn the engine room, though. He made a bit of a mess down there."

Raisa couldn't stop the playful grin from springing to her face. She punched his shoulder lightly, barely touching him. "It's about time the Hawk's engine room got a tune-up. She's been due for years."

"This is more like a complete rebuild..." Oleck's grimace faded into a reluctant smirk. "But the lad's managed to coax twice as much speed outta her. This little lady is now the fastest thing in the sky."

Raisa tapped the goggles she had pushed up on her head. "Hence the need for these things. Takes some getting used to."

"That they do," Oleck agreed. "But I guess a few adjustments aren't all bad." He studied her silently for a moment. "What did they do to you, Raisa-lass?"

A cloud descended on her mood at the reminder of how much she, like the Hawk, had been rebuilt. "Oleck... I... I don't want to talk about it."

"Fair enough." The big man picked up a length of rope and began coiling it neatly. "Seems to me, though... an experience like that... might be good to talk to somebody, if you can bring yourself to."

"Maybe." Raisa picked at a loose splinter on the railing.

"Well, I have to get down to the engine room, Captain wants to be off again soon as Mouse is settled."

Raisa nodded and Oleck tromped off. The restless feeling returned. She needed to move, to hide, to get away, high above it all where she could think in peace. With an easy leap, she was in the rigging, clambering up the familiar ropes until she reached her goal. She tossed herself into the crow's nest and then yelped and leaped back out, clinging to a rope like a frightened cat as the unexpected figure in the basket grunted.

"My apologies..." She trailed off as Ioan unfolded himself from where he had been lying down before she landed on him. He stood and faced her, eyes alight with merriment.

"None needed. I didn't mean to startle you. I just came up here to take a nap."

She narrowed her eyes at him. "Is there something wrong with your quarters?"

"No. They're fine. But I like the fresh air and the height. It's quiet up here, too. And since we were docked, I didn't think anyone would be using the crow's nest for a bit." He tilted his head to one side, squinting. "Guess I'm not the only one who likes it up here."

Raisa tried to quell the sudden kinship she felt with this stranger. They were from opposite worlds, she reminded herself sternly. Of all people, he... He was staring at her, she realized, and felt her ears grow warm. "What are you staring at?" she asked, her tone snapping more than she intended.

"I just... I've been trying to come up with a way to apologize."

"What? Why?" Startled by this completely unanticipated declaration, she dropped her guard in favor of honest curiosity.

He waved his hand in an aimless circle between them. "For what Lorcan did to you. From all that I've learned and the few things Lorcan said when we confronted him, I was his first success. Or rather, the first success he knows about. Whatever accident created... me... it gave him the key he needed to replicate the experiment. We should have stopped him in the mountains... we had him cornered, but he managed to escape. I let him escape." Ioan hung his head. "And because of me, he was able to continue his experiments on you."

A thousand emotions fluttered through her mind, followed by an intense numbness. "That is hardly something you need to apologize for," she muttered. "The madman has been making attempts for longer than you care to know. He's the one responsible for the durven, though he doesn't know it—well, he suspects, but he doesn't know how he managed it, doesn't remember them or where they are from—and he must never find out that his attempt to combine humans and leythan was successful. It was only a matter of time before he had another breakthrough. The important thing is stopping him and the Ar'Molon and the rest of the Igyeum from doing any more harm. And if that means tracking down another one of those cursed orbs... then that's what we have to do." Shaesta had filled her in on Dalmir's quest when she came to take Raisa's new measurements.

He nodded solemnly. "Duty binds us."

"Or revenge."

He gave her a quizzical look and Raisa suddenly wished she could melt through the base of the crow's nest and just plummet straight into the water below. She gave an uncomfortable and half-hearted shrug.

"You've..." Ioan began.

Raisa cut him off. Aware of the dangerous storm-system she had nearly driven herself into, she gave a wry chuckle. "Different perspective, same goal."

He studied her, a discerning smile unfolding on his lips. "I admire you. I didn't handle any of this half as well."

Now it was her turn to be caught off guard and she fumbled for a response to this sudden compliment. "I..." She stared down at her toes. "I'm not. Handling it well," she admitted. She didn't know why she felt compelled to tell him the truth, except that something in his earnest gaze seemed suddenly open and vulnerable. "I've spent the past lunats just fighting to survive." The words came out haltingly, her eyes remaining fixed on the ground. She dared not look at him. "I didn't have time to think about it. I was alone. And"—she paused and gnawed on the inside of her cheek for a moment, then let it out in a rush—"there weren't any mirrors." Shame mixed with fury at her own vanity and a deep sorrow she had quenched in the darkest corners of her heart rushed over her like a windstorm buffeting her from all sides. She squeezed her eyes shut against the onslaught, lost in the howling chaos of her own emotions.

A gentle touch beneath her chin startled her into opening her eyes. Ioan stared down at her. In the intensity of his gaze, she read a story that mirrored her own. An understanding she had never even hoped to see. And something else... admiration? Possibly. Her throat went suddenly dry. She could hear her heart pounding a strange rhythm in her head. She wanted to break away, to run, but instead she stood transfixed, frozen in the moment.

"Raisa..."

He whispered her name so softly the word barely existed, but it broke the spell. In a fluid motion, Raisa tilted herself backward over the edge of the crow's nest and plummeted headfirst toward the deck of the airship. She heard his startled exclamation of dismay, which brought a smirk to her lips as her gloved hand caught a familiar rope and she flipped in midair, riding the line down to land softly on her feet. She risked a single glance up and saw him staring down at her, leaning over the edge of the nest. The distance between them gave her back her courage and she shot him a jaunty salute before making her way back down to her quarters.

46

The foliage around Ferndale rustled in the breeze. Emerald leaves gleamed beneath the perfect summer sun of Avar. Dalmir stood in one of the gardens and breathed deeply. The last time he had been here, he had not taken the time to fully appreciate the serenity of the House with its clean windows and peaceful courtyards. Men and women arrayed in robes of soothing colors moved through and around the House quietly, their attention to detail surpassed only by the care and compassion they had for their patients.

Upon arriving at Ferndale, Marik had taken Mouse directly to the head physician while the rest of the crew tagged along.

"Another broken arm?" The physician glared accusingly at Marik over the rims of her round spectacles. "Perhaps you should pick a less hazardous occupation for yourself and your crew, Captain."

Marik gave her a flirtatious grin. "It isn't the occupation, dear Healer. It is simply that various members of my crew appear to have grown rather fond of you, and keep making up excuses to get me to bring them to visit."

The stern woman scowled, but a tinge of pink appeared in her cheeks, indicating that Marik's charm was not wholly wasted on her. Mouse had been bustled away, and the rest of the members traveling on the Hawk had taken this opportunity to evaluate their next steps. Shaesta disappeared into the nearby town for supplies. Ioan and Raisa had elected to stay aboard the airship but Oleck had eventually come ashore and settled himself to relaxing and enjoying the peaceful atmosphere of the beautiful gardens. Dalmir felt restless, and so he wandered out through a little gate and found himself on a well-worn dirt path that led him into a grove of tall birch trees.

He ambled along the trail, his pace languorous, taking his time to enjoy the staunch rows of birch trees surrounding him, their white bark hanging loosely in tatters, the long rays of evening sunlight shining between the trunks and coloring the air with golden brushstrokes. Peace settled into his soul, and he thought of Shiori; how she would love this place. He wondered when he might see her again. He hoped it would be soon, but he knew how difficult it had become for her to cross the worlds to get to Turrim. Or whatever it was that she did. He had never been able to quite grasp the idea of how she traveled, and she never spoke of her home. It took her a considerable amount of effort to visit, he knew, and she was out of practice. The smile in his heart faded. His fault.

He shook away the dismal recriminations. The time for guilt had passed. Now he must move forward, and thanks to Shiori, he had a direction, a mission—an impossible mission, to be sure, but it was better than drifting as he had for so many long years.

Consumed with his thoughts, Dalmir almost did not notice the young woman standing on the path in front of him until he had almost tripped over her. He stopped, backpedaling as best he could, catching a glimpse of silver hair from out of the corner of his eye as he and the woman danced about each other trying to avoid collision.

"Shiori?" Dalmir gripped her shoulders and stared into her face, but the joyful hope that sprang up within him died as his vision took in the delicate features. This was not Shiori, but rather a young girl with long, white-blonde hair and gray eyes. She stared up at him, her expression startled.

"Forgive me," Dalmir said, releasing her quickly. "For a moment, I thought you were someone..." He trailed off, memory stirring. Peering through the gathering dusk, he studied her face again. This time, his vision unclouded by disappointment, he realized with a jolt that he did recognize the girl. "It's you!" he exclaimed in a whisper.

The girl straightened, her hands smoothing out imaginary wrinkles from her simple garb. At his words, her eyes darted back to his face, her eyes widening in fear, which faded almost instantly. "You..." Her voice rasped like a gate allowed to grow rusty through disuse, yet still beautiful. "I know you." She paused, studying him intently. "But how?"

"You don't remember?" Dalmir asked, keeping his voice gentle. "We found you in the tower where you were being held prisoner. My friend and I freed you and brought you here."

The girl's eyes continued to gaze at him with disturbing intensity. "You rescued me. I... thank... you."

"No thanks are necessary. I'm just glad to see you on your feet."

She rubbed her arms and shivered.

"Will you accompany me back to the House?" Dalmir asked.

The girl nodded, her demeanor still guarded, but she no longer looked like a frightened gazelle about to flee into the sunset. They walked along in silence as the daylight faded completely and the stars began to wink into existence overhead. The girl did not speak, and Dalmir did not feel like breaking the peaceable silence of their companionship. Their feet padded softly on the path, the only sound of their passing until they came in sight of the House, its windows glowing with the warm light of comforting fires blazing merrily in their hearths. Lanterns hung on either side of the door, and the delicious aroma of roasting chicken wafted out to welcome them back.

Dalmir quickened his pace, but then stopped when he

noticed that the girl had paused. He glanced at her, frowning, unable to parse what her strained expression might mean. "What is it?"

She shook her head. "I'm not sure. I just feel... so cold. You carry doom with you. But this does not make sense, for... you are my savior."

Dalmir took a step back. "I am no savior. I merely seek to rectify a mistake I made many years ago." He peered at her. "What do you mean, I carry doom with me?"

The girl made a helpless gesture. "It is just... a feeling I have—a whisper in my ears. No, that's not right. Not in my ears... in my mind? Strange music. Where is it coming from?" She squeezed her eyes shut and rocked back and forth on her heels, obviously distressed.

"Shh, shh, do not worry. You do not need to explain it."

"But I do. There is power about you. Objects of power... they call to me, like echoes of my prison, echoes of... him... NO!" The girl's voice rose up in a shriek and she slumped to the ground, clasping her hands over her ears. She knelt on the path, moaning and rocking from side to side.

Perplexed, Dalmir lifted her in his arms, marveling at how light she was. She did not resist, but moaned, her hands clenched firmly over her ears as he carried her inside.

When he entered Ferndale, gasps filled the room and three young woman converged upon him, demanding to know what had happened.

"She disappeared from her room!"

"We did not know where she'd gone."

"We've been looking everywhere!" The cacophony of voices all speaking at once made Dalmir reel back a little.

"Calm down!" the head physician snapped, appearing at the door. "Master Dalmir, if you will please follow me, I will lead you back to the girl's room, and then I would like an explanation." She glared about at the women, her gaze halting on one of them. "And from you, as well, Criselda."

Dalmir followed the physician to the room she indicated. He laid the girl down on the bed. She had ceased moaning, and now just lay still, her eyes closed, her face a strange, ashy color.

"Will she... is she...?" He stumbled over his words, concern flooding through him as he wondered at this strange protectiveness that had sprung to life within him.

"She will recover," the physician said, her fingers light on the girl's wrist. "Let us leave her to rest." The woman strode from the room, and Dalmir and the other woman who had followed them barely made it through the door before she closed it firmly behind them. "Now, Criselda," she said, fixing the larger woman with a steely glare, "how did our young charge manage to slip past you? I did not think she had recovered enough to walk on her own."

"I did not think so either, Headmistress," Criselda stammered. "I only left her for a moment. I inhaled some dust and one of my coughing fits overtook me. I needed a glass of water. I was only gone for a moment!" She ended in a quiet wail. "She had not walked on her own. Except for eating what we give her she's been completely unresponsive for nearly two years! I never dreamed she would suddenly get up and leave Ferndale."

Dalmir shot a questioning glance at both women. The physician caught his look and fixed him with a pointed stare.

"Well?" she asked. "What happened?"

Dalmir cleared his throat. "I went for a walk through your birch glade. You have a lovely trail."

"And why did you see fit to remove our patient from her room?"

"What? No!" Dalmir waved his hands. "I was alone. The girl was already in the glade when I arrived. I found her there. We talked for a few minutes, but then it was growing dark so I offered to walk back to the House with her. When we got within sight of the door, she said she heard a strange whispering in her head and she fell to the ground. That was when I picked her up and brought her to you!"

"She spoke?" Criselda breathed. "Our fragile rose not only

walked far out into the birch glade on her own, but she spoke to you?"

Dalmir nodded, confused. "Is that so strange?"

"You have to understand," the headmistress explained, "Rosa has not spoken to anyone since she arrived. She has not sat up on her own, walked even two steps without assistance, nor reacted to anything or anyone. She eats what we feed her, but she never interacts, never even looks at anyone! She just stares into the distance with that look of hers."

"Well..." Criselda began, but fell silent at the headmistress's glare. "Forgive me for interrupting, Headmistress. But she did show a bit of a reaction when the airship pirate visited her."

The scowl on the headmistress's face smoothed. "Ah, yes, it was so long ago I had forgotten. That is true. A tiny sign of life that day, then gone, just like the pirate. Strange." The woman tapped a finger against her lips. "She appears to have formed an attachment to the two of you, which is not unexpected, since you rescued her from whatever horror she was trapped in. I would like for you and Captain Marik to visit her again in the morning if you have time. I think both of you together might have an increased chance of causing a reaction." Now she turned a smile on Criselda, who visibly sagged with relief. "This is good news. The girl is healing, something is breaking through the barriers she placed around her mind. It will be painful, but it is necessary."

"If you think it wise," Dalmir said, feeling hesitant. He wondered if he should mention the girl talking about doom and objects of power, but then he shook away the impulse. It had only been the mad ravings of a young woman who had endured more terror and pain than any human should have to. Guilt twinged in his heart. Of course, Uun was directly to blame, but he, Dalmir, had built the chains that this young girl had found herself trapped in. The prison had never been intended for someone like her... He frowned, remembering her words. Objects of power that whispered to her, reminding her of her prison? He had used the orbs to construct Uun's prison, all seven of them, in a mighty backlash of the power Uun had stolen and used to kill their brothers, power that Dalmir had briefly been able to wrench away from him and use to seal him inside his tower. Could the girl sense the orbs?

Dalmir made his way slowly back to the airship, his thoughts whirling. As he descended the stairs to the lower deck of the Hawk he heard low voices coming from the mess and peeked inside. Everyone was gathered inside having supper. Even Marik had already returned, having stayed with Mouse for most of the day, only departing when the orderlies insisted that he leave so that their newest patient could get some sleep. Dalmir's stomach rumbled and he realized he had not eaten all day.

"You were gone for a while," Marik said, peering at Dalmir as he joined them. "Did you go exploring?"

Dalmir nodded. "It is peaceful here." He ate mechanically, his thoughts awhirl with new ideas.

"Dalmir?" Ioan's query pulled him out of his reverie. "What's wrong?"

Dalmir ignored him and fixed his gaze on Marik. "Captain, do you remember the girl we rescued from the tower?"

Marik looked up at him, startled. "Of course I do. I visited her again the last time I was here. Why? What's happened? Is she well?" He half-rose from his chair, a look of concern clouding his features.

Dalmir motioned for him to sit. "She is... well enough. I spoke with her this afternoon."

"You spoke with her?" Marik asked eagerly. "Is she getting stronger, then?"

Dalmir recounted the entire episode, ending with his suspicion that the girl could sense more than one of the orbs. Even as he told them, he chided himself for what he was considering. The girl was not well enough to take with them, and even if she could sense the orbs, there was no guarantee she would be coherent enough to guide them.

"Why is it significant that this child can sense the orbs?" Raisa asked quietly from the far end of the table.

"I need the power of all seven to defeat Uun," Dalmir explained. "But I can only wield the power of my own. That is why it has been important to not only find the orbs, but also individuals who can wield each of them. I have recently discovered what Uun must have figured out long ago: the orbs of my brothers can be wielded by the descendants of the people they chose to shepherd—Grayden can use my orb, and Emilee can use Mulemo's orb, for example, and I believe Ioan can wield Edoran's orb that I took from Aubri Niveya, though we haven't yet had time to experiment—but this realization also leads us to our main problem."

"Why is that a problem?" Raisa whispered.

"Because Uun never shepherded anyone. While I and each of my brothers took a piece of Turrim and built universities and taught the people who lived in our countries, leading them and helping them, Uun preferred isolation. He devoted his time to experimenting and introspection, or at least, that is what he told us he was doing."

"What you're telling us is that there is no one alive besides Uun who can wield his orb," Ioan said flatly.

Dalmir nodded. "But if the girl can sense more than one of the orbs, perhaps she can wield more than one of them. She could be the answer I've been searching for. I hate to ask anything of her, but she might be the only one who can lead us to Uun's missing orb."

Raisa cleared her throat. "I wouldn't count on that."

Dalmir frowned. "Why not? I know her health is fragile, but with some time and care, I think..."

"That's not what I mean," Raisa interrupted.

All eyes turned to Raisa and for a moment she seemed to recoil from the intensity of their gazes, her shoulders hunching forward, her chin dipping down so that she appeared to be receding into the shadow of the hood she had pulled up over her head. She fiddled with a splinter of wood on the edge of the table, her fingernail sliding under it and pulling gently at it, making a faint scritch-scratching sound. With a long, deep breath, she straightened a little. "I can sense the orbs, too. All seven of them."

Dalmir's eyes widened. "What?"

Raisa placed her forearms on the table. Then, hesitantly, she raised her hands and slowly pushed back the hood Shaesta had picked out for her. "It's the true purpose behind Lorcan's experiments. One of them, anyway. I don't think it's his main objective, but it is Uun's top priority. As you have already suspected, the Ar'Molon has demanded the creation of a new class of warriors. But there was more to it than that. Uun has a group of highly skilled assassins who report directly to him called the Kotai. That was who you fought off in the ravine the other night." She paused and glanced at the Shipwright. "Davin told me that although they function as the Ar'Molon's personal assassins and are sent on various political hits, their primary function is to find and retrieve Uun's lost orb. It has been missing for hundreds of years, and he's frustrated that he can't find it. So he tasked Lorcan with another goal: to create in the Kotai the ability to sense the orbs so they can seek out its hiding place. I was merely the prototype." Her eyes drifted to Ioan, and a tiny line appeared between her brows.

Ioan gave a wry chuckle. "I was the accidental success."

The line on Raisa's forehead smoothed. "Ah. That's what he meant, then. I'm sorry."

"Don't be." Ioan lifted a shoulder. "I'm getting used to it. Can't deny there are some benefits, too."

Olin and Emilee met his eyes across the table and they shared a bit of a smile.

"Can you sense the orbs?" Raisa asked, leaning forward slightly.

Ioan frowned. "I'm not sure."

"We will test that theory in a moment." Dalmir broke in, impatience and excitement warring within him. He tilted his head to one side and regarded Raisa with new eyes. "How many orbs are on the airship right now?"

Her eyes grew unfocused, staring past him with a far-away look in them. After a moment she blinked. "Three." The word leapt from her lips with authority, but then she frowned. "Three?" Her eyes flicked to him for confirmation.

Dalmir nodded, hope coursing through him. He pulled the two orbs out of the inner pocket of his robe and he placed them on the table. He glanced at Emilee, who drew the third orb out and placed it on the table as well. "You can sense them. Can you use them?" Dalmir asked.

Raisa licked her lips. "How?"

"Just concentrate on one of them. Block out everything but the orb. Focus on how it calls to you. It might be a whisper, it might be a song, weaving through your thoughts. When you feel like you might almost understand what it's saying, whisper back to it in your thoughts with a simple command to glow."

Raisa's lips quirked to one side in an expression of skepticism, but she obediently lowered her gaze and stared at the orbs. After a few minutes, she reached out and picked up first the dull purple one that had been in Aubri Niveya's necklace, then the swirling blue, and finally the quiet gray. But though she stared hard at each of them, none of them responded to her in any way.

At length, Raisa sighed. "I can sense all three. But I can't use any of them." She frowned. "I'm Valleian, like Marik and Oleck. I'm guessing none of these are the Valleian orb?"

"Correct," Dalmir confirmed. "In fact, I believe the orb that Lorcan possesses was Avaleun's."

Raisa grimaced.

Dalmir turned to Ioan. "And you?"

Ioan's eyes bored into the table top for a long moment. Sweat began to bead on his forehead. A muscle in his jaw twitched. Just as Dalmir was about to tell him to stop, the purple orb flared to life, shooting blinding violet light out like a sudden wave that left everyone squinting. Just as swiftly, the orb dimmed once more, but triumph surged through Dalmir at the success. He lifted the orb and handed it to Ioan.

"Will you carry this for me?" he asked. "I will ask you to use it again, so make sure you practice."

Ioan accepted the orb reverently.

Marik spoke up. "Raisa, can you sense the orbs no matter how far away they are? Can you tell how far away they are? Are you always aware of them, or only when you focus?"

"Now that I know what I'm looking for, I can sense all seven of them," Raisa said. "I can't tell exactly how far they are, though I can tell that some are closer than others. The sensation is always there, but it's subtle; I can ignore it easily. The active ones are... louder than the dormant ones."

"We need to find Uun's orb before the Kotai do," Dalmir said. "Can you tell us which direction we should go?"

Raisa squinted, the uncertainty returning to her expression. "I can tell you which directions all the other orbs are in. I can't tell you which one is which."

"That shouldn't be too much of a problem," Marik replied. "Besides the three we have, we know that one of the orbs is in the Ar'Mol's scepter in Melar. One is with Lorcan in Palla. One is with the Kotai, probably heading back to Melar before they return to their search for the missing one. As long as the seventh orb isn't near any of the others, telling us the directions should help us know where to focus our efforts."

She nodded, then squeezed her eyes shut. The room fell silent. At length, her eyes snapped open. "The one you want is to the south. Far south. I think... if I had to guess, deep in Vallei."

Marik's eyes widened and he slammed a fist against his open palm. "Of course! I can't believe I didn't realize it before, but it all makes sense now!"

They stared at him.

"What makes sense?" Ioan asked.

Marik grinned. "I know who stole the orb from Uun."

47

Marik glanced around the table at his companions, trying to determine where to begin. "Most of you know that I grew up in Vallei. I spent much of my childhood alone, reading and studying, for my family expected me to join the military." His jaw tightened, his teeth clamping down on the memories. There were things he did not need to relive. "My favorite books were the ones about the men and women who spent their lives exploring the dangerous and undiscovered areas of the world. My favorite explorer was a man named Shurik Medvev who lived nearly three hundred years ago. He was Valleian and he was fearless. These two facts were enough to make him my hero, but he also went on exciting adventures and risked his life recovering lost treasures. He discovered lost artifacts and uncovered archaeological marvels all over Turrim."

"What does this have to do with Uun's orb?" Dalmir asked.

"I'm getting to that," Marik said. "Medvev garnered a lot of attention for his extraordinary finds. In the later years of his life, rumors started to circulate about the last great unexplored area of Turrim: the Whispering Wood. It was rumored that in the center of the wood sat an abandoned tower whose rooms were filled with precious gems of value beyond worth." Marik paused and gave

Dalmir a meaningful glance. "It was only a matter of time before someone decided it was worth investigating. In 714 A.L., Chieftain Cledwyn commissioned Medvev to take a team into the Whispering Wood to discover whether or not the rumors were true. Even though Shurik was already seventy-one years old, he agreed to the expedition. He led his team into the wood with great fanfare, and then simply... disappeared." Marik stopped and took a long draught from his mug.

"That can't be the end of the story," Raisa said.

Marik grinned. "No. Lunats later the team returned, ragged and starving and most importantly, empty-handed. Medvev reported his failure to the chieftain, claiming they had found the tower, but it was abandoned, empty, and completely haunted. He wove a story for the chieftain and his counselors about the strange, unexplainable things they had seen, the struggle it had been for him and his team to cling to their sanity, and of the ruined tower in the center of it all, where a malevolent ghost held sway. Thoroughly convinced by Medvev's words and the ragged state of him and his team, Cledwyn gave up on his dreams of finding fortune in the forest, and no other explorers were ever sent to repeat Medvev's failure." Marik grinned. "An eerie tale, it captured my imagination. And in spite of his failure, Medvev did bring his team home safely. I liked that about him. He always kept his crew safe."

Oleck narrowed his eyes at him. "A fine, spooky tale, Captain, to be sure, but what does this have to do with our present affairs?"

"I'm getting to that," Marik said. "When we made the exchange with the Kotai, I heard them use an interesting phrase. Do you remember?"

Oleck's expression took on a thoughtful look, but after a moment he shook his head. "There was a lot going on."

"I know it," Davin muttered. "I've heard it many times. 'May you find Sevalk.' It is their ritual greeting."

"And that was the final clue," Marik announced triumphantly. "Medvev called his team the Sevail-Kin—the

Falcon Riders. It's part of the reason I named my airship the Hawk. Dalmir, you said Uun must have seen the person who entered the tower and stole the orb? What if he did more than just see him? What if they spoke? What if Uun demanded to know the thief's name?"

"Then Uun would have known exactly where to look for his orb," Dalmir said.

Marik waved a finger. "But what if Medvev was too smart to give away his name? The stories about him agree that whatever else he might have been, Shurik Medvev was brilliant. In addition to being a builder and inventer and explorer, he was well-versed in politics and intrigue—he had to be in order to get the kings and warlords of different countries and tribes to let him dig around within their borders."

"So what are you driving at?" Ioan asked.

"What if Medvev gave Uun his team's name, instead of his own? Sevail-Kin. Or better yet, maybe he even shortened it: Sevalk. It would be close to the truth, but would have made it difficult for Uun to find him once he escaped. Especially if Uun didn't get out of his prison for another couple of decades, after Shurik died." Marik's excitement rose.

"It's a place to start," Dalmir said. "We don't have any other solid clues. Marik, do you know where this Medvev might have hidden the orb if he did take it?"

Marik scratched his jaw. "There are pretty good records that Medvev made his home in Vallei, though it doesn't narrow down our search much." He glanced at Raisa. "How accurate is your sense of these things?"

Raisa guessed at his true intent and shook her head. "I can't lead us directly there. I can sense the general direction and I know it's farther away from us than the others right now, but I doubt I could be as accurate as a homing pigeon, even. If we get close enough, within a couple hundred feet or so, then I might be able to be more helpful."

"Then we head to Vallei tomorrow," Marik said.

"What about Mouse?" Oleck asked.

Marik hesitated. "He'll have to stay here. That arm of his needs to heal, and this place will be safer than the Hawk."

"He won't like it," Shaesta said.

Marik nodded. "I'll talk to him."

Ioan ran a hand through his hair, causing it to stand up crazily. "Captain, I know I said I'd come with you, but I think someone needs to warn Telmondir about all of this. Our armies are completely focused on the incursions into Ondoura, but I've been speaking with Davin here and he believes that the battles on the Ondouran border are a distraction, and that Uun is readying the troops in the Weald to launch a full-scale invasion of Dalton."

"Why Dalton?" Marik asked.

"Because of me," Dalmir said, his voice quiet. "Dalton was my tower, my greatest achievement, the capital of my region. Of course it is the first thing that Uun wants to destroy. In his mind, striking at Dalton will be like striking directly at me."

"Then it is even more imperative that we get word to Lord Adelfried. If Uun is sure to besiege Dalton, we must draw our defenders there and fortify as best we can," Ioan said. He looked at Davin. "I would appreciate your assistance in this matter. Adelfried is a fair man, and like an uncle to me. I can help assure him that your intentions are not harmful to our people. Your intelligence from behind the Ar'Mol's ranks will be invaluable."

Davin's face paled, but he gave a firm nod. "Of course. I will help in any way I can."

Marik swung his gaze to Olin. "There's room on the skimmer for three. You should go with them. Your people are in Telsuma, they believe you are dead."

Olin glanced at his sister.

"I have given my word to assist Dalmir in his quest," she said in reply to his unspoken question. "But someone should let Mother and Father know that you are well. And it would be good to ready our people for war; our new neighbors may well need our help. You are best suited to help them understand the need."

Olin nodded. "Very well. I will go with Davin and Ioan back to Telmondir."

"Then it's settled," Marik agreed. "You, Ioan, and Davin will return to Gnupar to warn Telmondir. Mouse will stay here. And the rest of us will head to Vallei in the morning to track down Uun's orb."

48

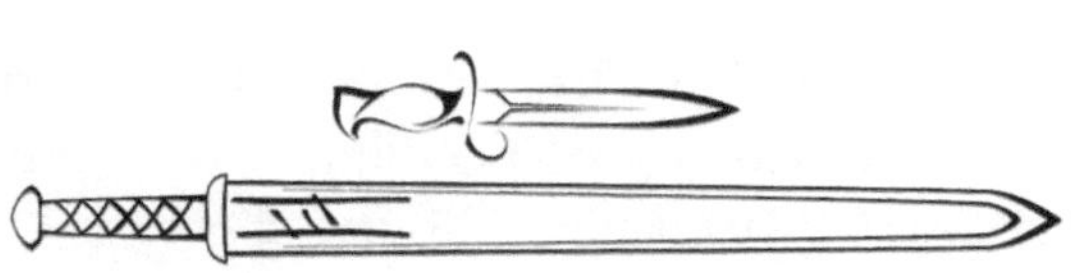

Grayden stared at the dark clouds below, the usual flock of pre-jump butterflies colliding together in his stomach. He barely noticed them anymore. His entire focus was on the mission and getting his men home safe. Turning, he addressed those standing behind him.

"You all know how dangerous this mission is. And you all know how important it is, as well. If we fail here, the Ar'Mol will bring his fleets to Telmondir and use his cynderblasts on our homes. We have to stop him here and now. It has been an honor serving with each of you, and I am certain that there are no forces in Turrim better qualified to do the job we have been given." Grayden tried to meet each man's eyes. "Ready yourselves, we jump on the signal."

The men regarded him solemnly, their grim faces barely visible in the scant light of the hooded lanterns lining the railing. This was not like their previous mission. Here, they would be jumping into the heart of enemy territory. There would be no friendly army marching toward them, ready to offer relief or aid. And while there was a plan to pull them out once the mission was complete, it depended on so many things going right that

Grayden could see that in spite of the fire in their eyes, they held little hope of surviving this mission.

A series of whistles sounded and the men began to leap out of the ship, disappearing into the thick clouds. Grayden met Beren's eyes and nodded, taking a deep breath, when a hand on his arm made him whirl around.

"Wynn?" he asked, looking at his friend's worried expression. "What's wrong?"

Wynn waved one of the hand cannons in a frantic gesture. "The altitude, or the clouds, or something…" His words tumbled together and Grayden saw panic on his friend's face.

"Take your time," Beren suggested.

"Moisture has gotten inside the chamber," Wynn explained. "It might impair the cannon's operation. The men will have to clean out the barrels and reload them—I can show them how— it's not hard and won't take much time, but if they don't do it, the hand cannons may be useless." His jaw tightened. "This mission was my idea, it's my responsibility to see it through."

"Calm down, it will be all right," Grayden said. "Just show Beren and me how to do it, we'll pass it along."

Wynn took a deep breath and nodded. "Right. That will work."

Suddenly, a cry went up from the other side of the airship. Grayden barely had time to wonder why someone would break the silence so blatantly when a beam of fire so bright it hurt his eyes and left spots dancing in front of his vision split through the clouds, lancing straight at the prow of their ship. The jumpship shuddered and lurched, throwing them to the deck. The sound of splitting timbers and a screech of metal resounded through the sky and the night air filled with the smell of smoke.

"What was that?" Wynn asked.

"We've been hit." Beren's voice was grim. "Scout ship."

The airship deck tilted at a crazy angle, sending them sliding toward the rail. Before they got there, the ship tilted back, righting itself, but still listing to one side. Grayden could hear soldiers shouting, and through the darkness he could see men running across the deck.

Another blast of fire seared through the air and the jumpship shuddered beneath them.

"We're going down!" The cry resounded through the troops.

"What do we do?" Wynn shouted.

"Everyone needs to get off the ship," Grayden hollered back, catching his friend's arm.

"But I don't have a skysail!" Wynn stared at him.

"I've got you," Beren shouted, lifting an extra harness from a nearby bin and shoving it into Wynn's hands. "Strap in!"

Wynn struggled into the harness. He fumbled with the straps, but with Beren and Grayden helping, he managed to get everything situated.

"What about the pilot and everyone else?" Wynn asked.

"Most of them have skysails, and those who don't will be jumping together like you and Beren," Grayden called back. "But hopefully they'll be able to get the ship to limp out of here, they're tough old birds, these jumpships."

"I don't know if I can do this," Wynn yelled.

"I've got you," Beren said, clipping Wynn's harness to his own.

Wynn threw a panicked look at Grayden. "Have you ever done this before?"

"Beren will get you both down safely," Grayden assured him as he checked his altimeter. "But we have to jump now, this bird is falling fast. I'll go first." He stepped off the platform and plummeted through the darkness. The clouds around him roiled gently, and as Grayden fell through them he thought about how many days they had waited for the conditions to be just right for this jump. They needed a cloudy night for the cover, but not a stormy one, and in this region in mid-Avar that was often a difficult combination to find. The wind rushed past his face, full of cool moisture and the thick, slightly salty scent of smoke. Then he was through the clouds, and he could see the lights of the shipyard far below. He checked his altimeter. Still fairly high up. His eyes scanned the ground, searching for his target. Could he still land on the platform below after the disastrous attack on their airship? Their element of surprise had failed; what awaited him below? Above him, he heard a crashing sound, and then something exploded and the clouds flooded with an eerie gleam of orange before dying back to their normal black.

Hoping that the wreckage of two airships were not about to come raining down on his head, Grayden turned his attention back to the ground. Based on the lights below, there were plenty of options for places to land. Gas lights flared along tidy streets and gleamed through windows high above the ground. As the ground raced toward him, he began to appreciate the true size of the complex.

The shipyards stretched across his entire field of vision now, and most of it flared with light. He could see enormous towers jutting up into the air, surrounded by a dozen or so docked airships bobbing gently in their moorings. His eyes scanned over them, searching... there! The largest central tower was the target of his and Beren's platoons. With a jerk, he pulled the cord to open his skysail, feeling the slight tug on his body as the black silk opened and caught at the air. Using the handles, he maneuvered himself closer to the tower; circling lower and lower, he descended onto the wide walkway that served as a dock. Several dark figures moved slowly along the platform and he hoped they were fellow defenders and not Igyeum guards.

Closer he fell.

Closer.

Then his feet touched down with a louder thud than he would have liked. Immediately, Grayden hit the clasp that released his harness, letting the black skysail billow away from him. He crouched on the metal walkway, glancing around as more of his men dropped out of the sky.

Catching sight of Beren's massive figure descending a few feet to his left, Grayden headed in that direction. His friends' boots hit the deck, and Grayden marveled at Beren's strength that kept them both standing. He stepped forward and helped Wynn detach his harness from Beren's.

Wynn turned to face Beren and gave a suddenly brilliant grin. "That wasn't so hard," he said.

Beren grinned back. "We have missed you, my friend."

Wynn started to shrug out of his harness, but Beren stopped him. "Keep it on," he instructed. "In case we need to jump to the ground."

Wynn frowned. "Why would the harness help with that?"

"We all have secondary skysails," Grayden supplied.

"Now, show us how to fix this moisture issue," Beren said.

Wynn deftly opened the barrel of his hand cannon and began showing them both how to swab out the interior. Grayden watched carefully. Once he was sure he had the process down, he turned to pace along the wide metal deck, peering into faces and taking a mental count of the men who had already landed.

"Shep, Joss, Flint, Hans, Jerky," he muttered their names under his breath. "Duster, Pen, Cooly, and Smith." As he passed each of them, he instructed them to check in with Wynn.

Debris lit by glowing embers began to plummet through the clouds and clattered on the cobblestones below. Not enough to make up an entire airship, though, which gave him hope that the jumpship had managed to get away.

"Tattered sails!" Grayden muttered under his breath at the noise. "Well, if the soldiers down here didn't know something was happening before, they do now."

A flicker of movement caught his eye and a man swung into full view. He just had time to catch a glimpse of a pale, frightened face, before the man's feet collided with the dock. A deafening clang filled the air and then the man's boots skidded across the surface of the walkway as a gust of wind caught his skysail.

"Release!" Grayden cried. He watched as the man's hand rose and fell against his chest to no avail.

The man gave a quiet wail as the wind tugged him sideways

and over the edge of the roof. Grayden lunged forward and caught him, his arms wrapping around the other's chest. He pulled the defender back to the roof, straining against the billowing skysail.

"Hit your release!" he gritted.

"I tried! It's not working!" the man panted.

Grayden wrestled the man back onto the deck, but he couldn't get enough slack in the lines to risk letting go with one hand to fuss with the harness clasp. Boots pounded toward them.

"Help," Grayden gasped out at the approaching man. "The clasp, it's stuck!"

Another set of hands suddenly appeared. "It's bent," Beren's voice grunted.

A blade flashed in the darkness. A sound of ripping fabric. And the skysail tore free, fluttering away and out of sight.

The man they had helped straightened and stared after his skysail for a moment before turning and giving a salute. "Thank you, sirs. Soldier Young reporting for duty."

"See that group of defenders?" Beren pointed. "Report over there to get your hand cannon sorted out. It needs to be dried before you'll be able to use it."

"Yes, sir." The man trotted away.

"We'd better get moving," Grayden said. "We've made a lot more noise than we planned for."

As if his words had brought them forth, a sound of metal sliding against metal reverberated into the night. A moment later, two large platforms suddenly appeared at the ends of the building, rising from out of the darkness, covered in blazing lanterns, and filled with soldiers.

Young screamed and staggered backwards, an arrow protruding from his chest. Too far away to reach him in time, Grayden watched helplessly as the defender he had just rescued stepped past the edge of the platform and toppled to the ground far below. Grayden grasped the hilt of his sword, but Beren's intake of breath arrested his motion.

"Hand cannons!"

In the suddenness of the attack, he had forgotten the new weapon at his side. Pulling the contraption out of the holster strapped just above his knee, Grayden fired into the oncoming enemy. They were close enough that the coria exploded on impact, throwing the foremost soldier back. He fired again and again into the oncoming enemy, alternating his shots with Beren so they could cover each other and reload, but more Igyeum soldiers continued to pour off the lifts.

The night around him filled with bright clicks and tiny starbursts of light as the men of Arta and Vector Platoons defended themselves against the onslaught. Despite their greater firepower, several of their opponents managed to make it through their ranks and onto one of the nearby docked airships, where they began working furiously to take off.

"We have to bring down that airship," Grayden shouted to the men nearby, "before it escapes."

A gleam of golden light suddenly lit a familiar grin. Before he could call out to Shep to be careful, the man hurled a glowing cynder through the air. It crashed down onto the deck of the nearest airship, and a moment later the sky filled with a rush of heat and light and flying splinters of wood. Grayden found himself plastered to the dock, flat on his stomach as the debris rained down around him.

"Tattered sails, Shep, are you insane?" he shouted. The roar of the explosion rang in his ears, drowning out his own voice. How had the man managed to bring along a cynder? And why? They barely functioned as weapons, though he had to admit that this particular application had worked spectacularly. Perhaps too spectacularly. Grayden shook his head to clear the ringing from his ears and pushed himself to his feet, only to find himself face-to-face with the glint of a drawn sword. He blearily fired his hand cannon at the enemy before him, blinking the smoke and grit from his eyes as the man stumbled back and fell from the platform.

A hand pulled him to one side. "You all right, Gray?" Wynn shouted into his ear, appearing out of nowhere.

He nodded. "A little deafened," he hollered back, "but yes. I'm fine."

The fighting raged along the dock. The scored cynder had been a gamble, but Grayden couldn't deny it had done the job: it had taken out two ships docked side-by-side. He rejoined the battle, pushing his way toward the next airship. Their mission was to take out as many of the airships as possible, and he had no intention of leaving any of them flight-worthy.

A fire suddenly roared to life on an airship at the far end of the dock, the flames illuminating the battle. Though not as impressive as Shep's explosion, the fire raced up the mast and flooded across the sails, filling the sky with light. A thunderclap rocked the night as a fireball soared into the sky far away at the northeastern side of the camp, and Grayden grinned, feral and fierce. Wylfen Company had been tasked with taking out the massive ships being outfitted with cynderblasts at that end of the complex. He hoped the explosion signaled their success.

Behind him, he heard a low hum, and he whirled to see one of the still-intact airships lifting away from its moorings, the golden gleam of cynder power shining along its hull and trim sails.

"No!" he shouted, loath to let even one airship of the Igyeum fleet escape. He took a few running steps in the other direction towards the ship's twin, still floating in its place. Perhaps he could get it airborne on his own, chase after the escaping craft. Maybe he could ram it, or...

A strange sound stopped him in his tracks. The air around him vibrated with a low-pitched buzz. Confused, he paused and glanced around.

The airship he had thought was fleeing had turned around and now swooped toward the battle. He frowned, trying to gauge their tactics. Was the pilot attempting to ram the building? He ducked as the vessel came closer.

A beam of fire shot out of the side of the airship, forging a path of destruction that tore apart the steel walkway and caused the entire building upon which the dock rested to tremble. As the fiery lance punched through the dock, Grayden lost his balance and stumbled to his knees. The airship spun away, the lance fading from sight as the sails billowed in the wind. A moment later, it swooped back into view.

"Watch out!" Grayden shouted as the beam of fire and death tore through the dock once more. The Igyeum soldiers threw themselves into the safety of the remaining airships, leaving the defenders to face the destruction of the cynderblast. Men were thrown into the air, disappearing over the edges of the walkway. Grayden watched in rising fury as the airship flew away from them. It would return in a minute.

Rain began to fall. It sizzled as it hit the still-flaming airships, and plinked as it hit the metal walkway.

"None of our intel said anything about the smaller ships getting cynderblasts!" Beren shouted, raising himself up on his elbows, his eyes wide and stunned, reflecting the orange flames.

"Doesn't matter," Grayden yelled back. "We have to get off this platform."

"But we haven't finished the mission," Wynn stammered.

"And we won't," Grayden shouted. "Not against that thing."

"What do we do?" Wynn asked.

"Secondary skysails!" Grayden barked at the men closest to him. "Beren, do you have Wynn?" He barely waited for the answering nod. "We have to get off this dock, now!" He shouted the order several times until he was certain he had been heard. A moment later, men began leaping off the tower, their secondary skysails unfurling above them. Grayden waited for several more breaths, then made the jump himself, pulling his release cord as he plummeted toward the street below.

49

Raisa lay on her bunk and stared up at the ceiling trying to quell the jittery feeling in the pit of her stomach. The gray light of predawn streamed in through her window, heralding the advent of a new day. Shaesta's deep, even breathing from the bunk below hers told her that her roommate was still asleep. She wished she could wake her and talk the way they used to, but though they all acted oblivious to her physical changes, Raisa felt that her crew mates were still tiptoeing around her.

A new adventure awaited, calling to them with the rising sun, but Raisa's stomach churned at the thought of chasing down another one of the cursed orbs. A thump on the deck above galvanized her into action. She leapt lightly from her bed, landing on the floor without a whisper of sound. Shrugging into the new clothes Shaesta had procured for her from the nearby town, she tugged a brush through her hair and crept out the door.

Up on the deck, she saw the skimmer already loaded with supplies. Marik stood near Ioan and Davin, chatting with them at the rail. Olin and Emilee were hunkered down by the mast, their heads close together as they said their goodbyes. In the misty dawn, Raisa could see lights flickering within the sychstal and she knew that preparations were already underway to move the patients to Dalton.

Davin glanced up and spotted her. "Raisa!" He strode over to where she stood. "Come to see us off, have you?"

"Watch out for pirates." She grinned. "I hear they're a dangerous lot."

Davin chuckled. "Thanks for helping me escape. I wasn't sure we'd survive. We came through a lot together, eh?" He glanced at the skimmer. "Never thought I'd..." He paused and looked back at her. "Thank you. For giving me the courage to... to start over."

"Thank you... for everything," she replied.

He gave her a tight smile and trotted back to the skimmer. Olin wrapped his arms around his sister for a final embrace before letting go and heading to the railing. He bobbed his head at Raisa as he passed and clambered aboard the skimmer, his face alight at the prospect of returning to his people. Ioan muttered something to the others and they nodded, then he strode over to her.

Raisa's stomach fluttered oddly as he approached and she suddenly wondered what had possessed her to get up so early. Why had she felt the need to say goodbye?

Before she could move or speak, Ioan stood before her. He took her hand gently in his own and lifted her fingers to his lips. Kissing her knuckles lightly, he gave her a roguish grin. "We are not done, my lady. Until we meet again." He raised his eyebrows slightly.

Before she could respond, he turned and jogged away. A moment later he had climbed onto the skimmer. The engines whirred to life and they shot away from the Hawk, speeding across the pool and into the gardens. A moment later they had disappeared behind the sychstal. Raisa stood staring at the spot where they had disappeared, her heart feeling like a wrung-out dishrag.

Marik came over and stood next to her. "Well." He grinned down at her, a teasing twinkle in his eyes. "They're off. Better get the others up, we've got a long ways to go before the day is out.

And I need to go talk to a certain cabin boy of ours before we leave."

Raisa nodded, a surge of anticipation shooting through her. Adventure lay before them. A treasure hunt like nothing they had ever sought before, and the stakes were higher than any they had ever faced. But if they succeeded, it could mean the end of an empire, the dawn of a new day, freedom for a people long enslaved beneath the merciless heel of a tyrant. At the very least, success would bring her a modicum of sweet revenge on the ones who had imprisoned and tortured her. And the journey would give her something to focus on other than the many lunats she had endured in the Weald. She grinned up at her captain, a surge of excitement coursing through her veins and chasing away the clouds.

"Thank you, Captain," she said. "For rescuing me."

"Of course." Marik shot her a lopsided grin. "Trying to find a new recruit with your skills would have been a nightmare."

His laugh mingled with her own ringing out across the pool and into the morning air. There were still many obstacles to overcome in the days ahead, and things could never be exactly the same as they had been before, but for the moment, she was home, and for now, it was enough.

50

"**B**ut I want to go with you!" Mouse tucked his good arm behind the sling holding his broken one and glared at his captain.

Marik shook his head firmly. "You have to stay here and heal that broken arm."

"Please, Cap'n. Don't leave me behind." Mouse's tone turned small and pleading.

"Mouse, we're not leaving you behind." Marik knelt down in front of the boy and placed a hand on his shoulder. "But the fact is, you're safer here. I spoke with the head physician last night. She promised to take good care of you. And they'll need your help, too. With the Igyeum army heading this way, everyone in the House is relocating to the sychstal in Dalton."

Mouse frowned. "Isn't that where Davin said the Igyeum is going to attack? How is that safer than going with you?"

"Ferndale is right in the path the Igyeum army will have to take to get to Dalton. Trust me, nobody wants to be here when they march through. Besides, Dalton is well defended," Marik assured him. "And it'll take them a couple of sennights at least to get there. And Ioan is going to warn Telmondir. They'll be ready for the attack."

Mouse pouted a little.

"Look." Marik lowered his voice. "The healers need your help. You've spent a lot of time on airships; you can help calm any of the patients who get a little nervous flying to Dalton. And I need you to keep an eye on Rosa for me, can you do that? She needs a friend, someone willing to just sit with her and help her get better, help her see that there might be something in this world worth coming out of hiding for."

"She was hurt pretty bad, huh?" Mouse bit his lower lip and squinted up at Marik. "What happened to her? Why was she in that tower?"

Marik shook his head. "I don't know if I can explain it. But yeah, she's suffered a lot. Do you think maybe you could try to be her friend?"

"How can I be a friend with someone who don't talk?" Mouse asked.

"Some children might ask how they could be friends with a boy with a broken arm." Marik tried to suppress the teasing grin, but at Mouse's startled glare, he couldn't help but let the smile spread across his features.

Mouse grimaced then gave a half-smirk. "Guess I can at least try."

"Thanks, partner."

"You will come back for me, though?" Mouse's lower lip quivered.

Marik drew the boy into a tight embrace. "I'm not abandoning you, Mouse. I will come back, I promise. Hopefully, we'll be in Dalton before the attack begins."

Mouse took a shaky breath and nodded into Marik's shoulder. "I'll do what I can then, Cap'n. I'll follow orders."

"Good lad." Marik held him at arm's length and tousled the boy's hair. "We'll be back before you know it. Your arm won't even be out of that plaster binding."

Mouse nodded again, but he was obviously fighting back tears. Marik gave him another quick hug. "Dalmir wanted to check in on Rosa before we go. Want to come along? I don't think you two have been properly introduced yet."

Mouse rubbed the back of his arm across his eyes. "Sure," he mumbled.

They met Dalmir and the head physician at Rosa's door.

"She is awake," the doctor informed them. "But there is no apparent change in her status. Whatever you witnessed yesterday evening appears to have been a solitary occurrence." She squinted at Dalmir, her expression guarded.

Dalmir scowled. "I assure you, madame, I did not make it up."

She pursed her lips and gave a tiny nod. "Well, perhaps that is so. Stranger things have happened. I must attend to our preparations, but there is a nurse in the next room, should you need anything."

They entered the room. Rosa sat facing the window, propped up in a wicker chair, her upper body engulfed in pillows. She did not turn her head or acknowledge their presence in any way as they approached. Marik pulled a second chair over and sat down next to her.

"Good morning, Rosa," he said.

"That is not my name," she replied without turning to look at him.

Startled, Marik glanced up at Dalmir, who gave him a mystified shrug.

"Oh?" Marik said. "Forgive me, that's what they've been calling you. What is your name, then?"

"Kayda," the girl said, her voice a hushed whisper. "My name was Kayda."

"Kayda. That is a beautiful name," Dalmir said.

The girl turned to look at Dalmir. Her demeanor remained calm. "You carry them still, don't you?"

Dalmir nodded slowly. "Yes. I apologize for upsetting you yesterday, I didn't know you could sense them."

"May I see them again?" Kayda asked.

Dalmir hesitated.

"I was unprepared before. They remind me... of... that place." A visible shudder rippled through her. "And yet... they also call me out of... the fog in which I wander. Please?"

Dalmir held out his hand, the two orbs glittering dully in the morning light pouring through the window. Kayda stared at them for a long moment. She raised a hand until it hovered over Dalmir's, then she glanced at him, her expression suddenly shy.

"May I?"

"Please," he replied.

Marik watched in fascination as the girl gingerly plucked the dull blue orb from the older man's hand. As she gazed into it, the jewel glimmered to life, a sparkle of light emanating from its center and slowly growing in intensity. Her head listed to one side, her eyes fixed upon it, and then she picked up the other, this time the dusky gray orb that Emilee usually carried. In her hand, it also began to pulse with an inner fire. Dalmir let out an awed gasp. Kayda stared down at her hand, the colors illuminating her face, the light growing brighter and brighter until it hurt to look at them. Marik glanced at Dalmir, wondering why the man did not say anything or try to put a stop to whatever it was the girl was doing, but Dalmir merely stared, his expression full of rapt wonder. Then Kayda closed her eyes and let out a long, slow sigh. The light faded and disappeared, and she handed the orbs back to Dalmir with a sad smile. She folded her hands in her lap.

"She was right, it seems to have helped a little. Perhaps it will be enough to keep the fog at bay when you leave," Kayda murmured.

"Who was right?" Dalmir asked in a ragged whisper.

"The woman with the silver hair," Kayda said, her voice wistful. "She helped me wake up the first time."

Dalmir's expression twisted into something that resembled a mixture of pain and joy. "I see."

"Thank you for coming," the girl said distantly.

"I might..." Dalmir stopped and cleared his throat. "Do you

think you might be able to do that again sometime? I might need your help in the future."

The girl nodded, her fingers clutching together, her expression tense. "I know. She told me. I will try. Thank you." Her eyes flitted to Marik and then back to Dalmir. "Thank you both, for rescuing me."

"It was no trouble at all," Marik lied. He gave her a wink and his best grin, then pushed his cabin boy forward. "Have you met Mouse? He's going to stay with you and help everyone get to Dalton safely."

She smiled softly at Mouse. "Hello. You remind me of my little brother, he... he would have been about your age now... I think." A look of worry and confusion flitted across her face. "I can't quite remember, it has been so long."

"Kayda." Dalmir knelt before the girl. "When this is all over, we will help you find your people. I promise you that."

Her gaze took on a faraway glimmer. "That would be nice. Thank you."

"I think our Rosa might need some rest now." Criselda bustled in, her demeanor full of authority.

Kayda looked up at the nurse. "Thank you for taking care of me," she said, her voice faint. "I think I would like to go to bed for a while."

Criselda stopped and stared, her jaw hanging open slightly. After a moment she recovered a little. "I... well... of course, dear, I'll just... help you over to your bed, shall I?" She tucked herself under the girl's arm and helped her stand.

"And... my name is Kayda."

The nurse's face relaxed into a gentle smile, and tears glimmered at the corners of her eyes. "That is a lovely name. Thank you for sharing it with me. Now, let's get you into bed, Kayda, it's been a while since you exerted yourself so."

"When I wake, can Mouse come see me again?" the girl asked.

"Of course he can." Criselda glanced over her shoulder at

them, her eyes wide but filled with joy. She mouthed "thank you!" at them and Marik steered them out of the room.

When they were back in the hallway, Marik gave Mouse a squeeze around the shoulders. "We will come for you in Dalton."

Mouse straightened, lifting his chin slightly. "I'll take good care of her, Cap'n. You can count on me."

"I know I can, lad." Marik grinned. "We'll be back before you miss us."

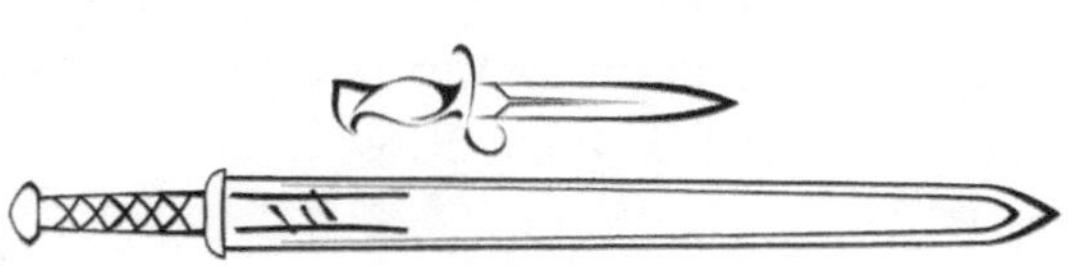

Leaping off the top of a building, even one tall enough to have an airship dock surrounding its summit, was not ideal. The shorter distance meant that the skysail had to open instantly and catch the wind just right to slow the descent to something that wouldn't end in a broken neck. As he jumped into the smoke-and-rubble-filled sky, Beren was grateful that Semiv and Argond had insisted they learn to skysail from multiple altitudes and in various levels of visibility. They had jumped from cliffs as low as thirty meters off the ground, quite a bit lower than the top of this building. Another blast of heat and fire seared through the sky above him as his skysail opened, and bits of the building erupted into the air, raining down around him. A few shards of flaming debris punched tiny tears in the canopy above him, but nothing catastrophic enough to send him plummeting unchecked to the ground. Strapped to his chest, Wynn did not make a sound.

His boots hit the cobblestone street with enough force to make his knees buckle, but his strength gave him the ability to keep himself upright. With a quick jerk of one hand, he released Wynn's harness, and the other stumbled away from him. Around them, members of his platoon dropped to the ground, though far fewer than he had hoped. Despite the rain, fires still blazed on the airships overhead, casting a fair amount of light on the street far below. That could become a problem later, but for the moment, Beren appreciated that he could identify the men nearby.

"All right, Badger?" he asked, squinting at the man who had just landed next to him.

"Yes, sir." The short, stocky defender nodded. "That was a bit more intense than training."

"How many of our men made it down?" he asked.

Badger shrugged. "I know Sergeant Dren and Major Fields both got caught in that first blast. I lost track of the rest of my squad, though."

"Make the rounds, find out who's still with us, and who needs attention."

Badger nodded and scurried off, disappearing into the night. The rain poured down, increasing in intensity. Beren shivered as it trickled down the sides of his face.

Something new caught fire overhead, and in the glow it cast Beren caught sight of Grayden a few meters away. He signaled and Grayden nodded.

"Stay low and quiet, and move fast," Beren's command whispered through the ranks. Crouching, hand cannons at the ready, they darted across the street and behind a second building as another blast of fire speared the top of the platform they had just abandoned. Twisted metal flew into the air and clattered to the street where they had been gathered a moment before.

Pausing in the shadow of the next building, Beren calculated where they were. The rendezvous site for extraction lay at the western end of town. The road they had landed on should lead them in that direction out of town, where they could meet up with the rest of the division. A burst of lightning scorched the sky overhead, followed by a distant rumble of thunder.

"This way." Beren gestured, but as he turned to move along the road, he heard the tromp of boots coming their direction. Filling the road, just to the west, shadowy figures that looked to make up an entire Igyeum regiment appeared, marching down the street in orderly rows. With a few quick gestures, Beren's men retreated back into the shadowy alley.

Badger showed up at his elbow, appearing out of the darkness so suddenly that it made Beren's heart jump a bit. "Vector's down twenty men," the man said, his voice sober. "And Arta lost about fifteen. A few might have made it to the ground with the initial jump, but if they did, we can't find them. Most of them fell when that airship started firing."

Beren's heart sank. Half their number, gone in a single skirmish.

"Form ranks, men," they heard the Igyeum commander bark from down the road. "Spread out, one platoon to each side street and alley. Deymash Pelyon, take your squad and quick march down to the control tower. Alert the guards and reinforce their positions. Anyone trying to leave Gavar in that direction will have to pass through those gates. No Telmondir scum is to get through, understood?"

"Aye, sir."

The soldiers marched as they had been ordered, blocking the direction Beren had hoped to go. The Igyeum commander continued to issue orders as more soldiers emerged from their barracks. In a few minutes, the streets would be crawling with enemies.

Beren ducked behind the building where he found Grayden waiting for him. "That road is no longer an option. We have to get out of here, fast. Dirk, Cole, see if you can find us a path to the west. Trinh and Badger, north."

Grayden nodded at two of his men. "Flint and Joss, scout a block south. Find us an exit."

On the other side of the building, the enemy soldiers were breaking into squads and marching closer. Beren unsheathed his great sword, holding it firm in one hand, a hand cannon in the other.

The men returned, breathless. "No good," Dirk panted. "All the roads going west are filled with soldiers."

"North is out," Trinh added. "Looks like the garrison is just a block that way. Igyeum soldiers are pouring out of a building at the end of the street."

"South is clear," Trinh said, skidding to a stop with Badger puffing along behind him.

"Then we'd best leg it around these buildings to the gates as quick as we can. We have to get to the western side of town and the rendezvous point somehow," Beren said. "Follow me."

They darted through the streets, keeping the massive supply buildings between themselves and their enemy as best they could. In this zigzagging method, it took them more than an hour to reach the edge of the compound, the night growing darker with every minute as the storm rolled in above them. Beren peered around the corner of a building and then sank down against the wet stone wall in dismay. A tall iron fence stretched all along the far side of a gravel road, well-lit by tall gas lamps that flickered with a warm, yellow gleam. The spiky tops of the fence had been wrapped loosely with barbed wire. A block away stood the only visible gates through the fence, separating them from the relative safety of the fields, but hundreds of guards stood between them and this portal, weapons at the ready.

"Can't get out that way," Stan muttered as they huddled under an overhanging roof, trying to stay out of the pelting rain.

"What do we do now?" Joss asked.

"Do you see any signs of more Skyborne nearby?" Flint whispered.

Beren tugged at his lower lip. "I haven't seen any trace of our fellow defenders in the past hour," he said. "They could be as close as behind that row of buildings on the other side of the road, but right now there's no way to know or reach them if they are." He caught Grayden's eye through the darkness. "Any brilliant ideas?"

Grayden rubbed a hand over his face. "We have several hours of darkness left, but once the sun comes up, it's gonna be a lot harder to hide. Looks like we need to take the long way around." He nodded east.

"The intel we have for that side of the compound indicated that the mountains made the terrain nearly impassable," Wynn objected.

"And our only hope lies in the word 'nearly,'" Grayden replied with a tight grin. "Besides, that just means our enemy will have a harder time following us."

Beren rose, ready to be moving toward a measurable goal. "Let's go, then," he said. "Before they catch us here. Keep your hand cannons ready and cover them if you can to keep them dry."

Staying low, the two platoons slipped east, away from the center of Gavar. These streets were not as well-lit, and the inky darkness and driving rain made their progress agonizingly slow. A hum filled the air and an airship slid over the building above them. It inched forward ponderously.

"Cover!" Beren hissed.

The men around him dropped to the ground, crawling and rolling to the safety of whatever shadows they could find as the airship hovered overhead. The crew would have limited vision from their perch, but all they had to do was look for movement in places where they knew their own soldiers weren't patrolling yet.

Beren's heart pounded in his ears like the surging of waves battering against a sheer cliff. He tried to quiet his breathing, but every intake of air seemed to shout their presence into the darkness. He forced himself to lie still, his body pressed up against the foot of the building.

Seconds ticked by.

His lungs screamed for him to breathe normally, and his rib cage ached as he kept his muscles taut.

And then the airship continued on, sweeping slowly north, following the alleys in that direction.

Beren took a deep breath, his lungs expanding gratefully. Pulling himself to his feet, he gestured to the others.

They continued on their way east, passing large granaries and more supply sheds until they reached a small copse of trees. Ducking into the cover, they took a moment to rest, taking stock of their situation. Grayden sent Shep and Jerky up ahead to scout what lay in that direction, while the rest of the men checked their hand cannons and took small sips of water.

"What if they don't wait for us?" Beren asked Grayden in a low voice. "Going east into the mountains to skirt around town could take us hours." If not days. But he kept that last thought to himself.

Grayden shook his head. "What choice do we have?"

"Sir." Jerky came darting through the trees with Shep right behind.

"What did you find?" Grayden asked.

"The forest is broken up by an old train road about a hundred yards further in," Jerky panted. "It's running about twenty meters off the ground. Then more trees right up to a village. Beyond that, looks like fields and sparse forests all the way to the mountains. Not a lot of cover, though."

Behind them the fire must have made it to the engine room of a crippled airship. A massive explosion sounded overhead as what was left of the vessel transformed into a ball of fire that fell from the dock and crashed into the street below.

"Cover or not, it's time to decide, men," Beren replied. "Listen."

They paused. Over the sound of the rain and occasional rumbles of thunder, they could hear the steady pounding of boots coming their way.

"We need to move while it's still dark," Grayden said.

"We could make a stand here," Badger argued. "There's cover, plenty of space to retreat to, and if we can hold out long enough, the rest of the division might show up."

"They don't know where we are," Flint replied. "It's just as likely they've already ducked around the northern end of the compound and reached the rendezvous point. If we don't show, they'll consider us lost in action."

"And if we get into those mountains we might actually get lost," Badger argued. "Better to dig in here and at least do some more damage to the Igyeum so they have fewer forces to send at Telmondir."

Flint opened his mouth to reply, but they never heard what he had to say. His expression turned startled, and then he fell forward, an arrow protruding from his back. Beren ground his teeth in frustration as the woods suddenly grew thick with crossbow bolts. Their voices had drawn the enemy straight to them.

The men flung themselves behind trees, their hand cannons popping with a quick staccato beat as they returned fire. Shouts filled the woods, and Igyeum soldiers raced into the trees, swords drawn. The ground here had grown mucky and slick in the rain. The battle raged as the enemy rushed to overtake their position, climbing over the bodies of their own fallen, unconcerned by the losses they were incurring. Beren slipped in the growing mud, but caught himself on a nearby tree branch. Badger grabbed him by the arm and propelled him forward, running in lockstep with him.

A plume of smoke billowed up into the sky and suddenly the Igyeum soldiers broke away, racing back the way they had come, fleeing the battle. Some of the defenders chased after them, hand cannons outstretched. The men at the back of the fleeing line of Igyeum soldiers fell, but the others did not pause to retrieve them.

The hair on the back of Beren's neck prickled at this odd behavior. With a sudden premonition, he broke away from his pursuit of the enemy.

"Fall back!" he shouted. "Get out of the trees! Fall back to the village!"

Most of his men heard him and obeyed. At the other end of the trees he could hear Grayden echoing his orders. The defenders dropped back, but not quickly enough.

Intense, searing heat blazed down from the sky as the airship summoned by the Igyeum soldiers burst into view overhead.

Branches flew into the air and whole trees twisted and ruptured, blasted into bits by the power of the cynderblast. He saw the men who had raced after the Igyeum soldiers flung from their feet, incinerated by the fiery spear.

The airship hurtled backwards through the sky, unable to withstand the force of its own weapon. But Beren knew it would circle around again for another blast. Their only hope was to move and keep moving.

"We can't fight that thing from the ground. Fall back!" he shouted again, and this time he heard the order echoed as if from the throats of every man at once.

They raced through the trees, bursting out from the other side of the forest and into the outskirts of a large village. The shadowy houses were dilapidated and run down, and Beren's mind registered the remains of a few larger buildings that may have once been a school.

"Through the village," he roared at his men. "Keep moving!"

Badger kept pace with him, and just behind them came Trinh, Cole, and Dirk. Together they raced down muddy streets, splashing through increasingly large puddles. Through a window Beren caught sight of a frightened face, but he didn't slow, urging the men to keep running. Behind them, he could hear the ominous hum of the airship sweeping toward them. Risking a glance over his shoulder, he saw the silhouette of the airship hovering behind, heard the sudden crackle of doom, and found himself flung sideways by the edge of the fiery lance that tore a furrow in the street where he had just been standing. He rolled over and found himself staring into the lifeless eyes of Badger.

Groaning with pain and grief, Beren picked himself up off the ground. Nothing felt broken, just bruised and scraped. His right arm and the side of his face were raw and blistered by the heat.

"Trinh? Cole? Dirk? You all right?" he called out hoarsely to the men lying on the ground nearby.

"All right, chief," Trinh gasped, rising to his feet. He wobbled a bit and Beren stepped forward to put a steadying hand on his arm. "The others?" Trinh asked.

Beren lowered his eyes. "Badger fell."

"Cole? Dirk?" Trihn choked out.

"Dirk is gone." Cole's voice was lifeless as he struggled upward, his jacket smoldering from the blast.

Beren ground his teeth. "There's no time to mourn. That airship is going to swing back around any minute now. We have to move!" He pushed himself into a lope, limping slightly, his men struggling along in his wake.

They burst through the final houses and Beren's heart sank as he saw a stretch of fields before them, nodding with the early sprouts of summer crops. Beyond this impossible distance, towering rock formations on the other side of the field jutted out of the ground like shadowy fingers reaching to the sky, too tight for an airship to maneuver between, too tall and solid for the cynderblast weapon to be as effective. Maybe they had a chance, after all.

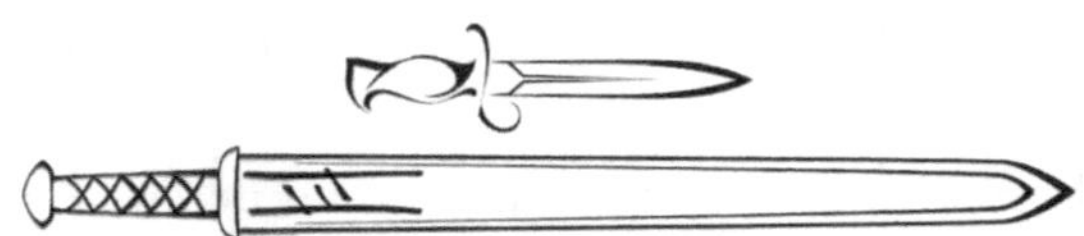

Grayden had never thought he would be grateful for those long runs their commanding officers had expected them to complete in Attatoire, but now he wished he could go down on his knees and tell them how thankful he was. He bounded across the field, wary of the uneven and slippery mud that threatened to trip him with every step. The enemy airship still soared behind them. He could feel it there, an ominous shadow in his mind. He expected every minute to feel a spear of fire through his shoulder blades. Far behind them, he could sense the faint pinpricks of discomfort that were the soldiers they had clashed with in the woods. For now, they were not approaching, but if they made it into the mountains, it was certain their enemy would send soldiers in on foot to track them, and it was equally certain that they would have better odds of outrunning soldiers on the ground than the airship and its deadly weapon.

"You aiming for those rocks?" Grayden panted as he drew even with Beren.

Beren nodded, never breaking stride. "Think we can make it?"

"We have to," Grayden replied. "Think it's safe?"

"Safer than back there," Beren said. "They might be able to blast through the rocks, but it will slow them down. They'll have to climb higher than they want. Hopefully we can lose them and get deeper into the mountains where they can't find us again."

"And if they just decide to level those rock formations while we're under them?"

"I'm sure that cynderblast can eventually level the entire area if it wanted to," Beren agreed. "But it won't be quick; the weapon throws the airship back every time they fire unless they anchor to the ground. If we're fast and lucky, we can get out of range before they can bring the mountain down on top of us."

It made sense. And it was their only hope. Grayden fell back, shouting Beren's plan to the men nearby, who relayed the message to the others. He didn't know who had made it out of the forest with them and there was no time to stop and count, but he could sense that their numbers had dwindled significantly. His legs churned and his lungs ached as they raced into the field. His shoulders burned where the heavy pack's straps dug into his skin. His sword, never awkward when he walked, seemed intent on unbalancing him as he ran. The rain pelted down, soaking him to the skin, but he blessed it and the darkness, as both made it harder for those on the airship to see him and his men running through the fields. The men had spread out and were running in straggling groups, making it difficult for the cynderblast to take them all out in a single shot. He pushed himself along, striving to keep up with Beren's long stride, unwilling to fall behind even as every muscle in his body begged him to fall to the ground.

They were nearly across the last field when Grayden slowed his pace and glanced around to check on the others. The rest of his men seemed to be doing well. Then his stomach clenched in concern as he spotted someone struggling at the rear of the group, his arms swinging awkwardly, his body lurching forward. Slowing even further, Grayden jogged over to him, one eye still on the airship above them. Why didn't it fire? What was it waiting for?

"All right, Wynn?" he asked as he got close enough to recognize his friend.

Wynn merely gasped for breath in answer.

"Almost there," Grayden assured him. "Maybe half a mile left."

"Might... as well be... the edge... of the world," Wynn wheezed.

"You can do it," Grayden said.

Wynn shook his head despairingly. "Maybe... just... leave me."

"Come on," Grayden ordered, linking his elbow through his friend's arm. "I'm not letting you stop now. Your ma will kill me if I don't make sure you get home safe. You can do this. We all make it to safety together."

He pulled Wynn along, refusing to let him fall any further behind. He felt his own strength failing, but he pushed his body forward, refusing to let himself falter. Out of nowhere, Shep appeared on Wynn's other side, taking his free arm and helping to propel him forward.

"Almost there," Shep panted.

Wynn gave a weary nod, but clearly didn't have the breath to say anything. Grayden's focus narrowed in on the task at hand as the whole world coalesced into the pounding of his feet hitting the dirt, propelling him forward through the rain.

Step. Step. Step.

He prayed against the lightning that might split the sky and give away their position.

Step. Step. Step.

His heart throbbed in his ears and he felt as though he were breathing through a reed. The ground beneath him hardened to packed earth and then rock as they darted inside the towering formations. Behind them, the roar of the cynderblast shattered the sky, razing through the great boulders. Unable to spot their prey through the darkness and the deluge, the crew had been waiting for them to enter the rock towers, thinking to cut off their escape or trap them beneath the rubble. Shards of gravel and stone flung high into the air and rained down around them. A piece of shrapnel seared across Grayden's face, causing him to stumble as the world blinked out in a blinding white haze of pain.

Then someone had him by the shoulder, propelling him farther into the relative safety of the overhanging rocks. The airship had fired too late: they were safe.

Gasping, his whole body trying to seize up and the side of his face on fire with pain, Grayden forced himself to continue putting one foot in front of the other. "Don't sit down," he gasped at Wynn. "Just keep walking."

Wynn nodded. Shep still held his other arm, and the three of them paced forward together behind the rest of what remained of both platoons. As the desperation in his lungs subsided, Grayden began silently counting the men. A new anguish flooded through him as he finished. Only eight men remained of the eighty he and Beren had set out with from the jumpships. He wondered how the rest of the regiment had fared and hoped their losses were not as great.

They hiked further into the rocks until they reached the actual mountains. Here the terrain grew much more rugged and difficult. The towering rock formations continued, strange arches and spires jutting up all around them. Idly, Grayden wondered what had caused them.

His brain began to whirl on, considering the difficulty they now faced. The problem spun in his mind as he examined it from every angle the way Wynn might with a schematic. They had food for a sennight, if they rationed it carefully. Water would be more of an issue, but a river did wind through these mountains, if they could find it. Steep cliffs would probably block their progress, making it difficult if not impossible to get to the rendezvous site, and even if they did, chances were slim that they would make it in time for retrieval.

That meant they had to find another way home. But how? The impossibility of the task before them was staggering.

They hiked on, following Beren's lead. Grayden continued to work the problem in his mind. Behind them, the airship had ceased blasting the rocks. He could sense that they were pulling away, though a scurrying prickle on his spine told him that the enemy would not give up.

Suddenly, he stopped dead in his tracks.

Shep, who had been trudging along behind him, ran into his back. "Sir!" he complained.

"Sorry, Shep," Grayden said, his thoughts miles away. "Wynn!"

"What?" Wynn's voice came from several paces away. "You all right, Grayden?"

"I'm better than all right," Grayden shouted. "I can sense the soldiers behind us."

"How close are they?"

"Not very." Grayden waved a hand. "But that's not the point. I can sense them, Wynn."

He stared at his friend, willing him to understand as Beren suddenly came swinging back to see why half of the men had stopped dead behind him.

"Grayden?" Beren queried. "What is the trouble?"

"No trouble, Beren," Grayden said. "But my sixth sense is back."

Wynn's eyes widened. "Back? What happened to it?"

Grayden shrugged. "We got to the Academy and it sort of disappeared."

"You never said anything," Wynn said.

"It seemed like a good thing at the time," Grayden admitted. "Using it always felt like cheating back home... a little."

Wynn gave a rueful half smile. "I guess I can understand that." He sobered. "But you're saying it just suddenly returned? I wonder why..." He trailed off. "Unless..." He glanced up at the sky. "Unless... Grayden. What if your sixth sense is linked to Dalmir's orb?"

"What?" Now it was Grayden's turn to be confused. "Why would you think that?" He paused, remembering how he had used Dalmir's orb to freeze water so many lunats ago it felt like another lifetime, another life.

"I've worked with Dalmir's orb quite a bit over the past year," Wynn explained. "And while I certainly do not understand it, it seems that people can be... attuned... to them. At least, that's sort of what Dalmir said. I'm not sure why, but you seem to be more sensitive to it. Maybe it's the reason for your unusual sensitivity to other things when it's nearby?"

"If that's true..." Grayden paused. "Then you think Dalmir might be close?"

Wynn shrugged. "It's possible. He and Captain Marik left a few lunats ago on a mission to rescue Raisa from the Ar'Mol."

"Raisa was captured by the Ar'Mol?" Grayden nearly bellowed the question, he was so startled.

"Right..." Wynn rubbed the back of his neck sheepishly.

"Wynn..." Grayden broke off, exasperated. "So, it's possible that Dalmir and Marik are up there somewhere right now?" He waved at the brightening sky.

"Well... it's possible," Wynn said. "Drengur writes me letters. His last one came before I left Dalton and he said Marik and Dalmir had left and were heading to Palla, but I don't know where they are right now. Or why they'd be coming this way."

"So if it's them, how do we get their attention?" Beren asked.

"Smoke?" Grayden suggested. He craned his neck looking up at the tall cliffs. "If someone could get up these cliffs, we might be able to spot the Hawk." He looked at Wynn. "Unless something happened to Marik's ship, too?"

"He crashed it," Wynn admitted, then flung his hands up defensively. "But I fixed it!" He chuckled. "I guess I'm not very good at telling stories, but we haven't had a lot of time to talk, either."

"If someone is going to scale that cliff, it should be Grayden," Beren said, looking as disgruntled as Grayden felt. "You're the better climber."

Without a word, Grayden removed his pack and extracted a coil of rope. He eyed the cliff face, wishing he had more gear, knowing that the rain and the darkness would make this ascent tricky. He reached up, found good hand-holds, and started his climb.

Hand over hand, he climbed; a sense of urgency filled him, but he did not allow it to rush him into making a mistake. His body protested every movement, still recovering from the long run he had just completed, but he focused all his attention on the task at hand, knowing their survival depended on his success. The rock face was wet and cold. Rain poured over him. He dug the toes of his boots onto tiny ledges, paused to search for another hand-hold, and slowly but surely moved up the cliff face.

Lightning split the sky, flooding the area with light for an instant. Grayden glanced up. Was that the shadowy form of an airship? Had the Igyeum found them? No, it was just a low-hanging cloud. He shook the rain out of his eyes and continued up, knowing that he had to keep going for his men waiting below.

Finally, the steepness of the rock wall began to taper off. The climb grew easier and there were far more hand- and foot-holds. Then, without warning, he pulled himself up over a ledge and found himself at the summit.

Working quickly, he pulled the coil of rope off his shoulder, secured it to a sturdy outcropping, and dropped the free end to those waiting below. As the others climbed up after him, Grayden gazed out into the storm.

Nothing.

Men joined him atop the cliff, scrambling up and over the ledge one at a time.

Lightning flashed once more. There! Coming out from behind a taller mountain, a small, familiar airship soared into view. Grayden waved his arms, and as the others reached the top he shouted for them to join him, but even as he yelled he knew it to be a hopeless effort. The night was too dark, the storm too fierce. Nobody on the airship could see them.

Wynn and Beren were the last to achieve the summit. They peered through the rain as Grayden pointed at the spot where he had seen the airship.

"Use the orb."

The words were so quiet that Grayden thought he had imagined them. "What?" he asked aloud.

"The orb," Wynn urged again.

"The orb?" Grayden repeated, feeling like his thoughts were stuck in a mire. "But that's... Wynn, you are a genius!"

Beren squeezed his shoulder. "Is it possible?"

Grayden had no answer. He had been able to make the orb react to his thoughts when holding it. And if Wynn was right and it gave him some sort of strange insight when it was nearby, could he make it do something if he wasn't touching it? If he was so far away? But if it was the reason for his extra sense, then maybe...

He could only try.

The others gathered around and watched as Grayden closed his eyes. Feeling a little silly, he tried to stretch out his thoughts in the direction of the orb. He reached for that prickling sensation he usually got when someone was sneaking up on him or following him, and tried to direct it back to the orb. He had made the orb freeze water once. Could he make it flare like a signal fire? Would Dalmir notice?

Sweat dripped down the sides of his face as he concentrated. A bright light. Warmth. Home and hearth. A signal fire. A rescue mission. Help us! He tried to funnel these thoughts directly at the orb.

A wild breeze whipped rain at his face. He squeezed his eyes more tightly shut and focused his mind, willing his thoughts toward the orb that he hoped was there. Light! Help us!

You can stop now. A wry voice penetrated through his concentration, echoing in his mind.

You can hear me? Grayden thought in surprise. Dalmir?

"Yes, I can hear you! You're like an entire off-key orchestra section down there. Tone it down a bit!" This time the voice came to him audibly. Startled, Grayden opened his eyes and found himself looking up at an exasperated Dalmir staring at him from above the railing of the Valdeun Hawk, a ball of blue fire flooding the darkness like a beacon in the older man's outstretched hand. The airship that now hovered just a few meters away from his mountain perch had never looked more beautiful. The smiles of the defenders on the mountaintop matched those of the pirates on the airship peering over the rail.

"You got my attention," Dalmir called, raising up a hand and holding out a gem that blazed with sapphire light and radiated with the heat of the sun. "Need a ride?"

ACKNOWLEDGMENTS

Thank you for reading! I hope you enjoyed the continuing adventures of Grayden, Wynn, Beren, Dalmir, Marik, and all the rest.

Please take a moment to review on Amazon and/or Goodreads to help your reader friends find this world (and others) of mine. Thank you so much for joining me here in Turrim for a little while.

This is the fourth book in this five-book series and *Turrim Archive* will conclude in book 5: *Towers of Might and Memory*. You can keep up with all my publishing news by subscribing to my newsletter, liking my FB author page, or following my Instagram.

J.L.S.